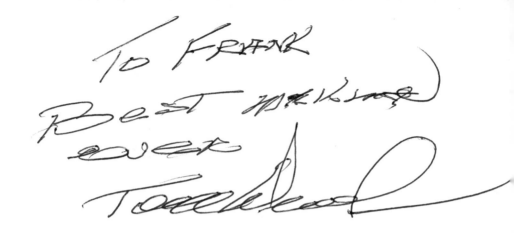

To FRANK
Best wishing
ever
Tomlin

PIOT

Thomas Denham

CHAPTER ONE

S cott Wilson, lying on the bow of the so-called cabin cruiser, was deep in thought. So-called, because she was an old well worn cruiser. Her hull was wood with many coats of paint. The interior was worn and the original mahogany was bubbling under several layers of paint. She had a compressor on board to fill his scuba tanks. But, she took them where they wanted to go without complaint. Her single diesel engine never missed a beat. They were somewhere in the Exuma Cays of the Bahamas. He didn't care where. The water was rippled with only a slight breeze, enough to keep from getting too hot. His mind drifted to the past with thoughts of his lovely wife Sarah Ann. He still wasn't over losing her to cancer just over one year ago. He had sold his financial consulting business to his partner, sold their home and left Kalispell, Montana. He spent a couple days with each of his two adult children then wandered, trying to get over the terrible emptiness he felt. He was thinking of the places he had been and the people he had met over the last eight months of wandering when suddenly a huge gray shape leaped out of the water right beside him! He grabbed his dive mask, yelled at the two Bahamians crewing the boat and dove over the side. They cut the power and leaped to the side rail looking for Scott.

There he was, about a foot under water with his snorkel just above the surface, face to face with the large gray shape. Scott was very still as was the gray shape. Then it swam slowly around him, dove down then straight up out of the water. The Bahamians were now laughing and yelling. Scott played with the porpoise for fifteen minutes before it swam off.

"Hey Mon," said Virgil. "We taut you gone crazy. Dat fish sur want to play."

Jackson was looking at him with a big toothy grin. "You scare us Mon" he said.

These were good people. Scott had flown from Ft. Lauderdale to North Eleuthera aboard a chartered Piper Aztec. He slowly made his way south until he ended up at Point Powell where he met the two brothers, Virgil and Jackson Russell. They promised him virgin diving spots if he chartered their boat for a week. Sleeping would be done outside on the deck so he didn't care about a fancy stateroom. What the heck. He was wandering, attempting to leave memories behind so his healing could begin. He gave them $600 to provision the boat and off they went the next day. They said he could pay the rest when they returned.

They headed southwest from Point Powell toward the chain of cays known as the Exuma Cays. For the last four days he dove for conch, lobster, grouper, snapper and anything else that looked good to eat. They cooked on a charcoal grill rigged out over the water for safety. The fish they cooked was very tasty, the best he had ever eaten. They would marinate it for a couple hours in sour juice, onions, peppers, tomatoes and chopped celery. The fish was sealed in foil with the marinate and cooked on one side for about 10 minutes. It was delicious. Sometimes they anchored in a secluded cove and cooked on the beach. They knew how to live off the sea. They smiled and laughed constantly. Scott even found himself smiling again, their good humor was infectious.

The next day started like the others since they left, a beautiful sunrise with a gentle breeze drifting across the turquoise water. They had anchored in a bay and after breakfast of eggs, fish and melon, headed further south in the chain. They found a promising looking reef and dropped anchor. Scott donned his scuba gear without his wet suit and rolled into the water backwards from the rail. He usually wore the suit to protect him from coral but decided not to this morning. He sank slowly to the bottom as he checked his gear for any problems. "My God this is beautiful", he thought. "I could spend a couple months doing nothing but this all day".

They had plenty of food but he had brought his spear on this dive anyway, never know when a granddaddy lobster might show himself. The water around the reef was about 55 feet deep with a sandy bottom and rose within 15 feet of the surface. The reef was particularly active with sea life and many types of coral. He passed over a large conch shell just before exploring the reef which was one of the most beautiful he had explored. There was a maze of tunnels through the coral with all sizes of fish darting in and out. A school of about 30 yellow-tail swam along 15 feet away as he began to circle the reef. A triggerfish with big front teeth was gnawing on a coral head. An eel poked his head out of its cave to investigate the disturbance only to stare at him as he swam by. Each reef had its own personality. This was one of the better ones with visibility over 150 feet. He continued to the far side where he found what appeared to be an arch doorway to the inside of the coral head. There was plenty of room to swim through even with his tank. Inside it was like an auditorium with a crowned roof about 20 feet above him. The entire room was a circle with several holes in the coral roof that let in plenty of daylight and made him think of stained glass windows in a church. What an amazing structure he thought as he explored the entire room. He felt special to find this and a spiritual feeling came over him.

The sound was faint at first. A hum that grew louder until he recognized it as another boat. He left through the arched doorway and looking up he could see it slowly pass over him and pull up near their boat. Were they friends of Virgil and Jackson? Maybe it was some kind of law enforcement from one of the nearby Cays. Don't spear a lobster now, taking them with scuba gear was illegal. Should he come to the surface and find out or stay down till they left? He had about 30 minutes of air remaining.

Suddenly there was a sound like a combination of a zing and a thud! Thung! Thung! Thung! He looked up and could see streaks in the water. Jesus Christ! he thought. Someone is shooting into the water. As fast as the bullets are coming it must be an automatic. What the hell is going on? Then a splash at the stern of his boat as something big went into the water. The water turned red. It was a person. It had to be Virgil or Jackson. The body didn't move. The red spread. Then a second splash. More blood. My God! They killed Virgil and Jackson. Jesus! Oh my God! What the hell is going on? What should he do? He had twenty minutes of air left. If he stayed down till out of air and came up they might still be there waiting for him. Did they know he was down here? A spear against an automatic. Some match. Think. This is life and death. What can I do to have the best chance to survive? How many are up there? Jesus! This is really happening! How could it be? He started shaking

4

as adrenalin rushed through his body. What the Hell could he do? They must be drug runners, the scum of the earth.

Whatever I do he thought, I better damn well get my wits about me. I can't just stay down here. I have to find out what's going on. I have to know the situation. Who are they? How many are there? Why, why, why. Why doesn't matter right now. They were good people. Now they are dead or dying from loss of blood. Blood! Jesus! How long before the sharks get here. I have to do something and now! His army special forces training started taking over. This wasn't the first time he had been seconds away from death.

He slowly made his way along the side of the boat away from his boat and made his way to the stern. His movements were muffled by the lapping of a slight chop against the hull. He heard shouting in Spanish. Someone on their boat shouted back. Were there more than two of them? The shouting stopped.

Think. The druggy in the drug guy's boat should have his back to him looking over at the other boat. What would the one in their boat be doing? Virgil and Jackson were both in the water. It should stand to reason that he would be rummaging around the boat looking for anything of value. If he could time it so the one in their boat was down in the cabin looking for booty he might have a chance, might.

He removed the knife and scabbard from the swim vest and stuck them in the back of his swim suit. He slipped out of the dive vest and tank, slipped the weight belt through the arm strap, slipped off his swim fins and let them all sink to the reef twenty feet below. When he reached the transom he found a swim platform with a ladder attached. He removed his face mask with snorkel attached and slowly lowered the swim platform. He gently placed his mask and snorkel on the platform and then lowered the ladder. He put his right foot on the bottom rung and brought one knee then the other up onto the platform. Kneeling, he cautiously raised his head above the transom.

The man was looking across to their boat, his back to Scott. He had a greasy pony tail, no shirt, dirty shorts and bare feet. His AK47 was propped on the deck beside him. No one else was in sight on either boat. Scott spread his knees apart for balance. He slowly raised himself up, drawing the spear to the maximum, and his eyes locked on the middle of the back. Fumswitch! Sang the spear as it left the sling, shot through the air, and entered the back an inch to the right of the spinal column half way down. The force drove it through the body and out the chest. No scream. Just the splash when it hit the water.

Scott jumped over the transom, grabbed the gun, and aimed at his cabin door. The man came out of the cabin and, as he raised his gun, Scott fired. The force of the bullets drove the man over the side and into the water. All was quiet. He thought of Virgil and Jackson. He went to the stern, looked over, the sight was sickening. Blood in the water, sharks.

The two boats had drifted about twenty yards apart when Scott smelled it. smoke. His old boat was on fire. The bad guy must have started it to destroy the evidence. It spread quickly. What would happen when it got to the gas tank? He hadn't noticed it before but the bad guys had not dropped anchor and had left their boat idling. He sat in the Captains chair and moved the gear levers forward and advanced the throttles to move further away from the other boat which was really blazing now. There was no explosion but a lot of flame until the boat sank out of sight. Scott pulled the throttles back and sat staring at the sea where their boat had been.

What had started out to be another beautiful day had turned into a nightmare. Four people were suddenly dead. Surprisingly he did not feel bad for the two he had killed. They were murdering scum who had killed two very gentle, kind men. He circled the area hoping for a miracle but his friends had vanished below the surface.

He thought about going after his dive gear but with so many sharks on a feeding frenzy, some may still be around. He slowly advanced the throttles further and headed south. He didn't know why. The after- adrenalin rush set in. He came out of it with a start. What the Hell am I doing? I'm sitting here dumb as a rock just driving this boat slowly south like I was on a Sunday cruise. You lucked out back there. Oh did you luck out. So don't do something stupid now. Think. Are there more bad scum around? Where did those two come from? Where did this boat come from. My God! They probably killed the owners, threw them overboard and cruised around looking for more victims. Not anymore. At least those two won't.

He decided he better check the boat out first. He ran through it so fast earlier looking for more scum after killing those two that he didn't really see anything. He looked around the captain's chair. Twin controls and instrumentation told him it had two engines. The fuel gauges registered half full. The boat was made by Hatteras. It was a real beauty. He found the owners manual in a glove box type compartment and found it was a Hatteras Sport Fisherman. It was a 1981 model and specs showed it to be 55' 8" in length. It had two 850hp GM diesel engines and could cruise at 20kts while burning 50gph. It further stated the fuel tanks held 1600 gals of diesel. Wow! This baby had long legs, 32 hours with full tanks. With half tanks he had 16 hours of fuel at normal cruise. He opened up every compartment he could find. He found many of the boating items you would expect to find such as life preservers, mooring lines, a flare gun with cartridges, ponchos, sun screen, expensive fishing gear, and so on. The one thing he was looking for he did not find. Navigation charts! Maybe they're inside. As he stepped inside he was impressed with the beauty of this boat. She may be a fisherman but she was also luxurious inside. He searched the galley and the three staterooms each with their own bath. Still no charts. He did find two complete scuba outfits with wet suits, spears and some clothes hanging in the closet that almost fit. Come night with the temperature dropping he could use a sweatshirt and pants. He put all of the items he believed belonged to the two scums into a diddy bag, added a dive weight and threw it overboard. He wanted nothing of theirs on the boat except for the two assault rifles, AK 47's with ten full clips of ammo. If more scum showed up he now had something with which to defend himself. This was a beautiful boat but still no navigation charts. He did help himself to a Kalik beer ,the beer of the Bahamas, from a refrigerator full of it. He sat down in the captains chair to think.

He thought of calling on the marine radio but if more bad guys were around they would hear him, that he did not want. At twenty nautical miles per hour he would travel 60 miles in three hours. He decided to go that far before looking for a place for the night. He should be out of bad guy country at that distance. If he saw a populated place before that, he would pull in. The chances of that were slim though, most of these small islands in the Exumas are uninhabited.

He wasn't worried about survival. There was plenty of beer in addition to the water in the fresh water tanks. They held 380 gallons and were three quarters full. There were juices and canned food in the pantry. Then there were the scuba outfits including spears like his so he could provide plenty of sea food. The main problem was avoiding any more bad guys. How far away should he go?

The boat was a real beauty. She handled well as her bow cut through the swells and slight chop. They had been heading south so he continued in that direction for no special reason. He experimented with the auto pilot until he could make it hold a course. He sat back with his hands folded across his stomach. With the throb of the engines and the gentle motion of the boat his head started to nod. He jerked his head up! Jesus! You dumb jerk. That's all you need. Fall asleep and run into the bad guys, or aground on an island, or a reef , or out of gas or any dozen other things and you've had it. You've been lucky so far. Don't push it.

He drank most of a large glass of water and poured the rest on his head. That helped a little but not as much as what he saw coming into view. It was an island higher than the rest with a beautiful sand beach. He would pass to the west of it between it and a flatter island off his right. The bottom started coming up so he throttled back reducing speed to five knots. The bottom was pure sand and leveled off at 10 feet. The owners manual had stated that the draft was 4' 10" maximum. First there were a few, then more and more. Then wherever he looked the bottom was covered with star fish. He had never seen so many. There had to be hundreds. As he passed the half way point between the two islands the sea bottom started dropping away and the star fish disappeared. He had seen no sign of life on the island so far. As the south end of the island came he turned east then north at the southern tip which came to a point.

His heading was now northeast as he maintained approximately 200 yards off shore. This gave him plenty of water under the bottom. There was a break in the shoreline ahead but he couldn't make it out yet, it appeared to be a small bay or inlet. He decided to climb the tower which provided a much better view. The tower was used to spot fish on the surface and was equipped with a full set of engine controls and helm. He moved in closer to the shore.

There was a finger of land jutting out that formed a sort of odd bay. He cut his speed to idle, barely making steerage and headed for the bay to take a closer look. It was then he spotted it, another boat. If he hadn't climbed the tower they would have seen each other about the same time. He wanted the advantage. He had no choice but to enter the bay. He estimated it to be less than a half mile deep. Water under the keel was steady at ten feet. Slowly he went in further, standing on his toes he could just see over the trees and keep the other boat in sight as it passed him 200 yards off the coast, just where he had been.

There were binoculars in a secured case which he removed. Careful not to let the sun reflect so the other boat would see the refection he focused and studied the boat. It was a good size Boston Whaler, identified by the lines and the helm in the center. The one driving the boat looked familiar with long hair in a ponytail, no shirt, dirty shorts and probably bare feet which he could not see. He could make out three other people, one with no shirt. Then they went behind the trees and were lost from view. They could have been more of the bad guys. He turned and studied the bay.

Almost at the end of the bay he saw what appeared to be a canal into the interior of the island. With the water depth still holding he eased the bow to port to face dead on west to the canal. Slowly he inched forward intent on not running aground. Then he was in the canal. It was about thirty feet wide which gave enough of room on both sides which were thick with pine trees. The canal turned gradually towards the northwest. The boat continued, slowly following the canal channel when the sight almost took his breath away. The canal entered a beautiful interior bay or lake. It was almost round with a half mile diameter. At the south end was a dock of some sort. He headed for it. Sure enough, a docking facility with three slips but no boats. There were several small buildings on shore at the head of the docks. Well, this is an emergency he thought, I'm docking. At least I will try to dock this big thing. It didn't make sense that this was a bad guy place or they would have turned in. Continuing towards the docks he kept a sharp look out.

He set the throttles just above idle then eased the right lever forward and the left back and spun the wheel to the left. Her bow started coming around. As the stern approached line up with the dock he eased the right lever into reverse also. Now very gently he controlled his direction with rudder and gears. He barely bumped the starboard piling as he went to neutral and jumped on the dock with the stern line in hand. The dock was long enough to give him plenty of room and there was ample water under the boat. He tied the proper line to the dock piling then ran forward, jumped on the bow, grabbed the starboard bow line and tied it to the proper piling. The same was done for the port side. Enough slack was left to allow for the rise and fall due to tide but not enough to let the boat rub against the dock. There, he thought, not a bad job. Now let's see if I can find out where I am and what this place is. I have to notify the authorities about Jackson and Virgil and what I did after. They also need to know about this boat, the Hey Mon, out of Ft. Lauderdale. At least that's what it said on the stern.

The Boston Whaler continued south at 30kts for another 15 minutes placing it 7.5 miles south of Scott. He was right. The one driving the boat was another scumbag as well as the shirtless one next to the other two in the boat. The other two came from the place where Scott had just arrived. "Where are you taking us?" asked Tim, the one with a bullet hole in his upper right arm. Steve, his friend, had doctored it as best he could from the boats first aid kit. He had to argue hard for them to let him use it.

"To our beautiful place gringo" replied the scum watching them with an Ak 47. "You will like it. We have lots of stuff to drink and smoke. Then we will decide what to do with you. Should we kill you sooner or later? Ha, ha , ha ha. I make a big joke. I should say, do we kill you fast or slow? How do you want to die gringos? With a knife or a gun? Ha, ha, ha."

Steve, whispering in a low voice, " Tim, we have to get these guys back to our place. We haven't checked in for over three hours so Mr. R should have the cavalry on the way by now. I think that is our only chance. These guys really plan to kill us. The one is not Columbian, he's Middle Eastern terrorist who is sending the drug money back to his buddies so they can kill more Americans."

Tim replied with a nod of the head.

"Hey liver lips" Steve yelled. "You should see our place. I bet it makes yours look like an out house. You probably don't know what an out house is do you. You crap on the whole world. We have a swimming pool and a couple of girls to serve our drinks and anything else we want" he lied. " I'll tell you what. We'll take you there if you let us live and you can have everything that's there including the girls. You won't find it unless we take you though. What do you say, let us live and we'll take you there."

Steve was counting on Mr. R having the troops waiting in ambush when they got there.

The two scumbags were looking at each other. Then they started grinning. " OK gringo" the Columbian replied. "You show us the way and we will let you go. Are the girls pretty?

12

"Oh yes", said Steve, "they are very pretty and with big booms" as he put his hands up to his chest with fingers spread.

This brought a grin to the face of the terrorist. He even licked his lips in anticipation. "Which way American" he said.

Steve pointed in the general direction hoping he was right about Mr. R. If he wasn't, God help the world if they gained access to the buildings. But that would be almost impossible with the built in security. If the troops weren't there yet, trying to break in would occupy the scums which would give the troops even more time to get there. Their lives depended on his assumptions. He had no way of knowing that Scott Wilson was there. Nor did Scott know there were more scumbags headed his way with two Americans as prisoners.

After Scott tied up the Sportfisherman he followed a path of flagstone and crushed shells through a thick forest of pine trees. Thirty yards later he came to a clearing. The sight was a surprise. There were buildings, very modern, large with some odd shaped and flowers everywhere which gave off a most pleasant smell. The first building he came to was a house. He knocked but no one answered so he entered through an unlocked door. The place was immaculate, nothing was out of place. The entryway led to a large great room with overstuffed and very comfortable looking furniture. At the end of the room was a large rectangular shaped dining table. Off that a doorway led to a very modern kitchen. Another room off the kitchen held two freezers and refrigerators. The house was air conditioned and felt cool to his skin.

Scott retraced his steps to investigate the rest of the house. He found three large separate bedrooms each containing a queen size bed, desk with computer table and computer, a large closet and each had it's own bath with shower and Jacuzzi tub. Very nice and still very neat. What he thought was going to be a fourth bedroom turned out to be a very big conference room with a table and one wall solid with computer equipment. "This is a strange place" he thought "not the home of a Bahamian or tourist."

He left the house with the intent of looking at the other buildings. One in particular caught his attention. It was three stories high, round and about 200 feet in diameter. He had only taken a few steps when he heard the outboard motor.

He ran toward the thick pine trees where he knew he could hide but still have a commanding view of the bay and dock area. He had the AK 47 with him along with a shoulder bag filled with the ten ammo clips. It was the Boston Whaler he had seen earlier. There were shouts coming from the boat. "Ernesto! Luis!" Then it dawned on Scott. The scumbags had seen the boat he brought in and thought their friends were here. They wouldn't be happy when they found out their friends were dead.

They tied their boat then stepped to the dock prodding the other two ahead with their AK 47's. He could see one was wounded and the other helping him. They were definitely not scumbags. Maybe they owned the boat he brought in. They were obviously prisoners and the one could barely walk he was so weak. One scumbag prodded the prisoners off the dock and onto land while the other, who looked more middle eastern than south American, was still securing the boat to the dock. The three entered the thick pines as Scott maneuvered himself to a position to head them off. Again he thanked his ranger and special forces training. The tall captive was looking around like he expected to see someone. When they were about 30 feet away the scumbag turned and yelled something to his buddy. As he turned Scott rose from his hiding place and caught the eye of the uninjured one. Their eyes met. Scott pointed at the ground with his finger then motioned with the flat of his palm in a downward motion. The uninjured one nodded then pulled his friend down to the ground with him. The scumbag whirled around when he heard the noise of his prisoners going to the ground. Scott had melted back behind his cover before being seen. But, his AK 47 sights were on the chest of the filthy, bad smelling scum. His aim was steady.

"Get up Americans" screamed the scum. " Hey Ernesto! Luis! Come and watch me kill two Americans. Ha Ha! They are of no use to us now. You do not want to leave the girls eh? That is alright, I will enjoy doing it myself, then I will show the girls what a real man is like. Ha Ha! Which one of you would like the pleasure of watching the other die?" He aimed his AK 47 at the injured prisoner. Scott fired! The scumbag was dead before he hit the ground.

Scott ran to the prisoners and told the uninjured one, "grab the gun and follow me." Steve picked up the gun and ran after Scott. The middle eastern scumbag had just stepped on land when Scott and Steve stepped out of the woods with guns pointed at him. Scott moved ten feet to the side of Steve so the scum wouldn't be tempted to get them both with a quick burst. "Drop the gun asshole or die like your buddy" growled Steve. Just then they could hear the whop, whop of helicopter blades as a big grey chopper appeared over the trees and settled to the ground. No sooner had it landed then five heavily armed men in fatigues burst from the open side door with guns at ready.

The scumbag, with open mouth, dropped his gun. The one who appeared to be in charge of the cavalry pointed his gun at Scott and said "drop your weapon, NOW! SPORT!"

"No way sergeant" replied Scott. "Not until you pick up that weapon our druggie may make a try for".

"He's OK" said Steve. " This is Rambo. He saved our lives. I don't know who he really is or how he got here but there were two other druggies driving that big boat this morning when they jumped us while we were fishing. What happened to them Rambo?"

"They're dead" was all Scott said.

"Jesus" Steve whispered, "you really are a Rambo"

One of the other cavalrymen picked up the terrorist's gun.

Steve turned to the head of the cavalry. "George, get Mr. R on the scrambler. We'll tell him what's happened and see what he wants to do."

"Right" said George, as he ignored the weapon in Scotts hands, walked to the chopper and dialed his scrambler phone. After seconds he yelled, "he's on Steve".

Steve turned to Scott. "What's your real name and residence address?"

"My name is Scott Wilson and I was from Kalispell, Montana but I left there about eight months ago."

Steve walked to the phone, spoke for about five minutes then hung up. He walked back to Scott and George.

"George", said Steve, " Mr. R wants you to take the middle eastern terrorist, in full restraints, back in the chopper along with Tim.

Plus, put the dead druggie in a body bag and take him along. Scott and I will stay here and wait for a call from Mr. R."

Steve turned towards Scott, "That OK with you Scott?"

"Sure, I'd like to know what's going on around here. I also need to report two murders of Bahamians and the killing of two druggies."

"We'll take care of that as soon as Mr. R calls us back."

Tim, under the care of a medic was now being loaded in the chopper on a stretcher.

As soon as they had the terrorist chained in and the body bag loaded the chopper lifted off and was quickly out of sight. It became quiet again. Birds were singing, a gentle breeze was blowing and the soft smell of flowers filled the air. The beauty was trying to erase the ugliness of what had just happened.

"Follow me Scott, we'll wait in the quarters for the call from Mr. R. I could use a cold one, how about you?"

"I'm so dry I'm a fire hazard," replied Scott.

"I hope you like Kalik, the Bahamian beer."

Steve got two cold ones from the house and Scott followed him to a pool. They sat in lounge chairs. Scott was thinking that Steve wanted him out of the house so he could take the call inside in private.

"Tell me what happened to you Scott and how you came to this place. Mr. R will ask me."

Scott told about his meeting the two Bahamian brothers and renting their boat and the encounter with the drug runners. When he had finished he said, "Steve, I need to call the authorities and report what happened. One of the brothers had a wife and children. Also, I would like to make some kind of financial arrangement for the family. I'm sure the boat was all they had. These were wonderful people. They gave me a peace I haven't known for some time. I want to do something for the family".

The phone rang. "I'll talk to Mr. R about it Steve". He excused himself and carried his beer to the house and picked up the scrambler phone.

"Hello Mr. R" said Steve.

"Hello Steve " replied Mr.R. "How are you handling the problem"?

"I'm okay personally Mr. R and I think Scott is too although he has been through a lot today. He appears to be a pretty cool character". Steve then repeated the story Scott had told him including his request to notify the authorities and financial help to one of the brother's family.

"I have a dossier on our Mr. Wilson" said Mr. R. "Fate works in strange ways. We considered him for pilot of the project but had to disqualify him as he was married at the time. The dossier is now up to date to the time when he left the mainland for Eleuthera. He owned a very successful financial consulting business which he sold to an employee shortly after his wife died of cancer. He lost both his parents at a young age, dropped out of high school and joined the army, forging what documents he needed in order to get in. He was accepted to ranger school and rose fast in the ranks. While in the army he received his high school diploma through GED and went on to complete enough college courses to give him an associate's degree in business. After the army he spent two years at the University of Montana and received a degree in finance. During this time he was married with two children. He married his high school girlfriend after army boot camp. They produced two children during the first two years of their marriage".

'While building his business" Mr. R went on, "he took flying lessons, received his pilots license with instrument and commercial ratings for both single and multi engine and is qualified and type rated in the P-51 and the Cessna Citation. Friends of his owned these high performance airplanes and checked him out in them. He also attended two different air combat maneuvering schools which the old timers know as aircraft dog fighting, as in World War Two".

"You know we have been looking for someone to replace Max since he fell in love and married", continued Mr. R. "Max has agreed to train his replacement pilot if it takes a reasonable period of time. He doesn't want to be separated from his new bride any longer than necessary. I want you to feel Scott out. He would be a valuable member of the team and the project could be just what the doctor ordered for him. As long as his attitude remains positive you can continue sharing the project information with him. You can also offer him the position of project pilot. If he accepts that, you can share all information with him. We will fly him over here for a complete physical and wardrobe. He'll be back in two days and we'll pick him up tomorrow. As for the unpleasantness of today, we will take care of everything including the financial aid to the Bahamian family. It will be best if they think Scott also perished. Please tell him that. Also, when we pick up Scott we'll bring a captain along to skipper the Hey Mon back to Ft. Lauderdale. Let me know as soon as he makes his decision".

Mr. R hung up without saying goodbye as he usually did when he was done talking. Steve rarely met with Mr. R in person and some of the project personnel had never met him. He must be a very powerful man to accomplish what he had on the project. It had cost a tremendous sum of money plus involving the mental giants in specialized fields. Steve was considered to be the most knowledgeable person in the world in his field, as was Tim. Tim's part in the project was 99% complete so his absence during recovery would not cause delays. The project itself was nearly done when one considered it was close to ten years since it began. That seemed like another lifetime ago to Steve. He had been on the project since the beginning. Steve knew his time was drawing to a close. He was financially rewarded very handsomely and could retire whenever he chose but hoped Mr. R would have another project. He loved the challenge. His thoughts came back to the present as he joined Scott poolside.

It was now the middle of the afternoon, clouds were building and the breeze was picking up.

"Why don't we find you some clothes, take a shower, and get you into something more comfortable than that swimming suit. After, I'll tell you as much about this place as I can. We may have some weather moving in so it's time to leave the pool anyway."

They found some clothes that fit along with underwear and sandals. Scott had been wearing his dive boots all day. It would feel good to get them and the swimsuit off and take a hot shower. The temperature was dropping with the weather moving in as Steve said.

"Do you want another beer?" asked Steve.

"No thanks, but I would have an iced tea if you have any" replied Scott.

"It will be waiting for you when you finish your shower" answered Steve.

CHAPTER TWO

Kim Jong Un, President of North Korea, sat in his raised leather executive chair, raised because he was only five feet three inches tall, behind a one of a kind huge, hand crafted desk. The tall middle eastern bearded man standing on the other side of the desk was beckoned to a chair. He gathered his robes and sat. Three body guards were positioned around Kim for protection.

"So, what you are asking," began Kim, "is a weapon of mass destruction, carried by a missile capable of reaching the United States. You prefer this weapon to be nuclear but would accept biological, is this correct?" Kim was trying hard not to smile as this would be great day if they made an agreement. He would benefit personally from the cash paid for the weapon and at the same time deliver the United States a severe blow. He was almost salivating at the thought.

"Yes, that is true," answered Mohamed Waleed Algamdi, one of al-Qaida's top lieutenants.

"Why do you want to do this?" Kim asked.

"Their way of life is evil. They are non-believers and must die for their sinful ways. The Westerner and the Jews must die."

"I am not of the Islam faith, do you consider me a non-believer?"

"There are non-believers who are our comrades against the Western non-believers. It is the westerners who live the rich sinful life who must pay with their lives. We work together against these sinful ones. It is our jihad to attack again and again until the infidels crumble. If all goes well we will purchase many more weapons from you. We will be triumphant in the end, you will see."

"We can provide what you seek. At this time we do not have the nuclear capability matched with the rocket to reach the United States but will in the near future. Although we are in negotiations to stop the start up of our reactor and disarm our weapons, we have no intention of stopping. In six months to a year we will have such a weapon for you. The price is five hundred million U.S. dollars. We will need one hundred million in advance to reserve your order. If someone gives us one hundred million before you, your order will be in second position, so it behooves you to get your deposit to us first. Of course, the price is not guaranteed until we receive the deposit. Do I make myself clear? The price for a biological weapon is three hundred million and that is available now. Which choice do you make?"

"I will wait for the nuclear weapon. It will cause much more panic among the westerners. They have frozen some of our bank accounts but we have many more and we are receiving more funds everyday. I will have your deposit wired to the bank of your choice tomorrow. Our drug sales alone will provide the money for additional weapons. The United States is so foolish they are providing us money through the sale of drugs to their people. We buy from the Central Americans and sell to the North Americans. The money just keeps coming in."

"Here is a card with the wire transfer instruction and remember please, there are others interested. The first to give us a deposit is first in line."

"You have made that very clear."

The Saudi arose and left the room. His thoughts were not kind towards the North Korean President. He had no use for the Koreans but they could provide him the weapon he sought. Soon, very soon, the Westerners will die by the thousands. We will also find a way to end the life of this little Korean.

When the Arab had been escorted out by armed guards, Kim rubbed his pudgy little hands together. He was thinking about the sum of money that would be added to his already bulging foreign bank accounts. When he checked the accounts this morning they totaled several billion dollars in U.S. equivalent value. He was so pleased with himself that he called for two of his actresses to meet him in the adjoining bedroom.

Kim Jong Un is the son of the former ruler of North Korea and demands that his people call him the Great Leader as his Father was called. He resides in a seven story palace of pleasure which includes a movie studio to make and view movies, a swimming pool, a library of over 20,000 movies, a bar stocked with the worlds finest wines and other alcoholic beverages, and any thing else he desires that his vast riches can buy. All this while his people are dying by the thousands of starvation. The vast sums of money he has personally accumulated come from the sale of weapons, including missiles to other countries. He is nothing more than a scab on the world.

The food his people eat come from a UN food-aid program. In this crazy world today, the good guys are feeding the bad guys people while the bad guy makes weapons of mass destruction that will be used against the good guys. Isn't it time that someone says enough is enough?

His plan is very simple really, it has to be. One must keep in mind that this is not a very intelligent person. He is playing a game called, confuse the enemy as long as you can. He says he has nuclear weapons, and then he says he doesn't. So, does he or doesn't he? The best course of action is to assume he does. But, what should really be done to stop this creature and by whom should it be done?

CHAPTER THREE

Steve and Scott sat in the room with the large over stuffed furniture sipping their iced teas. They had both showered, changed clothes, and were coming down from the high of the day's actions. A steady rain could be heard through the screened doors and windows. Scott was ready to doze off.

"Do you want to take a snooze Scott? We can have our talk later" asked Steve.

"No, I'll be fine, just had a sinker there for awhile. I am really curious about this place, there's plenty of time to sleep later."

"Okay, here we go. Tim, who was my fellow captive today, is known to be a genius on computerized systems. He designed the software for the propulsion system, navigation, systems analysis, attitude control and weapons just to mention a few. He is a member of MENSA."

Scott had heard of MENSA, the organization of those with genius IQ's.

"My specialty was the propulsion system. The goal was to design a propulsion system that did not use fossil fuels. More about that later. I want to back up and start at the beginning".

"Years ago some ancestor of Mr. R's did a huge favor or deed for British royalty at a time when Great Britain controlled the Bahamas. This island was deeded to that person and was forever a privately owned island. It ceased to be a part of the Bahamas even after they were independent. Mr. R is the only living heir of that person."

"Ten years ago six of us assembled in a conference room at a hotel in Miami Beach. Mr. R was on a speaker phone. We had all been interviewed previously by an organization hired for that purpose. We were all members of MENSA , single and had agreed to a ten year commitment wherever we were sent. We were told we would be working on a project never before explored. The salary was fantastic. The working conditions would be excellent and whatever equipment we needed would be there the next day."

"We were given one week to clean up personal affairs, then three of us met at a private airport where we boarded a helicopter and flew here. The other three would start working on the project in Florida. The building we are in now was complete as you see it. Computers are changed to regularly keep up with the latest technology. As the project proceeded, construction was started on the other buildings which you have not yet seen. It took two years to complete the buildings and transfer the entire project to this location. Some of the other buildings contain housing for special temporary workers from time to time. Right now you and I are the only ones on the island.

Oh, I hadn't told you, the Bahamian authorities found the headquarters of the drug scums and destroyed it. There were no more of them. Seems our middle eastern friend got diarrhea of the mouth when they opened the big side door of the helicopter at 1,500 feet. I wonder what worried him?"

"So, I have been here for ten years, with a week off every month to go anywhere I want. I have seldom left because there was no place to go that was as interesting as what was going on here. Scott, we have created an aircraft that is like nothing you could ever imagine. And now, because our pilot fell in love and married, we no longer have a pilot. I don't know how Max could give it up at this time. He had fifty hours of what he called the most unbelievable flying experience of his life."

"Now comes the part Scott that will surprise you. You were investigated two years ago as a possible candidate for pilot. You were dropped because of the requirement to be single. Fate works in strange ways though. You lost your wife, we lose our pilot, and you end up here. But, these events did happen, and you are here. Why? I don't know why. We need a pilot. Mr. R has authorized me to offer you the position. He kept your dossier up to date to the time you left the mainland for Eleuthera. You interested him. Think about it while I get us another iced tea. If you are leaning towards the idea, I can tell you more. I'll be back in a minute"

When Steve returned a few minutes later Scott was pacing the floor. "This is a big decision to make so suddenly" he said.

"Yup" replied Steve. "But that never stopped you in the past did it?

"Let's say I'm interested enough to find out more Steve"

"Fair enough. Let's head downstairs and take the underground passage to keep from getting soaked in the rain. You can not discuss what you see and learn. Except with the five of us, Tim, our pilot, Mr. R, me and about to be you."

Neither spoke as they walked through the passage to a door at the far end.

"Steve said "Hello door, I would like you to open so we may pass through".

The door opened and they passed through.

"The security we have here is voice controlled. If it were finger print or eye ball recognition or for that matter, any body part recognition, that part could be removed from a body and used to gain entry by anyone. You can't use someone else's voice. A voice can be imitated but never exactly. If you come on board your voice will be taped and computer analyzed. Even if you have a cold it will recognize it as your voice."

They went through a second voice activated door and entered a wide hallway. It appeared to circle a large center section as it curved and disappeared in each direction. Waiting was a vehicle resembling a golf cart without the roof. They got in with Steve behind the steering wheel and headed down the hallway.

The cart made no noise. "Electric?" said Scott

"Nope.

They continued around the large center section with various sized doors on each side of the wide hallway until they were back where they started.

"Round and round we go" said Steve. "I wanted to show you how big this center section of the building is. Now, let's walk over to that closest door on the right and see what's inside.'

As he opened the door for Scott he asked him a question. "What is the stealthiest shape from radar detection?"

"I don't know"

"A continuous curve"

They stepped through the door. Steve looked at Scott for his reaction.

'My God! You captured one" he whispered.

"What? No. No. We built one. This is the aircraft you will fly if you join us. This is what Max was referring to when he said it was the most beautiful flying he had ever experienced. This is the continuous curve.

Scott was speechless. It was a thing of beauty.. He walked up to it, reached up and could just touch the curved edge. It was smooth and hard like a polished stone. At six feet two inches he could walk under it without ducking. It had landing pads, not wheels. Wow! And they want me to fly this. There was now no question, who in their right mind wouldn't want to fly this.

He turned to Steve and said "I'm in." And a grin spread over his face.

Steve grinned back and held his arm out, palm up. "Let's go aboard". He opened a small panel on the underside, pressed a switch and a large panel with stairway slowly lowered and stopped six inches above the floor. Up they went.

The interior was like something out of Star Trek and the Enterprise. He could walk around standing up in the cockpit area. The front ahead of the cockpit was an all clear material as was the area over the pilot's seat. Visibility was outstanding. A second seat was behind and to the right of the pilot's seat which was in the forward center section. Behind those two seats were three more seats centered in the aft section. The entire cockpit was circular with a diameter of twenty five feet.

"Go ahead" said Steve. "Sit in the pilot's seat. You can adjust each seat to your own comfort by pushing the buttons on the seat's left side for more air, up, down, tilt or whatever. There is no instrument panel to obstruct your vision. Any information you want can be projected holographically wherever you wish, in front or off to the side. Just sit there for awhile and look around. What I have to tell you now is the most highly classified information you will conceivably ever hear. It is what makes this thing go. It is what runs everything in this complex, even the golf cart we rode in. In simplest terms it is called magnetic propulsion."

"Scientists have been working on this theory for years. I was fortunate enough to find some answers. If you try to force two magnets together with the same polarity they resist. If you loosen your hold on one of the magnets it will fly out of your hand. Newton's third law states that for every action there is an equal and opposite reaction. The theory is that for a force applied there is an equal and opposite reaction to that force. The earth, space and even the sun have a magnetic field. The suns magnetic field reverses itself every seven years. A magnetic field is made up of fluxes or masses of energy. Each flux varies in strength. That very difference in strength is what allows us to cross lines of flux. If we can capture this energy with magnets on a vehicle with a computer that can control the amount of energy used, we get a constant energy source. This energy force is then applied in a direction and amount opposite to that which we desire. The result is an equal and opposite force which is what we want to propel us in the desired direction. This direction is three dimensional, three hundred and sixty degrees, as in a sphere. You can go anywhere, anytime, as fast as you want to go and never run out of fuel. And if at night, no one will know you are there because this design is 99.99% stealthy. In the daytime they can see you visually if you are within range of whatever is looking at you. Even then, if you are edge on to them, there is a very small surface area to be seen."

"This craft has been developed for research and as a weapon" Steve went on. "This was the directive from Mr. R. In the right hands this could be a one vehicle air force with awesome fire power but, that's down the road a few years. Right now our job is to evaluate the flight characteristics to discover the limits of its operational capabilities. I rode with Max once and still can't believe what this machine can do and we are just getting started with the evaluations."

"It's now pushing seven o'clock Scott. You're flying out in the morning for two days of physical exams, pick up some clothing, fly back here and begin your check out with Max. He's anxious for you to be a fast learner so he can rejoin his bride. Can't say as I blame him, she's a real beauty. The room you used for your shower is now your room. Max and I will be in the other two rooms. I packed Tim's personal items away for him when he returns. By the time he does return I expect Max will be gone. Let's go prepare some dinner, then I have some work to do yet tonight."

They cooked a couple t-bone steaks Steve had removed from the freezer earlier along with a salad, rice and another Kalik beer. It was 9:00 pm when Steve handed Scott a thick manual and said "Here is a manual Max wrote on the aircraft which includes all the information learned to date. You will want to review this so take it with you for evening reading as your days will be full. Needless to say this is highly classified so lock it in your room safe during the day. The chopper will be here at 9:00 am to take you to the mainland."

"Right" said Scott. "It will make interesting reading." What an understatement.

"Yup" said Steve, "welcome to the project. I called Mr. R while you were cooking the steaks and told him you were on board. He was very pleased. I'm going to get some work done so I'll see you in the morning."

Scott stood there with the manual in his hand, anxious to start reading. At three in the morning he closed the book but was too excited over what he had read for sound sleep.

CHAPTER FOUR

Whop, Whop, Whop. The helicopter as it settled on the pad. Both Steve and Scott stood waiting to welcome the Captain who would return the Hey Mon to Ft. Lauderdale. Steve took the Captain down to the boat, Scott boarded the helicopter. The crew chief pointed to a seat and handed him a helmet. As soon as he was strapped in with the helmet on the crew chief gave him the thumbs up and the pilot asked if he was ready.

"All set," replied Scott.

The chopper lifted off and circled the complex which gave Scott his first bird's eye view of it. The paint scheme on the roof of the buildings did an excellent job of camouflaging the entire layout. The house and pool were uncamouflaged which made them look like any other island vacation home. They settled on a heading for the Florida coast as he sat back and closed his eyes. He realized he had not been thinking about Sarah Ann as much as before.

Suddenly he felt a bump and came fully awake. They had just landed among several buildings and the blades were winding down to a stop.

"We're here Scott", said the pilot. "There's transportation on the way to take you to the hospital for your physical. We'll take you back when they're done in a couple days. You won't mind all the probing if you get Dr. Kay. Her name is Dr. Kay Grant but everyone calls her Dr. Kay.

The Dodge Durango took him to the hospital dropping him at the front door. The driver was friendly and talked constantly about nothing. Scott just listened and looked out the windows. The buildings were attractive and the grounds manicured. They were obviously expecting him as a male orderly led to an elevator and ascended to the third floor. The orderly opened a door with the number 37 above the door frame. This was no ordinary hospital room. There was a living room, a small kitchen, a bedroom and bath and a pleasing view of the grounds.

"Do you have any luggage Mr. Wilson", asked the orderly.

"No " replied Scott. I don't even have a tooth brush or razor."

"They are in the bathroom sir. Have you had anything to eat or drink since midnight other than water?"

"No I haven't"

"Good. I'll draw some blood now, take a urine specimen and have that out of the way. Then you can freshen up, have some breakfast in the cafeteria and get some clothes in the clothing store."

"I'll be right back with the blood tray. There's a cup in the bathroom for the specimen".

"Right".

After the blood was drawn and the urine cup half full he had a breakfast of fruit, scrambled eggs and wheat toast. The clothing store turned out to be a well stocked facility for men and women. He picked out slacks, shirts, underwear, socks, shoes and a sport coat. He also added a couple swimming suits as his was looking well worn. When he checked out the clerk told him there was no charge and included an attractive duffle bag to carry everything.

He returned to his room where he hung the clothes or put them in drawers. He had just finished when the phone rang.

"Will you be ready to begin your physical in a few minutes Mr. Wilson?"

I'm ready now"

No sooner had he hung up than there was a knock on the door. He opened it for the orderly.

"I'm here to take you down to Dr. Kay" he said.

.He was sitting in the exam room when Dr. Kay walked in. She was indeed a real beauty.

"Take off your clothes!"

"What, no foreplay?"

"Sorry" she said. "I just came from a bad accident and my mind was elsewhere. I'll try again. I'm Dr. Kay Grant".

"Hello Dr. Grant. My name is Scott Wilson"

"Hello Scott Wilson. Take off your clothes."

The rest of that day and all the next was spent with Dr. Kay. By the end of the exams he was tired of it all even though most of the time was spent with her .The nights were spent reading the flight manual. The words "we are done Scott, and you check out okay on everything", were very welcome.

"You have a phone call and can take it on that phone over there" as she pointed to the phone. "I'll see you again in six months" She closed the door behind her as she left the room.

"Hello" said Scott into the phone.

"This is Mr. R, Scott. Congratulations on a clean bill of health. You will be a valuable asset to the team. I will be getting recordings of your flights so I can stay current with the evaluations. As you build confidence in the aircraft you will want to test its capabilities and yours. Do this in a very discreet and confidential way".

"Yes Sir", said Scott, as he wondered what he was talking about. Then the phone went dead.

That evening he was able to call his children to assure them that he was fine and they were doing well. He would call them again in a couple weeks but if they needed him they could reach him at a number given him by Steve.

CHAPTER FIVE

T he next morning it was on the chopper and back to the island. Steve and Max were there to meet him He had his duffle bag in one hand and the flight manual in the other. During the physical he had locked the manual in the room safe whenever it was out of his hands. Steve introduced Max.

"Okay Scott" said Max. "I see you have the manual in your hands. Stow your gear and I'll see you at the aircraft in fifteen minutes".

That whole day was spent on preflight procedures, pre-takeoff, in-flight, pre-landing, normal procedures, emergency procedures, systems, physiological, navigation, anti-collision, and anything else Max could think of. They took a break for lunch. After a full afternoon session Max told him they would takeoff at midnight and meet at the aircraft at 11:15pm. He said they only flew at night to avoid curious eyes and overhead spy satellites.

Scott could hardly sleep. There was only one machine like it in the world. He forced himself to think of diving the beautiful reefs in the area and finally fell asleep. The alarm went off at 10:30pm and he was at the aircraft by 10:45pm. He found Max there doing the exterior pre-flight.

"Ahhh" said Max. "Have trouble sleeping? Me too. I get so excited about flying this machine that I can't sleep either. I completed the exterior so let's climb aboard and defy gravity".

"Take the main pilot seat. I'm behind with a full set of controls. You will find a guarded red safety toggle switch by your left knee. Lift the guard and flip the switch to the up position. Go ahead and do it now."

When he flipped the switch he saw a movement out the top of the aircraft. The roof of the building was opening like a clamshell. He looked up.

"Ohhh! Look at that Max. There's a million stars out there".

"Well, let's get closer to them. Mind your controls and remember, all you have to do is think about what you want to do and it happens. That's how sensitive the controls are."

The controls were set up like a standard fighter aircraft. The throttle in the left hand control stick and aircraft maneuvering in the right stick. But, it is much more maneuverable than any fighter today as you will find out.

"Here we go", said Scott. "Ohhhh man" he exclaimed. "She's so smooth and feels like a feather." He advanced the throttle forward, pulled the nose up ten degrees, held that attitude and climbed towards the stars. He couldn't resist doing a few rolls on the way up.

They climbed to 25,000 feet where they leveled off. Scott slowly pulled the throttle back to zero power and they remained stationary. He moved the control stick in every direction which caused the ship to roll left, right, forward, backward, all while remaining in one spot.

"Go ahead and play with it" said Max. "That's the best way to feel out any new bird. You can't hurt it and the worst you can do is black us out. The anti-collision also prevents us from flying into the ground or another aircraft. We could fly through the mountains at night with our eyes closed and have no fear of running into Mount Granite. When landing we turn the anti-collision off at the last minute. If you forget to turn it off, you'll stop at three feet and you can't go any lower until it's off."

"What's the service ceiling?" asked Scott

"What do you want it to be Senior?" replied Max with a Spanish accent.

"And that means what?"

"Well Scott, would you like to go say hello to the boys in the space station?"

"You're kidding of course"

"No, I'm not. I don't think there is a service ceiling. As long as there is a magnetic field we can go there. From a safety standpoint we should be in pressure suits to fly above 50,000 according to the directive from Mr. R. Go ahead and take her to 50,000. Your pressure suit should be here tomorrow so, on the next flight we'll do some research on that subject.

A big grin came to Scott's face. He liked this man Max who was willing to try anything as long as it did not violate directives. Wouldn't that be something to fly to the space station? Can you imagine the looks on their faces? Hello there! Just thought we'd stop by for lunch. Unknown to Scott, this bird did have a docking collar hidden behind an external panel.

"I understand the airspeed is limited by the skin temperature but, at 50,000 feet and an outside temperature of -55 degrees, what is our maximum speed?" asked Scott.

"Approximately mach 7". However, once we leave the earth's atmosphere we have no limiting airspeed. So, if you want to get someplace in a hurry, climb as fast as your body can stand, in the direction you want to go, at maximum temperature. Once you are out of the atmosphere open her up. Be sure to plan ahead for the slow down and again, that's at a rate your body can stand. We have an excellent gym at the complex and I suggest you stay in good physical condition to withstand the constant G forces you're going to experience."

"Yah, I guess. With these high speeds and the maneuverability this thing has, I can understand that".

"Okay, play with it as long as you want but we have to head for home before daylight. We'll see if you can find home and land it in the hangar."

Scott played with the bird for another five hours. Scott then punched HOME on the GPS which gave him the heading to fly, the distance to get there, and the time based on present airspeed. Thirty minutes later he was letting down through the open shell doors . One hundred feet before entering the hangar he turned off the anti-collision system, continued his let down to a no- jar landing.

"Very nice" said Max.

"There is one problem that I see Max."

"And what would that be?"

"My landings are so smooth I'll need someone on the ground to tell me when I've landed".

"Right", said Max with a grin. "Let's give her an after flight walk around to make sure you didn't put any dings in her, then I'll buy you a beer".

CHAPTER SIX

I t was 6:00am when they walked into the house and there sat Steve with a big grin and three opened Kalik beers.

"Congratulations Rambo. I recorded the entire flight including voice. Mr. R also has a copy. What do you think Max, is he going to bend the bird?"

"Well, it was touch and go for awhile but, there's hope. One more flight tomorrow night with pressure suits may do it. He wants to say hello to the boys in the space station."

"Wouldn't that be a kick", laughed Steve.

"You're kidding Max. You don't intend to turn me loose with that mega-million dollar machine with only two rides do you?"

" I didn't have any dual when I flew it the first time. I was the first to fly it, period. I won't turn you loose until I know you are ready. But, I do believe you will be ready after our flight to-morrow night. You will then have over ten hours in the bird . Get a good night's sleep, review the manual, and we'll lift off at 11:00pm tonight. Now let's enjoy the beer."

They kidded each other for awhile, finished their beers then headed for their rooms. Again Scott had trouble sleeping thinking about being responsible for a one-of-a kind billion dollar aircraft.

He finally fell asleep and arose close to 2:00pm, brushed his teeth, put on a swim suit and headed for the pool. It was a beautiful afternoon with sunny skies, 85 degrees, and with that ever gentle Bahamas breeze.

He dove into the pool and swam laps. As he got out the others were setting a pitcher of iced tea with glasses filled to the top with ice and a tray of grouper sandwiches. Steve had been fishing that morning and caught several strawberry groupers. A guy could sure get used to this life.

After lunch they sat talking while sipping their iced tea. "To show you what a good guy I am" said Steve "I'll fix dinner tonight. I brought in six lobsters from our traps plus we'll have summer squash to go with it and a little butter pecan ice cream for dessert. That should be a non-gaseous dinner for you space travelers. I assume that's your plan for tonight's flight?"

"You bet it is" replied Max. "Anyplace in particular you want to go Scott?"

"Yes" he answered, "I'd like to know the fastest way we can get to the other side of the world and back again. Let's also do it in four directions to find the one best way".

"Alright, we'll find the fastest way" said Max. It was a strange request. He felt there was an ulterior motive. "Your pressure suit arrived this morning, try it on this afternoon for a comfortable fit."

They lifted off at exactly 11:00pm. Scott had found their opposite location and entered the lat long in the GPS. They climbed rapidly with an eye on the skin temperature. With the decrease in atmospheric pressure and a corresponding decrease in skin temperature, they accelerated in the direction the computer had calculated. They were soon traveling at the speed of the shuttle, over 17,000 miles per hour. They watched items float in space. They watched the sun rise and set. It took awhile to get over the view of the earth below.

Scott had calculated the time and distance to an altitude when they could accelerate to unlimited speed. He used a speed of 17,000 miles per hour at altitude. He had a theory about that speed which he would later verify. The earth's circumference at the equator is 28,739 miles. The computations came up with one hour and 41 minutes to circumnavigate the earth. Since they wanted to time half the distance, he divided one forty one, or 101 minutes, by two, which gave an answer of fifty minutes thirty seconds.

The first time they flew by the point and kept going until they were over their point of departure. They then circumnavigated the earth from north to south, flying over both poles. It was hard to believe he was actually flying around the earth in space the same as the astronauts but he didn't go through all the training the astronauts must endure before going into space. He asked Max about this and was told that Mr. R and his medical staff did not believe this was necessary. They felt that a person in good physical condition was prepared physically. It was not the mission of their aircraft to remain in space as the men and women do on the International

Space Station. Mr. R's pilots needed to understand the aircraft's handling in the atmosphere and in space. They needed to know the forces on the body and its limits, maneuvers to avoid so as not to bend or break the body. This was all part of the check out he was receiving from Max.

When they again returned to their original departure point they descended to just above the hangar and started all over. This time though, they needed to learn when they should start slowing in order to remain over the point and not overshoot it. They had to add two and one half minutes to their enroute time for a total of fifty-three minutes. Any distance more or less than the equatorial distance would be adjusted as a percentage more or less than the 28,739 miles circumference. Scott was able to compute the time and distance to start decelerating so as to arrive over an intended point without any overshoot.

"You handle this thing better than I do Scott, let's head for the barn" said Max. "It's 4:30am now so it will 5:30 by the time we button her up and do our post flight. A perfect time for a beer don't you think?"

"Sounds good to me Max", replied Scott.

"You've got something cooking in that mind of yours Scott. I don't have any idea what it is and I don't want to know but, you be careful hear?"

"Yup" .

Steve was up again with three opened Kaliks and a big grin. "You going home Max?"

"As soon as I can Steve. You don't need me here anymore and my sweet little bride is longing for my body."

"Yeah, right Max. Then go pack your gear because the chopper will be hear at 9:00am delivering Tim. You can catch a ride back on it", said Steve.

"Plenty of time to enjoy our beer first" answered Max.

CHAPTER SEVEN

They sat and watched the news as they had everyday. The more Scott watched it the more upset he became at the world situation. The president was fighting a battle on four major fronts, Iraq, North Korea , Iran and terrorist. Plus, and this is what really irked him, all the countries that always have their hand out, turn their head when he asks them for support. They know the United States will go it alone so why should they give their support and risk offending some neighbor or trade partner or some other lame duck excuse. Other than Great Britain and Australia most of the other countries are, to put it bluntly, limp dicks. Listen to them scream if North Korea nukes someone and they are showered with radioactive fall-out that kills thousands of their countrymen, or if Iran delivers biological attacks on someone and the fallout lands on other Arab nations. Our good friend Turkey has a change in political control which may cause them to cancel their agreement to let us use our bases in their country if we attack Iran. And we, as the world's watch dog, try to treat everyone with kid gloves. There are always those politicians who are afraid we might offend someone even if those countries are receiving substantial free aid. This President though, appears stronger than others, with the philosophy that we will do whatever needs to be done in order to protect our country. Steve, Max and Scott all agreed that we need to support the President.

Those of the Islam faith need to stand up and clean their own houses and stop looking the other way at the militant extremist in their churches. They must stop giving to that church if the funds end up with the terrorists. Instead, they whine about profiling. They expect airport security guards to strip search a little old lady with a thick southern accent in a wheel chair instead of some middle eastern twenty year old. And what makes it worse is that there are those in the U.S. that agree with that philosophy.

Max had insight concerning Scott.

The next morning the helicopter arrived. Tim moved into the room Max had vacated. He and Steve worked day and night in their respective rooms. The weeks passed as Scott flew every night to different places logging the flight profile as to distance and time. He flew in his space suit more and more. He became very comfortable in the aircraft while practicing many high performance maneuvers in the atmosphere and in space.

He had to know how well he was really flying in comparison to the best that was known today. He started flying over Edwards Air Force base where he knew the Lockheed Martin F-22 Raptor was undergoing Air Force evaluations.

CHAPTER EIGHT

One night he was near Edwards AFB when something was said on the radio that confirmed it was the Raptor taking off. Here was the latest Air Force fighter in the hands of an experienced fighter pilot, and here he was of inferior skill but with what he believed to be a superior aircraft. What would happen? He had to know, his future plans depended on knowing. He was sweating in anticipation. The new star-light screen gave him a daylight visual on the Raptor. He knew the 22 had a star-light night navigation system that allowed it to see terrain at night but not air to air like he had. That was a big advantage to him because both aircraft were stealthy and could not be seen on radar.

He slipped easily into the raptor's six o'clock position and stayed there during climb out. No one knew he was there. Oh man, this is crazy he thought. Here I am sitting within spitting distance of the most advanced fighter in the world and neither he nor his ground control know I'm here. They will shortly, and then the fun begins. He tuned his radio to that of the Raptor.

Raptor: "Control, Raptor level at flight level 350."

Control: "Roger Raptor, your target call sign, Spook, an F-4, is airborne, ete your area 12 minutes."

"Roger control.
"
Scott: "Hello double deuce, check six."

Raptor: "What? That you Spook? A little early aren't you? And if you're there why don't I paint you?"

"Because I'm not Spook" He then flipped his landing light on and off which illuminated the 22 and startled its pilot.

"This is Raptor. At my six o'clock say call sign"

"Call me Friendly and I want to play."

Raptor: "Ground this is Raptor. I have an unidentified on my tail that wants to play. Do you show him on radar?"

Control: "Negative Raptor. We show no returns in your area, and Spook is the only adversary scheduled tonight. We heard him on the radio, is he really back there?"

Raptor: "That's affirmative ground. He flashed his landing light at me. Tell Spook to stay out of the area until I find out who this guy is."

Control: "Will do Raptor. Let us know who he is and we'll violate him".

Raptor: "Roger control. I assume you copied that Friendly. So you want to play huh? Your ass is gonna to be grass when I identify you."

With that the pilot threw the 22 into a ninety degree right bank and tilted the exhaust nozzles up which caused a gut wrenching high G turn. Just as quickly he reversed into a left turn and looked over his left shoulder to get a visual on the other aircraft. Even at night something could show but the sky was empty. He continued the tight left turn rolling out on the original heading.

When the Raptor went into the high G turn Scott went high and rolled inverted where he watched the two high G turns then slipped silently back to the raptors six o'clock rolling back to top side up.

Raptor: "What happened to you Friendly? Spin out? Don't forget to punch out if you can't recover."

"Check six Raptor" He again flashed his landing light to verify he was there.

"What the hell you flying boy?"

No sooner were the words out of his mouth then he went vertical with burners on. That was intended to blind Scott as much as for speed. He pulled out of after burner and completed a three quarter loop. Then he set the exhaust nozzles full down, went into burner again and went nose over tail tumbling down.

Scott had anticipated the vertical maneuver and moved out to the side before Raptor cut in the burners. He watched the whole thing from the side maintaining the same altitude as the 22.

When the Raptor pulled out of the tumble Scott slid to his six again. This guy is really going to get pissed thought Scott. I can go in any direction or remain stationary. One more time for one upmanship as he grinned to himself feeling more confident and a little cocky.

"Very nice double deuce. Check six." And of course he flipped his landing light on and off to again verify he was really there.

Raptor: "Control is Dusty still active?"

"Roger, for another forty five minutes."

"Okay, tell them I'm on my way."

"Roger, will do."

Scott: "Where are we going Double Deuce?"

"Catch me if you can."

"Haven't had any trouble so far."

No answer from the 22 that time. The pilot pointed the nose down and accelerated to mach 2 heading for the dry lake bed. Over the bed he took the 22 down to 100 feet heading straight for what turned out to be a mobile control crew. Scott moved to five hundred feet and out to the side so the crew could not see an outline against the stars and since there was no engine sound they could not hear him either.. As soon as they were past the 22 climbed and Scott moved to the six o'clock position and turned on his landing light. He left it on a little longer this time so the ground crew could see the 22 illuminated. He turned it off and headed for home.

Ground crew: "We didn't see anything behind you but, you sure lit up like a Christmas tree. How did you do that?"

Raptor: "You don't want to know mobile and thanks for the look."

Scott: "Goodnight Double Deuce and thanks for the play time."

"Goodnight Friendly. I'd sure like to know who you are. Let's meet again, daytime."

Raptor: "Control this is Raptor. Cancel Spooky, I'm coming in. Meet me."

Control: "Copy that Raptor."

As Scott headed for home feeling a little chest-puffed, a big smile on his face, he felt assured he could handle any adversary in the air. This aircraft was without question way ahead of its time.

What else could it do he thought, as the smile left his face, replaced by a look of determination.

In the meantime, pilot Chris Denson taxied the Raptor to the hanger where the ground crew took over to put it to bed for the night. He entered the debriefing room and found the others were waiting for him.

"What went on up there?" said George Grey, head of the control crew and assistant director of the evaluation.

"That's what I'd like to know" said Chris. "I threw that bird all over the sky, did things I haven't done before, especially at night, and what do I hear? Check six! What the hell was behind me? We're supposed to have the most advance bird in the world then some guy waxes me, but good. I think we better find out."

"We have no idea Chris. We're as baffled as you. I'll call Air Force in the morning." Was all George could think of to say.

George did call Air Force, but not in the morning. He called that night.

"General Ragland", said George, "we have a situation down here. I can come there or you here but, either way we need to meet tomorrow sir. I'm not on a secure phone so I can't say anymore."

General Bart Ragland had known George for too many years not to know there was genuine concern in his voice. As deputy director of the F-22 evaluation he was sure it concerned that aircraft. Not now, he thought, we're well into the program and we really need that bird. He was looking forward to flying it himself next week. With 7,000 hours of fighter time he was well qualified.

"Clear the desk kind of thing George?"

"Yes General."

"Okay George, I'll be there in the morning. See you then."

"Click", went the phone and it was dead.

At 8:30am General Ragland called Edwards tower.

"Edwards, Air Force 578, two out initial, landing."

The tower knew who it was by the code passed from operations as soon as the General filed his flight plan. The General knew the active runway from the Airport Traffic Information System broadcast on a printed frequency.

"Ahhh, roger 578, you're number one, cleared to land. Left break."

"Roger, cleared to land, left break, 578." responded the General.

The General made a, "they're all watching the General from the tower", landing which was as near perfect as you can get. On his landing rollout the tower called him.

"578, ground one two two point five five when clear".

"578"

As he turned the F-15 off the active runway onto the taxi-way he switched his radio to ground frequency.

"Ground, 578 is with you, clear the active."

"Roger 578, hold position, a follow me is on the way."

"578 holding."

An Air Force blue pick-up arrived with a "Follow Me" sign in the bed, did a 180 degree turn and proceeded to the parking area with the General following. Ground crews were waiting for him as well as the Duty Officer, base commander and George. George was a full Colonel with a lot of fighter time in his log book. They all exchanged salutes as the General climbed down the ladder and stepped to the tarmac.

The base commander was a one star General by the name of Jack Jackson, a real hard-nosed fighter pilot who ran a tight no non-sense command. Do not call a jet fighter a fighter jet around him or you will receive a lecture lasting at least fifteen minutes telling you how the media has been screwed up for many years. His father flew F-86's in Korea and retired a two star. "They flew jet fighters not fighter jets. You would have been laughed at and thrown out of the officers club for such stupid nomenclature. What do you call a fighter with a propeller? A fighter propeller? Jet is the adjective and fighter is the noun!" Then he'd tell the story of the woman news-person who was showing the instrument hood a pilot was wearing when involved in a mid-air accident. She had the adjustable strap across her eyes trying to look through the holes, like the holes in a belt, and the hood sticking out behind her head. The tragedy was that she was serious and thought that was how they were worn. "So! We fly jet fighters, not fighter jets. If I hear you say fighter jets again you will be sent to a multi-engine outfit where everyone grabs a throttle and runs forward for take-off."

The duty officer was a young F-16 first lieutenant who had not spent much time around Generals and was obviously very nervous. The Generals excused him and off he went.

"General" said General Jackson, "if you will drop me by my of-fice the car is yours for as long as you wish"

"Thank you Jack," said General Ragland, "I don't know how long I'll be here but, you'll get it back by the end of the day and I appreciate the loan."

"My pleasure sir."

After they dropped General Jackson they drove to the hangar and office where George and the F-22 lived.

"Have a seat General and I'll play the disk while running the computer maneuvering software. The computer will show an animated aircraft going through the exact maneuvers the actual aircraft is going through synchronized to the recorded voice tape."

They ran the program several times. Afterwards they sat back and looked at each other, their minds trying to find an answer.

"You're right George, we have a situation. As far as I know the F-22 is not only the most advanced fighter we have but that anyone has. Whatever was up there with Chris would have flamed him. He must have some kind of air to air night vision system and be at least as stealthy as the 22. I know we are working on the night vision air to air but we don't have it yet. In fact we have a long way to go. And, whatever it was, kept up with the 22's maneuvers. Chris is a damn good pilot too. We had the best aircraft and an excellent pilot yet, we got waxed. Jesus! What's going on? Put the program on a disk for me and I'll take it to Washington."

"I taped it while we were running it including the reruns. Here's the tape General. I'd sure like to know if there's a bird better than ours."

"Me too. Give my regards to General Jackson George. I'm on my way to Washington. Keep the evaluation on schedule and I'll be in touch."

"Goodbye General."

General Bart Ragland flew to Andrews AFB and proceeded directly to the BOQ where he had a room and a change of clothes to a class A uniform. Transportation was provided him and he went straight to General Skip Hathcock's office, Air Force Chief of Staff at the Pentagon. Skip was a four star General and a good friend of General Ragland's. Since the F-22 was such an important project General Hathcock directed General Ragland to report directly to him.

"Good morning Bart", greeted General Hathcock.

"Good morning Sir. Thank you for seeing me on such short notice"

"It must be damned important by the tone of your voice."

"It is Sir," responded Bart. "May I use your computer to play this disk? It will explain why I'm here."

"Of course, go ahead and start it, then help yourself to some coffee while I watch it."

When the disk was done, including the recorded reruns, General Hathcock's comment was, "Jesus! What the hell was it? Where did it come from? You were right to bring this to me asap Bart. I'll get our analysis people working on this right away. Let's see if they come up with anything. The guy sounds American. You got any ideas?"

"No sir. Nor do any of my people. It's been a long day General. I'm staying at the BOQ tonight, dinner at the O Club if you need me."

"Good, and thanks for the heads up."

"Bart was surprised in some ways and not in others. He was surprised that the General knew nothing of another research bird as he had hoped but, not surprised because the General would have brought him in on it. He agreed the other pilot sounded American with no accent. It will be interesting to see if the analysis comes up with anything.

CHAPTER NINE

S cott was building time rapidly in the aircraft. He had over 550
hours now of extremely enjoyable flying. He had been all over
the globe. Gone into space orbit and calculated the maximum
speed he could fly without leaving the earth's orbit. He found,
by programming the auto-pilot to fly at 29,000 miles per hour at
a constant 1 G and a preset altitude of 150 miles, the bird would
stay in orbit without a tendency to leave it and shoot off into space.
There is an orbital speed at which an object overcomes the gravita-
tional pull of the earth and leaves orbit. Of course, he could always
fly back if that happened. One G allowed him to fly at a constant
altitude at 29,000 mph, get where he was going in a hurry, and
not worry about constantly adjusting altitude. With the top of the
aircraft facing earth, the result was a positive 1 G which avoided
the problems of long weightlessness at zero G. Nor did the aircraft
have the flaming high entry temperatures as did the space shuttle,
which had special tiles to absorb the heat. He could descend at
any angle, including vertical, using airspeed to control temperature
as he entered earth's atmosphere. When the shuttle re-enters the

atmosphere it is a glider, whereas he is still a powered aircraft with complete control over his re-entry.

Scott was sitting in the kitchen one morning after a six hour night flight, when Tim walked in and joined him for breakfast. Tim had been upgrading the weapons systems during the day. Steve removed the flight recording disks each morning and forwarded them via electronic transmission to Mr. R. They kept one copy for themselves, which they analyzed each afternoon after Scott arose. Steve walked in with the tape and joined them.

"How is the upgrading coming along?" asked Scott.

"Almost done" replied Tim. "I should finish it today. Some practice bombs are coming today and I'll want to load them later. I'll need the bird all night Scott so no flying tonight. You need a night off anyway. Why don't you and Steve take the boat out diving and bring back some grouper for dinner? You need some play time."

"Tell you what Scott" said Steve, "I have some work on the bird also. Why don't you hit the sack and I'll wake you when I'm done. It will be around noon and we'll head out then."

"You guys are smooth talkers, goodnight."

Back at the Pentagon the analysts had been busy studying the tape General Hathcock had given them.

"General Hathcock will see you now Major Rupard" said Jean Marshall, the General's secretary.

"Thank you Jean" he replied.

"Get some coffee Harvey then tell me what you have." welcomed the General.

"Thanks you sir but I just finished a cup. We feel certain the voice belongs to a man in his late thirties or early forties and he was raised in the northwest, Wyoming, Montana, Idaho or Washington, Oregon or even California. Because of his flying ability he may be ex-military. He's good and so is whatever he's flying. We don't know if he actually followed Chris through the maneuvers or positioned himself to jump on his tail at some point. This may have been a test by this pilot to see how he stacked up against the F-22. We think he got his answer so broke off the engagement and headed home, wherever that is. That's all we have General."

"Okay Harvey. It looks like we have to wait and see if he shows up again. Keep working on it. I'll need to brief the Joint Chiefs."

"Yes sir." said Harvey and left the office.

The next day General Hathcock showed the disk to the Joint Chief's of Staff.. Secretary of Defense Clayton also sat in on the meeting. After the showing of the disk he stated that the President must see it also, and he would see to it.

The Secretary of Defense Clayton, Secretary of State Painter, Secretary of Home Land Security, Ward, Chairman of the Joint Chief's, Air Force General Balanger and the president of the United States, President Barley, sat in silence for a short time after viewing the recording. "What I am told," said the President, "is that no one has any ideas about this. The F-22 pilot was not making it up because his aircraft was illuminated when flying over the mobile control crew in the desert. However, they could not see nor hear another aircraft. Is this correct?"

"That is correct," stated General Balanger. "Our analysts estimate he is in his late thirties or early forties, raised somewhere in
the west or northwest and possibly ex-military. That Sir, is all the
information we have."

CHAPTER TEN

S cott woke at eleven thirty, showered and dressed in a polo shirt, swim suit and sandals. As he entered the kitchen Tim and Steve were just coming in the house.

"Hi guys, how about a lobster salad for lunch? We have enough left over from last night."

"Great, good" they both voiced, thinking about their cholesterol with all the seafood they were eating. Oh well, they did have lots of vegetables and other meats too.

After lunch Scott and Steve loaded the Whaler with dive gear and a cooler of Kalik beer. Nothing tastes as good as a cold beer after breathing compressed dry air from a scuba tank.

"I'll take you to my favorite reef" Steve yelled over the roar of the twin outboards as he guided the boat at high speed through the canal and out to the ocean. "It's about three miles east southeast of here. Be there in no time."

They flew across the flat sea and came to the reef a few minutes later. They dropped and set the anchor then donned their scuba gear.

Scott looked at Steve and almost whispered, "The last time I went in the water like this, four men were dead a short time later. Hey Steve, see any other boats?"

"No other boats Scott. I'm a little gun shy too. Come on, let's do it!" They both went in the water at the same time.

They descended sixty feet to the bottom checking their gear on the way down. On the bottom they gave each other the okay sign and swam towards the coral reef using slow but powerful strokes to conserve air. The water was warm with excellent visibility in excess of one hundred feet. As they approached the coral they could see it was teeming with life. They passed over large fan coral with several flamingo tongues attached. Their orange and pink colors brightened up the fans. They circled the edge of the reef all the way around before exploring the center. Looking up under coral overhangs they saw lobster, large grouper and snapper. One large overhang was home to a six foot sand shark laying on the sandy bottom. It completely ignored them. They carried their spears but, by an unspoken mutual feelings, did no spearing. It was an hour of pure enjoyment observing the sea life.

After a decompression stop they climbed the ladder and stowed their dive gear. After Scott climbed in Steve opened the cooler and removed two Kalik beers. That good taste after breathing dry compressed air was a bit of Heaven.

"Well Scott", said Steve with a smile, "we're back in the boat, no other boats in sight and we haven't killed anyone or anything. I'd say it's a good day."

"Tim will be disappointed we didn't get any grouper"

Steve laughed. "I don't think he had much confidence in us, he took several filets out of the freezer this morning."

They finished a second beer while laying back in the seats enjoying the warm sun and deep blue sky. The distant sound of a helicopter grew louder as it came nearer and nearer, finally stopping overhead.

A loud speaker spoke from the chopper. "If you two are done we'll see you at the house."

With that spoken, it turned and headed straight for the complex as they watched. After stowing gear and anchor they too headed in.

"Wonder what this is all about?" spoke Steve. "Our R&R was interrupted but, it was sure relaxing while it lasted. If Mr. R assigns me to another project when I'm done here, I think I'll spend that week each month here now and then. This is sure Paradise."

After tying up the boat they rinsed themselves and the dive gear with fresh water from a dock side shower. Steve walked down the path towards the house while Scott carried the dive tanks up to the small building that contained the compressor used to fill the tanks. He placed them with the others that needed filling, a chore one of them would do later. It was then that he noticed a movement in the bushes behind the helicopter.

He pretended not to notice and walked casually to the house. When he entered he saw that the others were out by the pool having refreshments. He slipped into his room, grabbed the AK-47 and back out the door. He circled the other buildings until he came into view of the chopper. He then scanned the surrounding area, the brush and nearby buildings, and there he was, trying to open a hangar side door. Scott knew he couldn't get in so decided to observe him awhile. He was dressed like a tourist in white shorts and polo shirt, white socks with white sneakers. Not good camouflage for what he was trying to do. He soon tired of pushing on a door that wouldn't open and walked to the next door with the same result. Eventually he gave up and walked to the house. Scott followed him and when he joined the others he was able to slip back into his room unnoticed and hide the AK 47. He changed into shirt and slacks then joined the others poolside.

"Hey Scott, look who's here. Dr. Kay came slumming.

"Hello Scott. I've heard so much about this being paradise I had to see for myself."

"Hello Dr. Kay. glad you could come. It really is a sort of paradise though there is a lot that gets done," he said. She was wearing tan shorts with a white halter top, sandals and what a figure. He had trouble taking his eyes off her to look at the Air Force Colonel.

"This is Colonel Gary Tinsel" she said as she introduced Scott. "I met him on the helicopter. He won't tell me why he's here."

Scott and the Colonel exchanged greetings. He waived hello to the helicopter guys. The pilot said they had to leave in fifteen minutes to pick up supplies and return.

Scott looked at Colonel Tinsel and said, "Colonel, I need a word with you. Let's go in the house." He then turned and walked to the door leaving the Colonel to follow with a surprised look on his face.

"What's that all about?" said Steve.

"Don't know," replied Tim, "but I wouldn't want to be in the Colonel's shoes right now."

In the house Scott turned, "Colonel, I don't know who you are but you be on that helicopter when it leaves in fifteen minutes."

"What? Who the hell do you think you are?"

"When you were snooping around our buildings Colonel, did the hair stand up on the back of your neck? I had the sights of an AK 47 zeroed in on your back. You be on that chopper and don't ever come back here again." Scott turned and walked back to the pool. The Colonel did not follow.

"I believe a tall iced tea with a wedge of lemon would taste very good" said Scott as he walked to the refreshment table. "You care for anything Dr. Kay?"

"Make it two. Did you make a new friend or an enemy?"

"Unfortunately the latter"

" He was a jerk on the helicopter, really impressed with himself." She noticed that the Colonel had not come out of the house.

"You and Steve looked like you were enjoying yourselves in the boat. Sorry they called you back but the pilot had an important message for Steve. If you have time I'd love a boat ride."

"Uh. Well sure. When would you like to go?"

"How about right now?"

"Let's do it."

As they left the pool area Scott picked up a small cooler, put in four beers and two bottled waters along with ice. They followed a chipped shell path past the helicopter landing pad where they saw the Colonel sitting inside the chopper waiting for the crew. He pretended not to notice as they walked past. Scott helped Kay into the Whaler then checked gas quantity for the two outboards. He started the engines, untied the lines and cruised slowly across the lake and through the canal into the open water.

As they entered the open water Scott thought, what is on Dr. Kay's mind? Whatever it is, talking over the engine noise is difficult at best. I'll anchor at the reef Steve took me to earlier if I can find it. He headed in the direction he thought it would be and after a little zig and zagging he found it, dropped and set the anchor.

"It's more relaxing to anchor if you don't have a destination. We don't have to shout over the engines."

"I don't get a chance to do this very often. I can see why you love it here. I don't know what you do here and I'm not going to ask. Everyone that works for Mr. R knows better than to ask any questions about anyone. But, it would be nice if you can spend time enjoying the water. I love these Bahama waters." She then kicked her sandals off, removed her halter top, shorts and panties, then turned and faced him absolutely nude. He stood with his mouth dry and hanging open. MY GOD! he thought, she is beautiful.

"Take off your clothes Scott Wilson." she commanded, and dove into the water laughing. He stood for a moment not knowing what to do. She surfaced and with strong swimming strokes swam away from the boat. He came out of his shock, took his clothes off, hooked the ladder over the side and dove in. They swam and free dove for half an hour before returning to the boat.

He opened a compartment door and removed two towels handing her one. She walked to the bow of the boat, laid two bench cushions on the deck and covered one with her towel. She took his towel from him and covered the other cushion and lay down.

"It's much better to air dry than towel dry don't you think. But, before you lie down, may I have one of those beers please?"

He opened two beers and stretched out on the cushion beside her. "This is much better than diving with Steve" he chuckled.

"That's reassuring. I work hard long hours at the clinic with very little time off. That's of my own choosing though. I am paid very well and plan to return for my residency in heart surgery some day. I have two years residency in general surgery but, I'd like to specialize in the heart. I'm afraid I am a career woman. I don't want a serious relationship with a man but, I do have normal sex drives. Every so often there is a need to satisfy those desires. I pick and choose very carefully when that happens. During your physical and psychological exam you interested me. Now here I am." She set her beer down and turned to him. "By the looks of your friend there, it appears you have desires too. Make love to me Scott."

They made love. Their pent up desires brought them to a peak very quickly, almost too quickly. She stood and dove over the side. When she surfaced she looked up at him and smiled. "Come in the water and refresh yourself. You're not done yet."

They made love again, this time slower, followed by another refreshing swim. "This was the first time since you lost your wife wasn't it?" His reply was a nod.

"The memories you have of her are very special Scott. They belong in a part of your memory that is a special place, like a beautiful tranquil garden. You can call up those memories whenever you wish. No one will compete with them nor do they want to. It is possible to have new relationships that are not competing, that will not diminish those things you had with her. Hopefully, you will have wonderful experiences in a new relationship that will become special memories also. Then, you will be very lucky to have found another that will also give you happiness. It has been over a year since you lost her. Our meeting today was not all for me Scott. This was also meant to help you on the road to your recovery, doctor's orders. Now, I would like one of those waters please."

As he handed her a water he stammered, "Thanks Kay. Your words make sense. I have been trying to convince myself the same thing but without success. Hearing it from someone else helps. Our making love was a big hurdle I didn't think I could handle. I thought it would take something away from my memory of her. I was wrong. I feel I have come a long way this afternoon thanks to you."

"We helped each other Scott. It may or may not happen again but, it was special to me also. I now have a special memory of this afternoon that I'll tuck away thanks to you. Now, let's get dressed before that helicopter comes back. It wouldn't do to wave to them dressed as we are."

The helicopter landed while they were tying up to the dock. When they arrived at the pool area Steve and Tim had the fish cooking and the table set. The fare was grouper, green beans, fried potatoes and plenty of iced tea. No alcohol was around as there was flying and work after dinner.

They had a wonderful time telling stories and laughing. All too soon it was time for the helicopter to return with Dr. Kay on board. After the goodbyes the chopper lifted off and was gone. The three men returned to the pool where they made short order of the cleanup.

CHAPTER ELEVEN

When Colonel Tinsel returned to his motel room there was a message to report to General Ragland immediately. Since General Ragland's office was in Atlanta, home of the F-22 contractor, Lockheed Martin, he wondered how he was going to report immediately. That was Colonel Tinsel's problem not General Ragland's. The Colonel showered, changed into his class A uniform and booked the first flight he could find out of Ft. Lauderdale.

On the way to Atlanta he was thinking, I hope it has something to do with that mysterious plane the other night over Edwards. There was no runway there anyway and a helicopter couldn't fly as fast as they were flying so I have ruled them out as a suspect. I'm sure the General will be pleased with that information.

General Ragland had told his receptionist to inform him as soon as Colonel Tinsel arrived. He arrived at four thirty five and was shown directly into the General's office.

"Colonel Tinsel reporting as ordered Sir" he stated as he held a salute. The General kept him waiting longer than normal before returning the salute and, he did not tell him to stand at ease.

"Colonel", the General started, "what were you doing on that island yesterday, and why were you snooping around their buildings? How did you get an invitation in the first place?"

The Colonel was still at attention. "I used the office Sir."

"You used my office to get a social invitation?"

"It wasn't social Sir. They do so many secret things at that Company I thought I would check out their island facility to see if they were the ones involved with that mysterious aircraft. I ruled them out though because there is no runway and a helicopter couldn't do the things that bogie did."

"Couldn't you have found that out with maps or file photos or even fly over it yourself? You were observed trying to get into their buildings by one of their people who had a gun pointed at you. You embarrassed this office Colonel. That Company has done a lot of high tech development for the military. You were lucky you weren't shot."

"Did that pompous civilian puke tattle to his boss? He should be reprimanded for treating an officer of the military the way he treated me. I left because I didn't want to create a scene unbecoming of my rank. It took a lot of will power to keep from pulling rank and really chewing that guy out in front of his friends"

"You don't get it do you Colonel? You are the one in the wrong. You wrangle an invitation under false pretenses, snoop around their private property and nearly get yourself shot. That man would have been well within his rights to have shot you. You are no longer part of this command. I am transferring you to the Antarctic Command under Colonel Helton. I doubt you'll do much snooping around down there. Here are your orders Colonel, you leave tomorrow. That's all, dismissed'

The Colonel left the General's office in a daze. Had he done something wrong? He was the best investigator the General had, at least he thought so. He ruled out that piece of dirt in the Bahamas for him. Wait a minute, that's it, there's something going on in the Antarctic. He wants me down there to check things out. I'm no longer under his command for security purposes. Good cover General, I couldn't have done better myself. Look out Antarctica, here comes Colonel Tinsel. If there is something fishy going on down there, I will find it.

CHAPTER TWELVE

"You remember I'm working on the bird's weapons systems tonight don't you Scott? said Tim. Would you like to join me? I was going to cover the systems with you at a later date but we could get a good start tonight if you'd like."

"That's a great idea Tim" Scott replied. "I wondered what I was going to do tonight. I'm so used to flying every night, I'm lost when I don't."

When they entered the hangar Tim continued down the circular hallway to a door Scott had not entered before. Tim looked at him and nodded at the door, "You have never asked what's behind this door, even though it's not the "Green Door".

"I figured you guys would let me know when and if the time came."

"The time has come" said Tim.

They entered a building that was a twin of the main hangar. Inside was the bottom half of an aircraft similar to the one he'd been flying. Tim began an explanation. "This is the weapons pod. It holds ninety six two hundred and fifty pound bombs, twenty four air to air missiles, six thousand rounds of twenty millimeter ammo for four guns. It fits on the bottom of the aircraft with sixteen hydraulic bolts eight inches in diameter. This in no way adversely affects the stealth characteristics or the performance of the aircraft since aerodynamic lift and weight are not a factor with magnetic propulsion. The warheads on these bombs are filled with a new substance that gives them the equivalent destructive power of the old two-thousand pounder. Come over here, I want to show you the business end of these."

"What are these?" asked Scott. "They look like a miniature F-117."

"These are the bombs. A flaw in the F-117 and the B-2 bomber is when bombs are released the opening of the bomb bay doors and the weapon coming out can be seen on radar for a split second. If a really sharp radar operator happens to have his radar aimed that way he might pick up a signal. They could then direct everything they have at the estimated spot and perhaps hit our aircraft. The shape of these bombs makes them invisible to radar eliminating that problem. The bombs are stacked three deep. When the last bomb of the stack of three leaves the aircraft, a plate made of the same material as the aircraft's skin, snaps down into place which makes the skin smooth, no cavity where the bombs were."

"That's ingenious Tim."

"Everything about this bird is ingenious. We'll go over the targeting equipment when we go back to the plane but, notice the head on this bomb. This is an innovation of the Company that lets you select the point of impact on the target, in any weather, and once selected will remember even when you make your next target selection. The nose is made of a new metal alloy that if selected on your options panel, is a devastating bunker buster. Notice the tail, it has movable fins and a speed brake which gives you the ability to have several bombs hit the target at the same instant. For example, if you want to place six bombs on a building and have all detonate at the same time, you do so by a selection in the cockpit. The fins direct the bomb to the exact impact point selected and sensors in the tail operate a speed brake to keep them falling at the same altitude. You can also select an air burst or surface burst in addition to bunker buster. If you select bunker buster a solid rocket booster in the tail will ignite at five thousand feet and accelerate the bomb to mach 3 by the time of impact. That will propel it through a thick shell or many stories before detonation."

"To mate this to the aircraft" said Tim, "you fly the plane right down on top of it. You have alignment cross hairs that will guide you to the exact position on the pod at which time you activate the bolt switch. You are now one. A bypass switch will deactivate the landing pads on the aircraft, which allows the pod landing pads to take over. A few other housekeeping chores and you are ready to fly."

"I hope we go over this more than once" said Scott, " because that was sure a mouthful."

When they entered the aircraft Tim said, "come over here Scott, I want to show you how the docking collar works. This bird is equipped to dock with the space shuttle or the space station. If you stand under what appears to be a partially cut away cylinder, it houses the docking collar pressure hatches that lead to the pressure hatches on the shuttle or space station. We have two hatches, an outer one that opens after the docking collar is latched. This is opened to equalize pressure in the tunnel to that in the aircraft and the other vehicle. Both these hatches are eyelid type and are activated by switches behind this panel. The next switch opens the inner hatch."

"The space station is 240 miles high Tim. Can we go that high? I thought Max was kidding."

"Yes, we believe we can easily go that high. What we don't know yet are the operational limits of the bird. We'll keep pushing the envelope to get the answers. That's what you test pilots do isn't it?"

" My God, what are her capabilities?"

Scott opened the panel and noticed that the switches were labeled outer and inner. There was also a third switch labeled ladder. He questioned Tim about this and was told that a need would not exist for a ladder if they were in zero G environment, but if not, a ladder would be required to gain access to the hatches. He told Scott to activate the ladder switch.

What looked like the bottom of a rain gutter fastened vertically to the wall of the cylinder came away from the wall about twenty inches. This became the outside vertical part of the ladder. When this happened the horizontal rungs, which had been stored in a vertical position inside the rain gutter like channel, came down to a horizontal position. This was a copy of the Coolman Life Ladder used as an external fire escape on multi-story structures and was popular in the seventies.

"Go ahead and climb up, I'll activate the hatch switches when you get there."

When Scott was at the top Tim opened the inner hatch, then when he climbed to the outer hatch he opened that. What Scott saw was the evening sky as the sun was setting. This whole thing was unbelievable. Tim had opened the hangar roof so he was standing with his head and shoulders sticking out of the top aircraft looking at a brilliant sunset. He had to smile. Oh, how his life had changed since coming here.

"Okay Scott, I'm going to activate the docking collar now so you can see what it looks like and how it operates. Are your hands and arms inside the cylinder?"

"All clear" he replied.

He had seen the docking collar on the shuttle and this appeared to be identical as it came out from beneath the skin of the aircraft. It was still amazing to watch and to know they could dock with the shuttle or the space station.

"I'll show you the panels that let you select all the options we discussed. A quick review is all that is needed now."

"When you are docking there will be a second set of cross hairs which will represent the other vehicle's docking collar. When the two are overlaying each other exactly, you will see only one set. That is what you want for docking, you will be in perfect position. The holograph will increase or decrease in size. It is your choice for the most comfortable position and size for docking or mating with the pod.. We don't plan on any docking for quite awhile." Little did Tim know at the time how wrong that statement was.

"Let's move on now to weapons. The operation of the weapons systems has been greatly simplified with the intent of reducing the pilot's work load. That's not easy to do with a one pilot aircraft that has a weapons load greater than a B-52."

"You know how to use the air-to-air all conditions radar. The F-22 people are wondering what it was and where it came from."

"How did you know about that?"

"We are a small group with access to inside information Scott. How did you stack up against the Raptor?"

"This is the most fantastic machine anyone could imagine. You don't have to follow the other guy through all the gut wrenching maneuvers. I moved out to the side in a position that I could have launched a missile or even fired guns and taken him out. It was no contest. If I had to stay with him this bird is more than up to it. I wanted to try the easy way to see the results."

"Why did you turn on your landing light and illuminate him?"

"Primarily, because no one could see me due to the aircraft being so stealthy. I had to prove that I was there. Also, a little rubbing it in or misplaced ego."

"Okay, let's talk about shooting the bad guy down. You have a selector switch to call up guns or missiles. Select guns and you will see a sight picture appear as a holographic image in front of you. When you are in range the word fire comes up. That means you are in range with the correct lead. You can fire any combination of guns or all four at once. No matter if it is day or night, fog or smoke, you see the air-to-air by way of radar synthesized holographic display."

"The missiles are of our own design. They are good to one hundred and twenty miles with ninety seven percent accuracy. We use the same high explosive material as the bombs, so a hit or proximity detonation destroys. When you select missiles on the panel you get a different holographic display with different range options available. You center the triangle over the target of choice by use of the miniature joystick on the panel. When you press the button on top of the stick the missile's radar locks on that target. You can lock on as many targets as you have missiles. You can also select the order of launch. A smaller display shows the amount of gun ammunition left as well as the number of missiles remaining."

"When you select bombs on the panel, the same joystick you used for missiles is used for target selection. You have the choice of staggered or simultaneous contact as well as air, surface or subsurface detonation. The bomb targeting is a crosshair and when you press the button on top of the stick, the next bomb to be released locks that into its memory. You can even use the software to program targets before takeoff from our satellite archives. When you get to the actual target, all selections have been made. In autopilot/ target mode everything happens automatically, flight to target and bomb release. It really relieves the work load. Tomorrow morning we'll go inspect the range so you have a mental picture to compare with the radar image. It's eleven o'clock, what say we knock off and leave the dock at eight in the morning?"

"Sounds good Tim."

CHAPTER THIRTEEN

W hen Scott entered his room he turned on the TV for some late night news. Scott was upset. There was more stalling on the part of Iran. Was it their intention to take the fervor out of the countries supporting the inspectors, thinking that the stalling would only benefit Iran? Now the Navy is finding ships at sea carrying missiles to countries suspected of supporting terrorists. What a political nightmare for the President. Our country is so concerned about not offending others that that we leave ourselves vulnerable? Many of the countries we are trying not to offend are those with their hands out for the annual gift of aid. Iraq, Iran, North Korea, Libya, Somalia, Sudan, Yemen and Saudi Arabia are the main supporters of terrorism. The world needs a firmer "get tough" policy with these countries. The past performance of the UN has been pathetic. There has to be an answer.

Scott and Tim had a breakfast of fruit then left for the bombing island. As always, they carried scuba tanks and dive gear. It was low tide and the sand bar from their island to the bombing island was clearly visible. They tied the boat to a buoy just off-shore and swam and waded in. They had their water shoes on to protect them from the sand burrs. They walked a short distance through the trees bordering the beach and entered a large flat, treeless area.

"I've been working on this target for a week" said Tim. "It doesn't look like much but it should work for our purposes. I staked out the outline of a medium sized building with used old sheets supplied from the mainland. You won't get a depth return on the radar that you would on a real building but other than that it should be identifiable. We'll find out tonight."

They walked around the small island. The windward side shore was black-colored coral and very sharp. It had been eroded by wind and waves and with a rough sea could be very dangerous to a swimmer. Many small crabs darted about as they made their way across to where the sand began again.

"This is my favorite place for lobster," said Tim. "We have a fairly flat sea this morning so we can bring the boat around here before we head back and try our luck. We've been having so many guests lately our supply is about gone."

After walking the island, the swim to the boat felt refreshing. The sun dried them as they cruised slowly to the other side. When reaching the spot they dropped and set the anchor.

Tim said, "The water will be about eight feet deep so the snorkel will be fine. The waves have cut the coral so what you see on the surface is an overhang. Under it we should see the lobster. Ready?" They jumped off the boat holding their mask and snorkel in place with one hand and a spear in the other careful to keep it away from each other. Ten feet from the coral shore they dove under kicking to the bottom. The visibility was excellent. . As they approached the coral there was movement underneath. There were several large lobsters with their tentacles waiving. Tim motioned to go to the surface.

"You get three and I will too, that's enough for two meals for the three of us. We can always get fresh ones when we need more", said Tim.

Scott nodded and down they went again. Tim got three the first time and headed for the boat. Scott got two on the first dive and his third on the second and swam to the boat. Tim was already on board and took Scott's spear with the three lobsters on it while he climbed aboard.

"That was sure easy", said Scott. "Is it always like that? I usually have to hunt for them inside the coral heads."

"It's that easy if the sea is fairly calm but don't try it if it's rough. The visibility will be poor and the lobsters are way back under the reef. You could get badly cut on the coral and if it's rough there are other places to go on the lee side. No sense taking unnecessary chances."

The Whaler had a fish tank that they dropped the lobsters in and headed home. They talked all the way back about the target, the island and the spearing. The afternoon would be spent reviewing the weapons system, a nap, then dinner and takeoff about 9:00pm. This time of year it would be dark then so their coming and going would not be seen.

That night after dinner they discussed the news. Steve asked Tim, "What do you think of the actions being taken by the U.S.

regarding weapons shipments discovered going to countries considered friends? Do you consider Yemen a friend? What if they go to Somalia? Is their government considered friendly simply because they say they will fight terrorism? When is a country really on our side? We are so afraid of offending someone that we sometimes act irrationally. North Korea is talking of continuing nuclear production and research. They manufacture and export missiles and other arms to anyone because they need the money. They have such a huge military force it takes big bucks to support it."

"It's a Catch 22," replied Tim." We are damned if we do and damned if we don't. If we went in and bombed the nuclear facilities of North Korea and the weapons manufacturing plants, China and Russia would be steaming. No telling what they would do. But, something should be done by someone. If those facilities could be taken out along with ones in Iran and other terrorist supporting countries, there would be irate voices from many countries. But, secretly, they would be glad it was done and they did not have to participate or ruffle the feathers of those supposedly friendly to them. If only it could be done in such a way that the United States didn't take the blame. But who could do it if not us?"

"I agree with you both," voiced Scott. "The President's in a tough spot. He is a tough one though and has come out a winner so far. It's some of our congressmen I'm concerned about. A few give the impression they are more interested in their careers or their political party than the good of the country. Now, if you will excuse me, an hour's nap is calling. I'll be ready for a 9:00pm takeoff Tim."

Scott went to his room and lay on his bed. Their conversation really bothered him. They also were frustrated with the feeling our country's hands were tied in the struggle against terrorism. Someday it would be too late with a country suffering huge human losses. It could be a nuclear strike with fallout killing thousands of innocent victims of a neighboring country. The terrorists didn't care. Their objective is to kill as many people as they can regardless of who they are. The goal of the Islam extremists is unknown beyond the fact that they don't like the modern world. They are killing just to be killing and as citizens of countries lose their lives the attitude toward the religion of Islam is deteriorating. The Islamic world needs to root out the extremists and dispose of them or the world will turn against all Islam. Is this an action a single person should do if he could? Would he be considered another Hitler or Stalin? He was able to get in a half hour nap before the alarm went off.

The skies were dark by 9:00pm. They put on space suits and boarded. Scott had opened the hangar roof and rose to an altitude of 100 feet then maneuvered over the second hangar and opened the roof for first time coupling with the weapons pod. He took his time, kept the cross hairs centered and set the ship down softly on the pod. He activated the sixteen connecting bolts and they were mated. After that it was a normal lift-off into the night sky.

Tim said, "We have sixteen smart bombs without explosives in the weapons bay. Let's drop two from several different altitudes to see if accuracy is affected by altitude. We'll also try one while cruising just under mach 1 and the other when stationary. Climb out on a heading of 075 to an altitude of 80,000 feet. I want to test the accuracy at that height.

They dropped bombs from high altitude to low altitude. They set them for air burst, surface burst, and detonated multiple bombs simultaneously. The accuracy was right on.

"Wow", they both exclaimed.

"For research sake, take her up to 120,000 feet and we'll drop from a stationary position. Make the target the center of the panel. One bomb only."

When level at 120,000 feet with the cross hairs centered on the target, Scott toggled the release. It seemed to take a long time for the bomb to get there but when it did it was within a foot of dead center.

"Now let's see if you can tear up the panel with the guns. Come in from the west this time so if you over-shoot you'll hit the water. The casings go in a compartment where they cool down instead of dropping out the bottom to fall on something below. Since we are powered by magnetic propulsion, weight, is not a factor so we keep the casings on board. Use mach 1.2 and 1,000 feet. I'm hanging on so let her rip."

This is going to be fun, thought Scott. I'll clear the entire area first so I don't hit any watercraft. As he circled he picked up speed, switched to guns which changed the holographic picture. His trigger was on the right hand control stick, the target clearly visible and approaching fast. At 1,800 yards the word FIRE showed just below the cross- hairs. He pulled the trigger and poof, the target was gone. It was gone because he flew over it so fast.

"Holy Cow Tim, that happened so fast I don't know if I hit it. What do you think?"

"I think we need to do that again. That was a kick. This time anticipate the range so you start to fire as the fire command comes on. By the time you pulled the trigger we were almost past."

"I'll switch to just two guns firing until I get the hang of it. The area is still clear so hang on, here we go!"

This time he squeezed the trigger just before the word FIRE came on and he could see hits on the panel. About a half second of firing time was all he had.

"I'm going to come down on it from 5,000 feet this time and see if I can get a longer firing time. I'll also slow it to mach .9."

"Let her rip," replied Tim.

He cleared the area while climbing to 5,000 feet and turned west for 2 minutes then back east. The target was immediately acquired and cross hairs centered as he started a slight descent. Again he anticipated the fire command and squeezed the trigger. He leveled at 1,000 feet and flashed across the target which was now full of holes.

"Hot Doggies." Tim yelled. "You tore it apart that time. Safe the guns and let's head for home. Drop the weapons pod in the north hangar then park the bird in the south one."

"Roger that," replied Scott.

"Tomorrow I'll install a device that will prove very useful. We'll need to test it tomorrow night so let's plan another 9:00pm take-off. We can also do more bombing then if you'd like," Tim spoke through a yawn.

After dropping the weapons pod and putting the bird to bed in it's hanger, including a post flight inspection, they tiredly walked to the house, entered their own rooms and crashed into bed. It was 1:00am. The flight wasn't a long one but it was packed with learning new systems and operating them at high and slow speeds. Wearing the pressure suits added to the fatigue factor.

CHAPTER FOURTEEN

S cott slept till 9:00 the next morning. He found he wasn't obsessed with thinking about Sarah Ann as his busy schedule kept his mind occupied. He flew most every night then worked on the flight manual during the day. The session with Dr. Kay helped more than she knew as he had no feelings of guilt. Maybe he could cherish her in his memories and lead a life without her. He knew she would want it that way.

"We thought you might have died in there," said Steve. "Tim's so excited about a new gadget he and I came up with that he's out there installing it in the bird now. He told me to tell you about it so go ahead and get your breakfast while I do the talking."

"You know you can type on a computer in English and have it print out in a foreign language," he continued. "And you can talk to a computer and it will follow your commands including typing the words you speak. We combined the two functions plus some of our own ideas and now have a software program that will listen to a foreign language and speak it in English to you. Or, you can speak in English and it will convert what you say to a language of your choice. This can be done over the aircraft radio. For example, you can hear a foreign aircraft talk to another in Arabic but what you hear will be in English. You can talk to another aircraft in English but select the language you want it to transmit. You can talk to any foreign aircraft or ground station in their language and they will think you are one of them."

Steve sat there smiling as Scott stared at him. Finally he found some words, "You guys are amazing. The confusion one could cause in a foreign country is mind- boggling. Can it speak Chinese and Korean?"

"We figured you'd want those for sure plus the Arabic dialect of Iraq, Iran, Saudi Arabia, Libya and some others. They are all listed in the bird and you only need to select the one you want at the time. There is also a listening device for outside the aircraft but, we don't know the maximum range yet. The speakers and listening devices have a narrow cone to reduce any background noise but you will be able to converse in any language with people on the ground or just listen to them."

"This is really something Steve. My mind is thinking of all kinds of uses for this. Can we try it out tonight?"

"You bet," responded Steve. I'm going along too. I want to see if there are any bugs and what they are. I have my own pressure suit so I'll be raring to go at 9:00 tonight. I also want to see this baby fire those twenty millimeter guns and drop bombs with the accuracy Tim relayed. But now, I have to get back to work on another project for Mr. R."

Scott went out by the pool with his flight manual and lap top computer. He swam a few laps and just lay in the water till his fingers looked like a prune. Time to get out and get to work he thought. Ha. If this is work I'll never retire.

They all took a nap sometime during the afternoon and met for a light dinner at 7:00pm, then arrived at the aircraft at 8:15 for pre-flight of both the weapons pod and the bird. At exactly 9:00pm they lifted off and maneuvered to the pod's hangar where Scott joined the two together and silently disappeared into the night.

"Cuba is close," said Scott. "Let's go down there and talk to the tower or another aircraft."

"Sounds good," the other two voiced. "However," said Steve, "Miami is closer, and little Cuba is there."

"Right you are Steve," Tim laughed, "But there may be some English mixed in. I think there would be little of that in Cuba. Besides, it's a beautiful night for flying so why not go the further distance to Cuba. They are also a bit hostile and might launch a fighter against us. That would be interesting."

"Okay" Scott chuckled, "Cuba it is. We'll parallel the Florida coast line to avoid traffic and turn towards Cuba when we're well clear of the southern tip. You guys handle that new gizmo you designed and I'll fly the bird. When we get close enough I'll call Havana tower and you transmit what I say in Spanish. They may respond in English since that's the international language for all aviation radio transmissions. If he does I'll tell him I don't speak English. We will stay below mach 1 so there will be no sonic boom. That might put them in a panic thinking it's a US fighter."

Fifteen minutes later they approached Cuba from the south so as not to appear they were coming from the US. Scott had dropped the landing pads so they would appear on radar and pressed the radio transmit button on top of the throttle. "Havana, this is Cessna three ten, two five miles south, enroute to Florida. I would like to over-fly you, over." If their gizmo worked that would be transmitted in Spanish.

The tower operator took longer than usual to answer, probably shocked that someone heading for the US would call in for an over-fly with no flight plan. This was invading Cuban air space without prior permission. People got shot down for this.

"Cessna three ten," he responded in Spanish, "be advised that the radio international language is English. You must speak English. I have no flight plan filed for you. You are invading Cuban airspace without permission. You are directed to land at the Havana airport at once."

"But I do not speak English," replied Scott. "We both speak Spanish, so we will speak in that language and I do not want to land in Cuba. I am requesting to overfly you on my way to Florida."

"You do not have permission to overfly us. You must land at the Havana airport at once. We have you on radar. Turn to a heading of zero three zero and descend to one thousand five hundred feet."

"You do not understand Havana, I do not want to land in Cuba. I want to overfly you. Please keep us separated from other traffic. Thank you, Cessna three ten out."

"We got company just lifting off the runway," said Tim. "My guess it's a Mig twenty one"

"Got him," replied Scott. "We'll retract the landing pods now and disappear from radar. They'll be looking for us down low so I'm going to pop up to 3,000 feet."

"Cessna three ten, this is the tower, what is your position?"

"I am flying west of you down low. I do not want to land in Cuba. Please keep other traffic away from me. I will be over water soon and on my way to Florida. Good-bye."

The two men in the tower looked at each other. Finally one gathered his wits and spoke in the microphone. "Cessna three ten you are ordered to land. An interceptor will shoot you down if you don't obey. Cessna three ten do you hear me?" No answer.

"Havana tower this is Scramble One, what's his location?"

"We've lost radar contact. Last location was ten miles west heading north, two minutes ago. He must be down low heading for open water. Over."

"I will look for him. Let me know if he appears on your radar."

The Mig 21 turned north and slowed to two hundred and thirty knots, about fifty knots faster than the cruising airspeed of a Cessna 310, if it was a 310. At this speed his aircraft was barely staying in the air and was very mushy. His radar showed no returns other than a boat or two. These were moving too slow to be an airplane. He turned parallel to shore for one minute then turned left 180 degrees towards the open water which reversed his course but further out to sea. He was flying very low and concentrating on his altimeter and radar scope when his cockpit was suddenly illuminated by a very bright light. In his shock he fortunately pulled back on his stick instead of pushing forward toward the sea, it would have been his last movement.

"Is that you jet fighter coming to find me?" spoke Scott into his mike.

The pilot in Scramble One hadn't found his voice yet. When he did it was still a few octaves higher than normal. "Ahhhh, Cessna 310 return to Havana or I will be forced to shoot you down."

"No, I do not want to land in Cuba. I am flying to Florida. Go away," transmitted Scott.

Steve and Tim were trying unsuccessfully to keep from laughing. If they weren't completely stealthy it wouldn't be funny. Of course, they wouldn't be here if they weren't.

"I can not do that. You must return to Havana at once. The next time I will be forced to shoot you down."

There was no answer. There was still nothing on the radar. Where was this guy thought the Mig pilot? How did he get that close to me and what kind of light was that? It wasn't a Cessna landing light and even if it were he would have to be coming straight at me to shine like it did. No sooner did he have these thoughts when ZAP, his cockpit lit up again. This time he was startled but not like the first time. He climbed 200 feet but still nothing on his radar.

"Havana, do you have anything on your radar?"

"Nothing" replied the tower. "Can you not find him?"

"No, I am returning to base. I will make a report." There is something very strange with this intruder he thought. He does not appear on the tower radar nor on mine, yet he is all over me twice. If he were the interceptor I would be dead. It was just luck that I pulled instead of pushed the stick or I would have flown into the water. No, I will leave and let him go, for my own safety.

"We will report also Scramble One."

Scott turned east to fly to the east end of Cuba away from the airport and to less populated areas. "I'll drop down to 500 feet and slow to 100, let me know if you see a small village so we can test the external exchange. We can then check out the distance limit of your gizmo."

"Looks like something coming up at two o'clock Scott," said Steve.

He slowed the bird so it was slowly closing on the village. They were about a half mile out when voices started coming in over the receiver. They moved a little closer then stopped. The voices were in Spanish until Tim selected English on the receiver. The voices immediately switched to English. The conversation was local village doings.

One half mile was the maximum but, changes in humidity and temperature could affect that. They decided to continue the experiment in various weather conditions to see how great the differences would be. They would do that in the future.

Scott climbed to fifteen thousand feet and set course to pass south of the US coastline then northeast to the bombing island.

"Well," he said, "I believe your gizmo passed the test with flying colors, no pun intended."

"You really had that pilot going," said Steve. "Tim and I could hardly keep from laughing out loud. That wouldn't do for him to hear that in the background."

"I believe we have a go on the language exchanger or gizmo as Scott calls it," said Tim.

"Bombing and strafing range coming up. Tighten your seat belts. We're going to roll inverted and pull towards the ground to lose altitude then roll upright at 5,000 feet and fire the guns at 3,000 feet, then pull out with 500 feet to spare. Ready? Here we go!"

"WOW!," yelled Steve. This is better than any carnival ride. I want to be a pilot not a scientist. Go Scott!"

Scott pulled hard off the target in a six g zoom going vertical with a half roll at 5,000 feet then pulled back to inverted level flight, then another half roll and they were then headed in the same direction as the strafing run, level, and right side up at 5000 feet.

He could tell from the comments that Steve and Tim really enjoyed that. He never did things in an airplane with a passenger that made them nervous. These two were thoroughly enjoying it.

"I'm going to show you something that I think you will really enjoy. We have a solid under cast below us with a very bright moon above. As you can see it's almost like daylight. There are some big cumulus clouds we'll play with."

He flew directly at a particularly large cloud that extended very high. He timed his pull to vertical so that they flew right up the side of the cloud to the top where he performed a half roll then pulled back so they started the descent down the other side. Another half roll put the bottom of the ship against the cloud looking for the next cloud to start the climb to the top.. Steve and Tim reacted so excitedly that they did that several more times before getting back to business and running a few bomb runs. After using all the remaining bombs they returned to their base and put the bird to bed.

They sat at their table having a beer discussing the flight before going to bed. They told Scott how much they enjoyed the flight and how much they appreciated showing them the cloud maneuver. No one had ever shown them how graceful flight maneuvers could be. It was like a ballet in the sky. They were still so excited they didn't want to go to bed yet. And they had a new respect and admiration for Scott.

"Where do those bombs we use come from?" asked Scott. "Is it possible to get live ones?"

"Why do you ask?" replied Tim.

Scott stared at him. "I have a reason, but if you'd rather not answer, never mind."

"Mr. R can get anything we need and in any quantity." answered Steve. "How many do you want?"

"I need to have a meeting with Mr. R," said Scott. "Is that possible?"

Steve answered, "Not only is it possible but Mr. R has been expecting you to ask. Pick up the scramble, punch 17 and you will be connected to him."

"Thanks, I'll call him tomorrow."

CHAPTER FIFTEEN

A t 9:00 the next morning Scott picked up the scrambler phone and dialed Mr. R. He answered on the second ring. "Yes"

"This is Scott Wilson Mr. R. I'm calling to see if I may meet with you? There is something I would like to discuss."

"When do you wish to meet Scott?"

"Whenever it's convenient for you sir."

"There will be a helicopter to pick you up at 8:00 tomorrow morning. We'll meet at 9:00 and plan to spend the night at our facility. A car will meet you." The phone went dead. Mr. R was done talking.

Well, Scott thought, I better get the flight manual up to date and take it with me. He sat by the pool with his lap top, swimming occasional laps then back to the lap top. When he finished he printed the information, punched holes for the three hole binder and added it to the other information in the manual. Before he knew it his watch said 4:00pm and Steve and Tim were diving into the pool. Over a Kalik beer they discussed what to have for dinner. Scott wasn't flying tonight so he allowed himself to have one. Hamburgers on the grill would be a change from fish and lobster. Their garden provided large tomatoes and onions and the freezer yielded frozen Kaiser buns.

The next morning Scott was up and waiting for the helicopter when it landed. He had the small duffle bag and sport coat he picked up at the clothing store when he was at the facility for his physical exam. That seemed like a long time ago. The physical reminded him of Dr. Kay. He considered her a wonderful friend. He was grateful for her help with his problem getting over the death of his wife. Their intimate episode on the boat was part of the therapy. He wanted to see her while at the facility to thank her for all her help.

They landed at 8:45 where a car was waiting which took him directly to Mr. R's office. The building was the same architectural design as the others, tastefully done but not ostentatious, with stone two stories high. Palm trees, flower beds and grass surrounded all the buildings. It was very attractive with a comfortable feeling. When he entered the building he was met by an attractive upper middle-aged woman who asked if he was Mr. Wilson. Answering that he was he followed her to the elevator which they took to the second floor, the top floor. She introduced herself as Mary Stebbins, Mr. R's personal secretary. They turned right and walked to the end of the hall where she opened a heavy looking carved wood door. They stepped into an attractive reception room where she told him she would tell Mr. R he was here. The time was three minutes to 9:00am. Two minutes later she told him Mr. R would see him now.

He entered a very large office longer than it was wide. Along the entire left wall were mahogany book shelves containing hundreds of books with a mahogany wall behind them. The right wall was all windows with mahogany wooden blinds. Directly ahead was a very large mahogany desk and empty leather chair, matching credenza with cabinets along the entire wall. To the left of the desk were open double wooden doors leading to another room. It was from this room that a voice called beckoning him to come in there.

The first thing he saw was a large conference table with a dozen plush leather chairs around it. At the far end was the mysterious Mr. R, smiling and walking toward him with his hand out. It was a firm handshake but not the kind to bring one to their knees. Mr. R was about six four as he was two inches taller than Scott, with thick white hair and penetrating blue eyes and Scott guessed somewhere between sixty five and seventy. With blond hair and deep blue eyes, Scott and Mr. R could easily be father and son. A fact that did not escape either one. They were both of medium build and appeared to have no excess weight.

"Sit down Scott. I have been looking forward to meeting you. Your reports on the aircraft have been most informative and occasionally humorous. Would you like something to drink? The rest of the morning is set aside for us, then you will be taken on a tour of the facilities and acquainted with our numerous projects. We will meet again at 4:00pm. I've taken the liberty of informing Dr. Kay that you will be free for dinner this evening. I hope you don't object?"

"Not at all sir, I was hoping to see her again. Her analysis of my bereavement over the loss of my wife was most helpful, I want to thank her."

"Good, that's settled then. Would you care for a decaffeinated iced tea? I'm going to have one."

"That would be fine sir."

He walked to a small table containing a phone with intercom and asked Mary for a pitcher of the tea along with a dish of lemon wedges. Mr. R pointed out various buildings from the view through the many windows in the room. They made small talk until Mary left after delivering the tea. They each took a glass and coaster and sat at the table.

"Since you asked for this meeting Scott, why don't you go first?"

"Yes sir." Scott hesitated then began. "The aircraft is the most fantastic piece of equipment I could ever imagine. It is so far superior to anything in existence today that it is hard to put into words. You know all the unbelievable things it can do and we are just scratching the surface on its capabilities. With a machine like this, much could be done to help stabilize the chaos in the world. But, the United States could not be the one to do it. If it bombed North Korea's nuclear facilities both China and Russia would be furious and North Korea would immediately start their artillery barrage of South Korea. Thousands of lives would be lost and their million man army would head south. We have too many fragile relationships with many countries that would be shattered if we attacked North Korea, or bombed Iranian nuclear plants, or palaces in Iran or their suspected nuclear, biological and chemical storages while the United Nations inspectors are still there. The list of targets goes on and on if we include terrorists training camps in the Arab countries. If it could be done by an unknown country, the results may be a more stabilized world. To be struck by an unknown and unseen enemy would be a very big deterrent for a rogue nation. The support of terrorism would be dealt a major blow."

"Is it possible," he went on, "to nationalize your island as a Country with it's own constitution and all the things to make it a legal country? The world would not know where it is located or anything else about it. It would, by way of a video tape sent to the major news agencies in the world, declare war on the bad guys. I would make the video address with my face fuzzed out and a voice disguiser so there would be no recognition by anyone. I would state that my Country is not a part of any coalition, nor the United Nations, nor any other world organization, nor are we interested in joining. We have observed too much hesitancy by these organizations to do anything until it is too late. The future of my Country's safety is at stake, either from nuclear fallout, biological or chemical weapons. By a vote of our people we have no choice but to declare war on the following Countries; North Korea, Iraq, Iran, Libya, Yemen, Sudan, Saudi Arabia and all countries that in any way support terrorism. I would include Saudi Arabia to make more believable the innocence of the United States. The video would be thought of as a hoax, no one would believe it and consequently not be shown. But, after North Korea's nuclear facilities are completely destroyed, the video will be known worldwide. The United States will be blamed of course, but they will know nothing about it and will come across as truly sincere in pleading their innocence. There will always be suspicions but no evidence. As more strikes by our Air Force show complete vulnerability of these nations and no complicity on the part of the United States, they will start to believe there really is a country out there causing this damage."

"Another tape will be shown the following day with actual footage of the North Korean strike. Let's call the Country "Piot" for now. It stands for "Peace In Our Time". However, I will need intelligence help. Where are these facilities, the weapons manufacturing plants, the palaces, suspected terrorist camps and so on. This intelligence should come from several countries which will further deflect blame from the United States. After each strike a tape will be shown revealing the target and its destruction. I want to put a fear in these SOB's that will put a stop to unstable countries having weapons of mass destruction and giving aid to terrorist activities. I truly believe, with this aircraft, this can be accomplished."

All this time Scott had kept eye contact with Mr. R. When he was finished talking he kept looking Mr. R in the eye and could see a stone face looking back at him. Suddenly the stone cracked into a slight curve at the corners of the mouth, then a big grin. "My God Scott," Mr. R said. "I was beginning to think this day would not happen. What took you so long to bring this idea to me. Don't answer that, it doesn't matter. I know you had a lot of testing to do on the aircraft. The important thing is you did. It was my frustration at the daily news and wanting to do something fast that made me impatient."

"Everything has been done to make your island an independent nation except for the name. There is nothing pretty about the name Piot but it does indeed make a statement. We have a stockpile of weapons and will start the transfer to Piot immediately. I can't tell you how happy you have made me. To have this weapon and not be able to use it in defense of my country was maddening. They do not know it exists and we will keep it that way because they would not use it for the very reasons you stated. There is much to talk about Scott." He held out his hand and they shook in a warm, friendly and satisfying grip. Scott thought he could detect a moistening in the eyes of Mr. R. He himself was having trouble holding in the emotional relief he felt. This meeting could have gone either way, one way was him leaving without a job.

They spent the rest of the morning talking about logistics. It was decided that Steve and Tim would return to the mainland so if things went wrong they would not be implicated. A team of three people who had previously worked on the aircraft would be transferred to the island to serve as weapons specialists including loading and servicing. They would live in the building at the north end of the hangers and would seldom meet Scott. The less anyone knew about the plan the less chance for a leak. The three men would be there tomorrow and weapons shipments would also start then. A weapons storage building lay adjacent to the north hanger and would store five hundred bombs, one hundred missiles and ample twenty mike mike ammunition for the guns. A constant re-supply would be needed.

"It's now noon Scott. I have a lot to do that you can't help me with so why don't you go to lunch. Your driver is waiting and he can take you to your room first then to lunch. I happen to know that Dr. Kay is planning to lunch at 12:30 in the cafeteria. You may want to join her. Let's meet back here at 3:00 instead of 4:00. He had a big grin on his face when he said, "now get going so I can get started."

When he left, Mr. R sat at his desk for a few minutes before he started making calls. He was thinking that Scott could easily be the son he never had. He had to restrain himself from grabbing Scott and giving him a big hug after listening to his plan. The scary thing was that is was almost the identical plan he had devised.

As he left Mr. R's office Mary was just leaving for lunch also. "I believe there is a car waiting for me Mrs. Stebbins, may I give you a ride?"

"Oh, no thank you. I enjoy the walk to the cafeteria. Would you do me a favor though and call me Mary?"

"I will if you call me Scott," he replied.

"Deal," she said. They walked to the elevator and out the front door together.

"I'll be back at three instead of four Mary so I'll see you again then." They said goodbye and Scott climbed into the waiting car.

While being driven to his room his mind reviewed the conversation with Mr. R. The immediate problem was to avoid any implication by the United States. There had to be a plan before the strike on the North Korean nuclear facilities. Their northern border was with China and the very northeast bordered Russia. How could friction between North Korea and one of the other two be instigated. Although they were allies none of them trusted the other two. How could this be used to our benefit? If the United States was seen as innocent when their nuclear facilities were destroyed, would they hold off an attack on South Korea? They would if they thought the attack came from China or Russia. Their government was foolish but not foolish enough to attack either of those two. And, if they thought it was an attack by Russia or China, they would not attack the South as this might further provoke whoever it was. A slight smile came to his face as he thought of a possible plan.

When the driver arrived at his building he told the driver to wait. They gave him the same room he had when here for his physical. That seemed like years ago, he thought. Having the same room was comforting because of the feeling of being in a place before. He dropped the duffle bag with a change of clothes, put the flight manual in the safe, used the bathroom, washed his hands and face, combed his wavy hair and was back in the car in ten minutes.

"Would you mind dropping me at the cafeteria? Someone is to meet me after lunch for a tour."

"Will do sir," the driver replied.

When he walked into the cafeteria he spotted Dr. Kay seated at a corner table with another attractive white-coated person. She saw him and waived him to the table.

"Hello Dr. Kay," he greeted her.

"Scott, I'd like you to meet Colleen Hutchinson. Colleen this is Scott Wilson. Colleen is my surgical nurse. Go through the line then join us. We are on a tight schedule but would enjoy your company as long as we can."

"Nice to meet you Colleen."

"Nice to meet you also Scott," replied Colleen.

He was back in a few minutes with an iced tea and large chef's salad with ranch dressing.

"What, no sea food." Dr. Kay said grinning. "As much sea food as you appear to eat at your place, I better check your cholesterol."

"Yes Mother," he grinned back.

"If we can get flight authorization we need to visit these guys sometime. That is, if you can stand lobster, grouper, conch chowder, conch salad and so on. And, it's all fresh from the sea."

"Count me in Doctor, I love sea food. How long will you be here Scott?" Colleen asked.

"I believe till tomorrow morning unless something unforeseen comes up. And I do believe we have an arranged dinner date tonight Doctor."

"Not that I object but, he did surprise me by doing that. It's a first. I think he likes you Scott. Come to think of it, there is a strong resemblance between the two of you. Not just looks but personality also."

"Are you two in surgery this afternoon?" he asked.

"Changing the subject are we?" said Dr. Kay. "Yes we are, and speaking of that we better leave. We don't want to keep the patient waiting. Since I have a car and you don't, I'll pick you up at your room at 7:00 tonight."

"Good. I'll try to be ready on time. Nice meeting you Colleen. Give us a call to make sure we're home, we'd enjoy your visit."

The two women left and not a few eyes turned to watch them go then turned to look at him. He knew what they were thinking, what's so special about him that those two good looking gals eat with him?

Scotts tour guide showed up in the form of Hank Miller who informed him that a car was waiting for them and whenever he was ready they would begin.

The tour was interesting but he knew he was not shown the really good stuff. For example, he knew another aircraft was in the works but maybe this guide didn't have a need to know and therefore didn't know it existed. What else was he not shown?

At five minutes to three he was dropped at the front door of Mr. R's building after they swung by his room to pick up the manual.

"Good afternoon Mary," he said walking into the reception room. "Did you have an enjoyable lunch?"

"Yes, thank you. It appeared you did too."

He blushed as she opened the door to Mr. R's office for him.

They spent the afternoon discussing how the island was made a separate nation, its constitution, and how he should refer to it in his tapes. They played what if scenarios with North Korea, Iran and Iraq. Scott did not mention the plan that was forming in his mind, the one to take suspicion away from the United States when North Korea was attacked. It wasn't finished and he didn't want to present a part of a plan.

Before they knew it the clock chimed six o'clock. He was joking when he told Dr. Kay he would try not to be late but, if he didn't leave soon he would be.

"We have covered enough for today Scott and I don't want to make you late for your dinner date with Dr. Kay. I'd like to meet with you a week from today for more planning. I'm sure questions will come up between now and then. That will give me time to tie up any loose ends regarding the new Nation and put an intelligence net work in place. I have contacts in several countries that will not hesitate to help, in fact they'll be delighted. You two have a good time tonight and I'll see you a week from today at 9:00am. I enjoyed the day with you Scott."

"Thank you Sir, I too enjoyed it very much and will look forward to next week."

The driver was waiting and dropped him at his room. "Thanks, would you have someone pick me up at 7:30 in the morning so I can catch the helicopter?"

"Will do sir," replied the driver.

He was waiting in the lobby when Dr. Kay arrived. The evening was cool so the sport coat felt good even though he had worn it all day. He opened the passenger door and had to duck to enter the red Miata. "Nice car," he said, "for midgets."

"Nice sport coat" she responded. "Is that the only one you have?"

"As a matter of fact it is. It wasn't that long ago the only thing I owned was a bathing suit and a pair of dive booties. I picked up these clothes here in the clothing store and they wouldn't even let me pay for them. So don't make fun of a destitute man."

"Yeah right. I know more about you than you think I do. When you appeared on the scene Mr. R was more than a little interested in you. You know he had a dossier on you that was current up to the time you left the mainland for North Eleuthera. When Max decided to get married Mr. R needed a replacement. He wanted my opinion of you from your fitting in with the Company based on that dossier. He did not fill me in on the time frame from North Eleuthera to the time you showed up. He didn't tell me so I didn't ask. So don't tell me that you can't afford clothes Mr. Wilson"

"Jeez, that's like a beautiful woman you have never met walking into the room and saying "Take off your clothes".

"That comes later, right now I'm starved."

They had a delicious dinner at a steak house then to a cozy bar for an after dinner drink. "I apologize for the phone call during dinner but that's the life of a doctor. I'm afraid it spoiled the plans I had for you tonight. I have surgery at 7:00am. That means I take you to your room after this drink, go home to bed and no sex, a real bummer. When you come back in a week just be prepared because I won't ask you to take your clothes off, I'll rip them off."

"If you rip them I'll have nothing to wear, remember, I'm destitute."

She smiled, leaned over and gave him a tongue lashing kiss. "That isn't fair is it? I'm just making the frustration worse. Oops, are you going to be able to walk out of here?" she laughed taking hold of the protrusion in his pants.

He left the bar holding the sport coat in front of him. As they entered her car he said, "You would have to drive a roller skate, why not a van with fold down seats? It would be much more practical on a night like this."

They laughed and joked all the way to his building. "I'm not going to kiss you goodnight or goodbye and start your problem all over again. Goodnight Scott, we have a date when you return."

"Goodnight Dr. Kay. Thank you for everything, and I do mean everything."

He closed the car door and watched her drive off. Some woman he thought, She knows what she wants and where she is going. And to top it all off she has a beautiful face and figure to match. He let out a big sigh and went to his room.

The next day when the helicopter landed on the island Steve and Tim were waiting for him. He walked towards them with a big grin on his face, happy to see his friends again. They did not return the grin nor did they look happy at all. They each got on one side of him and walked him to the house.

The crewman in the back of the helicopter pressed the intercom button and asked, "I thought we were supposed to pick those two guys up and take them to the mainland"

The pilot responded, "I think we have a situation here." Just then Steve walked out the front door of the house and waived them off.

"Yup" said the pilot, "we do have a situation here. Standby to defy the gravity Gods boys, we're heading back without passengers." The chopper lifted off and was soon out of sight.

"Just what the hell do you think you were doing?" Steve said to Scott. "Do you think we are common sense stupid? Do you think we have no deductive reasoning powers? Are you forgetting you saved our lives, took us flying doing things we'd never dreamed about and would never have known if it weren't for you. And what thanks do we get for all this? We are to leave the island, our home, without even talking to us. We know what you're up to and we want to be a part of it. You can't do it yourself, you need us. And by God, the only way we're leaving this island is in chains. Now what have you got to say for yourself."

"Yeah!" said Tim. "That goes double for me."

"Okay, Okay." said Scott. "I apologize for not thanking you when I saved your lives. I apologize for not thanking you when I took you flying, and all the lobster I speared. But seriously guys, there could be repercussions from this. We could be tried for war crimes for bombing places that result in civilian casualties. This could escalate into world war three. We are going to do our best to see that none of this happens but, civilian casualties we can't avoid. I don't think you know what you are getting yourself into. We could end up in really deep shit. Mr. R must be protected at all costs."

"We know all that," said Tim. "We've had a lot fun since you joined us but now this is going to be serious stuff. We listen to the news and read the papers too. We agree something has to be done and we are not going to let you be selfish and try to do something alone. We are in, and that's the way it is."

"Have you talked to Mr. R?" asked Scott." He has to okay it."

"Yes we have and he said it's up to you. You would explain the potential consequences to us. You've done that, so what's your answer?" said Steve

"You guys really want to get involved with this huh? If I say it's time to bail you'll not argue with me, you'll do as I say?"

"Ya, Ya," they voiced in unison.

"Well okay but, no cooking for a month. No dishes for a month. My clothes are washed and it would be nice to have them ironed, especially the flight suit in case I'm shot down, I want to look my best."

"All right! All right!" Steve and Tim yelled. "But forget the other stuff. You're lucky we don't make you do all the cooking and dishes for a month, trying to get rid of us."

"Okay, serious time. Our biggest concern at the outset is to convince the world that the United States is not involved. World War Three could start very easily if other countries thought that. I have a plan I'd like to go over with you. Shoot holes in it, we'll revise it, then tell me if you think it will work."

Scott had deplaned from the helicopter at 9:00 that morning. It was midnight when they called it a night and went to bed. Their minds were racing. This was not make believe stuff. This was really going to happen. Their lives were in danger. Innocent civilians would be killed. It couldn't be helped, that was war and this was war. It was agreed that Scott would be the only resident, citizen of Piot. He would have dual citizenship, the United States and Piot. The other two would be consultants. Takeoff would be at 6:00am three days from now. It was still dark at 6:00 am during winter months and it was imperative they not be seen leaving or arriving from home base. Korea time would be 8:00pm the next day. Allowing for climb, acceleration, enroute, deceleration and descent, they should be where they want to be at 9:30pm the next day, allowing for the international date line. Actual elapsed time from takeoff to target would only be an hour and a half. The rotation of the earth would be in the opposite direction from their travel direction which would shorten their enroute time.

If they leave Korea at 4:00am Korean time, their estimated time of arrival over the home base will be 3:45pm allowing an extra fifteen minutes for travel in the same direction as the earth's rotation.

As long as they remained at altitude they were invisible from eye-sight, they were always invisible from radar whether day or night. They would park over the base till dark and use the time to write their mission debriefs. Tomorrow they would make a video for distribution to world wide-media. One copy would be carried that day by courier to the North Korean embassy in Paris.

CHAPTER SIXTEEN

The next morning they prepared to make the video by hanging a sheet over a desk and one on the wall behind the desk. They debated what Scott should wear and decided he definitely should not appear in western clothing such as a coat and tie. After experimenting they selected his blue blazer worn backwards. Since he would be sitting and not moving they could make it look like a high collar type of uniform. Through the genius of Steve and Mike , Scott's face was fuzzed out through lighting and reflectors. They also used a voice disguiser to mask his voice from recognition by anyone. They were now ready to record.

I am the President of a small nation that is virtually unknown to the world. Our name and location will be kept a secret for reasons which will soon be known.

We have become alarmed at the state of the world to the point that our people voted to take a drastic step and declare war of the following countries;

North Korea, Iran, Saudi Arabia, Libya, Yemen, Somalia, Afghanistan, Pakistan and any country that in any way aids terrorist activities.

In the event of a terrorist or rogue nation attack our Country could very easily be wiped out by nuclear, chemical or biological fallout. Because we are a small nation we would probably cease to exist. The world organizations are so slow to act against these rogue governments that we have decided to take matters into our own hands. We are not a member of any coalition nor are we a member of the United Nations. We will act alone in our own self-defense.

We do not consider ourselves war criminals as we are acting in self-defense. Our war is against the governments of these countries, not the people.

It would be a waste of time to convince you that this message is not a hoax. However, you will see otherwise by our actions in the very near future.

They played it back and all declared it was a take. Steve would see that a copy was transmitted electronically to Mr. R. If approved, his organization would have it in the hands of the media and the North Korea embassy in Paris today. They did not expect to see it on TV or in the papers, yet. With that done they started preparing for their first mission, two days away.

The North Korean embassy did receive the recording that day. They viewed it and immediately sent it by aircraft to Pyongyang for viewing by their President Kim Jong Un.

"Who delivered this to the embassy in Paris?" Kim demanded.

"It is unknown Great General," replied Jo Kang Ju, a trusted advisor.

"This is a trick of the United States," screamed Kim. "It is they who will attack us. Get our defense forces ready. If they attack we will attack South Korea when the first shot is fired. We will destroy the South."

"At once Great General," answered Jo.

.

Tim had checked the language translator, or exchanger as he called it, and reported that it was working fine. Without this piece of equipment the mission would be very difficult. Scott had to know the types of call signs used, such as red, yellow, blue, etc. He had to know what they called things such as an unknown aircraft. The USAF calls them bogies. When they are identified they are either bandits or friendlies. How did they express altitude and heading? They will need to know these things to make the plan work.

They spent the time reviewing all aspects of the mission. Knowing the bad guys can't see you certainly helps the pre takeoff nervousness but does not eliminate it all together. They knew so much depended on this mission's success. It could be the start of defusing world tensions, or starting a nuclear war. If they couldn't direct guilt away from the United States for what they were about to do, it could mean a war.

Scott went over his plan again emphasizing the need to be very flexible. If there were no fighters in the air he would have to bait them by becoming visible on radar. This was done by extending the landing pads as was done over Cuba. Each person would write down words or phrases used by the other pilots.

North Korea has many airfields and a very large air force mostly made up of outdated Russian fighters. They do have Mig- 21's, 23's and 29's as their primary air-to-air fighters and are based in the southern province for a quick attack on South Korea. The 23's and 29's are based around the capital of Pyongyang. Response time to the South is estimated to be in minutes but that's not our concern. We want all the action up north on the Chinese border to draw attention away from the south. The air fields they picked were the ones closest to the border.

The Chinese have a more modern air force with Mig-31's and Su-27 Flankers, all weather fighters. Most of these are based close to the Formosa Strait for attack or defense against Taiwan. China has many other fighters but these are the most modern and formidable. The intent is to stir up a hornet's nest between these two countries.

"How are you two coming with your radar identification of enemy aircraft?" asked Scott. Mr. R had given him photos of radar returns for various Russian aircraft which the two countries are flying. "Take them with you to help identify when we encounter the real thing." The day after tomorrow was the day. That would give ample time for the video to reach the major news media and the Korean embassy in Paris.

The night before they were to leave they slept, or tried to, until 4:00am and ate a light breakfast of mostly fruit and cold cereal. The jitters and excitement were running high. They had pre-flighted the aircraft the night before but gremlins had a way of coming out at night to screw up something that was fine before. Finding everything okay, no gremlin attacks, they boarded and began the struggle of putting on the space suits. That done they climbed in their seats, Tim to the right and behind Scott and Steve to the left and behind. They all had an excellent view of the holographic displays. They were strapped in their seats with the pre-takeoff checklist completed ten minutes before takeoff time.

"Anybody want to change their mind?" Scott asked. "Still time to deplane, no takers? Okay, hanger roof coming open. We attached the weapons pod last night so when we leave the hangar we're gone. We'll hold till exactly 6:00 am. Ten, nine, eight, seven, six, five, four, three, two, one, liftoff. Altitude three hundred feet and closing the hangar roof. Climbing on course, speed coming up, we are on our way guys. In case I forget to tell you, be sure your restraints are very tight and all loose items stored before we go into combat with the fighters. For now though, you can sit back and enjoy the ride."

"Right," grunted Steve as the acceleration pressed him into the back of his seat. Scott kept the G force at four since they weren't in a big hurry. He had allowed plenty of time for the mission.

The course to North Korea would be a great circle route using GPS taking them over Minnesota, to the Seward Peninsula, entering Russia and paralleling the Koryak Mountain Range, across the Sea of Okhotsk then north of the Kamchatka Peninsula , northwest of Sikhote-Alin Mountains then to the city of Sonbong on the northeast coast of North Korea. They would then follow the border with China to the southwest looking for aircraft activity on either side.

The check points seemed to click by very fast. They were over Alaska then heading for Russia. It was very dark with an under cast hiding any lights on the ground. At their altitude of 120 miles they weren't going to see any farm house lights but they would be able to see cities if not for the undercast.

"We are nearing our descent point at one hour fifteen minutes, we'll turn to face the way we came and start deceleration. I'll hold it to four G's and start a gradual descent. Everyone ready? Gear stowed and strapped in tight?"

A short time later Scott said, "we are now at flight level three five zero, mach .8 and following the border listening for radio traffic." They didn't have long to wait. Tim had the exchanger set to receive in any language.

"Tower this is Black One at four thousand five hundred meters, speed point 75, returning to base."

"Understand Black One, call when ten kilometers out for further instructions."

"Black One understands."

"Could you identify the type of aircraft Steve?" asked Scott.

"It appears to be one of their J-8s, an interceptor for bombers not fighters. Good looking bird with a speed of fifteen hundred miles per hour and made by the Chinese. They have a lot of these."

"We'll keep on trucking and see what else turns up. I'm starting to pick something up on radar at one o'clock, there are several small returns. Let's go down for a closer look. Steve do you show anything on the Chinese side near Hyesan? Anything within say thirty miles.?"

"Yes, there is a town and it's supposed to have an airfield. I can't pronounce it but it's something like Bongdian. Should be about five miles north of the border."

"We'll take a look. In the meantime see if you can identify any of the aircraft flying out of Hyesan."

"Looks like mostly more J-8's with a couple of either mig-29s or Su-27s, their signature is very similar."

"Good, now let's see what we have at Bongdian. Anything interesting on the radio from Hyesan Tim?"

Tim had turned the radio so only he could hear it to cut down on the chatter so Steve and Scott could talk without shouting over the radio noise. "I have some lingo for you when you're ready to talk Korean."

"Very good Tim. We're going in low over Bongdian to get a good look at the airport. The radar shows one bird lined upon the runway, probably ready to takeoff and one taxiing from the parking area. This could be what we're looking for. Those appear to be Su-27 Flankers, what do you think Steve?"

"Either that or Mig 29s. Either way they're good air to air fighters."

"Right, we'll follow the number two man and make it a three ship formation, but they won't know that. When we're off the departure end of the runway we drop the landing pads so everyone sees us on their radar, including the North Koreans. You know they are watching the Chinese if for nothing else than practice. We'll then head directly for the base at Hyesan. I need to be talking Chinese Tim."

The Chinese tower controller came on the radio. "Aircraft that just departed Bongdian say your call sign."

Scott responded, "this is Colonel Chen, you have my orders. They were delivered by special courier. I am Operation One, assigned to watch the North Koreans and stop them from entering our airspace. They are becoming belligerent and I am ordered to shoot them down if they violate our border. Does your radar show any close to the border around Hyesan?"

"Yes Colonel, there is a flight of two about to violate our border. Do you wish me to contact them"

"No," said Scott," I will take care of them. What is the course to intercept?"

"Turn to heading zero nine five. Their altitude is four thousand five hundred meters"

"I am turning and climbing to intercept."

Scott followed the climb and heading directions and increased speed to mach 1.5 or 1,070 miles per hour. He climbed a thousand feet above their altitude and had them clearly on radar. "Switch me to the North Korean's frequency Tim and set me to talk in Korean. Steve, you monitor the Chinese frequency to see if they call us for anything important."

"Roger," they both responded.

Scott pressed the transmit button on the throttle. "North Korean aircraft violating Chinese airspace, you must turn around immediately, I have orders to shoot you down if you do not obey at once." They turned toward him and locked on with their weapons radar. He doubted they carried weapons but he wasn't going to take any chances. He popped up into a high vertical maneuver right after retracting the landing pads. They were now stealthy. He cut power, did a half roll then pulled through the inverted position performing a split-S to come up on their six o'clock position. They were slow to respond when he disappeared from radar. That was a mistake as they were now well within range of his guns. The air to air daylight radar now showed them to be Mig-29s.

Scott keyed his transmit button again. "Check six pig eaters." He hit them with his bright landing lights when they were both looking back. "You have one more chance to turn back or I will shoot you down. You North Korean pilots are no match for us Chinese pilots." The lead aircraft yelled "break" into his mask. He broke left and his wingman right. Scott went vertical and rolled inverted to see what they would do. They continued around in a very tight high G three sixty and joined up again.

"Green two this is one, looks like our brave Chinese super pilot put his tail between his legs and ran. I think we will play around in Chinese airspace for awhile."

"That may not be too wise leader. We don't want the Chinese mad at us. Border relations are a little tense as it is."

"Stay on my wing number two."

When the two Migs joined up Scott slid in behind them. Going vertical, coupled with the daylight radar and the maneuverability of his aircraft, made the dogfight almost too easy. That would all change in the future as it always did but, in the meantime, he would take every advantage he could.

"No you won't inferior pilot," said Scott as he squeezed the trigger and watched twenty millimeter shells tear the tail off the lead Mig-29. The second Mig did a split S and ran for the border. He let the second Mig go. It was so easy he almost felt guilty.

"Jesus" said Tim. "You shot him down"

"That's what we came for," said Steve. "We have company coming Scott. Two birds lifted off Hyesan and the two that took off ahead of us at Bongdian are coming this way. They all have their throttles bent and their radars on."

One of the Chinese pilots called him to ask if he needed help. Tim switched the language exchanger so Scott would be heard in Chinese. He replied that he did because two more North Korean aircraft were headed his way. They should be able to intercept them. "I will give you the honor of shooting them down. I have already shot one down. They are easy but must be shown they can not violate our air space." The two Chinese pilots were grinning from ear to ear. This is what we train for they thought.

The two North Korean pilots were not grinning. They had lost one of their pilots and wanted blood. Both sets of aircraft turned towards each other and fired missiles but no hits. Scott, Steve and Tim were too engrossed watching the radar to speak. The four aircraft were going through about every maneuver in the book but there was a loser on both sides. The fate of the three pilots was not known. Two Korean and one Chinese were lost.

"Wow! How about that," Scott said over the intercom. "Things got hot in a hurry. Have you guys found your voices yet?"

"I'm still trying to find mine," said Steve. "That was really something. We just saw three aircraft shot down."

"Yeah," said Tim. "And we shot down one of them."

"We're going to sit up here for awhile and see what moves are made by who next. I think both sides are wondering what happened. They are supposed to be friends, but when fighter pilots are threatened they can't sit by and maybe get nailed themselves. Can't you just hear the communications between the Generals and politicians on both sides? You can both take a break. You'll have time to write down your view on what just happened. Stay strapped in tight though in case we have to move in a hurry."

Scott stretched his arms and legs. He had been tense and very focused for some time, the stretching felt good and helped relax his muscles. When he shot the Mig down he had used just two of his guns. The other two were loaded with explosive heads. While watching the battle calm down a plan was forming in Scott's mind.

An hour later Scott keyed his mike. "Time to get back to work guys. Stow your gear, tighten your straps and Tim I need to talk in Chinese. We are going near Bongdian so we can talk to them, then to Hyesan where we'll strafe every aircraft on the ground we can find. We'll use the explosive heads loaded in guns three and four."

"Okay Scott," replied Tim. "We're ready to go and you are set to Chinese."

"Bongdian this is Operation One. Do you show any more North Koreans invading our air space?"

"Operation One who are you? We have no orders for you. General Ghang has not heard of you or any special orders. He orders you to land at once."

"You tell the General to talk to his superior. Ghang was not informed of this special order. I don't have time to discuss this any further with you. Now answer my question, do you show any North Korean aircraft in the air?"

"Sorry Colonel. No, there are no other aircraft in the air that we show on our radar"

"I will complete my mission then return to my base"

"Time to switch to transmit Korean Tim" ordered Scott.

"You got it," he replied.

Scott flew over Hyesan at 1,000 feet. He saw no birds in the air but did see a lot of activity under lights. There was no traffic on the radio, it was strangely silent. They obviously weren't expecting a raid by the Chinese. The politicians must have put a stop to aggressive activity. Won't they be surprised!

"We'll go right down the runway at five hundred feet. I'll rotate the aircraft on its vertical axis so it's facing left while we go down the runway. This will give us good shooting all the way down. If the return fire is not too bad we'll do a one-eighty and come down the other side of the runway. Each of you count the number of destroyed birds and their type. Here we go. This could get rough."

Initially he slowed to one hundred and twenty knots to get a feel for the guns with the aircraft turned sideways. It took about three seconds to get the nose at the proper elevation to get the shells on target, then it was a matter of holding that position and distance from the target. The explosive tipped shells wreaked complete havoc on the ground. The aircraft exploded and burned as the shells tore into them. As he got more confidence he increased his speed to one hundred fifty then one seventy-five. Before he knew it he was at the end of the ramp. He turned one-hundred and eighty degrees to the right and started down the ramp on the other side of the runway. The light from the fires, now to their rear, were illuminating their aircraft as they flew down the runway with guns firing. They could see occasional tracers shooting past them from sporadic ground fire. Scott increased the speed and kept firing when suddenly there were no more targets. They had left the airfield behind them. He rotated the aircraft to the right so they were once again facing the direction of flight. He then started climbing and reversed course.

"Let's get a little altitude and see what damage we caused," said Scott with a dry voice.

"That ammo is powerful," transmitted Steve. "There isn't much left down there that's in one piece. Jesus! I've never seen anything like that, not even in the movies. The tapes are still running and have been the whole time so we can review everything when we get back."

"We do much more of that and it'll be, if we get back," voiced Tim. "Anybody want some water? I'm really dry." All three drank a full bottle.

"Let me know when you get all you want on video Steve. I was too busy to see all the damage but looking down now, we sure messed things up. Their leaders are going to be most upset. It's time to add a little more fuel to the fire. Switch me back to Chinese on the gizmo Tim. We'll pay Bongdian another visit."

"Are you going to erase that base too?" replied Tim. "You are now Chinese."

When they were ten miles from Bongdian and painting no airborne boogies Scott dropped the landing pads and pressed the transmit button, "Bongdian, this is Colonel Chen of Operation One, my mission is now complete. I am returning to my base. I will report that you were very helpful. Operation one out."

"Operation One, your superior wants you to report to him as soon as you land."

"I will do that Bongdian." Scott kept the aircraft low and retracted the landing pads when he was out of Bongdian's radar. He then set the GPS to fly to the nuclear reactor site at Yongbyon .

"If all goes well the Koreans heard that last transmission and will think the Chinese attacked their base," said Scott. "The skirmish between the fighters set the stage. Get some good pictures of the nuclear site Steve, we'll be there shortly."

They spent thirty minutes over the site taking video picture from every angle. When they felt they had enough Scott set in the coordinates of Pyongyang, the capital and home of their little leader. When they arrived, they held over the government buildings and the palace, recording the GPS positions of each for a possible attack later.

The radar showed no airborne aircraft. They flew over several airfields and also recorded the GPS positions of these. Three of these bases had hardened underground hangars and these were noted. They then flew down towards the DMZ to video all the artillery guns aimed at South Korea.

"Those people have a million man army along with nuclear, biological and chemical weapons, ballistic missiles, several hundred artillery guns pointed at South Korea, what chance do they have?" remarked Tim. "I don't feel sorry any more for those guys we shot down. What chance do they have if the North decides to attack? We have about thirty thousand of our guys there too. How did we let this get so far out of balance?"

"Good question Tim," replied Steve. "We need to put a fear into them that will bring them to their knees. What do you have in mind now Scott?"

"First we'll go back to that second airfield, give me the coordinates Steve. I want to see how effective these bombs are against the hardened hangars. I'll switch to bunker buster and see if it destroys what's in them."

A short time later they were over the airfield. "The daylight radar shows some hangars with aircraft in front, probably waiting to be refueled and pushed inside. I suggest we drop one bomb on a closed bunker. If they do refuel before closing the hangar, which we suspect, there should be a big fire or explosion inside. Does anyone have a better plan?"

There was no response. Scott lined up the cross hairs on the center of a closed hangar and released the bomb after making sure Steve still had the tape running. The daylight radar turned night into day and showed very good detail. The bomb landed dead center on the hangar roof and penetrated all the way through before exploding. The SU-27 fully loaded with fuel disappeared in a horrendous explosion and fire. Two aircraft being refueled still outside their hangars on either side also blew up. After the explosions the base was still strangely inactive. There were no aircraft taking off to find them or anti aircraft fire. Political phone lines must be running hot.

"Look at that," said Tim. "There's nothing left of the hangar but there is a hot fire where it was. It looks like these bombs will do the job."

"Let me know when you have enough on disk."

When Scott was told they had enough tape he keyed the intercom. "We're going back to the nuclear site at Yongbyon and drop a test bomb. The radius of destruction of our bombs is one quarter mile. I want to drop three eighths of a mile from the southern most building. This will have a two fold purpose. First, to see the results of the bomb based on the earth's structure around the site and second, it will let them know that we could have leveled the place if we had wanted. If they have any intelligence, which I wonder, the way their government treats the people, it could give those at the bargaining table a strong position. We're coming up on the site now. I want us all to agree that the cross- hairs are set on three eighth of a mile from the south building before release"

When Scott had centered the cross hairs he asked each one if they agreed the cross was in the correct position. When they agreed they were, Scott released the bomb from ten thousand feet.

They couldn't hear the explosion but could see the shock wave through the radar. If that building wasn't damaged it would be a miracle. It was all captured on video tape.

"How would you like to be working at a nuclear facility when suddenly a huge explosion shakes the building and the ground. How many do you think headed for the door before they realized it wouldn't do any good to run if there was nuclear explosion. No one could run that far and fast," remarked Scott. "Keep the tape running until after the dust settles. We'll have some experts look at it and advise us how close to drop if we just want to damage but not destroy. Maybe we can avoid a nuclear explosion. It's pushing four in the morning, time to head home. It's been a long and very successful night." He couldn't help a big yawn.

They dropped the pod in one hangar for rearming and the aircraft in the other hanger when they landed at home after dark. They opened three Kalik's and stretched out in the living room. Scott looked at the other two. " Did everyone get their after action report done?" They nodded affirmative. Scott laid his on the table and asked the others to do the same. "In the morning we'll read each other's to see how they compare then transmit them to Mr. R along with an after raid video we'll make. Be thinking of what should be said on this video which will again go out to the major world-wide news media. Now gentlemen, if you will excuse me, I'm going to bed."

CHAPTER SEVENTEEN

They had left a mass of confusion behind them in China and North Korea. After the dog- fight in which North Korea lost two aircraft and China one, the communication lines were hot. Kim sat with his advisors in his seven- story palace and the Air General of China sat with his aids.

"Explain to us your actions tonight Kim Jong Un. If it is not to our satisfaction we will launch an attack and wipe you and your advisors from the earth. Speak NOW," commanded the Air General of China, General Ni Xusan.

"We have the tapes General. We tape all our air communications for security purposes. Our tapes tell us it was your aircraft that shot and downed one of our planes first. When his wing man landed he confirmed that is what happened. They had accidentally entered Chinese air space and were returning when your fighter shot our lead aircraft down."

"What were your aircraft doing in our airspace? That was a violation that resulted in exactly what you deserved. You have been warned not to enter Chinese airspace have you not? And did not our pilot warn them to leave and they did not?"

"Yes General, we have been warned and the pilot responsible paid for it with his life."

"As it should be. Now explain why your fighters then attacked our aircraft."

"I can not give you a satisfactory answer General until I talk to the pilots myself. They are on the way to my headquarters now. I will call you as soon as I talk to them. I have been told another of our planes was lost and if that is so then there is only one pilot on his way here."

"I may want your pilot sent to me for interrogation. Your country shot down one of our aircraft and we demand reparations on your part. What those will be are for our leader to determine. He may decide to declare war on your country."

"We have already been attacked by your aircraft General. They attacked an airfield and destroyed twenty six aircraft on the ground along with much support equipment. They dropped a bomb on another airfield destroying a hangar and three aircraft there. They then dropped a bomb and nearly hit our nuclear reactor. It was fortunate they missed."

"I know of no such attacks. I will talk to our commander in that area. If this is true it is a small price you pay for attacking our aircraft. I will await your call after interrogating your pilot." General Ni Xusan slammed the phone down.

"You see," said Kim. "It was the Chinese who started this and are now blaming us. They can not be trusted. This pilot that is coming for interrogation, see that he has a most unfortunate accident resulting in his death. See that any pilot that comes within fifteen kilometers of Chinese airspace is executed upon landing. We can not win a war with China. This sword rattling must stop."

"I will see to it Great General"

CHAPTER EIGHTEEN

T he next day they arranged the sheets for the second video. Scott donned his blazer, Tim set up the voice disguiser and Steve the equipment to block out Scott's face. They took their time and discussed what to say and were finally ready to record at 3:00pm.

The scrambler phone rang. It was Mr. R for Scott. Scott listened for a minute then said, "We'll do it. Could you arrange for an Osprey to land on our helipad when we return so we can to transfer him to Bermuda? Also, we'll need to take Dr. Kay and a surgical assistant and they will need a surgical kit and pressure suit for each of them. We'll leave here an hour after dark, that's three hours from now, and I'll need the orbit location of the ISS. Yes sir, thank you sir." Scott hung up the phone and turned to the other two.

"Everything is on hold for awhile. A Russian on the space station needs an emergency appendectomy and neither Russia nor the U.S. have a bird ready to fly. Dr. Kay and a surgical nurse are coming with us and they may have to operate on the way back.

An Osprey will be here to ferry him to Bermuda. He'll wake up in Bermuda minus his appendix and remember nothing, if all goes well. We leave one hour after sunset. Can you two genius IQ's rig up an operating table that won't float in zero G? Dr. Kay may have to operate on our return trip.

It was 3:15 when Dr. Kay arrived and was met at the office door by Mr.R.

"Come in Dr. Kay. Have a seat."

"A Russian cosmonaut in the space station has acute appendicitis. Neither the Russians nor the United States have a shuttle available and won't have for at least a week. Our Company has a craft that can fly to the space station and return with the Russian. This is a secret of the highest magnitude, and one we want to keep that way. We can not leave until after dark and have set the scheduled take-off time for 9:00pm tonight. If the Russian is as bad as they say an emergency appendectomy may have to be done in the air while bringing him down."

"I'll be happy to standby where ever you bring him and can operate immediately Mr. R," said Dr. Kay with a puzzled look on her face.

" Will you go with our crew to the space station along with a surgical kit and a surgical assistant? If it weren't so important I wouldn't ask. Our craft has been in space many times but it has never docked with the space station. All of you will be wearing space suits as a precaution against depressurization. Our pilot assures me it can be done. You know him and the other two crew members, Scott, Steve and Tim. Scott is the pilot."

"You're asking me to go into space with no training and attach to a space station which has never been done before by this rocket and maybe do a surgical procedure in the air on the way down, if we ever get to the point of coming down."

" I wouldn't ask you if I thought there was a great risk involved."

"Only if there's a little risk, huh?"

"If you don't want to go just tell me and I will understand but, I'm sorry, I do need your decision now. There is a lot to do between now and 9:00pm. I will understand if you decline."

She got up and walked to the door but, turned took a deep breath, " I better find a surgical assistant and get my kit ready. Where do we get fitted for space suits?"

"The driver in the reception room who will see you get to the right places."

She told the driver to take her to the hospital. The receptionist told her Colleen was in the nurses lounge. Kay hurried down the hall and entered the lounge. When she entered the lounge Colleen was laughing with friends around a table. "Colleen, I need to see you right away."

Colleen hurried through the door. "What's the matter Doctor."

They entered Dr. Kay's office. "I don't know how to start but, here goes. Will you go in a spaceship with me to the space station and pick up a Russian who needs an appendectomy which we'll probably have to perform on the way back to earth? Of course it's top secret."

Colleen looked at her, "Sure."

"What do you mean, sure, I'm serious."

"I thought you were, I said, sure."

"Right. Okay, let's get our kit packed and a driver will take us for our spacesuit fitting."

With kit and space suits the two of them were taken to the helipad. "Remember Colleen, say absolutely nothing about where we're going."

On the way to the helipad Dr. Kay looked at Colleen. "You're nuts, you know?"

"Then what's that make you?"

Talking in a very low voice so as not to be heard by the driver, Dr. Kay said, "Remember Scott Wilson who joined us for lunch the other day?" Not waiting for an answer she continued, "We are going to a base somewhere near the Bahamas. Scott Wilson, who you met the other day is the pilot and the other two crew members are Tim and Steve. They are taking us to the space station to pick up a Russian cosmonaut who is having an attack of appendicitis. Supposedly, it is to the stage that we may have to operate immediately. That's as much as I know."

" Is that our helicopter?"

"They all look a like to me, but the driver is heading for it so it must be," said Dr. Kay as she felt the first pangs of stomach butterflies.

Am I nervous about this she thought? I can't let Colleen know. She's going because I asked her to go, so I must look confident.

They helicopter crew loaded the surgical kit and pressure suits aboard and announced they were ready for take off. "If you ladies will climb aboard we'll help you strap in and then we'll be off."

The trip would take approximately one hour. The two women were fastened tightly in their seats when the helicopter lifted off and turned east with the setting sun at their back. The coming night increased the intensity of the butterflies.

Colleen turned to Dr. Kay, "I'm not afraid but the butterflies are really flying in my stomach. I think it's the anticipation of the unknown ahead. I haven't felt like this in years, it's wonderful, I'm so excited. Thank you Doctor, thank you for asking me to go along. I'm so excited I'm about to pee my pants. I will have to go to the restroom before we leave."

"I have a few wings fluttering in my stomach too. I agree, it's the anticipation of the unknown. It must be safe or Mr. R would not have asked us to go. But I can't believe we are actually going into space."

When they touched down Scott and Steve were waiting for them. "Welcome ladies," they said. "Please head for the house where Tim is waiting for you. He'll show you to your rooms where you may perform any last minute activities before takeoff."

"They both hurried to the house where Tim showed them their rooms which were really his and Scott's rooms. A short time later they appeared looking refreshed and relieved. Kay made the introduction to Tim who looked at Colleen with more than a passing interest. Both women noticed Tim's reaction. "Scott and Steve are loading your gear in the aircraft. If you are ready we'll go there and start getting you ready. We have a little more time if you need."

They didn't need more time. They hadn't gone far when Scott and Steve approached. Since Scott had met Colleen at the cafeteria he introduced her to Steve. Like Tim, Steve noticed how beautiful this woman was. How nice it would be to have two beautiful women on board, he thought. Steve led the way up the stairs into the aircraft followed by the two women then Tim and Scott.

"Oh my gosh!" Colleen said. "This looks like the starship Enterprise. And look, they have an operating table with monitors set up. I had no idea something like this existed."

"Only a very few people do Colleen," replied Scott. "That's why we must take off and land at night. It is most important to keep it a secret. Steve and Tim will help you into your pressure suits, which you will wear until after we disconnect from docking. Steve and Tim will enter the space station and bring the cosmonaut through the tunnel to the operating table where you two will then take over. We'll be weightless and it will take a getting used to at first. We will descend to one G environment as soon as you give the all clear. When and if to operate is entirely your decision. Can you operate in zero G?"

"If we have to we will but, it would be better with one G. We'll know more after we examine the patient."

"Right. After you get your pressure suits on and plugged in Steve and Tim will check you over to be sure your life support is working properly as well as the intercom. Then we'll suit up and take care of some last minute pre-flight items and we'll be ready to go."

When the women were strapped in their seats with all connections checked and operating correctly the three men donned and checked their suits. They strapped themselves into their seats, set up their flight panels and Scott announced ready for take-off. "Wait a minute," said Dr. Kay. "Where is the rocket? You have to have a rocket to get this thing into orbit, then we glide down to a runway someplace. You don't even have a runway here. Where will we land?"

Colleen looked at her then Steve, Tim and Scott. "Hey, what about that? Where is the rocket? How are you going to get up there without one? Is this a joke to get us out here?"

"That's another secret you ladies will have to keep," answered Scott. "Hangar roof coming open, one minute to 6:00pm, all of you please check in that you are ready to go."

One by one they said they were ready. "Ten seconds. " said Scott. "Five, four, three, two, one and lift off. Two hundred feet, hangar door coming closed and pads retracted."

"Steve, what's going on?" said Dr. Kay. "Where is all the explosion, fire, smoke and vibration we see on television? That was so smooth it doesn't feel like we have left the ground, have we?"

"Part of the secret Doctor. We are going to increase speed gradually now but will keep the G forces to a comfortable level."

"Don't do that for me" said Colleen. "This is fantastic! Better than any carnival ride." Her butterflies were gone now replace by pure wonder and excitement.

"You boys do what you have to do," added Dr. Kay. "Colleen and I are just fine. Now that my butterflies are gone I'm starting to enjoy this."

"I still get butterflies before every flight," said Tim. "I bet the other guys do also. It's not fear, it's anticipation of another flight that only a handful of people have ever done. We five are going into space, two hundred and forty miles high, to rescue a Russian, and perhaps operate on him while returning to earth. What we are about to do is a first. This has never been done before. Ohhh Lord, don't let me screw up." Scott and Steve snickered over his cleaning up the phrase.

"The International Space Station is in an elliptical orbit which means its altitude is constantly changing. We have been given its position and altitude for the time we will arrive.

Scott continued, "We need to review our actions for after we dock. Steve and Tim will enter the ISS and bring the patient to us or wait at our hatch if the ISS crew brings him to our hatch. Steve and Tim will take him to the operating table where Dr. Kay and Colleen will strap him in and make the operation decision. The choices are; one, disconnect and operate while weightless; two, descend to one G environment and operate then or; three, return to base and operate there. After the decision is made the women will return to their seats and strap in for the disconnect. Then we will proceed with whatever decision the medical team has made. We'll stay flexible so if we need to make any changes we will. Does anyone have any additions, subtractions or comments?"

They all agreed on the procedure and the flight continued towards the ISS. When they were twenty five miles out and the sun had set, Scott keyed his transmit button. "ISS this is Rescue, over."

"Calling ISS this is a discreet frequency. Please change to another channel."

"ISS this is Rescue, we are twenty miles out requesting clearance to dock with you. We know neither the Russians nor the United States have a shuttle available to transport your sick crew member. We have the transportation and a medical staff aboard to care for him while returning him to earth, over."

"Whoever you are get off this frequency or you may be arrested. Play your hoax with someone else."

"ISS this is Rescue, we are now at your speed and one quarter mile abeam on your left. Do you have a visual on our lights?"

Chad, the ISS commander, an American, couldn't believe what he was seeing. "Hey guys," he said. 'Look at this and tell me I'm dreaming."

They looked. "If you're dreaming, so are we," they said. "Who is it? Where did he come from? No one but the Russians and the United States have space shuttles. I hope he's friendly."

Chad keyed his mike. "Ahhh, Rescue, we have you in sight. Who are you? Where did you come from? What country?"

"This will be hard for you to believe but we are from a small unknown Country on earth. We like our privacy and would have stayed unknown if it weren't for your problem. We can help you save that man's life if you will let us. Our docking collar is designed to match the ISS. As I said before, we have a medical team on board, actually they are a surgical team. If your man is as bad as you report, time is important. Check with your ground control."

"ISS this is ground control. Russia are you listening to this exchange also?"

"Affirmative U. S. It's not one of ours. Are you telling us it's not yours either?"

"That's affirmative. It's not ours and we have no ship ready to go. Break. ISS, does he show any markings?"

"Negative. It's dark up here now and all we can see are lights he has turned on."

"This is Rescue. Your talk is wasting time while this man's life is in the balance. His life is in your hands to take it from him or let us help. We are capable of operating the minute he is on board or taking him to a medical facility on earth. May we move in to docking position ISS?"

"Ground, what do you want me to do?"

"Has to be your call if Russia agrees Chad. You copy that Russia?"

"Roger, we copy and agree. You're the commander on site Colonel."

"Rescue, this is ISS. You ever docked before?"

"Not with you ISS. Rescue moving in for docking."

"Roger Rescue."

Chad turned to the others on the ISS. "Okay guys, cross your fingers and hope this Rescue character doesn't take us both out.

Don't open that pressure door until I give the okay. He's moving in now. Wonder where his docking collar is? There it comes out, you can see it in the lights. It's too dark to make out the ship though."

"Rescue, ISS, that's a strange place for a docking collar. Are you from earth?"

"Affirmative ISS. We're in position. Stand by for contact. Contact. Latches locking. Okay ISS, we show docked. How you?"

"Same Rescue. Nicely done"

"We are sending two men aboard to transport Vladimir. Chad, if you want to come aboard while the medical team examines him you may. Understand that if they need to operate immediately you'll have to return at once as I want to undock before they start."

"Ground, this is ISS. That okay with you?"

"Affirmative ISS."

"Rescue is opening hatches. Our crew will still be in pressure suits until undocking. Just a precaution against a hatch not sealing properly."

"Okay guys," Chad said. "Open them up and let the two men aboard."

The hatches were opened and pressure between the ISS and Rescue equalized. Steve and Tim floated up to the hatch and into the connecting tunnel. As they stepped into the ISS they all looked at each other. Steve raised his visor and opened his faceplate and smiled. "See, we're not little green men. We're earthlings, same as you. Next time let's have lunch, but right now let's get Vladimir through the tunnel.

They all jumped to it with Tim leading the way holding Vladimir's head and shoulders. Steve followed holding Vladimir's legs then came Chad. Once through the tunnel Steve and Tim took Vladimir directly to the operating table where the women were waiting. They strapped him down then set to work hooking up the instruments to monitor his vital signs. Chad was looking around in awe. He floated over to Scott and put out his hand. "I'm Chad Boomer."

"Call me Captain, Chad. Glad we could." He didn't get a chance to finish as Dr. Kay spoke with urgency.

"Captain, we need to operate immediately. I mean right now. No time to undock."

"Roger Doctor, understand. Steve and Tim, help them out of their pressure suits and you may have to hold them down while they're operating." Both women opened their face plates and donned surgical masks before removing their helmets.

Chad floated next to Scott while watching the women get out of their pressure suits. He couldn't help notice how beautiful the two women were even with their surgical masks on.. The two men sat on the floor with their legs around the operating table's cross braces and held the women's legs so they wouldn't float.

"This is unreal Captain. Things like this just don't happen in space. At least not yet. This ship is really something. Who are you? What country are you from?"

"I can understand your bewilderment Chad. We are a small Country with very advanced technology. The name of our Country is Piot. The location must remain a secret as you will understand in the next few days. We have declared war on several nations for self defense reasons. Those countries are North Korea, Iran, Libya, Saudi Arabia, Yemen, Somalia, Pakistan, Afghanistan and any country with an unstable government that possesses weapons of mass destruction or aids terrorists. Our Nation could be wiped out by fallout. We had no choice. If those countries don't know our location they can not attack us. That is why our location must remain secret."

"You say Piot is the name of your Country?"

"Yes, it stands for Peace In Our Time"

"And you are declaring war on all those countries?"

"That is correct Chad."

Chad looked at him like he was out of his mind yet, here they were in a shuttle much more sophisticated than anything operational by the United States. Well, it was their funeral.

Scott remained in his space suit along with Steve and Tim while the operation was in progress. "So much for plans to remain in our suits until undocked," remarked Scott. "It is important Chad that you do not reveal any particulars about us to anyone without a need to know. You can certainly tell them of the rescue by a vehicle from an unknown country. In fact, it would be helpful if you would emphasize that it was not from the United States or Russia. The other two men and I are leaving our space suits on to avoid any possible recognition in the future. The women needed theirs off to operate."

"Can you explain why you want me to emphasize that you are not from the United States or Russia?"

"In a few days you and the world will understand Chad. That's as much as I can tell you now but, I hope you will trust us. Our goal is world peace."

"After what you have done for us Captain, I have no reason not to trust you."

One half an hour later Dr. Kay said "The operation was a success and barely in time. The patient is doing fine but I would like to get him to Earth."

"Our thanks to all of you," said Chad with a big smile on his face. "I will relay to both the U.S. and Russia that all went well. Where will you be taking him?"

"We will call the interested parties when he is safely there and in bed," replied Scott.

"Understand," nodded Chad as he floated up to the hatch. He threw them a salute then disappeared into the tunnel. Tim floated up to the hatch to make sure he was clear before closing the outer and inner hatches. He then returned to his seat and noticed the others were already strapped in their seats.

"Please confirm crew and patient strapped in and ready for disconnect," spoke Scott. All responded they were ready including the patient with Tim's voice.

If the ISS positioning jets fired just when they disconnected there could be a sudden jolt. However, this did not happen and the transition was very smooth. "Nice flying Scott," said Steve.

"ISS, Rescue is disconnected and departing for Earth. We'll take good care of your man."

"Thanks Rescue, we really appreciate your help. ISS out."

"Rescue out."

"ISS this is ground control. What happened? We're sure Russia wants to know also."

"Roger control. Two of their crew came on board and carried Vladimir through the docking collar into their ship where they strapped him on an operating table. Because of his critical condition their medical crew was forced to operate immediately. He was stable and on his way to Earth when we disconnected. They will take him to a medical facility and inform someone where he was taken."

"Roger ISS, we'll debrief you when you return."

"Roger ground, ISS out."

"All of you did an outstanding job. This was a first for all of us and your performance was most commendable. How is the patient? Any problems we should know about?" said Scott.

"I can't believe we did this," said Colleen still full of excitement. "This is a first, an operation in space. You'll make headlines Doctor. This whole thing is amazing."

"Sorry Colleen," said Tim. "No public accolades for an unknown time. We cannot reveal to the world where this ship and it's people are from. We are letting them know the country is Piot but not where Piot is located. By the way, you were on Piot earlier this evening. It's location must remain very secret. You can't tell anyone what happened tonight. You can pretend to know only what you will read in the papers or hear on the news. Please understand that literally thousands of lives may depend on that."

"Turn the radio to interior speaker Steve," instructed Scott. "We can all hear what the ISS and the ground stations are saying. It will help us when we do our video."

"U.S. and Russia ground this is ISS."

They both responded, "go ahead ISS.

"Vladimir has been transferred and just in time. The surgical team performed immediate surgery as soon as the doctor examined him. It was close but he is doing fine and on his way back to earth. They will notify you where he has been taken. Over."

"ISS, this is Russia. Who are they? We must know where they are taking him. Over."

"Sorry Russia but they would not say. Who they are and location of their Country is a secret they want to keep. They did say the name of their Country is Piot, stands for Peace In Our Time. They were very professional and their ship is way ahead of anything we have. They did say that it was important for the world to know they are not from the United States or Russia."

"That's what we wanted to hear," said Scott as he turned off the speaker. "When we return to the base we'll land in the hangar so the Osprey crew can't see us. Steve and Tim will help you ladies transport the patient to them. They will have a medical crew including a doctor and will fly him to Bermuda where the U.S. and Russia will be notified of his location. Mr. R has seen that your schedules tomorrow have been cleared so you can spend the night on Piot and rest up. It might even be possible Colleen, to have one of those poolside lobster parties. Provided you two go lobster hunting with us."

"I'll go, I'll go," said Colleen. "I'd love a lobster party."

They could feel the forces of gravity start as they descended closer to earth. Soon they were over their base and very quickly inside the hanger with the roof closed. Transporting Vladimir to the Osprey went fast with no problems. As Vladimir vanished into the night aboard the Osprey, the five of them stared into the night.

"And just like that it's all over," remarked Dr Kay. "I can't believe it happened."

"That's because, thanks to all of you, everything went very smoothly," said Scott. "The only change was getting out of your pressure suits before disconnect and that couldn't be helped. I don't know about the rest of you but a cold beer and a swim will feel mighty good. You ladies have the run of the house. We three are staying in the dormitory by the north hangar. Help yourself to anything you want, see you poolside in a few minutes."

Colleen couldn't remember when she had such an exciting time. First the space ride and now a cocktail at midnight by the pool in an unknown Country called Piot and, she could tell no one any of it. She knew they could trust her completely but she felt there was much more going on that the men weren't disclosing. She understood there must be secrets but she was still curious. She felt Dr. Kay was also curious. Oh well, it was none of their business.

They called it a day at 1:00am and fell asleep as soon as their heads hit the pillow. All but Dr. Kay who lay awake for awhile wondering what this place really was. A lot more going on than meets the eye. These men were too cool today on this rescue mission. They have obviously been in space many times, but doing what?

The next morning after a light breakfast, they were relaxing by the pool when Scott asked a question that was also a statement. "Do you ladies mind if we use the house for an hour this morning? We have some unfinished business we need to complete. If we could use it starting at eleven we should be done by twelve in time for lunch. After that, it's in the boat and out to sea for lobster."

"Do you mind if we go for a walk while you are taking care of business?" asked Dr. Kay.

"Not at all," replied Scott. "Watch out for sand burrs."

At eleven the three men went in the house to tape the video. They decided to put the next flight to North Korea off for three days in order for the video to reach the news media and North Korea. They also needed the report from Mr. R on the nuclear reactor bomb. If they were to take it out they needed that information. They also wanted to see the worlds reaction to the tape they were about to make.

After hanging the sheets and Scott donning his blue sport coat, they were ready to start taping.

This is the President of Piot speaking to you, You now know the name of our Country but not its location. This is what we desire.

The first tape may not have been made public by the news media because they thought it was a hoax. That tape contained our declaration of war against the countries of North Korea, Iran, Libya, Yemen, Saudi Arabia, Somalia, Pakistan, Afghanistan and any country that supports terrorism in any way. One such tape was delivered to the North Korean embassy in Paris before the attack you are about to see. Our reason for this declaration of war is self defense. Although we are way ahead of the world in certain areas of technology, we are a very small Nation. In the wrong hands there could be fall out from weapons of mass destruction that could end life in our Country. We can no longer stand by and watch the world situation deteriorate.

Two nights ago we made our first attack on North Korea. This was after they received our tape declaring war on them. This attack has not been made public until now. It started with two North Korean Mig 29's crossing the border into China. They have been warned by China not to do this. We pretended to be a Chinese aircraft and ordered them out of Chinese airspace. They engaged our aircraft as you can see from the tape of the encounter. It was night time but our technology converts night into day. We have converted the languages to English. A short air combat followed and as you can see, our aircraft shot the tail off the North Korean Mig 29. It was at this moment two aircraft from China and two from North Korea engaged each other while we watched and recorded the fight. The result was one aircraft from each country shot down.

We then proceeded to this airfield in North Korea where we destroyed many of their aircraft on the ground. You can see the total destruction. Again, this was not made public until now.

The rest of the film covers our bombing of a hardened hanger to observe the effectiveness of this particular type of bomb. The hanger and several more of their aircraft were destroyed. We then dropped an intentional near miss on their nuclear reactor for a specific reason.

To Kim Jong Un we have this to say. You must start immediately to shut down your reactor and deliver the rods to either China or Russia for safe keeping. We will then destroy the site. If you do not we will destroy the site with the rods in place which will contaminate the area for many years. We will also destroy all your weapons manufacturing buildings, all of your aircraft and missiles.

We will be informed when you receive this tape. You will then have twenty four hours to begin removing the rods and evacuating your people. We will attack very soon after that. *Your nuclear reactor will be destroyed.*

Yesterday we docked with the International Space Station to bring to Earth a very ill Russian cosmonaut. Neither the United States nor Russia had a shuttle available to fly. The Russians have now been informed of the whereabouts of Vladimir. He is doing fine but lost his appendix when our surgical team removed it while we were still docked with the ISS.

Our Country does not depend on any other country for its survival. We can and will act without thought of offending another country. We do not care what the opinion of others may be, we are doing what we must do for our survival.

"That should do it Scott," said Tim. "The news should start carrying the story about Vladimir any time now. With that plus the two videos there should be a lot for the news people to talk about. They will be interviewing the leaders of the U.S. and Russia about this unknown shuttle. Hopefully this will convince the world and especially North Korea that the U.S. is not involved."

"That's the reason for everything we have done so far Tim," he replied. "After you make a copy Steve, will you see that its gets to Mr. R?"

"Will do Scott," replied Steve.

That would be done electronically direct to Mr. R for his review before going to the news media and to the North Korea embassy in Paris. It should be in their hands this afternoon. It was now nearing noon and time to rejoin the ladies.

The three men left the house for the pool and found the women in deep conversation. "Are you ladies getting hungry after your walk?" asked Steve. "Our business is finished, now we're ready to play. How about you two?"

"We are starving," answered Dr. Kay. "But before we eat can we listen to the news? Our little trip should be a topic of discussion today."

"Good idea, let's go in and listen to the TV news while we get lunch ready," said Tim.

It didn't take long to find a station talking about the rescue of the Russian cosmonaut. They all listened intently. Scott, Steve and Tim were interested to find out if the news media was biting on Piot as a nation and not casting suspicion on the U.S. or Russia. Obviously the information he told Chad, commander of the ISS, about declaring war on those other countries was relayed to ground who then released it to the press. Now they are showing the first video delivered to the media several days ago. After that they interviewed top level U.S. diplomats who confessed they knew nothing. There were interviews with the Secretary of the Navy and Air Force. No one knew anything but voiced that there was a logical explanation and they did not think it would take long to find it. There were also overseas interviews with Russia, Germany, Great Britain and Japan. They even interviewed Chad from the ISS. He said he thought he was current on space equipment of the world and didn't know that such a vehicle existed. He further stated that he was in the craft during the operation on Vladimir and was very impressed with the professionalism of the entire crew. He would have to hold comments on the shuttle itself until cleared by his superiors. He was told by the commander of the shuttle that they were from a country called Piot, which stood for Peace In Our Time, and they had declared war on the countries previously mentioned. He had complete confidence that Vladimir was in good hands. This turned out to be true as Vladimir is recovering very well in Bermuda. That was pretty much the gist of the ISS interview.

"There is something you haven't told us about," said Dr. Kay. "What's this about declaring war on all those countries?"

"Right. Well we have, but the only thing we can tell you is what you hear on the news. I'm sorry but that is the way it has to be. If this upsets you we can call for the helicopter to come early. Or, we can go on with our plans for the lobster dinner. This will probably be the last free time we will have for awhile. The choice is yours and whatever it is we understand," explained Scott.

Colleen and Dr. Kay looked at each other. "I vote for the lobster," volunteered Colleen.

Dr. Kay turned and looked at the three men waiting for an answer. "Lobster it is then."

Tim turned the TV off as he knew the second video could be aired anytime and he didn't want the women upset further.

They finished a light lunch and the men cleaned up while the women changed into their swim suits. The men told the women they were going to the dormitory to change and would meet them at the boat. Thirty minutes later they were moving towards the canal with a cooler of liquid refreshments and their diving gear. It was 1:30 pm, the sky a beautiful blue with a few puffy cumulus, the water an inviting turquoise color and calm with an air temperature of 82 degrees. A typical beautiful Bahamas day. Who would ever think these three men were in a shooting war?

The President and his Joint Chiefs of Staff were in a meeting at the same time Scott and his friends were diving for lobster, when there was a knock on the door. A Colonel handed a video to the Army Chief of Staff, the person who answered the door. "Looks as though we have another video Mr. President. Would you like me to play it?"

President Barley nodded his head. The video was inserted and the play button pushed. They sat there not believing what they were seeing. "My GOD!" the Air Force Chief of Staff exclaimed. "Is this real? We've heard nothing. There has been a high overcast over North Korea for a few days which blocks out our satellite but, how could this happen? Do you suppose this has anything to do with the F-22 encounter with an unknown that night?" Giving no one a chance to answer he continued. "He absolutely leveled that airfield. Why haven't we heard about this from North Korea or the Chinese? That near miss on the nuclear reactor was intentional. Look at what happened to that hangar, a direct hit. And then, and then Mr. President, he actually goes into space and docks with the ISS to save a Russian."

"Well gentlemen, let's be thankful for one thing, his enemies are our enemies. This aircraft or shuttle or whatever it is must be way ahead of us to do the things it's done. He seems to be trying very hard to turn the blame away from us and Russia. Since we know it's not us, could it be the Russians? Why would the Chinese attack North Korea. The Russians are in meetings for the purpose of de - nuking the North. Are the talks going that bad? Put your best feelers out on this one and report any feelers coming to us from others. This story could be true."

"We'll get right on it Mr. President," they all voiced.

Each person went their office and started making phone calls. One call went to Colonel Tinsel ordering him to report to the General as soon as possible. Another call went to Mr. R.

They had ten medium sized lobster, enough for two each. The men dove while the women watched from above while snorkeling. It had been a wonderful afternoon. There was no talk of war. The day had been beautiful and full of laughter which continued as they made their way back to the dock. The men put all the gear away while the women headed for the shower.

"You know, that Colleen is very attractive," volunteered Tim. "I think I'd like to see more of her."

"There wasn't much left to see with that bikini she was wearing," laughed Steve.

"You're right," chuckled Tim. "They both looked mighty good in bikinis."

"You're drooling boys," said Scott. "We better check in with Mr. R and see what's happening in the world. We've raised a lot of dust lately."

While the women were in the shower they called Mr. R on the scrambler phone in the computer room. He asked that Scott accompany the women that evening back to the mainland and Scott alone was to come directly to his office for a meeting. He also asked Steve to start preparing for a transfer as he was badly needed there. This was a bit of a shock to Steve as he was enjoying himself so much on the island. He had also grown very fond of this quiet, extremely competent man Scott. Even though Scott was the last to join the group he had quickly, with no reluctance on the part of either Steve or Tim, become the leader. They assured Steve that he was welcome to visit whenever he wished. You don't even need to call, they told him, just show up. They had become close as flight crews do during war. But just like flight crews, they would adjust.

The helicopter was due at 7:00pm so dinner was planned for 5:00. Colleen was beside herself with enjoyment. Her two lobsters never had a chance and Tim introduced her to a Goombay Smash. A very potent island drink made famous by Miss Ellie on Green Turtle Cay. Two was all he would let her have and they were enough as their effect was apparent. She was far from drunk but was most mellow.

Scott and Dr. Kay enjoyed a walk through the woods to the other side of the island. They held hands as they waded in the shallow water, neither speaking but enjoying the silence and serenity without feeling they had to make conversation. Their friendship was growing stronger each time they met. "You know that I know what you're doing and I have only one thing to say. Please be careful, very careful. You have become a friend Scott, a good friend, and I don't have many of those. I don't want to lose you."

"I'll do my best to see that doesn't happen. If you don't mind, I'd rather change the subject. I'm going back with you this evening to meet with Mr. R. The meeting will probably run late and you have to work tomorrow so I don't know when I'll see you again. If we get a lull in the schedule it would be fun to have you and Colleen come back. I believe Tim has more than a passing interest in Colleen. Have you picked up on that?"

"I think the feeling is mutual. Maybe two people looking for something suddenly find what they are looking for in each other. She's a wonderful person, she deserves the best."

"Tim is a fine man Kay. Give it time and we'll see what happens. I hate to cut our walk short but I need to change and throw some things in my duffle. Our ride will be here in fifteen minutes."

When they landed at the Company pad there were two vehicles waiting, one for Colleen and Kay and one for Scott. Scott saw the women to their car then entered his. He asked the driver to take him to Mr. R's office. Ten minutes later he was knocking on the office door.

"Come in Scott." said Mr. R. "Let's meet in the conference room. I have the material you requested and that will give us room to spread out. Did you have a nice day with Colleen and Kay?"

"Yes sir we did. Colleen asked for a lobster dinner by the pool and who could refuse such an attractive woman. As I told you on the phone, the women performed most admirably on the flight. It was the least we could do to show our appreciation."

"I've done a little to show my appreciation also."

Scott didn't ask but was sure it wasn't a little.

CHAPTER NINETEEN

"Here is the analysis of the bomb you dropped near the nuclear reactor. It is believed that six bombs, one at the top, one at the bottom and two on each side, impacting simultaneously one eighth of a mile away will cause the walls to be blown inward by the overpressure with the ceiling falling on top. This is the best way to avoid a large release of radioactivity. There would be no nuclear explosion. The other buildings should receive a direct hit. If they haven't removed the rods, this area will be contaminated for many years but can be contained."

"That all sounds good," said Scott. "Do you have a feeling what they will do when their reactor is destroyed? What I'm asking is this. The targets are the nuclear facility, Kim's palace, communication centers, government buildings, the missile sites, the weapons manufacturing plants, the dock area including ships that haul those weapons, the airfields to take away air superiority and the artillery guns aimed at the South. When the bombs start falling will they launch an attack on the South? Do they have a long-range missile with a nuclear warhead? If one is launched toward the United States can we intercept and destroy? What is the best target order to dissuade that attack? These are the questions I need answers to before the next mission."

"Analysts can give the answers," replied Mr. R. "I can get those without arousing suspicion. The War College is studying North Korea presently and it will make a good assignment for tomorrow's class, like a pop quiz, turn in your papers at the end of the day. We'll have our answers tomorrow evening and can review the papers to come up with the best target order. These officers are well versed on Korea and their answers will be more analytical than the Pentagons."

"As you requested, here are the photos of all these targets plus the exact coordinates of their locations. These were taken by satellite very recently. There is also a written analysis of each target as to construction, height of detonation for maximum destruction, number and type of aircraft located at the various airfields, and so on. The information is very informative and will help you decide which missile sites and airfields to hit first. We don't believe they have a missile capable of reaching us at this time. However, they are working hard on increasing range and accuracy so time is very important. It would be most uncomfortable to know they had such a missile and are sick enough to use it."

They spent the next two hours going over each photo and discussing the targets. Mr. R must have had a lengthy briefing as he was very well informed on the targets, including which government buildings housed what.

"Sounds very good sir. Today is Monday, I'd like to fly the mission Thursday night or Friday at the latest. We should have our answers by then. I'd also like to discuss Iran with you as well as other things..

"Talk to me about Iran first."

"Russia is helping them build a nuclear facility. I believe it is a mistake to allow any country with a history of supporting terrorism to have such a facility. Korea is a good example. How long will it take them to make a nuclear bomb? If they have nuclear weapons and they support terrorism, how long before a terrorist organization ends up with a bomb. If terrorists have such a weapon they will not hesitate to use it. They hate the world as it is now and all they want is to kill people and they don't care who it is. The countries that are timid about joining a coalition to invade a country with that same attitude would be very sorry if a terrorist act killed thousands of people in their country. Iran is such a country as well as Iraq. I would like GPS coordinates and photos of this site. I firmly believe now is the time to destroy it, not after it is up and running."

"I will also have that information for you tomorrow evening."

"Iraq is another problem," said Scott. "If they have sent their weapons of mass destructions to Syria I will need to add them to the list of countries with whom we are at war. If the location of this storage can be discovered, should it be destroyed? I don't want the escape of bacteria killing thousands of their people because the warehouse was bombed. Should we consider helping the coalition? Things are moving fast which is good. The faster we move the less world opinion can gather momentum against what we're doing. In one week I would hope to neutralize North Korea and destroy the nuclear plant in Iran. We can then see how Iraq plays out. I can start night searches over Afghanistan, Pakistan, and Iran for terrorist training camps. On a dark night the listening device and language translator will be very useful in identifying the bad guys."

"After North Korea and Iran we will meet again to plan future strategy," said Mr. R. "We'll meet tomorrow evening at 7:00 to review the new information. In the meantime I would like you to get measured for clothes. There is a formal dinner at the White House a week from Saturday night and a representative from our company has been asked to attend. I have never gone to such affairs but feel it important we be represented. I'm asking you to be that person. This will be after the attacks on North Korea and Iran so you should find the conversation interesting."

"Mr. R I'm not really good at those kind of things. Can't you find someone other than me?"

"I have a specific reason for wanting that person to be you. I want you known as being with the company. It is important you start making contacts in high places as these contacts will pay off in the future. My crowd is getting older and we are losing them with age. The people your age are the leaders in a few years. Now is the time to cultivate friends and to know who your enemies are. I have plans for you Scott, this is just the beginning."

"I have asked Steve to be ready to transfer here," continued Mr. R. "Progress on the second craft is to the stage where his expertise is needed. In another month or two we'll need Tim here also. Can you spare them?"

"The missions can be flown with only the pilot but, it does make it easier when things start moving fast to have two people. It may be a good idea to transfer Steve before the next attacks. He'll scream like a banshee but he is too valuable if something goes wrong. I'm not saying that Tim isn't just as valuable but the second bird needs Steve now. Tim and I can then plan these next missions with just the two of us doing the air work. I hate to lose either one of them let alone both. We've become very close friends."

"I know you have and that pleases me very much. See William at the clothing store tomorrow so he can measure you. He'll then have your measurements on file so we can order clothes when needed."

"One last thing Scott. General Ragland, who is the director of the F-22 project, thinks there is a connection between the aircraft that mixed it up with his bird over Edwards one night and this country called Piot who docked with the space station. He has called in an investigator to start putting the puzzle together, a man called Colonel Tinsel. I believe you two have met."

"Ahh yes. The nosey nooser Colonel. I'll be on the lookout for him. If he wants back on the island do I have to welcome him?"

"Absolutely not. That is private land legally belonging to another Country and he has no authority there. Of course, we don't want to tell him anything other than it's private land. He could put two and two together if he knew it was land belonging to a foreign nation other than the Bahamas."

"Good. That's a relief. What will you do if he wants to snoop around Company property here?"

"He'll be shown only the things we want him to see. There will be an escort with him at all times."

"Well sir, if there is nothing else, I'll get a room and hit the sack."

"You'll find a room waiting for you in your name. You may also find a bottle of Crown Royal on the table. You're not flying tomorrow so help yourself. Goodnight."

A car was waiting for Scott when he reached the lobby. He was dropped at the Company motel and was shown to his room. "This is your room from now on Mr. Wilson," explained the night manager. "No one but you will occupy this room except you. If you want to leave things in the closet or refrigerator you may. There is no need for you to check in or out in the future."

"Thank you," answered Scott. "That is greatly appreciated."

The room had a large living room with a kitchenette and separate bedroom. The bathroom was quite large and the living room had a sliding door to a deck that over looked the complex. Being on the second floor gave him an excellent view.

CHAPTER TWENTY

Meanwhile there was a very upset and confused little man in North Korea. His pilot did indeed meet with a most unfortunate accident resulting in his death, if you can call a pistol held to the back of his head when fired an accident. Kim Jong Un was talking to General Ni Xusan, General of the Chinese Air Force. They had both seen the tape made by Piot.

General Ni Xusan did not like Kim Jong Un and was not bashful about showing it. "You see little one," said General Ni Xusan, "we did not start the fight, it was Piot. You continued it by attacking our aircraft and shooting down a pilot on his first night flight. How brave of you. You will make financial reparations to our country and the family of our pilot."

"Yes General," replied Kim. "Who is this Piot that has declared war on us and is causing all this trouble between us? He is going to bomb our nuclear reactor. What can we do?"

"You are the one that has caused the problems. You sent home the inspector and shook your sword at the world. What did you think they would do, run like a dog with it's tail between it's legs? You are biting the hand that is feeding the people of your Country while you spend millions on yourself and threaten them. You are a foolish person. You are on your own."

"But if Piot attacks me I don't know where they are so I can counter attack."

"That is a problem isn't it?" replied the General.

"I will attack the South. That should confuse them, everyone," said Kim.

"That would be most foolish. That space vehicle does not belong to the United States or Russia. Our intelligence would know. They say neither country has a craft like the one that rescued the Russian cosmonaut. You have aroused the anger of an unknown with your foolish nuclear threats."

The phone conversation ended with Kim not knowing what to do. He was hoping, like a child, that the problem would go away on its own. Even though he had quit smoking he desperately wanted a cigarette but settled for another glass of cognac instead. He summoned his Generals who put the Country on full alert. If anyone dared to strike his Country he would strike back at someone. He then summoned his new actress. It is said that Kim owns over 20,000 movies on tape and sometimes produces his own. The actress who now stood before him was not there to make a movie.

CHAPTER TWENTY-ONE

The next morning Scott was measured by the Company tailor who meticulously wrote down the numbers for his file. He showed Scott several choices of formal evening wear but ended up making the decision himself as Scott requested. Scott had never been to such an affair and had no idea of the current style. He did though pick out a pair of comfortable-looking flight boots that caught his fancy. These kinds of things he knew about but not the other.

He made arrangements to meet Dr. Kay and Colleen for lunch at the cafeteria. As he was walking that way he noticed a dark threatening sky moving in from the southwest. If they were in for some bad weather with low visibility it could be possible to take off and land without being seen. He would have to stay in the clouds for a fair distance out to sea so a passing satellite could not connect him leaving from any particular land mass. He would check the weather forecast for the rest of the week this afternoon. Taking off, flying and landing in weather was a piece of cake in his aircraft due to the radar enhanced visual cockpit display. He would be going east when flying to Iran versus flying west to North Korea. It would be convenient to have a base at Diego Garcia for rearming. Or better yet, another weapons pod there so he could drop one for rearming while he hooked up the second and flew another mission. He would think about that. The North Korean engagement would require multiple missions but, Iran was unknown at this time.

He entered the cafeteria and saw the women waiving him to their table. Not only were they a pleasure to look at but also to be with.

"Good morning Ladys," said Scott.

"It's past twelve so, good afternoon to you," said Colleen. Dr. Kay smiled a warm greeting. She was even more intrigued by this man after their flying adventure. Everything had gone so smoothly thanks to his calm commanding way. She now knew who that was on the tapes that the news people were showing over and over. She could not tell from the disguised voice and blocked out face but, she knew. She also knew he was the one flying those dangerous missions over North Korea. That made him all the more interesting. He wasn't doing it for the glory because no one knew it was him. No, he was doing it for the love of his Country, the United States.

"And what have you been up to all morning?" asked Dr. Kay

"Getting measured for a tux for some kind of dinner evening wear. I've been asked to represent the Company at some affair in Washington. I tried to get out of it but, Mr. R wouldn't take no for an answer."

"Just be yourself and don't drink anything alcoholic," offered Dr, Kay. "Alcohol loosens the tongue and can make an ass of a person very fast. Did you ever wake up in the morning and wonder what you said the night before? And when you find out, the hangover is nothing compared to the embarrassment. We can forgive that in our youth but not as responsible adults."

"Is that coming from a friend or a doctor?" grinned Scott. "Is that the voice of experience talking?"

"Been there done that," said Dr. Kay

"Me too," voiced Colleen.

"Since we're all confessing, me too," laughed Scott.

They had an enjoyable lunch with light conversation. The women asked if he had heard how their patient was doing but that was the only mention of their adventure. He heard on the news that Vladimir was doing fine and remembered nothing. Both seemed to be working very hard not to discuss it. Fortunately they had each other to talk to until they came back to Piot, then they could all relive the event. Scott told them the next time on the island he had a special grouper recipe cooked the Bahamian way which he would happily cook himself. Suddenly it was time for the women to return to the hospital. They said their goodbyes not knowing when they would see each other again. Colleen asked him to tell Tim to be careful.

Scott returned to his room and made notes on things he wanted to discuss with Mr. R. This evening would be the last meeting before flying to North Korea. He wanted to be sure he covered all contingencies he could conceive. After that he stretched out on the bed and fell asleep. Two hours later he awoke, showered to get the cob webs out of his head and dressed in fresh clothes for dinner, then his meeting with Mr. R.

The meeting with Mr. R started at 7:00pm and lasted until midnight. They covered each target in detail. The papers from the War College had arrived and provided valuable information in selecting the order of targets. It was decided to bomb the communication center in Pyongyang and two nearby sub-stations first. The immediate next target would be the seven story palace residence of Kim. Ideally the palace bombs would detonate within two minutes of the communications centers bombs. This could be accomplished by pre-programming the targets and using bunker busters on the palace. The rocket boosters in these bombs would accelerate the bomb to mach 3 speed and substantially shorten their air times allowing them to detonate within one minute of the communications bombs. The next target would be the nuclear reactor then the missile sites. The reactor target would take the most time as Scott wanted to be sure the bombs struck simultaneously in the right places. The ensuing shock waves would push the walls inward with the roof collapsing on top of them. Scott was assured this would not cause a nuclear explosion. After that the missile sites. The intent was to hit the sites as quickly as possible before generals could recover from the initial bombing and give launch orders. The faster these were hit the less chance of the launch orders being successful. All this time they would be monitoring for any missile launch which seemed to be aimed at the United States. If that happened, they would give chase with the intent to intercept and destroy the missile. If the missile was armed at launch there could be a nuclear detonation when their missile intercepted. If that happened, their fate was unknown.

After that, the weapons manufacturing plants would be bombed. With these shut down the flow of income would slow considerably.

Then the airfields. The goal was to destroy as many aircraft as possible whether in the air or on the ground. If they had time left, the next targets would be the docks then artillery and troops aimed at the South.

When Scott left Mr. R's office he was loaded down with documents. His driver took him directly to his room where he briefly reviewed the pile. At 1:30 am he turned in, sleep coming with difficulty. He was up at 6:00am then met the helicopter at 7:00am landing on the island at 8:15 am. There he met Tim who informed him that Steve had been recalled last evening. He was not a happy camper. "I know, but they really need him on the mainland working on the new bird," said Scott.

They spent the morning going over targets and plotting their bombing route so as to hit the greatest number of targets in the least amount of time. The afternoon was spent in the aircraft programming all this information into the software. Steve was glad Tim had stayed as he was an expert in this field. Scott knew how to turn a computer on but was lost when it came to programming. They checked and re-checked the program.

Next they checked the aircraft systems and supplies and preformed a very thorough pre-flight inspection. After that they went to the pod hangar where they checked all the weapons and the pod itself. The next morning they did the same thing over again. Satisfied they were as ready as they could be they took the afternoon off. Sleep was out of the question as they were too primed for the mission. They sat by the pool talking and taking an occasional dip. A lot could go wrong. North Korea could be on a short fuse and attack the South with the sound of the first boom. The North could launch an intercontinental missile, which they would attempt to intercept with possible catastrophic results. They would be engaged with enemy aircraft and anti-aircraft fire. Takeoff time was set for 5:00am in the morning to make use of the dark. That would be 7:00pm Korean time. They decided to fly at 65,000 feet to stay well below space on the way over. They had plenty of time as they planned their first bomb for midnight Korean time. They would wear their space suits the whole mission. They thought of putting them on when over Korea but decided against that in case the action began as soon as they arrived. It was best to be prepared for that contingency.

All they had for dinner was a chef's salad as food was not high on their list at this time. They watched the news and listened to the newscasters describing the actions of North Korea. They were belligerent and seemed to be working diligently to bring the reactor on line. It was obvious they were not heeding the warning on the videotape, or maybe they didn't believe it. This made Scott and Tim all the more certain their mission was a just one. It gave them confidence they were doing the right thing.

They were up at 3:00am and arrived at the ship at 4:00am. They took their time struggling into the space suits then went through the pre-takeoff check list. They brought all systems on line and checked each one several times to satisfy themselves that all was a go. Time was now 4:40am.

Scott opened the hangar roof of both hangars. They lifted slowly out of the ships hangar into the black night and moved over to the pod hangar. The ship settled slowly onto the pod and the locking bolts all moved into proper position. They ran another check on the weapons and when satisfied it was 4:59:30am. Scott started counting at 4:59:50am. They lifted off at 5:00am and climbed straight up to 65,000 feet where they once again checked all systems, it wasn't too late to abort. When satisfied, they set a great circle course for Korea. Their radar showed early morning air traffic well below them but the anti-collision system was activated as a safety precaution.

When they left Alaska and entered Soviet air space a prickly sensation went up the back or their neck. "Do you have a prickle on the back of your neck?" asked Scott.

"Sure do. I thought I might be the only one. I kind of miss Steve don't you?"

"Yes I do, but he's really needed at the Company. We'll drop one on the palace for him."

"I have us now over the Shelikhova Gulf at this time Scott."

"Roger Tim, I concur. The island of Sakhalin should show up next."

"Roger," replied Tim.

They slowed to arrive over North Korea no earlier than 9:00 pm. When there, Tim turned the language translator to Korean but found no unusual traffic. If they were expecting them tonight it was sure quiet. They flew over the nuclear reactor site but saw no unusual activity on the radar. If they hadn't removed the rods by now it was evident they weren't going to. They flew to Pyongyang and again saw no unusual activity. The country side was almost void of lights due to their poor power system. The city itself had very few lights away from the center. They flew over the missile sites trying to identify which one or ones might have intercontinental missiles. They could not tell the difference. Maybe they didn't have any. That would be a relief. Time was now 11:15pm.

"We're going to sit right over a spot between the palace and the communications center and look and listen. If you hear any air traffic let me know Tim. The radar shows nothing moving so I'll descend to 25,000 feet and we'll check again."

"Roger. I'm picking up what sounds like a couple of night training flights. I don't think this guy believes we are going to bomb him. I'm not picking up any ground to ground radio traffic between headquarters and front lines to the South. That's a good sign."

"Roger," said Scott. "We'll bomb from this position Tim. At 25,000 feet I can put the cross-hairs on the communications building and the sub station then move them to the palace, all from this one spot. After we drop, we want minimum time to the nuclear reactor, then the same to the missile sites. We'll come back later and check for bomb damage. My time piece now reads 11:55pm. Strap in tight, we'll be moving soon."

"I'm ready Scott."

"Roger. Aiming now."

"Six BOMBS AWAY on the communication center and one on the sub station. Moving cross hairs to the Palace. Bunker busters on first four bombs set for simultaneous hits, BOMBS AWAY. Four more on the palace set for contact detonation, BOMBS AWAY. Heading on course for the reactor."

"Couldn't see the hits Scott."

"Roger. Approaching the reactor, holding steady directly above and still at 25,000 feet, set for simultaneous impact, cross hairs moving around building. SIX BOMBS AWAY. Now moving to the three out buildings, contact detonation set. BOMBS AWAY on out build-ings. Now let's make tracks to the first missile site. Keep a lookout for any missile launches Tim."

They pulled a four G acceleration on the way to the first site. It wasn't far and only took them eight minutes to get there. Scott turned the craft to face back the way they had come and pulled another four G's slowing down. They wore G suits under their space suits which permitted them to withstand much higher G forces than without. When pulling G forces, bladders in the legs and stomach of the G suit would inflate with air to restrict the flow of blood from the brain to the lower body. There is a point, which varies with in-dividuals, that even with a G suit blackout occurs.

"Cross hairs on target, I see no activity, contact detonation set, BOMB AWAY. Off to the next site."

They hit the 2nd, 3rd, 4th, 5th and 6th missile sites. They were on the way to number seven when Tim spoke in a tense voice. "Visual at one o'clock. Looks like a missile lifting off."

"Good eyes Tim. Hang tight, we're going to give chase. That thing is accelerating fast. I'll set a course to intercept with a missile of our own. We'll be pulling some high G's. Tense your muscles as much as you can and don't forget to yell, it can help."

Just after Scott said that, they were pulling six G's and going to seven. Both were grunting and straining to keep their muscles as tight as possible. They also found the yelling helped some.

"Launching missile one," said Scott. "It fell short. We are too far away with that much acceleration. We'll have to risk it and get closer. Now it's tipping over a little and headed out the way we came in. That means Alaska or the lower forty eight, depending on its range. We're gaining a bit Tim. I'll close in and launch another missile when we're about a mile out. After launch we'll have to pull some high G's to get out of the blast. If it goes nuclear we won't have time to clear. Just about there, I'll count down, cross your fingers, 5, 4, 3, 2, 1, FIRE!"

Both were graying out, the warning that full black out was close as they tried to put as much distance between them and the missile. They watched on radar as their missile hit the North Korean missile. NO nuclear explosion! The missile fell harmlessly toward the Manchurian Russian border.

"Luck was with us there Tim. We'll head back and finish those missile sites."

"Hold it Scott. Check eleven o'clock. Is that what I think it is?"

"Yeah. Missile number two. Let's hope our luck holds. I'm going for more altitude now. We pushed our skin temperature to the limit on that last missile by going too fast at too low an altitude. We'll level at 50 miles. It's on the same track as the other one but this one looks different. What's different about it Tim?'

"I think it's much bigger, longer. It must have more range and a bigger payload. I'd guess it could reach the lower forty eight."

"Jeez! That thing is moving. We got altitude on it and our speed is coming up to match it. I'm going close enough so you can video tape the thing Tim. We may need the evidence in the future."

"Right. Providing it doesn't go nuclear when we kill it. Tapes are running, we're getting good pictures but turn your landing light on it, most of what we're getting is rocket flame. There, good, oh look at that, it even has the North Korean flag painted on the side. How's that for evidence?"

"Cross your fingers again Tim. We're backing off enough for our missile to acquire and kill. Coming up on one mile behind. I'll count down again, 5, 4, 3, 2, 1, FIRE! Missile is away."

This time Scott went high and as fast as the skin temperature would allow. They watched the radar as the missile hit. The North Korean missile went into a tumble with no explosion except their missile, which hit the tail causing the tumble.

"Don't look at it Tim. If it goes nuclear the brightness could blind you. Drop your sun visor down and look off to the side. Hopefully it will splash harmlessly just off the Sakhalin coast in the Sea of Okhotsk."

It did, but only fifteen miles off the coast. There was a blinding flash of light far below them. It was a nuclear explosion.

"Did you get the detonation on tape Tim?"

"Sure did. That thing went nuclear when it hit. Jesus! Those guys really launched a nuclear missile at the United States. They are crazy. I don't think the Russians are going to be too happy with North Korea either. There will be damage and fallout on their soil. Maybe they'll badmouth us less for taking out the North's reactor. On the other hand, they may be upset with us for not waiting until it was over the U.S. to kill it."

"If our missile had hit any place but that bird's tail feathers, I'm afraid we'd be toast."

"I thought about that too."

"Well, no sense worrying about things that didn't happen. Let's get back to North Korea and hope there are no more missiles. We have three missile sites left to destroy then we need to check on the reactor and palace damage. We may have destroyed additional long-range missiles at sites we've already hit. I hope so."

They returned to North Korea and destroyed the remaining missile sites with no more missile lift off scares. Returning to the reactor site they saw trucks and figures running about.

"Do you think they're foolish enough to try and remove the rods?" asked Scott.

"Don't know, but there is one sure way to stop them," replied Tim. "After launching a nuclear missile, I wouldn't put anything past them. It's even more imperative we destroy any nuclear capability they have. They are nuts."

"Setting for air burst, BOMB AWAY."

This time they could watch the detonation. It was awesome. It further made the reactor building into a pancake and completely mowed down anything within a quarter mile radius. No more people running about.

"I'd say you put a stop to their messing around with that reactor building," remarked Tim.

"Now we'll see what downtown Pyongyang looks like." Said Scott.

They went into a fixed position half way between the palace and the com building.

"The com building is a pile of rubble and the substation doesn't exist anymore. Not even a small pile of rubble. The west half of the palace is gone. The east half looks like a couple of floors are still standing."

"Not for long Tim," he said as he dropped two bunker busters. Now there was nothing left standing. "If Kim was in there I don't see how he could have survived. We have two weapons manufacturing plants to take out now Tim. Ready to move on?"

"Let's do it," replied Tim.

The plants appeared idle at night which pleased them because that meant less civilian casualties. Rail lines passed through the center of the complex at each site. They must have liked the layout as they appeared identical. Four bombs were dropped on each of the plants reducing them to piles of junk. Next they headed for the airfield with the hardened hangars. Some were even below ground.

"When you were a kid did you ever poke a hornet's nest with a stick?" asked Scott.

"Sure did. Is that what you think we've been doing to these jet fighters?"

"Yup. We've been bombing their country causing confusion in the higher ranks and they can't see us. They can't see who is attacking them causing all this damage. They also know their two missiles were destroyed and, they have to be getting nervous about Russia's reaction to the nuclear explosion just off its coast. They know it's not a big force or the destruction would be more wide spread. They are probably looking for half a dozen enemy aircraft. But even so, why aren't they up here looking. Something doesn't make sense."

Tim answered, "What may have happened was a typical failure of a communist government. When the leaders are unable to communicate with the rank and file masses, they are unable to make decisions on their own for fear of doing something wrong. The wing and squadron commanders are afraid to scramble their aircraft without direct orders from above." This worked in Scott and Tim's favor, at least for awhile.

"We're coming up on the airport where we dropped on that hangar. We'll lay a string of bombs on the hangars down the west side then back up on the east side. Expect them to throw up everything they have. Try to find some ground to ground communications helpful to us. Here we go."

They flew at 12,000 feet dropping a bomb on each hangar. The destruction was complete. The twelve hangers on the west side were completely destroyed. They could only assume the hangars contained aircraft. As they turned east at the north end they dropped one bomb on the operations building then turned south when lined up with the twelve hangars on the east side. Down they went, dropping a bomb on each hangar. As they were leaving, the night sky erupted with tracers criss-crossing the night sky. It reminded them of the air attack against Baghdad on the opening night of Desert Storm. They had dropped a total of 25 bombs on the airfield.

"Looks like the troops finally woke up," said Scott.

"And not just here. I'm picking up air to ground and air to air radio traffic. I'll try to find out what's happening down there. It sounds like they are putting up a protective cap over the other airfields."

"Our counter shows we have twenty seven bombs left. Subtract ten for use on the way home leaves us with just seventeen more for the next airfield," informed Scott.

"What target is there on the way home?" asked Tim.

"I'll tell you on the way there so you can study the photos," answered Scott. "We're on our way to the other airfield with hardened hangars. We'll show them that all that concrete does no good against our bombs. If they have staggered altitudes on their CAP we'll fit right in among them. When the bombs detonate, the light from the blast may illuminate us momentarily, that's when they'll look for us. I hate to sound repetitious but be sure you are strapped in very tight. There are going to be a lot of aircraft in the area and with our anti-collision activated there may be some violent G force. It has no G force limit. The important thing is to get us out of harm's way and it does it without regard for Gs."

"Let's go get 'em," replied Tim.

The target airfield was only 80 miles away but they took their time getting there in order to monitor radio traffic. Radio discipline was falling apart as the CAP pilots, with minimum night time, were getting confused and flying too close to each other.

"We may be able to draw some away from the field if my idea works," said Scott. "Turn on your magic box so I speak North Korean."

"You're on," said Tim.

"HELP, HELP, we are being attacked. We are over Sariwon. Hurry, we see them."

"Aircraft calling over Sariwon identify yourself," said another aircraft or a ground station.

"Hurry, we shot one of the dogs down but there are more. Hurry"

"Aircraft calling say call sign," the station or aircraft said again.

"This is Green Leader, he is too busy to talk to you. I am taking my flight to Sariwon to help."

"Green leader this is ground control, maintain present position."

No answer.

"Green leader this is ground control, do you hear me?"

Still no answer.

"Give me a call sign you've heard used Tim."

"Use yellow flight Scott."

He keyed his mike. "Ground control, this is yellow leader," said Scott. "Green leader is not going to answer you. He is going to Sariwon to help. I too am going to meet the enemy. Yellow flight, set course for Sariwon."

"Yellow leader, this is ground control, do not leave your cap position. Do you understand?"

Scott did not answer him.

"Green leader and Yellow leader, this is ground control, do not leave your CAP position."

The real Yellow leader answered. "Ground control, this is Yellow leader, were you calling?"

Scott answered. "Yellow leader, this is ground control, you are to proceed at fastest possible speed to Sariwon to engage the enemy."

"Understand," replied the real Yellow leader.

Scott then keyed his mike to block out other transmissions so air and ground could not communicate. He held the mike switch down for two minutes then let it up.

"Aircraft holding transmit button down, release it," came a command from ground control. "Any aircraft hearing ground control answer now."

"Is there anyway you can tell the approximate location of an aircraft transmitting on the radio Tim?"

"It's approximate. Who do you want?"

"Yellow lead. Give me direction and distance if you can," replied Scott.

"Yellow leader this is ground control, do you hear me/"

"Ground control, this is Yellow leader, I hear you."

"Got him," said Tim. "Heading 065 at 30 miles."

"I have him on the radar, good job."

Scott pressed his mike. "Yellow leader this is ground control, what is your present position?"

"Yellow leader is in a left circle orbit at 7,000 meters."

"Understand Yellow leader, continue your orbit." Scott wanted to keep him talking so the real ground control could not break in. "Where is the rest of your flight Yellow leader?"

"They are stacked above me at 8, 9, and 10,000 meters."

Scott transmitted while Yellow leader was saying the word "meters" to prevent ground from getting through. "Understand Yellow leader. What is the type of aircraft you and your flight are flying?"

"Yellow leader, Yellow leader, you are not talking to ground control. Who is that talking saying they are ground control," transmitted the real ground control. Yellow leader did not respond to Scott's question soon enough to block him out

"Yellow leader, what type aircraft is your flight flying," transmitted Scott as he placed the twenty millimeter sights on him and pressed the trigger for a short burst. The shells found their mark causing flame to pour out the tail of the North Korean aircraft.

"Ground control, this is Yellow leader," transmitted Scott in an excited voice as an attempt to sound like Yellow leader. "I have just shot down one of the enemy."

"Congratulations Yellow leader, you will surely receive a medal for such bravery. Continue to orbit." came from the real ground control.

Scott climbed a thousand meters higher to slip on the tail of Yellow two. He reminded himself that these people launched a nuclear missile against the United States this night. He and Tim had determined the aircraft were Mig 29's. The cross hairs settled on the Mig followed by a short burst. This Mig blew up.

"I SHOT ANOTHER!" yelled Scott into his microphone. "This is Yellow leader, I shot another enemy. He blew up."

"Yellow leader this is ground control, do not yell into the transmitter."

"I have shot two of the enemy down," Scott transmitted excitedly trying to imitate the North Korean pilot. Immediately after flaming the last Mig he climbed another thousand meters to get on the tail of number three. With his radar converting night to day this was not difficult. In addition, since his aircraft was stealthy, they could not see him. The nuclear missile launch erased any feelings of guilt over the great advantage he enjoyed with this aircraft. A short burst flamed number three of Yellow flight.

"Ground control this is Yellow three, I just shot down an enemy," transmitted Scott again in an excited voice.

"Very good Yellow three. Congratulations. Continue in your orbit."

Scott had moved quickly to the tail of number four. The cross hairs settled on the mid-section of the Mig 29. A short burst with hits was followed by the ejection of the pilot. Now is the time to drop the sixteen bombs.

They settled on 25,000 feet as their bombing altitude. This airfield was laid out very similar to the other, showing their lack of creative originality. It shouldn't take long to take out sixteen hangars. If they came back here there would be forty less hiding places counting hangars destroyed at both airfields.

"Ground control this is Green leader, my radio stopped working for awhile. We can join Yellow flight in their orbit."

"No green leader, orbit 40 kilometers south."

"Green leader will orbit 40 kilometers south," responded Green leader.

Scott wanted to down Yellow four before dropping bombs so he would not be silhouetted against the light from the explosions. It appeared Yellow flight was the main air CAP over the field and with them out of the way they were clear to bomb. The result was sixteen hangars destroyed in less than five minutes..

"Ground control this is Green leader, I just saw a number of explosions about where the airfield is. What is happening?"

"Ground control this is Yellow leader, where are you located. There were bombs dropped on our airfield. Are you down there?" transmitted Scott in Korean.

"Wait Yellow leader, we are located in Haeju. I will try to find what is happening."

"Green leader, what is your aircraft type?" asked Scott, again imitating ground control.

"My aircraft is an SU-27. Green flight is flying the only four we have. Nothing can out-fly us. Who is asking?"

"Oh Oh, that sounds like a challenge that I'm sure will be answered," laughed Tim.

"You are about to meet a superior aircraft Green leader," transmitted Scott.

"Did he talk long enough to get a fix on him Tim?"

"Roger, twenty five miles south, heading 170 degrees, altitude 24,600 feet."

"Got him," replied Scott. "So that's what an SU-27 looks like on radar. Now we know Tim. Okay, he's flying high cap and the rest of the flight is below him. We'll go to twenty- five and drop in behind."

Scott entered an orbit four hundred feet above the orbit path of Green leader. When Green passed beneath him he descended and took a position two hundred yards behind and slightly lower than the other aircraft. When settled in position he raised the nose a little and placed the crosshairs on the hot exhaust coming out of the Su-27's tailpipe.

Scott pressed his transmit button two seconds before he pulled the trigger. "Better eject Green leader."

Green leader had no time to reply before the shells entered his tailpipe and disintegrated his engine. He was lucky enough to eject immediately before his aircraft exploded. His thoughts turned to his flight flying CAP below him. The concern was not for them but for him falling through them without being hit. He separated from his seat but delayed pulling his parachute deployment lanyard until lower when the automatic opening device would deploy the chute. He made it through them without being hit but one of his flight was not so lucky. His ejection seat hit the number two man shearing the vertical stabilizer and rudder off the tail. The aircraft flew for two seconds then went completely out of control forcing the pilot to eject. Green three and four went to afterburner and left the area.

"Before we go after anymore aircraft or airfields, let's look at the dock area Tim. If they're loading any missiles on a ship I'd like you to take them out. It's your turn, I'm passing control of the bomb panel to you. First we'll look at the Wonson harbor on the east coast. We're going down to 5,000 feet."

As they approached the harbor and dock area Tim was looking intently at the radar and visual optics sight when he suddenly let out with a yell, "HOT DOGGIES! Look at that. I see four, five, six, six missiles on the dock next to a freighter. They're in the process of loading her. Which one do you want to take out, the missiles on the dock or the freighter?"

"How about we watch for awhile and see if we can tell which warehouse those missiles are coming from. If we determine that we'll take them all out."

"That I like. It will give me a little pay back for what these guys tried to do to our Country tonight. They're loading another one on the ship now. And look at that, another missile is leaving that closest warehouse by truck. I'll wait till the truck is on the dock unloading that missile then take out the warehouse first, next the dock then the ship. Do you agree?"

"Sure do Tim, that's the way I'd do it. Let them fall when you're ready."

"Roger, it won't be long now. They're starting to unload. How many on the warehouse?"

"What do you think?"

"Two."

"Okay, do it."

"I thought you wanted to save some bombs for the target on the way home."

"We'll still have enough," said Scott. "Two on the warehouse, one on the dock and one on the ship. That will leave us with six, should be enough."

"All right. This is going to feel so good. Here we go. BOMBS AWAY, two of them on the way to the warehouse. Moving the cross hairs to the missiles on the dock. BOMB AWAY! I'm going to hold on the ship, it's not going anywhere. I want to watch the warehouse and dock go up first. Oh what a beautiful sight. Look at those explosions! Beautiful. Just beautiful. The ship is on fire, do you want to waste a bomb on her?"

"Drop one right in the middle of her. We don't want to risk a recovery of her cargo."

"Right you are. BOMB AWAY! Getting closer and closer. WOW! It blew the ship in half. Look at the secondary explosions. They had some bad stuff on that boat. Thanks Scott. I can't tell you how good that felt."

"Good job Tim. I know what you mean. Let's hit another airfield. We have 29 missiles left and a whole lot of 20 mike mike. I want to destroy as much of this military as we can. If Kim is dead, which I think he is, we don't want to leave a tempting military for some power-happy general to step in and create another problem."

Their conversation ceased as they listened to radio traffic on the way to an airfield north of the capital. Aircraft were being diverted to this field due to the damage done to their own fields. That should make for a very congested and crowded situation, thought Scott. Too bad they were low on bombs but, they could still do a lot of damage.

As they approached they could see on their radar the number of aircraft in the traffic pattern. Scott keyed his mike, the translator was still set to transmit in Korean. "My engine stopped. I am declaring an emergency. I need landing priority, emergency landing!"

"Aircraft calling with engine out, this is the tower, say identification and position."

"I am two kilometers from landing, clear the runway for me." transmitted Scott.

"All aircraft, extend your patterns to make room for an engine out on final approach." radioed the tower.

Scott was lined up on an aircraft flying an extended downwind leg. He was still in guns mode with the crosshairs on the enemy's exhaust as he again keyed his mike. "LOOK OUT! LOOK OUT!" he yelled. "YOU ARE GOING TO HIT ME." One second later he squeezed the gun trigger. The aircraft exploded. Again he pressed the mike button. "MIDAIR! MIDAIR!" he yelled.

The tower operator lost it. "Who had the midair? Who had the midair? Answer me. Who had the midair?"

"They can't answer you. They crashed." someone answered.

"What happened to the aircraft on final with his engine out?" asked the tower.

"He crashed short of the runway," said Scott.

"All aircraft, extend your spacing from each other," radioed the tower.

"Minimum fuel. Minimum fuel," said Scott.

"You keep that up and that operator is going to have a nervous breakdown." said Tim.

"He sounds pretty frazzled now doesn't he?" responded Scott. "I think we'll let them get all bunched up on the ground then use our missiles and twenty mike mike. If we get fires going the damage should be substantial."

"Aircraft calling with minimum fuel what is your position?" radioed the tower.

"He crashed." said Scott into the mike.

There was silence for awhile on the radio until the tower spoke. "Aircraft continue landing."

Scott and Tim moved far enough away to be out of the traffic area but close enough to monitor the radio. Aircraft after aircraft was landing at the air base thanks to the destruction they had caused at other air bases. When the traffic dwindled to a few in the local traffic pattern they moved in.

"What do you see Tim?"

"It looks like a parking ramp on the east side of the field only. It's really packed but nothing on the west side. What's the matter with these people? We've been bombing them all night yet they park their aircraft wing tip to wing tip. Before they wise up and move them let's strike."

"Right. I figure we'll get just one run before the sky is full of lead and no place for us to be. You take control of our missiles and I'll handle the twenty millimeter. Our best route is north to south between the runway and the ramp at an altitude of six hundred feet above the ground. We'll try 150 knots air speed with the ship rotated ninety degrees, facing the ramp parking area.

If it gets too hot by the time we get to the end we'll increase airspeed. Any comments?"

"No. I'll fire all missiles before we run out of targets. Time for more revenge. I'm ready."

"Okay, here we go. Altitude six hundred feet, airspeed coming up to one five zero, rotating ninety degrees, parking area coming up, fire when you're ready."

Scott fired all four guns with three second bursts. Tim was firing their missiles one every second. He figured they would be over the parking area for thirty seconds and with twenty nine missiles he would have to fire one every second. The damage was complete. There were many secondary explosions that caused more explosions. The four twenty millimeter guns were tearing the aircraft to pieces, the missiles caused the initial explosions. They could hardly believe the damage they were causing. Suddenly there was nothing, they had crossed the airbase boundary. They were out of missiles and almost out of twenty millimeter ammunition and not a shot was fired against them. Another indication that the leaders were cut off from the troops and the troops were afraid to make a decision on their own.

"My God Scott, we tore that place apart."

"We're going back through at 2,500 feet for a tape only run Tim. We need this on film but let's wait fifteen minutes to let the dust settle. Look at those secondary explosions still going off. We may have to wait longer."

"That's fine with me, I like to see the destruction continuing."

Thirty minutes later they made their pass over the field with the tape running. They were so fixated on the damage they couldn't speak until well clear of the base.

Finally Tim spoke. "How many aircraft do you think we destroyed?"

"I really don't know except it's a bunch. That's why I wanted the film pass so we can get an accurate count later. We really did it Tim. We hurt them bad."

"I love that kind of talk."

"I'm climbing to 80,000 feet for a cruising altitude to our next target." Scott opened a map case and pulled out a file. "Here's the target information. We are set on a great circle route to it now. Our course will take us across China, Afghanistan and the width of Iran to the Persian Gulf. We could go higher and get there faster but I need to stretch out for a bit. We can use the time in route to discuss the target and get our energy recharged. It's the nuclear plant under construction in Iran."

"You may be aware of what I'm about to say but let me say it anyway," continued Scott. "On June 7, 1981 Israel destroyed the French built Osirak light water nuclear reactor near Baghdad. If they had not, think of the problem we would have today. In 1974 Germany began building a nuclear plant at Bushehr, Iran on the Persian Gulf. During the Iran-Iraq war, Iraq attacked the plant three separate times as they saw it as a threat to their security. Now Iran is paying Russia $800 million to act as a consultant and furnish joint labor to build the plant again. Iran, just like North Korea was, is a signatory of the Nuclear Non-proliferation Treaty. They are no better than North Korea and their word is worth nothing. This is supposed to be the first of several plants of the Iran-Russian cooperative building plan."

"Why is Russia so blind or so antagonistic as to continually doing things like this?" added Scott. "They act like the big, dumb stupid person who keeps giving criminals weapons. The world is going to wait until it's too late, as they did with Korea. We can't afford to do that again, that's why we're here now. Destroying the plant will hopefully give them second thoughts of starting again. Also Tim, they are supposed to have anti-aircraft missile batteries surrounding the complex. We are low on weapons, which means this will probably not be the first strike we'll have to make. We need to put our bombs right down the throat of that big round reactor dome. But first, we need to stretch and get our second wind."

"Sounds good. We've been pretty busy since we crossed the North Korea coast inbound. Come to think of it, seems like we've been here several days tonight. It's hard to believe all the damage we've done and we're just one aircraft. Think what a whole squadron of us could do."

"Yeah. As long as they can't see us. When they can that will change everything but, until then, we've got the upper hand so we need to do the right thing with this advantage. I feel we did the right thing with North Korea and that feeling was validated when they launched the two missiles at the U.S. Kim had to go as their leader."

They both stretched out as the craft flew towards their next target. They were lost in their own thoughts, even dozing off now and then. Before they knew it they were slowing to a stop over the next target, the nuclear site under construction in Iran.

Over the years Russia has sent their S300 air defense missile to various countries. The S300 has various modifications ending with the S400 which has a range of 250 miles at a speed of 8.5 mach. Huge trucks transport the missiles along with a radar semi-trailer truck which has advanced high and low level tracking. Unconfirmed intelligence has Iran's nuclear facilities ringed with clusters of these weapons. They are supposedly able to track stealth aircraft.

Before takeoff Steve and Tim briefed Scott on a new weapon called the lethal decoy. This is a modified bomb capable of flying with a version on the magnetic engine that can be controlled from the ship or programmed via GPS to destroy a target. Or, it can loiter in the area under control from the mother ship.

It was decided that when they reached Iran they would stay at a high altitude to give them room to escape if one of the missiles locked onto them. They would deploy a decoy to buzz the facilities and identify the location of the sites as they lit up their radar to lock on to the decoy. They would program the site locations into the computer so they could target them when they wanted. The plan was to program the location of the sites at all the facilities first then take out the missiles before bombing the targets themselves. The risk from these missiles would then be eliminated.

"Well, here we are Tim, more nuclear facilities in an unstable country. Iran has no business becoming a nuclear power even if it is supposed to be for electric generating purposes only. Look at North Korea, theirs was to be for electric generating only. Ha! It didn't take them long to come up with a couple bombs did it? No. We need to take care of these now rather than later."

"There are several people at the site, do you want to see if we can pick up any conversations?"

"Good thought," countered Scott. "We'll go down and get as close as we can. Sing out if you see one of those aircraft batteries."

There was no construction going on tonight so the only conversation they picked up was between the guards and that yielded nothing of interest. They saw two missile batteries but the crew was stretched out on the ground. Did they have a surprise in store for them.

"Log that battery into the computer Tim. Let's climb to altitude and start the decoy."

The decoy worked great. Four missile batteries lit their radars and their locations logged into the computer. The decoy survived and headed for the next facility. Here the decoy was damaged by a near miss so Tim directed the decoy to the guilty site and destroyed it. But, they were able to log three others for destruction later. Site facility three was like site one without loss of the decoy. Facility four was like two in that they lost the decoy but destroyed the missile site after programming others into the computer

"Okay Tim, tell me when you are ready to start bombing the missile sites. We'll start with the last one then move on to number three, two and one in that order."

"I'm ready Scott. I'll tell you when to head for the next facility. Bombs are away on this one. Okay to go to the next."

In less than fifteen minutes all missile sites at the four facilities were destroyed. It was now time to bomb the facilities themselves.

"Okay you busters, do your job. BOMBS AWAY! Two bombs set to BB with simultaneous impact on the way. Now we're going to move way out to the side towards Bushehr so we're clear if they fill the sky with ordinance. We'll also be able to see the hits."

The site of the bombs hitting inside of the reactor dome was unusual. It looked like a volcano erupting with the fire and debris coming out the top. After the initial explosion they could see a fire burning inside but the sides of the dome were still intact. The air suddenly filled with anti-aircraft fire but no missiles. They were above the effective range and since they were stealthy there were no lock-ons. So much for the stealth capability of the S400 if there were any left operational.

"The ground fire has stopped and the fire inside is barely burning. Tim, are you ready to drop two more?"

"You bet, let's do it."

They moved back over the target and set the cross hairs on the mouth. BOMBS AWAY!

These were set for surface detonation with the intent of blowing out the sides of the dome. They blew some large chunks out but the majority was still intact. Again they had moved out to the side and watched the missiles fly. When things calmed down again they moved back over the target to drop two more bombs. One was set for surface detonation and the other for bunker buster. The result was something to see.

The bunker buster penetrated the area beneath the dome that had been severely fractured by the previous bombs. When it exploded the fractures gave way and the pieces were blown into the dome itself just when the surface set bomb went off. All that debris was propelled horizontally by the exploding shock wave into the walls of the dome. The result was instantaneous, the walls disintegrated, the dome was no more.

They destroyed the other four facilities the same way.

"Yahoo!" Yelled Tim. "They're gone. I bet they think twice about building those again."

"Let's hope so," said Scott, as he accelerated on a climbing course towards home. Their course would take them across central Europe, southern England then the Atlantic all the way home. Considering the time changes, the time over North Korea, the time enroute to Iran, the time over Iran and the enroute time home, they should arrive just after dark. It will have been a very long and intense day.

They stretched out on the way back and wrote their after action reports. That would be one less thing they would have to do when they arrived.

"I know it's been a long day Tim but I would like to make the video and get it sent to Mr. R tonight. That way it will get to the various world news media in the early morning hours and be on the air soon after. Are you going to be up for it?"

"If I can have a beer while we're doing it."

"Wouldn't you love to hear what Iran has to say to Russia? Those air defense missiles we purchased proved to be worthless" laughed Scott.

"We may even have a bartender if my hunch is correct," said Scott. "I believe Steve knew our plans and could be waiting to meet us with two beers in hand in exchange for a complete review of the mission. If that's the case he can help us with the video."

"That would be great," responded Tim. "I actually miss the guy."

They finished the reports and talked about the narrative that would go with the video. Time passed quickly and suddenly they were home. The weather was overcast with misty light rain and a little fog. Visibility was restricted and a dark night had settled in over the island. Radar showed no aircraft or boats within 50 miles. They landed in the pod hangar where they disconnected the pod then popped over to the other hangar and put the bird to bed there. They cleaned up the crew area, hung their space suits then decided to walk to the house in the rain. It would feel good and the tapes were in protective containers.

When they opened the door to leave the hangar there stood Steve with a big grin and two beers held out to them.

They shook the rain off on the porch and entered the house. Scott felt a warm sensation go through his body as he looked around. This really was home in his new life. He had grown to love this house, the island, the aircraft and these men who stood with him now. They just looked at each other and tipped their beer up. Scott and Tim had a powerful thirst after the long mission but Steve had no excuse.

"You guys look thirsty," said Steve.

"Not to be repetitive but we are so dry we're a fire hazard," said Tim.

"One more," said Scott, "then we have work to do. We could sure use your help Steve in making the after-mission video to send to Mr. R. By doing that you'll get a thorough briefing of everything that happened."

"Of course I'll help. You guys sit back and drink your beers while I set up the studio. But first you've got to tell me something, did you kick ass?"

"Steve, we kicked ass like you can't believe," replied Tim. "Just wait til you see the videos."

During the editing of the video Steve kept muttering, "Oh Wow!, Look at That!, Geez!, You Guys Really Did That!, That's Unbelievable!, I should have been with you."

When the editing was done it was time for the narrative. Scott was primed for this as he again was the speaker for Piot.

"This is the voice of Piot, spoken by it's President.

In the last twenty four hours our Air Force has conducted raids on two countries. The first was North Korea. As you can see by the tapes the first target was the communications center and it's sub station followed quickly by the palace of Kim Jong Il. The next target was the nuclear facility and it's out buildings. This was done to disrupt the communications abilities while we destroyed the nuclear plant. These three things had to happen very quickly, the communications, the palace and the nuclear reactor. We accomplished this as planned.

We then targeted the missile sites which went well until we detected the launch of an intercontinental missile from one of their sites. You are now seeing the downing of the first missile which must have malfunctioned as it fell harmlessly out of control. There was no nuclear explosion when it struck the earth. The second missile was larger, faster, and on course to hit the United States. Note that a crew flew along side the rocket and photographed it, clearly showing the emblem of North Korea. Our Air Force shot an air- to-air missile into the tail of this rocket and caused it to tumble towards earth. When it crashed there was a nuclear explosion fifteen miles off the coast of Russia. We do not know the extent of casualties the North Koreans have caused to Russia.

Our air force then continued targeting the remaining missile sites before going back to the nuclear reactor, dropping another bomb to ensure it's destruction. The same was done to the palace. They then moved on to Wonson Harbor. You can see the destruction of missiles being loaded on a ship in port as well as the warehouse and the ship itself."

Next, our Air Force destroyed airfields and aircraft in the air. It is estimated that over 100 of their best front line fighters were destroyed. We sincerely hope that civilian casualties were kept to a minimum. We also strongly encourage the people of North Korea to enter into immediate talks with South Korea regarding the unification of the peninsula . If a military force takes over with the intent of continuing a government as before, we will strike again and again until a peaceful settlement is agreed upon for a unified Korea with a democratic government.

Our Air Force also bombed a target that has no place in this world. The nuclear plant at Bushehr, Iran. We will continue to destroy such targets of mass destruction and the means to deliver them. As we stated earlier, Iran is one of the countries we declared war against.

We are prepared to continue our raids for the safety of our country. We will not tolerate unstable leaders with weapons of mass destruction.

Be it known that we have no friends in the world. No one knows of our country other than its name and no one knows our location. That is the way it shall remain. We will attack any country that poses a threat to world peace.

"Play it back Steve and let's critique it before we send it to Mr.R," Said Scott. "Put your two cents in guys. This is going to be a real shocker to the world, the launching of nuclear missiles."

"First impressions are usually right and I like it," said Steve.

"Me too," voiced Tim. "I was there and that's the way it was."

"But I have to tell you guys, it's hard to believe you did all that," said Steve in awe. "I believe you did it, it's on video but, my God, you wiped out two major world problems in one night. And in addition, you stopped a nuclear missile from reaching the United States. It's unbelievable. The free world owes you a debt of gratitude they could never repay. Plus, I didn't get to go."

'I'm sorry Steve. That wasn't my decision," replied Scott.

"I know it wasn't Scott. All good things come to an end. By the way, Mr. R wants us all back on the morning flight. I'll get this tape to him right away." When he finished and returned to the living room the others were sound asleep in their chairs.

CHAPTER TWENTY-TWO

When Mr. R received the tape he was ecstatic. His contact in Washington received it a few minutes later. That contact was also very pleased. He in turn saw to it that the right person received it. Thirty minutes later there was a meeting in the President's office.

Present at the meeting was the Secretary of State, Secretary of Defense, Chairman of the Joint Chiefs, the expert on North Korea, the expert on Iran and the President. As they viewed the tape words were uttered like, "Jesus, look at that, Oh my God, I can't believe this," and a few others. When it was over they sat in silence for a few minutes. Then the President spoke.

"Can we confirm this? Did a satellite pick up the explosion? How about seismic readings? What verification do we have?'

"Mr. President, the nuclear explosion is confirmed, just off the coast of Russia. Our satellite will be passing over North Korea in three minutes, the film will be brought to us as soon as it's ready. The destruction of the nuclear plant in Iran is confirmed by satellite. Someone is doing us a very big favor," remarked the Chairman.

"Piot, whoever they are, says they are responsible. We can't very well doubt them with the video as evidence," said the Secretary of State.

A knock on the door was answered by a "Come". An envelope was pressed into an outstretched hand and the door closed. The envelope was opened and handed to the President.

"Oh my! Oh my! Gentlemen, here is our answer to the North Korean nuclear reactor."

The satellite photos were passed around the room. The comments were much the same as when the video was viewed.

"This certainly authenticates the video," said the President. "Whoever Piot is we owe them a debt of gratitude. Not only did they save the United States from a nuclear missile but they took out the nuclear capability of the country that launched it. And in addition, it appears they killed that Country's leader. If this is all true, which we have no reason to doubt, they accomplished in one night what would have taken us months and billions of dollars without any guarantee of success. Why can't we find out who these people are?"

"Maybe," answered the Secretary of Defense, "it's best if we don't know. They don't seem allied with anyone. I think they want it that way. So far we are not taking the blame for previous happenings. Let's see how the world reacts to this tape. It's probably already in the hands of the world news media."

"Agreed," said the President. "But I still want to know who they are."

"We have people working on it Mr. President," responded the Secretary of State.

"Let's call it a night gentlemen. I think I'll sleep pretty good with a couple of the world's problems solved for us. Good night."

"Good night Mr. President," they all voiced.

The situation wasn't quite so happy in Russia. It was in fact just the opposite. The premier was livid. "If that runt wasn't killed in the bombing of his palace I want him brought here and I will personally shoot him. It would give me great pleasure. That's an order. If he is alive I want him here in my office."

Fortunately the area where the bomb detonated was sparsely populated and the prevailing wind carried the radioactive fallout out to sea. The loss of life was expected to be less than fifty people. That was still fifty people too many. But what about the nuclear reactor in Iran. They had sunk $800 million into the project and it was four months from going online. Fortunately the rods had not yet arrived.

"General," he told his intelligence chief, "I want to know who this Piot is. They shoot down a missile that lands in Russian waters, blow up the nuclear reactor we helped build in Korea, then blow up the reactor we were building in Iran. The only good thing they did was bomb the runt's palace. They owe us for our investments. Find out who they are and where they are."

In North Korea there was much confusion. Their leader's body was found in the palace rubble. No one knew what to do as they had always been told what to do. It would take awhile but someone would eventually poke his head out. It wasn't even known by the military heads that two missiles had been fired. Most didn't know the reactor no longer existed. As news of Kim's death became known the world would be watching to see who would take his place. Hopefully, the new leader would have concern for the well being of the people and not for his own pleasures.

When Japan viewed the tape they were elated. Secret plans were being formulated to attack North Korea to eliminate their nuclear capability and the means to deliver them. It now appeared they could put the plans on hold waiting to see what direction the North would take. This was another government whose leaders would sleep better tonight even though the future was still uncertain.

In Israel, the leaders were meeting to discuss the bombing of the Iranian nuclear facility. The mood was jubilant but questions were being asked. Who did this? Who was this Piot? What had Mossad, the famous Israeli intelligence agency discovered?

Mossad had recruited a high ranking United States Air Force officer who was in a position to pass on information regarding the latest aircraft advances. He had reported that the F-22 was the best there was. That might change if the encounter with an unknown over the Nevada desert could be confirmed by their mole. The new joint strike fighter had not developed to an operational evaluation program. The choice of aircraft submitted by manufacturers had been made but the real test flying had not begun. He had further reported that nothing led to the United States being involved with Piot but he would keep digging.

The next morning Tim, Steve and Scott arrived at the Company and were driven to Mr. R's office where he was waiting for them. He greeted them very warmly. They gathered around the conference table where coffee, tea and breakfast rolls were served.

"You three have served your Country in a way that may never be known. What you have accomplished in such a short period of time is nothing less than amazing. We knew we had something very special in this aircraft but the way you have used it, what you have achieved, is more than I could have hoped. Steve, I'm sorry you didn't get to join Scott and Tim on this latest mission but you were badly needed here. Think what we can do when the second ship is ready."

"I'm glad you brought that up Mr. R," said Scott. "When it is ready, the first bird should be brought in for a thorough going over. There is nothing wrong I know of but let's not get any surprises while in space. If we do find a problem we can also fix it immediately on the second bird. We have pushed the first bird several times to the known limits. If there are no stress problems perhaps the "do not exceed limits" can be increased."

"That's a good point Scott," responded Mr. R "Now tell me about the mission in your own words."

Scott and Tim covered the mission in detail. Steve was hanging on every word, as was Mr. R, even though he had heard it before. There were questions and answers and suddenly it was noon.

"Gentlemen, it is noon and I believe there is a doctor and a nurse waiting for you at the cafeteria. I thank you for coming. Your Country doesn't know it but it thanks you also. Tim, we need you here working with Steve. Please plan to be moved back by this coming Monday. You can return to Piot any weekend you wish but right now we need you here to help on the second bird. I'd appreciate it if you would return after lunch Scott, there are a few things I need to go over with you."

"Yes Sir," said Scott. The three of them then left for the cafeteria. The women were waiting and there were hugs all around. They knew what the news media didn't know, these were the men responsible for the bombings.

"We are so glad to see you safe. Those videos they have been showing are frightening. We were so worried."

"We are fine ladies," said Tim. "We shouldn't talk about it in public though. Let's put it on hold until we are sitting around a pool in the Bahamas having a lobster dinner. I will be moving back here next Monday but Mr. R said we could return any weekend we wish." Tim and Colleen made plans for that evening but Scott didn't know what Mr. R had in mind so arranged to call Dr. Kay when he knew. Maybe they could all have dinner together this evening.

After lunch Scott returned to the office of Mr. R. They sat in a conversation area of his office in overstuffed leather chairs. It was like being in a comfortable home library except no brandy snifter. Scott sunk down in the chair and felt a wave of relaxation come over him. The rigors of the last few days were catching up with him. "Would you like a brandy?" asked Mr. R.

Scott smiled and declined knowing if he did he might fall asleep. That would not make a good impression with his employer. That's funny he mused, he had never thought of Mr. R as his employer before, more like a father image and a wise advisor.

"There will come a time Scott when I will step down as head of the R Company. I have no heirs to leave all this to and I want this company to continue doing the wonderful things it does. You have seen only a small piece of the projects and humanitarian programs in which we are involved. Some charitable programs are completely anonymous. We don't seek nor do we want the public relations accolades. We do it because we can, thanks to this great Country. I know you want to continue flying and I also want you to continue. There are still hot spots that need your attention.

If the schedule permits, I would like you to spend two days a week here with me. There is another office off the reception area that will be yours. I don't expect an answer from you now but as you learn more about this company and its purpose I will need an answer."

"I'm sure you have come to the realization that as the other craft gets closer to completion we will have the need for another pilot. Max is permanently assigned to the development of the training program including the simulator. Has anyone come to mind?"

"Mr. R I don't have the training, experience or ability to run a company like this. I am very flattered you considered me but I don't have the qualifications."

"I do have the experience and the qualifications to make that judgment Scott. In time you will see that I am right. Now, is there a pilot whose background information you would like to see?"

"Yes Sir, I was thinking about Chad Boomer, commander of the ISS."

"Yes, a good choice. I'll see that you have the information to-morrow. Stop by the office tomorrow morning for a brief meet-ing then why don't you take the rest of the week for some R & R. Come back Monday with Tim and we'll meet again at 10:00am. I want to share some information with you before your formal affair Saturday night in Washington. By the way, Dr. Kay was informed on her return to the hospital after your lunch that she was accepted for her residency. Would you allow me to make a dinner reservation for you at my club? Correction, our club. You are a member also. Will there be two or four of you?"

"Things are moving pretty fast Mr. R. There will be four of us."

"Mary will give you the address and phone number. Will 7:30pm be good?"

"Yes sir, that will be perfect."

"Good. Why don't you get some sleep this afternoon, you look tired. By the way, you will find a few more clothes in your room than when you were there last. Coat and tie is required at the club. Enjoy yourselves and I'll see you in the morning, say 9:30am."

As Scott left the office Mary gave him a slip of paper with the name, address and phone number of the club. She also gave him a warm motherly smile. He was sure she knew exactly the conversa-tion that had taken place in Mr. R's office.

Scott called Dr. Kay when he returned to his room. She was de-lighted to hear the dinner plans and would take care of informing Colleen who in turn would tell Tim. He stretched out on the bed and fell into a deep sleep awakening at 5:00 feeling fully refreshed. Guess I did need some sleep he thought.

When they entered the club they were in awe at the beautiful furnishings and the décor. It was done as a replica of an old southern mansion except the furniture was comfortable. The ceilings were twelve feet high with fans turning slowly to draw the warm air up even though the temperature was very comfortable with air conditioning, something the old mansions didn't have.

The matre de met them in the foyer with a "Good evening Mr. Wilson, my name is Charles, welcome to the club. I hope you find everything to your satisfaction. If you will follow me I will show you to your table. I put you in the main dining room but if you prefer I can seat you in one of our private rooms."

The main dining room was beautiful with crystal chandeliers hung strategically to give light to the tables. "Oh, this is so beautiful Scott, let's eat in here," said Dr. Kay. Colleen and Tim were so struck with the beauty they hadn't said a word.

After they were seated Charles informed them that Mr. R had requested the honor of taking care of their dining this evening. "And I have taken the liberty of choosing a very fine champagne."

While the champagne was being poured they were given menus with prices conspicuously absent. Since they would probably be eating seafood for the next few days they all decided on meat. Colleen had pork chops with an apricot brandy sauce, Tim braised tenderloin tips and Scott and Dr. Kay ordered filets wrapped in bacon. The champagne and food were excellent and the conversation focused on the beauty of the club until Dr. Kay announced her residency at Johns Hopkins. They had another bottle of champagne to celebrate her dream coming true.

While they were talking, Charles approached their table asking Scott if he would mind if one of the members introduced himself. Out of curiosity more than anything else Scott agreed. Charles nodded at a man sitting at a table by himself who then rose and approached their table.

"Thank you for allowing me to introduce myself. I am Dr. Christopher Thomas. My father and Mr. R are very close friends. I do feel that I am the victim of a plot by those two that arranged this evening so we would meet."

Scott rose to shake his hand then introduced him to the others at the table. "Won't you join us?" said Dr. Kay.

"I'd be delighted on the condition that you call me Chris."

Charles was there with a chair and Chris's drink which was a tall water with ice and a lemon twist.

"Would you by chance be Senator Dr. Christopher Thomas?" asked Tim.

"Guilty," replied Chris. "My father was a senator for a number of years. He and Mr. R went to school together. My father went into politics and Mr. R into business. They have remained very close friends through the years. Are all of you associated with the R Company?" He already knew the answer to that but wanted to appear he knew nothing about them.

They visited for about fifteen minutes then Chris excused himself and left the club. When he had left the table Tim remarked, "That was no chance meeting. You two were supposed to meet Scott.

You know he has become quite a powerful man in the senate for his age. Some even say he is a future candidate for President. Can't you just see it, a Thomas and Wilson ticket?"

Scott was horror struck. His face went white and all at the table noticed. "He was just kidding Scott," said Colleen. "Tell him you were kidding Tim. You were weren't you?"

"I thought I was until I saw Scott's reaction."

"Something you're not telling us?" said Dr. Kay.

"No. No," said Scott. "It's just that the thought of politics is petrifying. That's the last thing I would want to do."

When they left the club Scott and Tim took the girls home as they had an early morning surgery. They agreed they would spend the weekend at the island. Scott and Tim would leave tomorrow after Scott's meeting in the morning with Mr. R. The women would follow that evening as they had arranged for a three day weekend.

CHAPTER TWENTY-THREE

S cott arrived at Mr. R's office promptly at 9:20am. Mary insisted on showing him the other office that was his. It was nothing like Mr. R's but it was very nice with paneled walls, mahogany furniture and overstuffed brown leather chairs. It also had a six-place conference table with matching brown leather chairs. He was very impressed.

"Any secretarial duties you need give them to me," said Mary. "If I 'm busy there is a secretarial pool downstairs I can tap. Behind that door is a closet with two file cabinets in which I recently filed all your investment correspondence from your investment advisor friend in Kalispell."

"Thank you Mary. I don't expect to be here but two days a week."

"Right," she replied. "Oh, hello Mr. R. I was just showing Scott his office."

"It's very nice Mr. R but, I'm beginning to feel a little uneasy. Things are moving too fast."

"Then we'll slow them down. Come into my office and we'll have a little chat. Did you enjoy yourselves last night?"

"Very much and thank you. The others asked me to express their thanks also."

After they were settled in the conference pit Mr. R began. "The people at the affair next Saturday night will consist of military heads and representatives of military contractors as well as politicians including Senator Thomas whom I understand you met last night. A good man Scott. I mentioned to you that my cronies are getting up there in years and will soon be dropping out of the picture. You need to make friends with tomorrow's leaders. Look around to see who might be the leaders of the military in the future. The same goes for politicians. Senator Thomas is a fine young man who can help you in this regard."

The meeting ended at 10:30. Scott returned to his room and called Tim. He was ready to go and would pick up Scott then head to the helipad where the chopper was waiting for them. They arrived at their island home shortly after noon. After the helicopter lifted off for the return trip they walked to the house. When they came out of the trees they stopped and just looked at the house. They both had a warm feeling go through them. This had become their home, a small piece of permanency, it had become their roots. They looked at each other and smiled knowing what the other felt.

Tim broke the silence first. "Let's get our dive gear and bring home some fresh lobster and conch for dinner."

"Sounds good if we take some iced-down Kalik for after the dive."

"Absolutely," said Tim.

Thirty minutes later they were in the boat headed for the channel. The day was beautiful, perfect for diving. The sky was a brilliant blue with fair-weather alto cumulus clouds looking like cotton balls. They anchored near one of their favorite reefs and helped each other put on their dive gear.

Steve and Tim had placed lobster traps months earlier and there was always plenty of lobster under them. After they explored the reef they raised the corrugated metal which rested on two by fours. This gave the lobsters shelter and they could come and go as they pleased. They raised one end and propped it up with a cement block placed there for that purpose. They confirmed at least a dozen of good size and returned to the boat where they slipped out of their vests with tanks attached and tied them to the boat. They placed several pounds of dive weights on the swim platform as they needed to lighten up for free diving. They had placed spears and Bahama slings on the platform earlier which they now took with them as they dove down. Soon they each had four lobsters on their spears, which they had agreed would be enough. They removed the cement block, surfaced and returned to the boat where they retrieved their dive vests and tanks.

Scott was still in the water so suggested that Tim drive while he held on to a tow rope. Tim would go slow towing Scott and when he saw a conch on the bottom he would yell, then dive down, grab the conch, then hand it to Tim when he surfaced. It didn't take long to get four, which was all they would need for conch salad. Scott climbed in the boat and stretched out to let the sun dry him.

"You ready for a Kalik now?" asked Tim.

"You bet I am," replied Scott.

They lounged on the boat drinking their beer not feeling a need to talk. It just couldn't get more relaxing than this. One more beer and an hour later they headed back. They cleaned their catch putting the lobster and the minced conch in the refrigerator. They then showered, dressed and sat by the pool waiting for the helicopter that would bring the women. At 6:30pm they heard the whop, whop of helicopter blades and walked to the landing pad. No sooner had the women deplaned than the helicopter was off for the mainland.

"The boys hoped you would understand their hasty departure but they have social plans this evening," said Dr. Kay. The women looked like twins dressed in blue blouses and white slacks.

"Well, well, if it isn't the Bobsy Twins," said Tim. They all laughed as they walked to the house.

"I would like nothing more right now than to sit by the pool with a relaxing drink," said Dr. Kay as she held Scott by the arm trying to walk in step with him. "Then we want to hear about your flight to North Korea and Iran."

Tim and Colleen followed behind holding hands. "That relaxing drink by the pool sounds good," added Colleen. "We'll drop our overnight bags in the room then join you by the pool."

"Take the west side bedroom, that's the one on the right," said Scott. "It has twin beds and it's own bath." The women went in the house while the men went to the pool to make the drinks.

It was a wonderful evening. The food was excellent and the companionship even better. They called it a night around 1:00am with each going to their own bedroom. That's the way the evening ended. It wasn't awkward, no thought about the male- female sleeping arrangement. If something was going to happen it would happen. And, it would be a private natural thing.

The next morning after breakfast Tim and Colleen went for a boat ride leaving Scott and Dr. Kay in the kitchen loading the dish washer. "Let's get our suits on and sit by the pool," suggested Kay.

"Sounds good, I'll meet you at the pool."

As Scott was getting his suit from the towel bar in his bathroom he heard his door open and close. When he looked to see who it was, there stood Kay, in her suit, her birthday suit. They were dressed alike. He stared at her beautiful body as she walked toward him, her bathing suit in her hand. Their bathing suits fell to the floor as they embraced. She took him in her hand and led him to the bed. Their love making was slow, vocal and passionate. They knew what the other liked.

An hour later, dressed in bathing suits, they were relaxing by the pool with a tall iced tea. "I will be leaving the end of next week so I don't know when we'll see each other again. I know I'll be very busy at the hospital without much time for social life but, if you are ever in the neighborhood I'd love to see you."

"I don't know what my future holds. I want to keep flying but Mr. R has plans for me that will gradually leave less and less time for flying. He has me headed for management which I don't think I want. I'll give it a try though if I can keep flying. I hope I am doing the right thing in what I do with the aircraft. There is so much terrorism and so many ruthless heads of government that the free world wants to eliminate but finds their hands tied with world opinion. I can accomplish things they can't because Piot doesn't give a rip about world opinion. But, I want to know I am doing the right thing and not stepping over the line, not going too far."

"You have Mr. R to consult with and you have your own conscience. I respect the judgment of both. I know you will do the right thing, make the right decisions, and when the major problems are solved listen to Mr. R concerning your future."

An hour later Tim and Colleen returned from their boat ride. It was obvious they had a most enjoyable time. These two were very serious about each other."

The rest of the weekend passed all too quickly with Monday morning's arrival and the flight back to the mainland. Scott arrived at Mr. R's office at 9:20am for the 9:30 appointment. Mary was all smiles as she told Mr. R of his arrival. "Send him in Mary," said Mr. R.

They spent the morning acquainting Scott with the holdings of the R Company and the various projects underway and those planned for the future. The company was much larger than Scott had ever imagined. The holdings stretched around the world. How could one person manage all of this? It took highly skilled managers of the various entities who reported every two weeks, much the same as the President of a large country keeps a finger on all the pulses.

In the afternoon they visited all the important buildings on the grounds. He saw Max and was brought up to date on the status of the simulator. He saw Steve who showed him the progress on the second aircraft. He saw the laser weapon that would be fitted to the second aircraft and retrofitted to the first. There were many projects of things that were only a figment of the imagination of most. This was truly an amazing company. The next day was a repeat of the first but with new subjects and buildings and projects. It was mind boggling.

"I wanted you to become aware of the many projects the company undertakes and the large geographical area it covers. Geopolitical considerations must be taken into account in all decisions. You needed to know this before your affair Saturday night. You are coming from a position of strength. Those who are there that count, know this to be true and you needed to know why."

"What did you think of the report on Chad Boomer," asked Mr. R.

"It was as I expected. He is very capable as well as a good man."

"If he joins us you have made a good choice. Have you thought of the amount of monetary inducement you will offer?"

"We will discuss it the same way you and I did."

"Which means you won't discuss it at all?"

"Yes. If he joins us it won't be for the money."

"He will be returning from the ISS soon and I can arrange a meeting with the two of you. In the meantime here is the information you requested on the head of Syria and the dossier on George Hutcher, head of our swat team security."

"Thank you Sir. If it's all right with you I'll go back to the island tomorrow morning."

"Of course. Mary will have all the information for the affair Saturday night. Come in Monday Scott and tell me all about it."

"Is 9:30am okay?"

"That's fine Scott. Have a good time. It's late in the afternoon and I'm sure you are anxious to return to the island. I'll see you a week from today."

The helicopter was waiting when Scott arrived at the helipad. It was 6:00pm when they dropped him on the island. The first thing he did was to check the aircraft and the weapons pod. Both were ready to go. He decided to write a letter of commendation praising the ground crew, whom he seldom saw, for a job well done. He then entered the house to study the two files Mr. R had given him.

He opened the Syria file first which contained detailed information on the President, Ali Shibabi. He was 53 years old and had risen rapidly through the ranks of the politicians through fear and murder. More than one superior had met with a mysterious death yet nothing could be pinned on Ali. He was clever and ruthless and feared by many. But, he had a fault. He was a creature of habit. Every Thursday night he traveled in a seven car convoy to a home outside of Damascus for pleasures of the body. One car traveled a half mile in front followed by two cars close to each other, followed by Ali one hundred yards behind. One hundred yards behind Ali's car were two more security cars followed one half mile behind by the seventh security car. There were four security guards in each car. In Ali's car was a driver and one security guard in the front with the driver. Ali sat in back by himself.

Scott studied the file for three hours. When he was through he had what he thought was a good impression of President Ali Shibabi. This was Monday night on the island which was Tuesday morning in Syria. The convoy left Damascus at 8:00pm Thursday which was noon on the island. He couldn't leave a couple hours before noon unless it was overcast with very limited visibility. The weather forecast was for clear skies, so that meant a 5:00am Thursday morning takeoff. He would then be able to spend a few hours over Syria doing reconnaissance. If all goes well President Ali Shibabi, you and I will meet Thursday evening.

Scott was so intent on planning the mission he hadn't opened Chad Boomer's file. That would have to wait until Friday, after the mission. He wasn't leaving for D.C. until Saturday morning.

Scott was up at 3:00am, showered then a breakfast of cereal and fruit. He preflighted the aircraft and weapons pod one more time then donned his pressure suit. The interior preflight was complete and the aircraft was ready, time was 04:55am. He opened both hanger roofs, lifted off and moved to the pod hangar and connected the two, time 05:00am. He climbed into the dark night on a northeasterly heading.

Meanwhile the Joint Chiefs of Staff were taking their showers and a fresh uniform was laid out for another day of sweating through major crises. Several of them were thinking, thank God for this Piot country, several very major problems were solved. But who were they? Where do they come from? Some so called experts were even saying they were from Atlantis, or the Bermuda Triangle. So far the United States had not taken the blame for Piot's acts. If it hadn't been for the ISS incident the world would be pointing their finger at the U.S. Some were anyway. It was a subject that was consuming their time. They now believe the aircraft that jumped the F-22 one night over Edwards was from Piot. They were going crazy not knowing this country's location nor how they could be so far ahead technology wise to have an aircraft that could do all the things theirs appeared to do. Who are they?

Scott was sitting over Syria at an altitude of 350,000 feet. The day was clear of clouds, haze and sand which gave unlimited visibility. The aircraft's optical equipment could take pictures or videos of things as small as an automobile license plate from this altitude with the numbers plainly visible. He recorded things he thought may be of interest to military intelligence or the CIA. It was now 7:30pm Syria time and time for him to get in position. The sun had set with night falling quickly and with no moon it would be a very dark night. The spot he picked had been well studied from the air and should provide the perfect place for an ambush. It was ten miles out of town, in the desert, with no building or people within three miles in either direction.

He stayed at three thousand feet above the ground until the convoy was spotted. That didn't take long after 8:00pm, it was coming now. He picked up the convoy and flew parallel to it along the highway at an altitude of 200 feet with the aircraft rotated on it's vertical axis so it was facing the convoy. As dark as it was they could not see him. The ambush spot was approaching rapidly as these guys were really moving.

He selected missiles on the armament panel and locked on each of the cars excluding Ali's car. An eighth of a mile from the ambush site he pressed the fire button. Six missiles left the aircraft headed for their targets. There were six explosions and six cars including their occupants gone. Ali's car skidded to a stop before colliding with the wreckage in front of them. He set one twenty millimeter gun site on the front seat of Ali's car and squeezed off one round. It entered the passenger side traveling through the passenger and the driver exiting the drivers side door. Ali was now the only survivor. The translator equipment was on and the speaker beam narrowed and aimed at the rear seat . Scott pressed the transmit button.

"Step out of the right side of the car President Ali and do it NOW! If you don't I will blow up the car with you in it."

The President stepped out of the car and leaned against the door. He was visibly very shaken and even more so when Scott turned on a spot light centered on the President.

"Listen to me and listen well Ali, your life depends on it. Your life is now in my hands and unless you do exactly as I say I will take that life from you. You are nothing but a runny pile of camel dung. You are dishonest, immoral, a liar without any integrity or regard for human life other than your own. I should just kill a vermin like you instead of giving you a second chance. I will give you a second chance with certain conditions. If you screw up just one of these conditions I will take your life. Don't think you can hide from me because you can't. Do you have any idea who I am? Answer me!"

"No."

"Do you know what happened to Kim Jong Un of North Korea? Do you know what happened to their nuclear facility? Do you know what happened to their front line aircraft? Do you know what happened to Iran's nuclear facility? Do you know who rescued a Russian cosmonaut needing an operation from the International Space Station? It was the Country of Piot. That is my Country. I can find you anytime I want so listen very carefully because if you don't do exactly as I say your life will end."

"You will immediately imprison all terrorists in your country and close your borders to any more. You will freeze all their bank accounts. You will turn over to the coalition force in Iraq all known or suspected Iraqi people who have sought shelter in your Country. You will start downsizing your military to a skeleton force. You will call in the UN to dispose of all your weapons of mass destruction and don't say you don't have any because we know better. Then you will consult with free world advisors for the purpose of converting your government to that of a democracy. You can stay on as President until a free election is held. You do all these things or die, the choice is yours. What is your answer?"

Ali hesitated, thinking about these terrible things he would have to do. Scott fired one twenty millimeter round into the window beside Ali. It exploded and brought more than the anticipated result, he wet himself.

"Are you ready to die like your body guards Ali?"

"No. No. Please, I will do as you say. I don't want to die."

"I will be watching you very closely Ali. If you do not do exactly as instructed you will die. You must start by noon tomorrow with the terrorists and the Iraqi Nationals. The car you are leaning against will run and get you back to town as soon as you remove the bodies."

Scott turned the spotlight off and climbed the aircraft into the starlit sky. It was 8:25pm Syria time and 12:25pm island time. When he arrived over the island he parked the aircraft at 250,000 feet , stretched out and took a nap. When it was dark enough he landed, completed his after mission report, reviewed the video of his meeting with Ali, then made dinner, a steak and baked potato. He wanted the President of the United States, and only he and Mr. R, to see the video. Senator Dr. Christopher Thomas might help him accomplish that.

CHAPTER TWENTY-FOUR

The Company plane flew him to Washington where he was met by a black Lincoln Town car. The driver looked familiar to him.

"Do I know you from some place? You look familiar to me."

"We have sort of met Mr. Wilson, or should I call you Rambo? I led the swat team that arrived just after you came on the island. You had just killed the one drug runner and had the Middle Eastern man in your sights. You had just saved the lives of Steve and Tim. I'm George Hutcher."

"Oh yes. I remember you now. I don't believe we were ever introduced. What are you doing up here playing chauffer?"

"I asked for the job. I was also a Ranger, then CIA before Mr. R talked me into joining the Company as head of security. I do a lot of classified jobs for Mr. R. including investigations, bodyguard and some black ops."

"Okay. That doesn't explain why you're here driving me. Why did you ask for the job?"

"I've read your file, that's part of my job. I was impressed. And now, the things you've accomplished since joining the Company are even more impressive. Don't worry, knowing what I know and do, it was obvious what was happening and by whom. And now, it looks like Mr. R is grooming you for a bigger position with the Company. I'm concerned about you. You're naive about your importance so, like it or not, you need protection. You will want to know more about certain people you meet and that means a background investigation. Many people, especially in Washington, are not who they appear to be. I'll get the information for you. You're climbing and I want to watch your back. Okay?"

"You really think I need protection?"

"Yes. Until you get more experience, other than flying aircraft, trust me. Please. Mr. R agrees with me."

"Okay. We'll give it a try. Since you do investigations and background checks, there are three people I'd like you to check, thorough background checks. The first is an Air Force Colonel Les Tinsle. He's on the guest list for tonight. Second is Senator Dr. Christopher Thomas. Third is you. Don't leave anything out." He didn't tell George he already had the dossier on him, he would see if the two matched.

George smiled to himself as he thought, that was a good move Mr. Wilson, give you the background information on me. If I'm not thorough you'll know and my honesty will be in doubt. If I'm thorough you'll know everything there is to know about me. Well, how bad do I want this job? You'll get everything about me Mr. Wilson, everything. You need my protection.

"Here's the apartment building Mr. Wilson, it's number five on the second floor. I'll help you with your things."

"No thanks, I can get it myself."

"Right, let's do it together. I want to check the apartment."

"Is this part of my protection?"

"Yes, this entire building is owned by the R Company so they can control who the tenants are. It's very secure and in the best part of town. However, I still go in first to check it out."

After George was satisfied Scott entered the apartment. It had two bedrooms and two baths, kitchen with a separate dining room, utility room with laundry facilities and a very large living room. It was tastefully furnished and not ostentatious.

"Your evening's entertainment begins at 7 o'clock Mr. Wilson, I'll be out in front at 6:30. Is there anything you need before then?"

"Yes, a double to take my place."

As George closed the door upon leaving the apartment he was thinking about what Mr. Wilson had said. "A double to take my place." This guy was something. Most people would give anything to be going where he was going tonight. The President would most certainly be there and would undoubtedly visit with all the guests.

He shook his head as he walked to the car. He had three investigations to complete as soon as possible and four hours before returning to pick up Scott. If his contacts were in their office's he may have enough time.

He dialed a number from memory on the car phone. A voice answered and simply said "Yes?" George recognized the voice immediately and visualized the face on the other end of the phone, a face that was rugged and sat on top of a six foot three inch solid frame.

"Hello Bird Drop." This nickname came from an incident in a combat situation when they were frozen in position because the bad guys were very close. A bird perched on a branch above Chuck, his real name, relieved itself with the droppings landing squarely on the face of the frozen Ranger who never moved a muscle. Since that day he was known as Bird Drop but only to his Ranger friends. No one else dared call him that.

"George! You son of a gun, how are you? How are things at the R Company?"

"Everything is going just fine. I'm breaking in a new boss and need some help. This guy is one of us, a Ranger and a real Rambo. Unless I miss my guess this man is the future head of R Company. He's a winner Bird Drop and I want to help him all I can."

"Since he's one of us George, tell me how I can help."

"He's requested a complete dossier on three people. An Air Force full Colonel by the name of Sid Tinsel, Senator Christopher Thomas and me. I have a hunch he already has a dossier on me and wants to check it against the one I give him, sort of a credibility test."

"How soon do you need these?"

"I believe your files are pretty well up to date on these three. Would two hours be too soon?"

"Ya, it would but, I'll do my best."

"Thanks Bird Drop. Meet you at the same place?"

"Right. Two hours from now."

The same place was a rest area three miles from Bird Drop's office. It would be good to see his old friend whom he had not seen for six months. It would take an hour to drive to the meet so he had an hour to spare. Plenty of time for a late lunch. He stopped at a small café one half hour from the meeting place and enjoyed a delicious chicken ceaser salad.

He arrived at the meeting place with ten minutes to spare. Bird Drop pulled up next to him five minutes later. The two close friends gave each other a hug as only two combat veterans who have faced death together can do.

Bird Drop handed George a brown paper grocery sack containing the three files. "Here you go George, all up to date including yours."

"Thanks Bird Drop. I think you will see a star rise. What makes it so special is that he's one of us."

"Just let me know when you need anything George, we owe you man. Now I gotta get back to the office. This Piot guy has us scrambling trying to identify him."

"Making any headway?"

"Not yet but we'll keep digging," he said as he closed his car door and drove away.

George sat in his car and read the files. It was what he would expect on the Senator and himself but the Colonel was a real surprise. This guy was a double agent working for us and Mossad. How about that. My man must have a good sniffer for suspicious characters. I wonder if the Colonel knows we know? He had plenty of time to drive back to the apartment to pick up Scott, arriving there at the agreed upon time.

"Please sit in the back on the right side Mr. Wilson, you'll be on the correct side when we pull up to the White House."

"We have to get one thing straight right now George. I was a sergeant in the rangers the same as you, so call me Scott. If you insist on the Mr. Wilson, do it only when we're around others in a formal situation."

"Will do Scott. The files you requested are on the back seat and a reading light is positioned on each side."

"Thanks George, that's fast service. You still have friends in the right places I see."

"Some old Ranger buddies Scott."

He read the files on the way and was also surprised at the Mossad connection with Tinsel. That must be why he was snooping around the island. He too is trying to find out who and where Piot is.

The other files contained no surprises. George's file matched the one he had with no major differences. George was a good man and very competent. He was lucky George wanted to look out for him. He put the files back in a very attractive soft leather burgundy briefcase.

"Nice briefcase George."

"Thanks Scott, I hope you enjoy it."

"What do you mean?"

"It's a gift Scott. You need a handsome case and now you have one."

"Thank you George, that's very kind of you."

"Two minutes to the gate. Leave the briefcase on the seat. I'll see nothing happens to it."

When they pulled up to the gate the guards looked the car over carefully and checked ID and the invitation list. Cameras were also running with security people monitoring the displays as they had pictures of all the guests and their drivers. When all of them were satisfied another guard climbed in the front seat and rode with them to the entrance where Scott slid out of the car when the door was opened by the guard.

When Scott entered the White House his heart was beating to the flutter of butterflies in his stomach. Take a deep breath he thought, it's going to be okay.

As he entered the room Senator Dr. Christopher Thomas came up to him. "Hello Scott, good to see you again. The first thing we do is head for the bar to get a drink in your hand. That gives you something to do with your hands instead of sticking them in your pocket." They both had a chuckle as they made their way to the bar. Scott ordered a tall water with ice and a wedge of lemon. The senator ordered a club soda with lime.

As they turned to leave the bar a very attractive brunette came up to them. "Senator," she said, "I haven't met Mr. Wilson."

Scott was staring at her. She was beautiful in a way that a woman who needs no makeup can be. She had a heart shaped mouth with a turned up nose and light olive skin. The Senator had introduced them but Scott didn't hear a word. When he regained his senses he realized he was staring at her. She was looking at him with her head cocked to one side and a smile on her face.

"Oh, I'm sorry, I guess I was staring."

"Should I be flattered?" she said. "Or do I remind you of someone?"

"Flattered," he responded.

She didn't say anything but studied Scott more closely as the Senator introduced them again.

"This is Beth Howard. Beth is the daughter of the Air Force Chief of Staff whom you will meet shortly."

"Why not right now?" said Beth. "Let me take charge of Mr. Wilson."

"Careful Beth, he's the strong silent type."

Scott's face turned red as the Senator walked away. Beth did a double take as she saw Scott was indeed blushing.

"I'm sorry Ms. Howard, I'm completely out of place here. I told Mr. R I didn't want to come but he insisted. I'm nervous and afraid I'll screw up somehow."

"Let's walk over here by this painting and visit a bit before any more introductions. What you just said is very refreshing. Most people try so hard to make a favorable impression that they come through in a sickening way. You're just the opposite."

"I was told to be myself but, that seems so inadequate."

"Mr. R is one of the most respected men by the politicians and the military. Do you really think you would be here representing him and his Company if he thought you would, as you put it, screw up?"

He looked at her with a smile on his face and said, "No Mother."

They stood there smiling at each other for a longer than normal period of time when someone cleared his throat behind them.

"Hello Father," she said. "I'd like you to meet Scott Wilson. Scott, this is my Father, General Hathcock."

"How do you do General, it's a pleasure to meet you."

"Likewise Scott. May I call you Scott?"

"I'd appreciate it if you would General."

"Scott, I would like you to meet General Frank Jones Army Chief of Staff."

"Very nice to see you again Scott. It's been a long time. Any chance of you changing your mind and coming back to us?"

"I don't think I could cut it anymore General. You kept us in excellent physical condition that only a younger man can maintain. I've been following your career Sir, and I am very happy for your well deserved rise to the top. Congratulations."

"Thank you Scott. It appears you have done well yourself. You're here representing the R Company I understand. That's a fine Company, always comes in at or under budget which is very unusual for government contracts. Also, your quality control is the finest. How do they manage to do all that time after time?"

Scott started to say something as an answer but thankfully Beth interrupted him. "Now gentlemen, don't monopolize Scott, he has many more people to meet." She pulled Scott away as the General's aide whispered something in the General's ear.

"Why did I start calling you Scott instead of Mr. Wilson? I hope you don't mind."

"I don't mind at all Mother," he said. They looked at each other chuckling again.

When they were out of earshot General Skip Hathcock asked General Frank Jones, " How do you know him Frank?"

"He worked for me in black ops. There was none better Skip. I offered him a commission but he refused. I think he was afraid I would take him off missions. He was one of the finest solders I have ever commanded. Every mission he led was successful. Every one of his men came back. I saw the way he and Beth looked at each other. He's at the top of the quality ladder."

She introduced him to the important people ending up by the Senator. "I'm returning Mr. Wilson to you Senator. He's been intro- duced to all the right people and is undoubtedly tired of my hang- ing on his arm." Now why did I say something stupid like that, she thought.

"I'll take him for awhile," said the Senator, "then we'll see who else we can pass him off to."

"Thanks you two," laughed Scott. "I will try really hard not to be any trouble."

Scott couldn't take his eyes off her as she walked away. He sud- denly felt lonely. "Penny for your thoughts my friend," said the Senator. "She is indeed a very lovely woman. Her husband was an Air Force pilot killed in an accident ten years ago. It was a mechan- ical failure and he stayed with the plane to steer it away from a populated area and crashed in a vacant lot. Not long after that she lost her Mother to cancer. Since then she attends all the functions with her Father. It started out as mutual support and has contin- ued through the years. She acts as his hostess when he entertains and attends others as his companion. She hasn't looked at another man for ten years, until tonight," he added. Scott looked at him questioningly.

Scott changed the subject. "If I gave you a strip of film, would it be possible for you to give it to the President without looking at it or anyone else seeing you do it?"

"We'll know soon enough, the President just entered. Slip it to me, everyone is looking at the President."

Scott handed him a small plastic rectangular shaped container which housed the film. The senator slipped it in his pocket. "We'll see what we can do Scott. It goes without saying that this is very important.?"

"Very," replied Scott.

The Senator caught the eye of the secret service leader and went to him. They conversed briefly in hushed voices then Scott saw the Senator hand the tape to the man who immediately put it in his pocket. First step done thought Scott, now we'll see what happens next.

Out of the corner of his eye he saw Beth approaching with the President. It had to happen sometime, he thought. He felt the butterflies flying in his stomach again.

"Mr. Wilson, I would like to introduce you to the President of the United States. Mr. President, this is Scott Wilson who is representing the R Company."

"How do you do Mr. President, it's an honor to meet you sir."

"I'm happy to meet you Scott. May I call you Scott?"

"Of course Sir."

"Beth tells me this is your first visit to the White House. She's been here so often she'll make an excellent tour guide. You'll have to make arrangements Beth so he'll feel more comfortable here. Being your first time it can be intimidating. It was for me the first time. Oh excuse me, I'm getting the high-sign that I'm needed. Nice meeting you Scott, I'm sure we'll meet again."

"An honor to meet you sir," Scott replied as the President walked towards the secret service leader. A few words were whispered then the two disappeared. Unknown to Scott they went to the Oval Office where the leader inserted the tape in the player then left the room. He was told by the senator that it was for the President's eyes only.

"That wasn't so bad was it?" Beth asked Scott

"Fortunately it was a short visit. I didn't know what else to say."

"Don't worry about that, he knows what to say. He leads the conversation in the direction he chooses. He is really a very nice person."

"I like the job he's doing as President. I have a lot of respect for him."

Out came the secret service leader walking straight towards the Senator. They whispered a few words then looked directly at Scott. The leader left the room but returned shortly and approached Scott who was still talking to Beth.

"Would you please follow me Mr. Wilson. Please excuse us Ms. Howard." They were orders not questions.

"Excuse me Beth, I need to follow the man," said Scott with a smile that the leader couldn't see.

Beth looked at him with a bewildering look like, what's going on?

A few people noticed Scott and the leader leaving and wondered, why? What's going on?

Scott followed the leader who, after a short walk, opened a door and motioned for Scott to enter, he then closed the door without entering with Scott. "Oh boy," he said to himself, "I've done it now." He was standing in the oval office looking at the President.

"You're getting to see more of the White House sooner than you expected Scott. Come over here and sit down, we need to talk."

"Yes Sir," replied Scott.

"You had a reason for giving this tape to me, did it come from Piot?"

"Yes Sir, it did. Piot wanted you to see it. They need intelligence to know if Ali is complying with their ultimatums. Their on the ground intelligence is limited to what they pick up on aircraft receivers. They don't know what your people are doing and don't want to step on any toes that would compromise your operations."

"They have been working hard to direct suspicion away from us haven't they? Why is that? Who are they? Where are they?"

"Mr. President, they are a country that does not want to reveal their location for obvious reasons. They are afraid that terrorist activities could eventually result in the use of weapons of mass destruction which could result in catastrophic harm to their country. They are a small country that could be wiped out under the right circumstances. Your evil countries are also theirs but, they are not concerned with world opinion as the United States must be. As you know, they have declared war on a number of countries with the hope they won't be considered war criminals. They don't care what other countries think. Their mission is to rid the world of terrorism and leaders of countries that support it. I ask that you respect that and not ask me to reveal the answers to who or where they are."

The President thought about that for a minute then replied. "Alright, I'll respect that. We go through you as the middle man, is that correct?"

"Yes Mr. President, you will be in contact with each other through me. They also ask that we be the only ones that know about this arrangement. We can't risk a leak."

"They have done a tremendous service to the world Scott. I ask that you convey that to them. The raid taking out the North Korean leader and his nuclear facility was brilliant. Because of the rescue of the sick Russian cosmonaut, the suspicion that we were involved was diverted. I slept very well that night."

The President paused then continued. "I know the R Company has a scrambler phone so I'm going to give you a number that only you will have. It will go through a security switch board. Give the person answering the phone the code name "hand." If I have a message for you it will start transmitting. If you have a message for me it will ask you to start recording. You can check in as often as you wish. If it's an emergency message use the code name "bright hand." If you need hard copies, such as maps or other documents, they will be transmitted on your fax scrambler. You will need to give us that number when the request is made so if you have a need to change it we will have the current number."

The President was thinking that this man standing before him was Piot. He was the pilot of the aircraft that was ridding the world of the axis of evil. He watched his manner, the way he handled himself and the conviction in the good Piot was accomplishing. Gone was the nervous man he had met earlier with the other guests. This man had an aura of confidence when he spoke now. The President was impressed and relieved. He was relieved that the person or persons behind Piot were stable and not some kind of extremists. The world was becoming a better place in which to live.

"Do you have anything else to discuss with me Scott?"

"Yes Mr. President, I do, but not now. There is a matter of great economic interest to the United States and the world but, I would like to establish a trust between us before discussing that subject. By trust I mean your trust of me. I, of course, trust you explicitly and I didn't mean to imply otherwise."

"In that case, let's get back to the party before tongues start wagging but, obviously they are already doing that. I will turn the tape you gave me over to our Middle East intelligence. They will find it extremely interesting. Thank you Scott and please thank Piot."

"I will pass that on Mr. President, thank you."

You don't walk into a room with the President of the United States and not be noticed, especially with his hand on your shoulder.

The last thing the President said to him that evening was when they entered the room, "Later Scott."

The Chairman of the Joint Chiefs of Staff as well as his Joint Chiefs were all sneaking looks at Scott wondering who he really was. Who was this guy that went into a private meeting with the President for twenty minutes then comes out with the President's hand on his shoulder. Something is going on here and they all wanted to know what.

Scott walked over to the Senator who was just leaving a conversation with a couple generals. "Thank you for the delivery Senator, I really appreciate it."

"From the way things happened it looks like the President appreciated it also Scott. Maybe he'll give me a pat on the back too," grinned the Senator.

"Well, well, and here is this shy, I don't belong here, Mr. Wilson who just spent almost a half hour alone with the President at his request," said Beth. "You have my father wondering who you really are."

"Tell him that if I can get checked out in the F-15 and F-16 I might tell him," chuckled Scott.

"You came here tonight with the purpose of meeting alone with the President, didn't you?"

"I meant what I told you Beth. I have never been in the White House. I am very uncomfortable at this function and I have butterflies in my stomach. But, when I am one on one with a person, I am not uncomfortable, except with you."

"Oh? And why are you uncomfortable with me?"

Just then General Hathcock, Beth's father, joined them. "Am I interrupting anything?"

"No General, in fact you came to the rescue. I was painting myself into a corner."

"We males do have a way of doing that don't we? How long will you be in town Scott?"

"I'd go back tonight General if I could catch a ride in an Eagle. That F-15 is one beautiful airplane."

"He told me he would tell all if you would check him out in the Falcon and Eagle Daddy."

"Did he now? Would it be worth the risk of two very expensive airplanes?"

"Are you checked out in them General?" said Scott trying to change the subject.

"Yes I am, and they are fantastic birds. Why?"

"Just curious is all. How do they compare with the F-22?"

"Did you meet General Ragland yet? He's the project director for the F-22. Let's ask him."

"I'll see if he can join us," said Beth. "Excuse me, I see him talking with a group just over there."

Beth returned with General Ragland a few minutes later and made the introductions to Scott.

"Scott asked me how the F-22 compared to the Falcon and the Eagle, Bart. You're in the best position to answer that. Scott represents the R Company so you can share some facts but not all."

"Yes Sir. I'm familiar with the R Company Scott. You people have done some mighty fine work for us in the past and it's greatly appreciated. The Raptor enters a new realm of flight in both maneuverability and continuous high speed, called supersonic cruise. There is no aircraft that can compete with it in air-to-air combat maneuvering. We are extremely pleased with its operational abilities. It's superior to anything we now have in inventory."

"Has it ever been beaten in air combat maneuvering General?"

"We have nothing that can beat it Scott."

"I would like to see a friendly duel sometime General."

When he said the word "friendly" both Generals went silent and stared at Scott. He got the reaction he wanted and waited to see what they would say next. General Hathcock broke the silence.

"Thank you Bart, I think you covered the subject very well."

"Yes Sir", he said as he turned and walked away wondering who this Scott fellow really was. I'll have a word with Colonel Tinsel about him.

"Do you fly Scott?" asked General Hathcock.

"Yes Sir, I do," he replied.

"Somehow I knew that. Why don't you come to our house for breakfast in the morning? We'll see you have a full stomach for your flight back."

"Thank you General. I accept if it's all right with Beth."

"Of course it's fine with me," she said but wondered why her Dad had asked him. He'd never asked anyone for breakfast before. There was something about this man Scott that intrigued her father as well as herself. It will be an interesting morning.

A short time later as Scott was leaving the party a General's wife came up to Beth. "Who is he Beth? Everyone is wondering who this tall brown haired man on his first trip to the White House gets called to the oval office for a one-on-one with the President."

"He represents the R Company Carol. Beyond that I don't know."

George was waiting for him when he left the White House and Scott wondered how he knew when to be there. He told George about the breakfast invitation he'd accepted and gave him the address.

"Good for you. That Beth's quite attractive isn't she?"

"I hadn't noticed."

"Right," George grinned as he looked at Scott in the rear view mirror. "I'll pick you up at 7:00am."

The next morning Scott packed his clothes and left the apartment as he had found it. George was waiting for him and loaded his things in the trunk. Thirty minutes later they arrived at the home of General Hathcock and his daughter Beth.

"I shouldn't be more than an hour and a half George."

"Don't rush it Scott. I'll be back at 9:30," said George. He waited until Scott was in the house before leaving.

Beth met him at the door. "Come in Scott and welcome to our home."

"Morning Beth. The house sure smells good. What are you baking?"

"You'll know when it's time. Daddy's in his study. Follow me and I'll show you the way."

She led him down a short hall to a room with the door open. "Daddy, Scott is here."

"Come on in Scott. I'm doing some paperwork I need ready for tomorrow. Have a seat. Beth will let us know when breakfast is ready. What are you baking Beth? It sure smells good."

"You're the second one to ask. We're having home made biscuits and gravy."

"Umm. She makes the best biscuits and gravy you've ever had Scott."

"I'll call you when it's ready," she said heading back to the kitchen.

"Did you fly all these aircraft General?"

"Sure did. I go back a few years. Most of these aircraft are in the bone yard now. I cut my teeth on the F-4 Phantom then flew everything in the fighter inventory after that. What have you flown Scott?

"The usual civilian single engine, some multi-engine, the P-51, the Citation and Lear but no jet fighters. I'd sure like to fly that Raptor."

"That wasn't a chance remark last night was it? The one where you slipped in the word "friendly."

"No it wasn't. Making any progress on who Friendly is?"

"No. Nothing firm yet unless it's from that country called Piot. I won't ask how you know about that encounter because I know you wouldn't say. It's impossible to keep a secret very long. We'll find out about Piot soon. Whatever they're flying it's got to be one fantastic bird and I'd sure love to fly it."

" Who knows General, maybe someday you will."

"What do you hear about Piot? The military and the politicians are getting nowhere. How about private business, do you hear anything?"

"I've been out of the gossip loop General and I've heard nothing from anyone who has any leads. Tell me what you think of the raids by Piot. Do you agree with what they have done. If so, and you were Piot, what other actions would you take?"

"That's an interesting question. I'd have to think on that a bit. Oh, there are a number of actions that need attention but, what are the most important? Which ones will become the biggest problems in the future if not stopped now. We try to analyze each situation to come up with the answer. Piot took care of North Korea and the nuclear plant in Iran. Saddam was removed from power in Iraq. These were major concerns that consumed many hours of "what if" planning. That now allows us to spend our time on other problems."

"I would say International Terrorism is now our biggest problem," he continued. "This means Syria, Iran, Pakistan, Afghanistan, Libya and Sudan for starters. If this President feels our Country is threatened he won't hesitate to attack. We still have to consider world opinion so we're not thought of as a bully type who wants everything his way. The Bekka Valley is a real cesspool of terrorist organizations. Syria needs to clean that up and cease giving refuge to the scums of the earth. Is this what you and the President were discussing?"

"Daddy," scolded Beth, "what they talked about is their business. Now let's change the subject. Where do you live Scott? I mean, in a small town near the Company Headquarters?"

"No, I live on the grounds part time and on an island off the coast other times. It's a quiet research house full of computers. It's very peaceful and relaxing. Sometimes our research engineers spend time there away from interruptions that always occur around headquarters. Do you like the ocean Beth?"

"I love it. Daddy was stationed several places in the Pacific and the Mediterranean while I was growing up. We both took scuba diving lessons and spent many hours diving together. Didn't we Daddy?"

"We sure did Angel and I miss those days."

"Why don't you both come down to the island and spend a couple of days? Our Company plane flies here fairly often so you could catch a ride to our headquarters then a short helicopter ride to the island. If you will let me know when you both can get away I'll make the arrangements. We have plenty of dive gear, a boat and many good dive sites. We'll spear our own lobster and grouper and have a sea food feast. Would that be of interest to you both?"

"That sounds wonderful, doesn't it Daddy?"

"It sure does but, let me ask you Scott, do you have an ulterior motive in asking us?"

"Perhaps but, do you have one in accepting?"

The General laughed. "Touché," he said. "A good answer, I like that. We accept. We'll check our schedules and see if they fit with yours. Do you have a number where I can reach you?"

Scott handed him a business card. It was fresh from the box Mr. R had given him just before he left for Washington. He hadn't looked at them and was curious what was on it. He'd look at them later as he didn't want to look foolish looking at them now.

The two hours had gone by very quickly but it was time to go. He excused himself to look out the window and there was George, waiting for him in the car.

"This has been most enjoyable and greatly appreciated, I thank you and hope you'll let me return your hospitality. I'll look forward to hearing from you."

They said goodbye at the door and Scott entered the back as George held the door open for him. When they were out of sight of the house Scott told George to stop the car. He then got in the front seat.

"I feel ridiculous sitting back there when we're not going to some function where you want to appear as my chauffer or body guard or whatever. Are you flying back too?"

"Yes I am. I'm afraid you'll have to get used to seeing a lot of me when you leave headquarters."

"That doesn't include the island I hope."

"No, it doesn't but, we'll have it under close surveillance."

"Good, the General and his wife are going to visit sometime soon."

"We'll increase security when they do but you won't know it. We'll be invisible."

"Fair enough. What are you going to do with the car at the airport?"

"We've a man there who will take care of it."

When the car was out of sight Beth turned to her father, "Well daddy, tell me what you're thinking."

"He's a very confident and interesting man. I really don't know what to think but, I do believe we should take him up on the offer for a visit to his island. I believe we'll find out more about Scott Wilson if we do. Now tell me what you think."

"If it weren't for his brown hair he'd be the tall dark silent type. Two out of three's not bad."

They both laughed and he knew he wasn't going to get anymore out of her.

After landing in Florida at the Company, Scott went to Mr.R's office where he briefed him on the trip.

"You did well Scott. You met with the President, established a line of communication with him, made a friend in Senator Thomas, caused tongues to wag and people to notice this unknown who met alone with the President and, invited General Hathcock and his daughter to the island for a visit. He's curious about you Scott. He's the type that has everyone positioned, they were all a known. You are an unknown, he can't place you in his organized mind and that bothers him. Don't misunderstand me, he's a good man but, he won't rest until he has you figured out."

"I'll be on my toes. Now, if you don't need me Sir, I want to see if I can get a ride to the island."

"I thought you would Scott, so it's waiting for you."

When Scott left the helicopter and walked toward the house he had that "Oh, it's good to be home" feeling. He got on his bathing suit, opened a Kalik beer and sat by the pool reviewing the weekend in his mind. He liked the General and was looking forward to playing mind games with him. Beth was another matter, he felt a cautious attraction to her. Why hadn't she found another man in the ten years since her husband had been killed? She was very attractive with a wonderful personality. Was she looking, and if so what was she looking for? Time will tell.

Then he thought about the General's answer to the biggest problems facing the Country today. Syria and the Bekka Valley were big problems in combating terrorism. No wonder the President was so interested in the tape. Scott needed intelligence information on the activities of Ali. Was he doing the things Scott had told him must be done. If not, a surprise visit would be made. He'd talk to George, maybe he could get information from his CIA friends. Mr. R could also get valuable information and he had a phone number to call. He'd start work on that tomorrow. Now it was time to check the bird.

He walked into the hangar and stood there looking. She was beautiful and she was deadly. Lethal might be a better adjective. Her natural color was black but the bottom of the ship and the weapons pod was a bluish white in order to be less visible from below in the daylight. He had a feeling of comradeship with the craft. He lowered the stairs and entered, a familiar smell of the interior filled his nostrils. He sat in the pilots seat and thought of the flights they had made together. Some were getting acquainted, some were fun, some were mission planning , some were hairy and one was even a flight of saving another's life, a mission of mercy. The day would come when another would sit here and take his place but, he would put that day off as long as possible.

The next day he made the calls to George, Mr. R and the number the President had given him, all to get as much intelligence on Syria and Ali. His first call to the President went like this:

The phone rang one ring and was answered by a single word.

"Code."

To which he answered, "Hand."

"Go," said the voice.

"I'm requesting intel on whether Ali has started complying with the instructions given him. Also, need GPS location of known bad guys in Bekka Valley, no women or children. Out."

He would now wait for incoming information. He went to the weapons hangar to check the load of bombs, missiles and twenty millimeter. All was in order and ready for the mating to the aircraft. If no intel came in today he decided he'd take a joy ride this evening. Too bad Tim and Steve weren't here to go along, maybe they'd go back to Cuba and harass the tower controller again.

He did go flying that evening after it was dark. He flew without the weapons pod as this was a pleasure only flight. He stayed up for five hours trying new maneuvers then decided to see what was happening around Edwards Air Force base. There wasn't much radio traffic when he arrived so he decided to call for Raptor.

"Raptor, this is Friendly, do you read?"

There was no answer, but that didn't mean no one heard him. Assistant Director Colonel George Grey, working late in his office, heard the transmission. His head snapped up from his work.

"He's back," he said to no one as he was in the room alone. He spun his chair around and picked up the microphone lying on the table by the radio.

"Hello Friendly, go to 122.6."

Scott changed his radio frequency to 122.6 then transmitted, "Friendly is on 122.6 Raptor, do you read?"

"This is Raptor's nurse Friendly, were you looking to play tonight?"

"Roger, can he come out?"

"Not tonight Friendly but another night would be good. When do you plan to be back?"

"Never know. When do you plan to fly again?"

"The fifteenth, seventeenth and nineteenth. We'll look forward to your return."

"Roger Nurse Raptor. Friendly out."

Maybe he would come back and maybe not. It depended on the Syrian activity. He could find out the schedule through his new friend General Hathcock if he decided to return at a later date.

When he returned to the island the intelligence information had arrived by secure fax including the information from the President. Instead of complying with the demands Scott had given Ali, he had increased the security around himself thinking that would prevent Scott from doing him harm. The man needed to be taught a lesson and given one more chance, maybe.

There was information on the Bekka Valley from all three sources. He compared the data then listed possible targets that all three confirmed were terrorist leaders or cells. The GPS figures matched perfectly. He again requested information from all three sources as he needed intel on Ali's comings and goings. That information would determine the details of the next mission.

He lay in bed thinking of the problem areas and trying to formulate a plan to make those problems go away, or at least help in resolving them. Syria was the most pressing and the one to concentrate on first. A plan started to formulate, a plan that would require the blessings of Mr. R. If he approved, it would open up a whole new arena. Did he really want to do that? Should the President know the whole story, that the island was Piot and he was the only pilot of the only craft in Piot's Air Force? Could the United States be kept away from guilt by association?

He rode the helicopter to the mainland the next morning for a meeting with Mr. R. They discussed his plan in detail playing the what if game. After two hours they concluded that the project had been extremely successful to this point but, where did it go from here? Should they bring the President in on the whole story? This was not the time to put the project in the hands of the President to make all the decisions. Those decisions would be based on the same criteria and possible repercussions on which present decisions are based. Because he respected the President he didn't want to burden him with the weight of the project on his shoulders. The project's future was up to he and Mr. R. They would continue to make the decisions, they would continue spreading the word that Piot was real and only they were responsible for the attacks. However, he did have a plan to divulge the whole story to a man who would be an asset to the Company now and in the future. This plan he would discuss with Mr.R.

After explaining the plan's concept to Mr. R he returned to the island and began laying the details. The Raptor would be flying tomorrow night, and so would he. The Syrian mission was set for the following night.

Using his cell phone he called Colonel George Grey, Deputy Director of the Raptor project.

"Colonel Grey speaking."

"Hello Nurse Raptor, this is Friendly calling."

"Well hello Friendly, you coming to play?"

"I'll be there tomorrow night. Will General Ragland be there?"

"I'll make it a point to ask him and General Hathcock."

"What's the takeoff time?"

"Eleven pm."

"I'll join up passing through five thousand feet."

"Our pilot, Chris Denson, will look forward to it."

They both said goodbye and hung the phone but, Colonel George Grey was busy dialing again.

"General Ragland, this is George. Friendly just called and wants to play tomorrow night. I thought you may want to be here."

"You bet I do. What's the Raptor's takeoff time?"

"Eleven pm General. He'd like General Hathcock to be there also."

"I'll call him. See you tomorrow evening George and thanks for the heads up call."

"Goodbye General."

A few minutes later General Hathcock received a call on his scrambler phone. "This is General Hathcock."

A mechanically disguised voice said, "General, this is a representative of Piot. I am the pilot of the aircraft who will be meeting the Raptor tomorrow evening, would you care to fly with me?"

The General almost fell out of his chair. He couldn't believe it. They had been trying to find any kind of lead that would tell who these people were and here he was, an offer to fly in their aircraft against the Raptor. Before he could answer the voice went on.

"There are conditions General. You must not tell anyone you are flying with me. Second, I would like you to accompany me on a combat mission the following night. You will stay with me beginning with the flight against the Raptor until after we return from the mission. My man will pick you up at your home at 8:00 pm tomorrow night. Are you agreeable to these conditions?"

The Generals mind was racing. How could he refuse such an offer. "Done," he replied. "I'll be looking for your man tomorrow night."

"You must not tell any one where you are going to be or what you will be doing. Not even your daughter. You must agree to that General."

"I agree," he said.

The General had no more than hung up the phone than it rang. It was General Ragland informing him of the event tomorrow night and could he be there.

"Can't do it Bart, a prior meeting. Record everything you can."

Little did Bart know that he'd be there, in the Piot aircraft. Of course, he couldn't tell him that.

"Will do General, sorry you can't make it."

Scott hung up the phone and called George to arrange the pick up and rendezvous site. That taken care of he went back to work on the Syrian mission. He wanted this to go very smoothly to impress the General. He decided to add a stop to another country on the way home. The purpose of this stop was to let this country know they could be next for an all out aerial attack. The country was Iran.

At 9:00pm the following night it was very dark as Scott hovered over the rendezvous site waiting for George and General Hathcock to arrive. He didn't have long to wait before he saw headlights approaching. George parked at the edge of the pick up site and walked the General to the middle. Scott lowered the landing pads and slowly settled to the ground and lowered the stair. As soon as the General was inside the stairs closed, the craft slowly climbed as the pads retracted. At 1,000 feet Scott stopped the climb and turned to face the General. He was dressed in his pressure suit with the visor closed. He spoke to the General with the voice scrambler on.

"Welcome aboard General. Behind you you'll find a flight suit, G suit and pressure suit. Please put them on and we'll be making tracks to Edwards. I'll continue climbing slowly while you're dressing. If I don't have to dodge traffic the climb out should be smooth."

The general looked around him. This was like something from outer space. It looked to be far beyond, from a technical standpoint, anything he had ever seen. He was spellbound.

Fifteen minutes later the General was strapped in the seat behind and to the side of Scott. He had been looking around the craft and continued to do so as he said, "Does that altimeter read one hundred and twenty thousand feet?"

"Yes, that's why the pressure suit. We'll accelerate and arrive Edwards well ahead of time. Watch the airspeed and skin temperature gauge. That's the only limit to speed. We're approaching mach 7 now. We could go higher and fly much faster but there's no need, we have plenty of time."

"This thing is amazing," said the General in awe.

"You haven't seen anything yet General."

"What makes this thing fly? There was no noise when you picked me up, there's no noise now?"

"That's a "tell you later" question. You'll have a lot of questions I'll answer after we leave Edwards. In the meantime I'll show you some of the systems."

Scott was still explaining systems and aircraft control when it was time to meet Raptor. The General was having trouble accepting how far advanced this ship was compared to anything he had in the Air Force, including the Raptor.

"Nurse Raptor this is Friendly, over."

"Hello Friendly. Let's go 123.76, over."

"Roger."

"Nurse Raptor, Friendly on 123.76."

"Roger, read you five by five Friendly. Raptor will come up this frequency when cleared by departure control. He's taxiing to the active now."

"Roger Nurse. We'll be looking for him."

Scott brought up the tower on another radio so he could monitor Raptor. They were now at 1,500 feet south of the runway with traffic monitoring radar and the anti-collision on.

"Raptor you are cleared for takeoff. Runway heading to five thousand then right turn to three five zero, continue climb, report clear the area."

"Roger, Raptor is cleared runway heading to five thousand right turn to three five zero continue climb report clear the area."

"Roger Raptor, have a good flight."

"Raptor rolling," said pilot Chris Denson.

When Raptor was climbing through 600 feet Scott joined up in echelon right formation, tucked in as close as he could. His aircraft was much larger by several times than the F-22.

"Tighten your straps General, the fun's about to begin."

Scott turned on the daylight infrared and projected the outside scene in three dimensional in front of them. The F-22 appeared close and clear.

"Jesus," said the General. "We are a long way from having that perfected. The Raptor doesn't have a chance, he can't see you but you can see him."

"Precisely General, that's one of the reasons I wanted you along. You'll see some amazing things tonight."

Scott then performed several barrel rolls around Raptor. The other aircraft could not see him. He then moved in front of the F-22 and rotated about the vertical axis until facing backwards, looking directly at the other aircraft from a head on view. The General's mouth was hanging open, he couldn't speak. Scott then moved back in formation on Raptor's right wing as they were climbing through 5,000 feet.

"Raptor, Friendly is echelon right."

"Roger Friendly, it's a pretty black night, can't see you but I'll take your word for it."

Scott turned on his landing light illuminating the F-22. He quickly turned it off again.

"Gotcha Friendly. You don't have much of a radar return, in fact you don't have any."

"Same for you Raptor. Your lead, I'll follow."

While he was still talking Chris did a half snap roll, pulled the stick back causing the aircraft to head towards the ground at high speed then another half snap with a pull back on the stick into a vertical climb in afterburner. At thirty thousand feet he again pulled back on the stick and directed the exhaust nozzles full up which caused a gut wrenching change of direction from vertical climb to vertical descent. He turned on his landing light but there was nothing there. Scott had moved out to the side watching the maneuvers on the daylight infrared display. He anticipated the vertical reverse and moved into the six o'clock position when the Raptor was pointing straight down. He turned on his landing light.

"Gotcha Raptor. Very nice flying. Against any other bird you would win." He turned the light off.

Both aircraft leveled off at twenty thousand feet when Scott looked at his other radar, the standard radar, the one where the Raptor should be invisible, but there it was.

"There's skullduggery afoot General. They've rigged the Raptor to show on standard radar which can only mean he has a friend up here. He just did something that caused that to happen."

Scott pulled into a large loop ending up five miles behind and level with the Raptor. There he was, a second Raptor, sitting in a position to try to identify Friendly as to the type of aircraft he was. Scott took up a position one hundred yards off his left wing.

"Hello Raptor two, gotcha!" He then turned on the landing light startling it's pilot. He quickly climbed on a reverse course from the Raptors.

"Nurse Raptor this is Friendly"

"This is the Nurse, go ahead Friendly."

"Scratch your two raptors. You're sneaky Nurse but, it didn't do you any good. We'll be leaving the area now. Friendly out."

"Can't blame a fella for trying Friendly. Nurse out."

They climbed to 150,000 feet and set course for the island. "Okay General, your aircraft, play with the controls, base line course 135 degrees."

"This is something, this is really something. I can't believe this. Those Raptors didn't stand a chance."

The General was a quick learner, he played with the ship for thirty minutes growing more fascinated with each minute.

Scott removed his helmet and turned off the voice scrambler. "I've got the aircraft General."

The General looked up. "It's you, I should have known. Scott Wilson. That explains your visit with the President."

"No it doesn't General. He thinks I'm a go between. I got a tape to him and he wanted to discuss the source with me. The source was Piot. He now has a way to communicate with them, through me. What else he suspects, I don't know. You are going to learn things tonight that only eight people in the world know and I must insist on absolute secrecy. The temptation will be great at times to say something that could reveal a lead to us. I must have your word on it General."

"You have it Scott. I understand fully the need for complete secrecy."

"How about a cold Kalik beer General. We're at our destination letting down for a landing with a cold one waiting. We only come and go when it's dark or socked in with very minimum visibility."

Scott opened the hangar roof and set the bird gently on the pads. He closed the roof and the silence returned.

"Welcome to Piot General where I am the President and the only citizen. It is a legal country complete with a constitution. You can call me Scott if I can call you Skip or you can call me President and I'll call you General. Your choice."

"Hello Scott."

"Hello Skip. Now that that's settled let's hang up our pressure suits, we'll need them tomorrow. Let's give the bird a post flight and , hey, you haven't seen it yet from the outside have you. Follow me and we'll do the post flight together. The weapons pod is in the other hangar. We'll give the pod and the aircraft a thorough pre-flight tomorrow."

Skip could not believe what he was seeing. The only descriptive word was saucer, or plate. He knew the best stealth was a continuous circle and that's what he was looking at. But what makes it go. There were no engines that he could see. He was also looking at the vehicle that transported the Russian cosmonaut from the ISS. Amazing was the only word that kept coming into his mind.

"Hey Skip, let's get that beer now and I'll fill you in on everything after you answer a question for me."

"What's the question?"

"Not before we have a beer in our hand."

Scott gave Skip a tour of the house stopping at the refrigerator for the beer. He pointed out the bedroom that was Skip's then they settled in the great room in comfortable chairs.

"When your tour as Air Force Chief of Staff is over what are your plans?"

"This is the last career stop. I don't have anything planned for certain. Why do you ask?"

"I want you to join the R Company. We need your skills. We'll exceed any financial offer you have. You will also find this an exciting second career. You got a taste of it tonight. Tomorrow will be even better. I need your answer now Skip before I can reveal anything else about us."

"You don't waste any time do you? What if I say yes and then change my mind before I retire from the service?"

"You won't."

"No, you're right, I wouldn't. You're not even going to give me the night to sleep on it are you?"

"No. We have a lot to cover if the answer is yes. We have no more to talk about if the answer is no."

"Do you have any iced tea?"

"In the kitchen, I'll show you."

Skip made a glass of tea then returned to his chair. He sat there in silence for a minute then said, "Okay."

Scott walked over to him and they shook hands on it. The next two hours were spent reviewing everything from the time Scott started out with the two Bahamians in the old Chris Craft to the present. Skip didn't say a word the whole time, he was mesmerized.

"We have been trying to find out who Piot is, what they were flying, and here it is, 135 miles from the mainland, right under our noses. And Colonel Tinsel was here, you kicked him off the island. I'd love to be the one to tell him someday."

"Maybe you'll have that chance Skip."

"The truly amazing thing is the magnetic propulsion breakthrough. My God Scott, you never have to refuel. You don't have to carry the weight of fuel. Think what this can mean to the world."

"I have Skip and, it's wonderful and frightening at the same time. We will no longer be dependent on Middle East oil. No country will be dependent on their oil. But what will become of them. Their only source of income will be cut off. What about all the gas stations in the United States and those millions of people in the oil business, the refineries, the manufacturers of internal combustion engines, the list goes on and on. We have the breakthrough of the century but how do we introduce it to the world without destroying the economy of the world?"

"Yes, I see what you mean."

"When the time comes to tell all to the President, I'm sure he'll bring in the economic minds to plan the best strategy. I wish I believed that. We'll have time to talk more on the subject later. Let's get to bed, tomorrow will be a busy day."

"I doubt I'll get much sleep after what you've just told me."

"There is a warm front due through tomorrow. That's good news if it really socks in. It will mean we can leave without waiting for night fall. Why don't you call Beth in the morning, see if she can come down the day after tomorrow. If she can, I'll have her picked up and flown to the island. Good night Skip."

"I'll do that. Goodnight Scott."

When they awoke the next morning it was solid overcast, rain with a quarter mile visibility. A great day for flying, if you're flying the Piot aircraft.

"I put a copy of the tape I gave the President in the player for you to look at after breakfast. It will bring you up to date on the Syrian problem. But, let's have our breakfast first. Since we'll be spending a lot of time at altitude I suggest nothing heavy. I usually have fruit and a muffin along with good Florida orange juice."

Skip was thinking about all the training they put their astronauts through before letting them go into space. And now, here he was, no training, heading for space and combat. Life sure has a way of changing in a hurry. Life hadn't been this exciting since Desert Storm. He was feeling young and full of panther piss as he did when given his wings many years ago.

Syria time is ten hours ahead of local time which means noon here is ten o'clock at night there. They would depart at noon and with two hours to target would put them there at midnight Syrian time, the perfect time for what he had planned.

At precisely three minutes to twelve they lifted out of hangar one, closed the roof and moved to hanger number two where they mated with the weapons pod. At exactly twelve noon they departed the island climbing through thick fog then solid cloud to eighteen thousand feet. The radar showed no traffic within one hundred miles which allowed them to climb further without detection. They accelerated as they climbed leveling off at one hundred twenty five miles high. The view was fantastic.

"Like the view Skip?"

"I wonder if this is the view from heaven. This is something I never thought I'd see, while still alive anyway. I'm too old to be an astronaut and we have nothing other than the shuttle that can go this high. Look, it's getting dark ahead."

"Won't be long and we'll start letting down over Syria. Be sure you're strapped in tight Skip, I have a feeling a trap has been laid for us, like high cap cover. If so, we'll take them out first then see what protection he's traveling with now days. I"ll level at thirty five thousand and have a look."

It didn't take long until he spotted them, two sets of two, what appeared to be Mig 29's flying high cover for something below. That something had to be Ali, the Syrian President. The scanner picked up the frequency they were using and with the voice translator on they were able to understand the transmissions.

"Blue flight, are you showing anything on your radar?"

"Negative yellow leader, nothing on the screen."

"I will move a hundred kilometers west and set up an orbit there."

"Understand yellow leader."

As the two ship formation headed west, Scott slipped in behind the remaining two Mig-29's with the daylight radar on.

"My God Scott, what an advantage, the same as the other night against the Raptors. Now what?"

Scott keyed his mike, "Blue flight, this is ground control, return to base."

"Understand ground, Blue flight is returning to base."

"Yellow flight, this is ground control, return to base."

"Understand ground control, Yellow flight is returning to base."

"That takes care of that Skip, now let's go down and see if our friend Ali is where he's supposed to be."

"Very clever, not a shot fired and four Mig 29's taken out of the picture."

"We may not be able to be so gracious in a few minutes. We'll keep the voice translator on and see if we can pick up transmissions between Ali and his escorts."

As they descended the voice transmissions became more audible. They must be using short- range radios. That was good as it would limit listeners. Scott narrowed the beam on their external transmit and receive frequency and channeled it through the language translator. When they found Ali he could aim it like a rifle so Ali could hear and not the goons in the front seat.

"He may be driving blacked out, if so ,our daylight radar will pick him up without him being aware. Sing out if you see anything Skip, I smell a trap even with the Migs gone."

They followed the highway which was deserted this time of night. Anyone traveling it would be suspect and stopped by the military who ran frequent patrols. They knew that Ali was out tonight so it was expected that he would be the only one traveling this road. And sure enough, there he was, ten miles ahead with three helicopters flying escort and four armored vehicles, two in front and two in back. The radar showed no other returns for twenty five miles.

"We'll move in within a mile and raise Ali. If it's a trap something should happen soon. Here we go."

It was a very dark night which allowed them to slip between the helicopter and fly two hundred yards abeam Ali's car. Scott put the transmit cross hairs on the back seat and pressed the transmit button.

"Hello Ali, remember me, I'm the one that spared your life and gave you a chance to put things right in your country. You've disappointed me, you've done none of the things we agreed upon. Your life is in imminent danger, what do you plan to do about it?'

No answer. Evidently Ali was springing the trap or too stunned to speak.

"Answer me Ali or a missile will vaporize your transportation. You have three seconds."

Three seconds went by and still no answer nor any sign of a trap being sprung. Then it dawned on Scott. Ali wasn't in the car, he was in one of the armored vehicles. He put the missile cross hairs on the car and fired. The explosion completely destroyed it and anyone inside. He then moved the cross hairs to the armored vehicle directly in front of the destroyed car and moved the transmit cross hairs to it also.

"Hello Ali, we know you weren't in the car that exploded but you are in one of the armored vehicles. A missile is about to be fired at this one, talk to me fast or you're dead."

No answer. The armored vehicle exploded.

"Jesus Scott. What if Ali was in that thing. You killed him."

"Relax Skip. He wasn't in that one. We'll move to the one directly behind where the car was."

"Hello Ali. You have three seconds to answer me or die like the people in the car and the armored vehicle. Speak now."

"How can you talk to me? I am surrounded by thick armor."

"You have not kept your end of our agreement Ali. Do you want to die now?"

"No! No! I will do it. I promise"

"You promised me last time. This is your last chance Ali. I will not talk to you again. If I have to come back there will be no talk, I will kill you. Do you understand that?"

"Yes. Yes I do. I will do as you ask starting tomorrow."

"No. You start tonight Ali. If you don't you will be dead within a week. Your Migs, helicopters and armored vehicles do you no good against me. Do you want to die?"

No! I will do as you say. Please do not kill me. I will start tonight. You have my word."

"Your word is your life Ali. If you don't keep it you will die. Goodbye Ali, this may be the last time we speak, the decision is yours."

Scott climbed to an altitude of fifteen thousand feet keeping a sharp lookout for fighters. He turned to a westerly course for the Bekka Valley, Lebanon. The valley of several terrorists factions and located 86 kilometers from Beirut, Lebanon, a short flight from outside Damascus. The intelligence Scott received from the several sources gave the GPS coordinates of the worst of the terrorists head-quarters. He wasn't totally comfortable with this information so decided to check out the sites himself.

"Okay Skip, we're going down close with our receiver beam and language translator on again. Let's see if we can verify this as a terrorist house. Listen carefully to the conversation, I need you to confirm it as a target."

"Will do Scott."

They closed within a half mile slant range to the target and fine tuned the equipment. Voices started coming in, garbled at first then clear.

"Ahh, so you were the money man in that operation. How successful was it?"

"Very. Thirty people were killed including five Americans. It is always a pleasure to kill the Americans. Sometimes our brothers must die with the Americans but they do not mind I believe, so long as Americans die."

"How many are in there Scott? They're sure bad-mouthing us."

"We'll climb back up to five thousand feet and drop from there, I've heard enough to confirm it's a target."

Scott set the weapons selector for two bombs, roof penetration before detonation. The structure wasn't large so two bombs should level it.

"We're ready to drop, laser locked on and GPS confirms, BOMBS AWAY!"

The night below was suddenly turned to day as the bombs detonated. It looked like a huge orange explosion even from this altitude. It was five miles to the next target. They wondered if the terrorists at the next target could hear or see the explosion. They dropped down to monitor any conversation and were rewarded to hear anti-American and terrorist talk, again confirming the target. They climbed back to five thousand feet and released two bombs. They confirmed three more times thus eliminating all five targets. They both had a good feeling knowing that a minimum of fifteen terrorists were removed from any terrorist acts in the future. It was now time to fly to Iran.

"I have to admit that felt very good to eliminate those terrorists without a lengthy expensive trial and the chance of them getting off through some technicality. They got a taste of their own medicine, blowing themselves up and killing innocent men, women and children," said Skip.

Skip found himself shaking his head. Five terrorist cells taken out just like that. They never knew what hit them. The ease that this was accomplished was unbelievable.

The route to Iran was east across Syria and Iraq on a course of 085 degrees. This would bring them to Tehran and the Mehrabad Air Base. In addition to being the largest air defense base it was also the primary maintenance facility plus overhaul and manufacturer of spare parts. Before the fall of the Shah the Iranian Air Force was a proud and effective organization flying F-4 Phantoms and F-14 Tomcats. Most of these were grounded for lack of spare parts now. The radio scanner was not picking up any transmissions nor was

the radar showing any airborne traffic. They identified the maintenance and parts manufacturing buildings. The plan was to destroy
both of them which would cause a further reduction in the number
of operational aircraft.

"We are going to take out those two buildings," said Scott as he
locked the radar beam onto the target. "They're laid out in such
a way that a string of bombs placed a hundred yards apart will destroy them. We'll drop from five thousand feet so we can see the
results as they happen.

The results were confirmed when a close inspection showed
both buildings gutted. There was still no radio traffic with any
Iranian aircraft.

"We have two more targets while we're here skip. I'm sure you
know what they are but you guys don't know what to do about them
without adverse world opinion and possibly offending a couple of
so called allies. That's the beauty of being Piot. I can do what I
think is best for the free world without concern of world opinion
and I don't have any so called friends to worry about offending. So,
let's go get those two nuclear facilities all of you are having such a
fit about and remove them from your thoughts. All we need is for
the Iranians to have nuclear capabilities. Those so called religious
clerics are nothing but power hungry radicals."

One facility was 150 miles north of Esfahan, and 25 miles southeast of Kashan. The complex has two 25,000 meter halls built 8
meters deep into the ground with concrete walls built 2.5 meters
thick with another concrete wall outside of it. This facility could
be used for the production of highly enriched uranium for nuclear
weapons. The underground facilities are sized to hold over 50,000
centrifuges. There was no fear of a nuclear explosion as the facility

was not yet fully operational. This was the perfect time to destroy it. They set course for the first one and still no sign of aerial defense.

"It appears we were not expected. There's no defense of any kind, so far anyway. Would you like the satisfaction of taking out the first site Skip?"

"You bet I would."

"This needle points the way to the GPS coordinates, follow it while I set up the bomb data. Then all you have to do is put the cross hairs on the various preselected aiming points and hit the bomb release switch. We'll drop from 25,000 feet and set the bombs for deep penetration and simultaneous detonation. Those underground buildings are heavily reinforced but the bombs will hit mach 3 before hitting the target. We may have to do it a second time to be sure we get deep enough to take out those deep underground buildings. When we're sure they are destroyed we can take out the surface buildings."

"You have no idea of the satisfaction this will give me Scott. The nuclear capability of Iran has been a nightmare of mine for several months now. And here we are, ready to bomb the site into yesterday with no blame directed at the United States, at least outwardly. The cross hairs have all been set with the preprogrammed software, I'm ready when you are."

"I'm ready also, bombs away on your call."

"BOMBS AWAY. Take out the target you beauties."

The bombs found their altitudes with each other then simultaneously fired their engines built into the tail. They accelerated to mach 3 before hitting the target and penetrated the outer and inner concrete protection before detonating. All that money and labor to build the underground structures was destroyed in an instant. There would be no need for more bombs on this part of the target, it was completely destroyed. The surface buildings were also obliterated before they left for the next target. Mr. R would be pleased with the results accomplished with his bombs.

The second nuclear facility was not far from the first as it was located 150 miles south of Tehran near the town of Arak. This site was used for the production of heavy water to support a reactor for producing weapons grade plutonium. This site had towers 3 meters thick, 48 meters high with 70 mesh trays, another formidable target.

"This target is yours also Skip. We'll have you sleeping like a baby very soon."

"I'm ready for that. The software is up, targets identified. Jesus those are big towers. I'm ready when you are."

"Before we release let's think about what this site could do. Iran denies Israel's right to exist and is a sponsor of Hezbollah. How long before a nuclear weapon could be in their hands?"

"A long time if these weapons have anything to say about it. Are you ready for bomb release Scott?"

"Roger, I'm ready, bombs away on your call."

"BOMBS AWAY," said Skip.

Very little could be seen from 25,000 feet as the detonations were under the outer shells of the dooms. When the dust drifted away there was very little left of the target.

"Let's go down for a closer look and make sure we destroyed everything important. We'll stop our descent at 5,000 feet and bomb the other out buildings from there." Since they had plenty of bombs they dropped two on each building. When they observed the site from 1,000 feet they whistled at the destruction, it was complete.

"Hot diggity," yelled Skip. 'This will set them back to the stone age as far as their nuclear program is concerned. Thank you, President Scott, for allowing me to come on this trip. I can hardly wait for the satellite pictures at the Chief's of Staff meeting. I'll be thinking to myself, I did that, I pressed the bomb release that destroyed those targets. The world thanks you Piot, but they don't know how much they owe you. I understand what you have done with your other missions and why. It's an honor to have flown with you Scott and I thank you for letting me see first hand the tremendous service you are performing for the good of the world. I look forward to working for you after my retirement."

"I'm glad you understand Skip. It's important that you feel as I do about the threat of evil in the world and that we should act because there is no one else that can do the job as we can. If there is a target in the future that is causing great concern and it would be a perfect solution to have it destroyed, well, I don't need to say any more. Take us home Skip, the GPS is programmed to give you the course. Fly at any altitude you want and any speed as long as you don't exceed temperature redline. I'll start filling out our after action report. Mr. R gets a copy and a video as soon as we land."

"Roger. Climbing and accelerating. What a fantastic bird you have."

After landing they completed the post flight, made a copy of the video and transmitted it along with the after action report to Mr. R. When that was done they opened a Kalik beer and stretched out in overstuffed chairs.

"Do you mind if I call Beth? She'll be wondering where I am."

"Why don't you ask her to join us tomorrow. I can have her picked up and flown here to the island. She should arrive early afternoon in time for a scuba diving adventure. We'll get fresh lobster for the grill."

"I think she would love that. I'll do it."

The helicopter landed at 1:30pm and a very attractive Beth was helped from the cargo bay. She was dressed in khaki pants, a tucked in white blouse with the sleeves rolled up and a navy blue cardigan sweater over her arm. One of the crew carried her luggage into the house while she gave her Father a big kiss on the cheek and a polite hug for Scott. But even that polite hug had an effect on him.

"You two have some explaining to do. You disappear without a word, which isn't like you, then you end up down here with Scott, whom you barely know, call me out of the blue and have me whisked down here on a private jet and helicopter to a private island off the coast of Florida. What is going on between you two?"

"Why don't we let Beth get her bathing suit on and we can talk about it in the boat on the way to the dive site?" suggested Scott. "I'll show you and your luggage to your room. If you will follow that shell path when ready it will take you to the dock where Skip and I will be loading the dive equipment."

"I'll do that but you two are not off the hook," she responded as she wondered about Scott calling her father Skip. Only his closest friends and fellow combat veterans called him that. Something was definitely going on here and she meant to find out what.

CHAPTER TWENTY-FIVE

As they helped her into the boat Scott couldn't keep his eyes off her. She was extremely attractive even in the modest swim suit she was wearing. Skip noticed the look in Scott's eyes and grinned to himself. "Good luck" he thought, "there have been many a man smitten by her over the years but she hasn't found one to get serious with. Who knows, you could be the one Scott."

They left the canal heading for one of Scott's favorite dive sites where he had placed a lobster trap. Beth broke the silence by asking, "Which one of you is going to tell me what is going on between you two?"

"I'll let your father tell you Beth."

"Alright, go ahead Daddy."

"Scott has offered me a job with the R Company when I retire from the Air Force. I accepted. He convinced me that I would be a valuable asset to the Company in an administrative capacity. When the time comes it will mean our moving to Florida. I estimate that time will come in six months."

"I thought you wanted to work for an aerospace company."

"I will be. The R Company is one of the leaders in aerospace technology, a fact that is known to only a few."

"Okay, now what aren't you telling me?"

Skip looked at Scott with a questioning look. "Before we go into that," said Scott, "let's get our gear on and catch dinner. I'll answer your question afterwards."

"Fair enough," replied Beth.

After putting on their dive equipment and checking each other they entered the water backwards off the side of the boat then surfaced and gave each other the okay before descending to the bottom. The depth was only twenty five feet so a decompression stop would not be necessary when surfacing at the end of the dive. The water was warm with excellent visibility which made spotting the trap easy. Scott lifted one end and propped it open with a cement block he had placed near the trap. They lay flat on the sandy bottom and looked underneath, they saw at least fifteen good size lobsters and a couple crabs. Beth was the first to shoot her spear and was rewarded with a large one speared through the head. Skip and Scott followed until each had three on the end of their spears. Scott removed the cinder block and lowered the trap. There would be even more lobsters the next time. Scott signaled them to lay their spears on top of the trap then made a horizontal circle with his finger and pointed at the reef. Beth and Skip nodded their heads and they swam towards the reef to circle it. Thirty minutes later they were back at the trap where they surfaced with their catch of lobster. When back in the boat with the dive gear stored, Scott opened the ice chest and offered a Kalik to the other two. They eagerly accepted, settled into a comfortable position and waited for Scott to answer Beth's question. Skip knew that any explanation would have to come from Scott.

"What I'm about to tell you Beth is classified information of the highest category. The safety of the United States depends on you keeping what I am about to tell you a secret. You may have discovered other classified information because of who your father is but, none of it compares with what you are about to learn. I must ask you for your answer that you will discuss the information with no one. So you swear?"

"Yes I do, and I do have a top secret clearance."

"Good, and this information is way above top secret. The reason I am going to tell you is because you would always be curious what your father was doing and why. Beth, when you stepped off that helicopter a couple hours ago, you stepped on foreign soil. You were on the island of Piot. I am the only resident and I voted myself as President."

"You," she gasped. "You are the one who has been bombing all those horrible targets?"

"Guilty," he said. "The latest one was last night. Your Father went with me and in fact, dropped some bombs himself. You may have seen it on the news this morning before you left."

"Father? My Father went with you on a combat mission? Are you out of your mind Daddy, flying a combat mission at your age?"

"It was important that he see first hand the capabilities of our aircraft. There was only one way to do that. Whenever you're ready for another Kalik, help yourself. I'll start at the beginning Beth."

He gave her the same explanation he had given her Father as they cruised slowly back to the dock. He continued while they rinsed their dive gear and walked to the house. He finished as they sat by the pool. Beth had listened intently without interrupting once. For a time, after he finished, she didn't know what to say. She was thinking about this man sitting across from her, what he had done for his country that only a very few would ever know. She thought how he had risked his life many times in an experimental aircraft, flown into space on a humanitarian mission, been in combat with enemy aircraft, all for the good of free nations worldwide, and now he sat there calm and unassuming, as if all he ever did was dive for lobster. This was an unusual man, the only one since her late husband that interested her. She wanted to get to know this man better, much better.

"I can now understand why you took a job with this company and this man Father. You will still be on the leading edge where all the action is. I was worried you would get bored after retirement but not anymore. I wish I could play a part in your quest for peace."

"Ahhh but you can Beth," said Scott. "There will be many functions to attend in the future and a beautiful woman with social graces at my side and the side of your father would be a wonderful shoulder to lean on."

The sun had now set and darkness was rapidly closing in like a shade being drawn. They started walking towards the house.

"This is sounding better all the time," she answered as a strange sounding ring came from the house.

Scott jumped and ran to the house as the others followed, wondering what could cause Scott to react the way he did. He opened a secret panel in the great room and picked up the receiver of a red phone.

"Yes! Right! I'm on the way!" He hung up the phone and sprinted for the door heading for the hanger with the other two right behind him.

As he sprinted across the hangar floor to the aircraft's stairs he yelled! "You two stay here!" He was glad he had left the munitions pod attached, that would save several minutes. He retracted the stair and opened the hangar roof and was airborne closing the roof when he noticed the two passengers still strapping into their seats. "So much for obeying the President of Piot," he thought.

"The phone that rang is for extreme emergencies only. That's the first time it's rung since I've been here. Our helicopter spotted three fast moving boats ten miles from our island heading this way. When they tried to turn them around they took heavy fire damaging the chopper bad enough that they had to pull off and are headed towards us hoping to make the island. So it's up to us to stop those boats."

"How will you do that? asked Beth.

No one answered her.

"I have them on radar, now going to 3D daylight mode and projecting in front of you."

"Looks good Skip. Those boys are really moving, radar shows 75knots."

Scott placed the cross hairs twenty feet in front of the lead boat and fired. The boat tore through the water spouts without slowing. He then selected bombs, flying over the top he dropped one fifty feet in front of the same boat. The result was different this time, the water spout and concussion caused it to somersault backwards landing upside down.

"One down two to go," said Scott.

Suddenly the night sky was full of tracers as the boat gunners fired blindly into the night as they continued towards the island. This left Scott only one option.

"No choice now Skip. We'll take the new lead boat first, these guys have pure evil intentions."

This time the twenty millimeter wasn't aimed in front of the boat. A short squeeze on the trigger and the boat disintegrated. The third boat still headed towards the island but not for long as it too disintegrated under the twenty millimeters deadly fire.

"Nightbird, this is Chopper Two, over."

Nightbird was a coded call sign. "This is Nightbird Chopper Two, go ahead."

"Roger Nightbird, we're three minutes out, say situation, over."

"Under control Chopper Two. Take a look at the capsized one for any survivors but, I don't think you'll find any."

"Will do Nightbird."

"Check for company within 100 miles Skip. I think those boats were radio controlled by an airborne controller."

"Checking, and there he is. Sixty miles out on a heading of 170 degrees, flight level one nine zero, ground speed 475knots. Has to be a jet of some kind."

"We'll find out very soon," replied Scott as he accelerated in a climb to the same altitude. "Put him on the 3D daylight mode."

"Done," replied Skip.

There he was, in and out of the tops of cumulus clouds not knowing anyone was within 100 miles. Scott keyed his mike with his radio tuned to military guard frequency which transmitted on all frequencies. He thought they would be monitoring the military channels in case an intercept was scrambled against them.

"Hello Lear heading 170 at flight level one niner zero."

The blood of the two pilots in the Lear suddenly ran cold. They looked at each other then outside their side windows, then at their radar, nothing. They were Arab drug runners, raising money for terrorist organizations. They went into a hard climbing turn to the left then back to the right on the same base course. Immediately they were in the glare of a powerful landing light.

"No where to go Lear. Turn to a heading of two six five now, you're going to Miami or you can make a big splash in the ocean below. Your choice."

To help them with their decision Scott fired a missile across their nose. They turned to a heading of two six five.

"Take control of the radio Skip and call your fighter boys to escort our friend into Miami."

"My pleasure," he replied.

He also transmitted on guard. "Tyndall alert, this is Nightbird, go two one six point five five."

Skip switched to the frequency just before a voice said, "Nightbird this is Gator alert, over."

"Gator, this is Nightbird. We have a drug Lear that needs escorting to Miami. He's monitoring military guard, heading two six five degrees on the Miami reciprocal, flight level two four zero at one five zero distance. Authority code Backlight four six six seven three, over."

There was a short pause while authentication was verified then, "Gator one and two rolling."

Scott now keyed his mike. "Lear, you have two fox fifteens joining you for escort to Miami. If you don't obey their every command instantly they have strict orders to shoot you down. Do you understand?"

"Lear understands," was the only reply.

They backed off and watched as the two F-15's took position on each side of the Lear and made radio contact. There was nothing more for them to do so they turned towards home.

"Your aircraft Skip. Take us home and put her in the hangar. We'll leave the pod on for now."

"Roger, I have the bird."

"You have the bird," replied Scott.

"Well Beth," said Scott, "this wasn't exactly the introduction to the aircraft I had planned. Need I say that this carries the same high classified designation as the other subjects we discussed earlier? This craft is so far ahead of anything but dreams that it gives us a huge advantage over any known defenses but, we don't know how long it will last. We have a lot to accomplish in as short a period of time as possible before we lose that advantage. We can be a big help in Afghanistan and Iran in putting down terrorist activities. We have destroyed three of Iran's nuclear facilities but there are several more known that must be destroyed."

"Sounds like you may be busy for a long time."

"Yes, and it's very important that there not be a connection to the United States. Piot must remain a known country but it's location kept a secret for obvious reasons."

"I understand completely Scott and I appreciate your trusting me with the information."

"Since your Father and I are going to be working together I felt you should know what we're doing and why. Now if our pilot can get us down in one piece and you're not too tired, we can still have that lobster dinner."

"I'm too wound up to sleep and the lobster sounds good. After all, I speared the biggest ones."

"Right," Scott and Skip said simultaneously.

"Questions will be asked about your involvement tonight Skip. What were you doing there, why no radar return, just to mention a couple."

"I've thought about that but I can handle it, no problem."

"Speaking of problems, let's give the area a good look before landing. Do a fifty and twenty five mile radius search. The damaged chopper should be on our helipad and the crew gone with the second chopper. They'll be back in the morning to fix it."

Thirty minutes later they were in the house with the lobster pot on the stove, they had decided on boiled lobster and a salad. Scott had reported to Mr. R so all was right in their world for now, time to relax and enjoy each others company.

Scott was up early the next morning checking the bird over for any damage a stray bullet may have caused. While inspecting Skip walked in.

"Thought I would find you here. Any damage?"

"No, she looks good. By the way, nice landing last night."

"Thanks. Coming from you I appreciate the compliment. No one on earth has more time in a ship like this than you."

"I talked to the mainland this morning and Steve, Tim and Tim's fiancé, Colleen, will be coming on the repair chopper. Due in this morning at 10:00 o'clock. Better wake Beth by 9:15 so she'll have time to get ready. They'll leave tonight on one of the choppers."

"No need to wake Beth. When I came out here she said breakfast in 30 minutes. That's 20 minutes ago."

"Great, let's head in, I'm hungry."

Shortly after a breakfast of scrambled eggs, sausage and grits the helicopter arrived with Steve, Tim and Colleen. It was like old home week. Scott had filled Skip and Beth in on the part Steve and Tim played in the development of the aircraft. Without them it would not have happened. They also had learned of the part Colleen played in the rescue of the Russian Cosmonaut. Everyone met at the pool after changing into swim suits.

It was with relief they could all talk freely about the aircraft and the missions it had flown. Beth was the newest member of "those in the know". The "those in the know" list was growing out of necessity. It was good for Skip and Beth to see the quality of the people involved in the project.

They spent two hours talking and talking. It was good for all of them as they had kept their knowledge of Piot and the aircraft bottled up with no one to talk to about the project and their experiences. Scott suggested he show Beth the rest of the island while the others went in the boat for snorkeling and diving.

"Tell me what you're thinking Beth, after hearing all the tales."

"I think it's the most exciting thing I've ever been involved in and the flight last night was my first of many, I hope. Oh Scott, what you are doing is so right for our country and the world. I understand that by using Piot you are protecting our country from blame but sooner or later the truth will be known."

"I know, that's why we have to accomplish as much as we can in the shortest time possible. The President thinks I am the go between Piot and him. I want to keep it that way. So far the hot spots we've attacked have been furnished by the press. "

"Are you asking my father to supply you with that information?"

"Definitely not. I don't want him to pass any classified information to me. However, there is information published and available to the general public that the press has not printed. The public does not know it's available. I need to know what those publications are and where I can gain access to them. But that's far from the reason I wanted your Father to join the Company. He has a brilliant mind and his knowledge in the areas of economics and administration just to mention a couple are of tremendous value to us. Mr. R is grooming me to take over the Company someday. I need to build a staff of highly qualified people in whom I have absolute trust. I don't have the organizational abilities that Mr. R has nor the expertise in so many areas. That is why I need men like your Father so we can continue the work of the R Company. I have no idea when that time will come but, I believe Mr. R knows something he is not sharing with me. Do you understand now?"

"Yes, and forgive me for questioning you. You're a man of honesty and integrity and I should not have doubted you. I'm sorry, please forgive me."

"There is nothing to forgive Beth. You were concerned for your Father and that is admirable. Now, there was a coded call from the President during the night asking me to come to Washington for a meeting. I want you to go with me. There will be a social event and he and I will slip away as before for a meeting. Will you go with me?"

"As an employee of the Company or as your date?"

"Which do you prefer?"

"As your date."

"I was hoping you would say that."

CHAPTER TWENTY-SIX

The helicopter left at 8:00pm with everyone on board including Skip and Beth who were anxious to return to Washington and begin the thought process of leaving there and living in Florida. The General had a number of projects to finish before his retirement as did Beth. He decided to retire four months from the end of the current month. He was excited more than he had let on about coming to work with Scott and the R Company. Scott would put the alone time to good use mentally selecting those who would make up his advisor circle. He was also thinking about the upcoming social at the Whitehouse. The world of terrorism seemed to be losing the battle to the good guys, at least that's what it appeared but, little did Scott know that just the opposite was true.

Saddam's ex-generals and Al-Qaeda terrorists were hiding in the hills between Afghanistan and Pakistan. Their assets were measured in billions of dollars in banks around the world and cash stashed in cities throughout the world. This money would be used to bring terror on the West. They had the funds to unite terrorist organizations into one force. The hatred of the West had grown so strong that they were insane with hate. They would use their financial strength to acquire nuclear and biological weapons and attack the West with them.

Late the next Friday afternoon George picked Scott up at the airport and drove him to the Hathcock home where he freshened up and enjoyed a brief visit with the General.

"Who is going to attend your gathering tonight Scott?" asked the General.

"I don't know Skip. We were told it would not be formal and beyond that I have no idea."

Just then Beth came downstairs looking lovely as usual. She was dressed in an emerald suit with a mid-calf skirt and gold accessories. She was very beautiful.

"Wow!" said Scott. "You are absolutely beautiful."

"Why, thank you kind sir," she replied. "If you two are done talking, I'm ready to go. We don't want to keep the President waiting."

The guards at the gate to the Whitehouse knew George but nevertheless they were given a thorough security check. As they approached the front door it was opened by a Marine security guard who welcomed them by name. Just then the President and First Lady entered the entry way and greeted them.

"So nice to see you both again," they said

"President and Mrs. Barley, thank you for asking us," they responded.

"Let's go in this room for cocktails or whatever you wish to drink and hors d'oeuvres." As they entered the room they saw only one other couple, Secretary of State Sam Painter and his wife Esther. Introductions were made and small talk began. This was it, there were no other guests coming. Why was he invited? Best course is to try and relax and see what comes.

Small talk lasted about half an hour when it was announced that dinner was served. Once seated and Grace said the conversation started again.

"Did you know, Scott," said the President, "that Sam has a PhD in economics and taught at Princeton before becoming my Secretary of State? He is considered an expert on world economics."

"No, I did not know that Mr. President, that's most impressive. It raises an economic question I would like to ask, if I may Mr. Secretary?"

"Of course Scott, ask away," said a smiling Secretary.

"What would happen to the Arab world if the demand for oil was reduced by 70 to 80%? The second part of the question is, what effect would that have on the rest of the world?"

The President interjected a comment, "Now that would be a relief, not having to depend on Arab oil."

"How do you anticipate that happening Scott?" asked the Secretary.

"Let's say that a method was discovered to generate energy that could be harnessed to provide power to drive engines. It would eliminate the need for consumable fossil fuel and internal combustion engines such as automobiles, trucks, buses, trains, generating plants, etc. What effect would that have on the Arab world first, then the rest of the world?"

The President was looking at Scott while the Secretary and Scott were looking at each other. "My God," thought the President, "Does he have such a power source?"

"That's a good question Scott and one I'd like to hear the answer to but let's not bore the ladies with it. We'll talk about that after dinner," said the President. He didn't want any distractions when that question was discussed.

After dinner and dessert they were discussing the announced retirement of Beth's father when the President suddenly said, "Ladies, would you please excuse Sam, Scott and I for a few moments? Something has come up that I need to discuss with them."

"Of course, of course, we'll have another cup of coffee," replied the Presidents wife.

"Thanks, we won't be long."

As the door closed Sam was wondering, "What's going on here? Who is this young man who suddenly appeared on the scene and who has the President's ear just like that?"

The President looked Scott squarely in the eye and said with a voice almost a whisper, "Do you have such a power source Scott? You do don't you?"

"Another country is involved Mr. President, and because of that I can't answer your question at this time. It would be against international law to do so.

"Is that country Piot?" asked the President.

"Please forgive me Mr. President but again, I can not answer."

"Mr. Wilson, the President has asked you a question and by God you will answer it!" barked the Secretary.

"Calm down Sam", said the President. "He would tell us if he could. I respect him for not breaking his oath of secrecy. But I do want answers to the two part question he asked during dinner. Please see to it Sam."

Sam was one of the good old boys who would retire involuntarily after the next election regardless of who won. His feathers were ruffled at this young man having the ear of the President. If he weren't so upset he would realize that there were unspoken words between Scott and the President. As it was they went unnoticed.

When they returned, nothing was said about the closed meeting. Sam did not bring up the questions Scott had asked. The fact was, he had no answers but, he knew he needed to put heads together who could come up with them.

They joined the women and an enjoyable evening followed. On the drive back to Beth's home she wanted to ask him about the meeting with the President but refrained until they were inside. Skip joined them and he told them about the meeting. They agreed whole heartedly that it may be time to bring the President in on the power source if it could be used as an advantage to the

United States against the terrorists. Two points had to be considered; 1. By not divulging the power source he would continue to have a huge combat advantage for the foreseeable future. 2. If he did divulge the power source this knowledge could be used with great leverage against the Arab world in negotiations.

What they didn't know, and the President did, were the details of the terrorist's plan to create a large group to wage war on the free world. The President needs a strong lever to win the aid of the Arab world in defeating this new group. That meant cutting off the funding and their bank accounts as well as their help in apprehending the guilty ones.

The next morning he contacted Tim and Steve and arranged to meet them for lunch in his office. He took their sandwich and drink order, added his to it, and asked Mary to arrange for their delivery at noon. He needed their Mensa connection.

They finished their sandwiches during small talk and knew the reason for the meeting would soon become apparent. He brought them up to date on his meeting with the President. He then said, "Do you know anyone in Mensa whose main talent is economics? We need the help of someone who can answer those two questions."

Steve and Tim discussed his question for a few minutes then asked if they could get back to him. They had some possibilities but would like to check them out through other Mensa friends.

"Thanks guys, I appreciate the help. I'm very hesitant to talk about the power source without some economic answers. Too many people could be hurt. Let me know when you have a name or names." They said they would and the meeting ended.

He met with Mr. R that afternoon and brought him up to date on his meetings and possible missions. After listening to Scott for over an hour he made comments on some areas and generally agreed with his activities. Now it was his turn to bring Scott up to date on an important intelligence intercept.

"Saddam's old generals are trying to organize a single terrorist group with them as the leaders. They are trying to bring all the groups into one large organization. Their main goal is to attack the West and primarily the United States. The President is obviously aware of this intelligence and will be interested in what Piot can do to crush this threat. If he thinks you can be an asset, you will have access to any intelligence you need in order to crush this force. Good luck Scott, keep me up to date as always."

"I will Sir, and thanks for the information. I have given much thought whether to tell the President the whole story of Piot and reveal all the information about the aircraft. I have decided not to reveal anything, He thinks I'm a middleman between he and Piot so I'll let it stay that way unless you disagree."

"I agree Scott. I believe it is premature but, the right time will come and it will be obvious."

CHAPTER TWENTY-SEVEN

T he day was now Wednesday. Tim and Steve had flown to the island in the morning and spent several hours checking all the systems in the aircraft including updating some that had more advanced technology. When they were done they briefed Scott on the updates and reported that all systems were in excellent condition and ready to go. Tim had checked the space under the cockpit floor and the skin of the aircraft and was pleased with his findings. He didn't say anything to Scott yet but they were very close to an operational laser. If he ever ran into another missile the laser would take care of it without having to get close and endanger their lives by a nuclear explosion. The space was more than ample for the installation of such a weapon.

This was a joint project with many companies such as General Atomics, Raytheon Company, Northrop Grumman Company, PEI Electronics Inc., Armstrong Laser Technology Inc. Saft America, Boeing and others including Lawrence Livermore Laboratories who designed a prototype tactical weapon. It is being mounted on the Army's Humvee and considered part of their FCS (future combat system). A few more weeks here and there and they will mount one in the bird. Tim decided to wait until it was operational before telling Scott.

Scott flew more missions to the Bekka Valley and destroyed several more terrorist hideouts. The days passed quickly with everyone busy on their projects. Steve and Tim were putting in long hours on the new bird. Skip and Beth were busy winding up their affairs in Washington and would start looking for a home near the Company headquarters. Dr. Kay was busy with her internship at Johns Hopkins and Colleen was busy with the hospital and her time off spent with Tim.

Scott found himself spending those two days a week at the Company office. There were seven days in a week, Tuesday or Sunday, the name didn't matter. He flew or was in the office. The days had no names. The only way he knew it was a weekend was the office was empty. He was learning so many things about the Company and meeting management and staff of the different subcompanies. He wished Skip were here but he also knew it would be good for him to go through it all again when Skip physically joined the Company. He was also looking forward to Beth moving closer.

They had attended a couple boring Washington cocktail parties where so many were trying to impress each other with their importance. They slipped out of those early and did their own thing. Once they went to a small lounge with a piano bar and sat there listening to old songs. They sat in silence each with their own memories. Finally Beth looked at him and said, "We can't live in the past can we but, it is nice to have those fond memories."

"Someone else told me that once and here you are telling me also. It is true. I didn't necessarily agree with them at the time but I now know it to be true. We can hold those we loved in the past in a special place and life does go on. There can be love again in the future."

Scott noticed a tear roll out of the corner of Beth's eye. She had a funny ache in the pit of her stomach. She wanted to crawl inside this man next to her. "Oh God", she thought, "Am I falling in love again? After all these years I never thought it would happen but, I think it is." She excused herself and went to the powder room to freshen up.

When she returned Scott took her face in his hands and kissed her tenderly on the lips. Uhh, it felt like someone hit him in the stomach. It must be catching.

When he took her home they went in the house for a social visit with her father. Skip noticed a difference immediately. For one thing they couldn't stop touching each other even if it was a hand on the back or shoulder. A short time later he excused himself saying he was tired and going to bed. Beth thought that was funny as he never went to bed this early. They sat on the couch holding hands until it was time for Scott to leave. He hadn't courted since high school and didn't know how. Beth giggled to herself like a school girl at his awkwardness.

When he left, the ever faithful George was waiting. He also noticed the change in the two of them but didn't say a word.

His meeting with Chad Boomer happened sooner than he'd planned. It happened at one of the cocktail parties, one planned by the military and NASA to welcome Chad's return from the space station. Beth was unable to attend so Scott went by himself. When Scott was introduced to him he wondered if Chad would recognize him in some way. He was relieved when he didn't, one reason for his coming was answered.

It was inevitable that someone would bring up the rescue of the Russian Cosmonaut and Scott was curious to hear Chad's account of the transfer.

"Vladimir was very sick, we suspicioned it was appendicitis but what could we do. We had no skills nor knowledge how to operate. We flat did not know what to do. Neither the United States nor Russia had a vehicle that could arrive in time to save him if it was appendicitis. If it was something else we had no idea what or how serious it could be. Then out of nowhere came this voice over the radio calling himself "Rescue." Given this situation what would you think? We thought it was some hacker on our frequency."

"When we looked out and saw the lights we couldn't believe it. There was something out there. That something said they could help us and asked permission to dock. The United States and Russia left it up to us to make the decision. We approved the docking. We're not true believers in aliens so thought this craft had to come from earth, where we didn't know. Vladimir was in bad shape so we really had no choice."

"As they told us, their docking collar matched ours and it went very smooth. Two of their people came on board and carried Vladimir to their ship. I was invited aboard to watch the transfer. Suddenly the doctor, who was a most attractive woman, said she had to operate immediately. Her assistant was also a very attractive woman and removed her space suit as did the doctor and began operating. They both wore surgical masks. Since we were weightless the two crew members who brought Vladimir on board held their legs to keep them from floating. The operation didn't take long and the doctor said she wanted to get back to positive gravity as soon as possible. I was asked to return to the ISS and was assured Vladimir would be well cared for."

"I had no doubt that was true. They were most professional and well trained. Their aircraft commander kept his space suit on so I never saw his nor the two crew members face. Nor did I see the faces of the two women because of their surgical masks. They were most cordial and concerned and spoke English. Their ship was out of science fiction. It was nothing like ours in your wildest imagination, far ahead of anything we have."

"That's pretty much it. Since it was dark we never saw their ship from the outside. The commander told me they were from a country called PIOT and they had declared war on terrorists and countries that supported them. That's the end of it. We heard later that Vladimir was in Bermuda and doing very well."

"Someday I would like to meet a member of their crew to thank them for their unselfish rescue. I would also like to see their space craft again."

More questions were asked as Scott moved away from the group. A short time later Scott and Chad were both ordering water with a twist at the bar. They were alone. Scott introduced himself and asked if he could have a private meeting with Chad when it was convenient. Chad suggested 8:00pm in his room, number 315. Scott agreed.

At 8:00pm Scott knocked on Chad's door.

"Come in Scott," called Chad. He was making them a tall water with a twist.

"Hello Chad. Thanks for seeing me."

"I must admit I'm wondering why a top executive from the R Company would want to see me. A friend told me who you were before we met at the bar."

"I was listening to your ISS venture concerning Vladimir."

"The world has certainly heard of Piot since then. At the time I wondered what difference a small unknown country could make. I found out along with the rest of the world."

"I'd like to talk to you about the R Company but, I would like to do that on my turf. I live on an island off the coast of Florida. Would you accept an invitation to come down for a few days. I would like to discuss a proposal with you."

"No hints ahead of time?"

"No. Let's talk about it when you arrive. Would it be convenient if our plane picked you up Friday noon at the executive jet terminal?"

"Wow, you move fast don't you? All right, I accept your invitation and look forward to it."

"Great. I'll see you Friday evening for dinner. A helicopter will meet your flight and bring you to the island. The dress is very casual and bring a swim suit. Goodbye."

"Good bye Scott"

Scott returned to his Company office spending the next day and a half going over more of the Company's many businesses. Thursday night he left for the island aboard the evening supply helicopter. Oh how good it was to be on the island again.

He opened the freezer with the intention of having a steak for dinner when he saw the bottle of Sky vodka. It had been there all along but he had paid no attention to it. Why not, he thought. It's been well over a year since I've had a vodka martini and it use to be a favorite of mine. He made a very dry one with four olives, sat in a big easy chair in the great room and called Beth.

It was good to hear her voice but he got that feeling of being hit in the stomach again. She was busy packing and keeping her father focused. She said she hadn't seen him so excited since he checked out in the F-15.

"You have certainly given him a purpose in life Scott. He wasn't sure what his job would entail after leaving the military and was apprehensive. Now I have to keep him on the path to getting his project completed or assigning competent people to finish them. I, on the other hand, have a more focused person, I mean reason, for moving down there. I miss our time together Scott."

The conversation went on for another thirty minutes and after hanging up he missed her more than when he called.

The next morning he put on his swim suit, loaded scuba gear onto the boat and cut a wake across flat turquoise water. He found a new patch of coral and anchored the boat. The wind was calm and the air and the water was warm. Another perfect day.

One rule of diving is never dive alone. But if you are alone and want to dive what other choice did you have besides not diving at all? Anyway, the depth was only fifteen feet which was perfect for free diving but he wanted to stay down longer and explore the coral.

He checked the anchor was secure and would hold. It would be embarrassing to surface and find your boat had drifted away. This far from shore it could also be dangerous. He had this happen once when he and a friend were diving in a small fresh water lake. Fortunately they were able to swim to the boat among cheers from other friends on shore.

Scott swam slowly, expending very little energy resulting in his tank lasting over an hour.

" Wow! Did that feel good."

He had two nice size lobsters on his spear which he tossed into the boat. He then dove down and brought up two conch shells placing them in the boat also.

He climbed on board, opened a Kalik beer and stretched out in the bow of the Whaler. His thoughts went to Chad and how he would react to his offer tonight. Then he thought of Beth and wondered how long it would be before she moved down. It couldn't be soon enough to suit him.

Chad fell in love with the place when he arrived. It was hard to take in the beauty of the whole scene. He just kept saying Wow! He quickly changed into a swim suit and started swimming laps while

Scott cooked lobster. He had made the conch salad that afternoon which would preceed the lobster dinner with boiled new potatoes and fresh asparagus.

They had an iced tea together before dinner, nothing alcoholic in case they flew that night, and enjoyed small talk. They were quite a bit alike in that there was no B S nor chest pounding. It was straight out and honest. Some people you hit it off with right away and others it takes time. Then there are those that you never do find the right chemistry. These two hit it off in the first fifteen minutes.

During dinner they talked about the food, diving, Chad was also a diver, and the waters around the island. After Dinner Scott asked if no alcohol was okay with Chad until after their discussion.

"No problem Scott," he said. "I would not have accepted if offered until after we talked."

"What would you do if you weren't in the military?" Scott asked

"I've given a lot of thought to that Scott. I have over 20 years and a Brigadier General heading for Major General within the next five years, if I keep my skirts clean and kiss a behind or two now and then. I'm back up pilot for the next shuttle launch to the ISS sometime in the next twelve months. Another space flight is my primary goal right now. After that, I'll just have to see what happens. Flying is what I really want to do but, they also want to give the younger guys the opportunity to get shuttle time so, one more flight is all I have, if that. Only time will tell."

"The R Company is quite advanced in the aerospace industry and looking for a pilot. We don't want young hot shots full of panther piss, we want experienced stable pilots. We prefer those with space time in their log book but it isn't necessary. If you thought we had a shuttle nearly ready to go and offered you a spot as its pilot, what would be your reaction?"

"That's a lot of ifs Scott."

"Okay, let me put it this way. We have a bird ready to fly. You can be its pilot."

"Jeez. What can I say, of course I would take the job. However, I do have a commitment to NASA for back up pilot of the next shuttle. As I said, sometime in the next year, I couldn't join you until after that. Would that be acceptable to you?"

"Are you saying that after the next shuttle flight, whether or not you fly, you will join the R Company?"

"Absolutely, I'll put it in writing if you like. I didn't believe something like this could happen. I'd resign from the service in a heartbeat if I can still fly in space. Who wouldn't?"

"No need to put it in writing Chad. In fact I'll make you an employee of the R Company now and put you on special leave of absence. Is that acceptable to you?"

"Yes, yes, of course. This is a dream come true Scott. I don't know how to thank you."

"Well, lets just shake on it."

Scott stood in front of him and put his hand out. Chad stood with a big grin on his face and shook Scott's hand.

"By the way Chad. You and I have met in the past. You are also shaking hands with the pilot of the craft that picked up Vladimir from the ISS that night."

Chad just stared at him. "You? You? It was you? But how? Piot! You are Piot? My God Scott!"

"Follow me Chad," Scott said as he turned and walked out the front door towards the hanger.

When he arrived at the hangar door Chad was right behind him. They went in together and entered the section where the craft was parked. Scott watched Chad to see his response. He wasn't disappointed.

Chad stood with his mouth agape, unable to say anything. Slowly he approached the craft, put out his hand and touched the skin.

"Beautiful," he whispered. "Beautiful," he kept repeating as he walked completely around its circumference. 'I've never seen anything like it. So this is what it looked like when you picked up Vladimir. It is real, you are real, this is it."

"You have much to hear Chad but first, would you like to fly her?"

"You're kidding right? No you're not are you?"

Scott lowered the stair and invited Chad to board. Scott sat in the forward seat and Chad in the seat slightly behind and to the right. Scott explained various systems but felt Chad was in such awe he wasn't comprehending, so Scott decided to go flying. This brought Chad back to reality.

When the hangar was clear and closed they headed into the night. Scott confirmed that Chad was strapped in tight before he put the craft through maneuvers.

He accelerated to mach 3 and tumbled the craft tail over nose three times while continuing on course at mach 3. He then reversed the tumble three times. Scott then rolled it three times left then three times to the right. He then rotated the craft on its vertical axis so they were facing in the opposite direction from which they were traveling. He then slowed the craft as rapidly as possible, without being uncomfortable, until they came to a complete stop.

"If you had a space suit we could visit the space station and be docked thirty minutes from now. Wouldn't that be a shocker to them to have you poke your face in there again?"

"I'm way behind Scott. Slow things down and start at the beginning. Go through the controls with me."

"Follow me through on the flight controls while I explain how they work."

Chad was a fast learner and was soon flying the aircraft in such a way that Scott was able to relax and enjoy the ride.

"Play with it as long as you want Chad. When you want a break and you feel confident enough to put this bird in the hangar, go ahead," encouraged Scott. He was setting the hook to reel in a highly qualified pilot to be happy of the decision to join the R Company.

When they arrived over the hangar Scott showed Chad how to open the hangar roof, lower the landing pads and line up the cross hairs for landing. Chad set it down like a feather. He was hooked.

"Before you ask any questions, lets go in the house, open a Kalik beer, and I'll explain everything from the beginning. He did just that plus facts about the R Company. Chad sat fascinated and didn't interrupt once.

"Lets spend tomorrow relaxing, talking and getting to know each other better. We can help you with your notice to NASA as we have close ties with them. They, of course, don't know we are Piot or that we have the aircraft. Needless to say everything we do is highly classified for the main purpose of protecting the United States and allowing us to strike the bad guys when world terrorism raises it's ugly head. We are six months away from having a second ship so the sooner you make the change the better. I'm ready to hit the sack, how about you?" asked Scott.

They spent the next day diving and talking. The two felt very comfortable with each other. Chad left the following day and Scott flew to Detroit to visit one of the companies owned by the R Company. The real purpose of the visit was not shared with the Company personnel other than the company president.

The Company building was just completing a 100,000 square foot addition as they were contemplating a new product manufacturing facility. Which product was yet to be determined. Scott studied the addition carefully and decided the building would be perfect for the purpose he had in mind. He and the president talked of what would be needed to turn it into a specialized manufacturing facility. When Scott left he told the President that he would send plans by special courier and to set the plan in motion upon receipt. In the meantime he would discuss his plan with Mr. R.

CHAPTER TWENTY-EIGHT

S tanding in front of the terrorist leader was Mohamed Waleed Algamdi, the terrorist lieutenant who was responsible for the transfer of one hundred million U.S. dollars to Kim Jong Un. He was very nervous and perspiring freely. The leader stared at him and said, "So you are the one that threw away a huge sum of our money which is now being used by North Korea to rebuild their Country and create closer ties with the West." It was not a question but, an accusation.

The Lieutenant did not answer but stood very still.

The leader nodded to one of the guards in the room who immediately shot the Lieutenant in the back of the head. He was dead before he hit the floor. He was just as viciously sick as he ever was, if not more so now that he no longer ruled the extermination squad of Iraq. He was insanely hateful of the West and especially the United States and was becoming a force that would need to be reckoned with. The only good news was the sky rocketing cost of oil which resulted in very high gasoline prices around the world. The economy of several western countries was hurting. The Arabs still held the world hostage with control of oil. This made the terrorist smile. He loved the Muslim style of justice.

Several weeks passed with Scott spending more time at Company headquarters in meetings with Mr. R. He was learning more and more about the entire Company and meeting managers and department heads of it's many interests. An international meeting of management personnel was scheduled on Paradise Island, Bahamas at the Atlantis Hotel in three weeks. He had asked Skip, Beth and Chad to attend. In the meantime Mr. R had approved Scott's plan for the manufacturing facility in Michigan. Both Tim and Steve were there working with the facilities president to help in designing the production line. It was a giant step between the electromagnetic motor in ground transportation and the truly magnetic propulsion system in the aircraft.

During this time the Syrian President was gradually moving in the direction Scott had mandated to him, however, it appeared another visit was needed in order to speed up the process. The North Koreans have agreed to unification with the South with the South taking control of the economically depressed North. Funds would be needed to build the infrastructure in the North which was practically nonexistent outside of a handful of cities. Iran still could not be trusted as there were rumors of renewed nuclear facilities which so far remained secret. The terrorist organization was a growing threat to the free world even though no act had been committed as yet. And as always, there were countries suspected of providing terrorist support whether financially or with secret training camps.

Two weeks before the Paradise Island meeting Skip and Beth flew down on the Company plane to look for housing and a meeting with Mr. R and Scott. The purpose of the meeting was to discuss the power source. Since Steve and Tim were the scientists who perfected the system they were also included. The main subject of the meeting had been weighing heavily on Scott's mind to the point that he would wake in the night thinking about it.

The meeting started at 9:00am with Mr. R welcoming everyone and giving a review of the Company and it's achievements over the past year. He included a well done to the aircraft and its accomplishments and praising those involved. He then turned the meeting over to Scott. It was becoming apparent that Scott was the successor to Mr. R and this pleased them.

Scott opened with, "Thanks to Steve and Tim, we are in a very unique position regarding the advantage enjoyed with the aircraft in its mission to combat terrorism. Although many Countries suspect the United States is involved there is no proof so there have been no repercussions against them. We will continue our efforts in that direction."

"Chad Boomer, who will be joining the Company soon, rode in the aircraft one night not long ago. After the next shuttle flight he will be joining the Company as a second pilot."

"The power source was not explained in any detail to him other than the fact that fossil fuel is not used for propulsion. I believe all of us would love to share this with the world. We think of all the good it could do in primitive areas and in irrigating fields for crop production where people are starving. We could also put an end to the world oil shortage problem and the resulting hardships it causes, not to mention the kowtowing to the oil producing countries. When we look at the motor used in ground transportation and the propulsion system in the aircraft they are a long way apart. We could share the motor and not jeopardize the magnet propulsion system. How does everyone feel about making the ground transportation available to the US auto industry? They are in a world of hurt and the motor could be their way out of this dilemma."

"But think about the jobs that would be lost when the power source replaces engines in automobiles, trains, boats, anything with an engine. A source the size of two shoe boxes could provide plenty of stand alone power for a large home including heat, air conditioning, appliances, lighting, etc. There would be no need for power lines and poles criss-crossing the country or for power generating plants. What would happen to the economy of the OPEC countries who depend on oil income? Steve and Tim have contacted Mensa economists and the Secretary of State has sent us his views through the President's office. The general consensus is that they can't say for sure. They agree that it would take several years and be a gradual transition to the new motor. There would be a need for gas stations for 5 to 10 years in the future. We would start out providing motors for new cars only. When production is able to meet that demand we can start producing for retrofits. We should consider licensing present internal combustion manufacturers to produce our engines which would protect their employees jobs. We could then, after we take care of our auto industry, license our true friends in the world to produce the motors in their country. I'm talking about countries like Australia, UK and Canada to begin with. We might be surprised at the countries that would become our friends if they didn't have to depend on Russia for their oil.

A two hour discussion of the subject followed with many questions being raised and few answers. They decided it was paramount to keep the aircraft power source top secret for the foreseeable future. They also agreed it would be wise to hold off on a power source for homes and commercial businesses until the auto industry was running smoothly. They agreed to another meeting after Steve and Tim had the facility in Michigan able to produce motors. Following lunch they all left and went their own way. Scott caught a helicopter to the island, Skip met Beth to house hunt and Steve and Tim went back to their projects.

Something bad was about to happen, he could feel it. Everything had gone very smooth, too smooth. Things just don't work that way. What was that saying? Forewarned was forearmed. If something bad was about to happen, why not try to figure out what, where, when and by who.

Think, where was the most likely place trouble would come from? It had to be terrorist as governments were beginning to co-operate with the United Nations, finally. What would the crisis be about? What was the worst thing? It had to be either a nuclear or biological weapon in the hands of terrorists and no question about their plans to use it. That was it. He felt certain that was it.

After sleeping over night he still felt the same way in the morning. He called skip and left a message for him at the hotel where he and Beth were staying, compliments of the Company. Thirty minutes later Skip called.

"Hello Scott. We just returned from breakfast and found your message."

"I need to see you right away Skip. Can you get away for a few hours? I'll have you back there this afternoon."

"Of course Scott, you sound concerned."

"The helicopter is waiting for you at the Company."

"On my way. Bye."

Skip landed shortly after 10:00am. Scott met him and asked the helicopter crew to return at 3:00pm to return Skip to the mainland. A large pitcher of iced tea was waiting for them by the pool, thanks to Scott. As they settled in chairs Skip said nothing, waiting for Scott to begin the conversation.

"Skip, I have a very strong premonition that something terribly bad is about to happen if we don't do something about it. It is so strong that it's eerie. I believe it has to do with terrorists who have a weapon of mass destruction, either nuclear or biological. We have to do something, now, before it's too late. I'm not asking you for intel, but you can at least tell me if I should call the President on the secure coded line."

They sat in silence for a few moments before Skip said, "Let me use your secure phone to make some well placed calls. I can at least see if there is cause for alarm."

"Thanks Skip. I appreciate that."

He placed one call and gave the person on the other end one hour to get back to him. That one person put another dozen with the right connections on full throttle to gather fact and rumor.

"The wheels are turning Scott, they'll call back in an hour."

"Thanks Skip. It's too strong a feeling to ignore."

An hour later the phone rang. It was for General Hathcock. Skip spoke for just a few minutes then hung up the phone. He walked back to where Scott was sitting.

"Make your call Scott, then call the chopper for me please. I'll be heading to Washington as soon as possible. All I can say is, I'm glad you didn't ignore your feelings."

Scott made the call immediately to the number the President had given him. A voice said "GO". Scott responded "HAND." The voice said "State your message." He explained his premonition and offered the services of Piot in any capacity that would be helpful then hung up the phone.

Five minutes later the scrambler phone rang again and Scott answered. A voice said, "Please accompany General Hathcock to Washington at the earliest." Then line then went dead.

After Scott called for the helicopter and arranged for a Company plane to Washington they both were ready to leave. Skip found Beth and she promised to have a bag packed and waiting for him at the Company jet hanger. They were in the air on the way to Washington at 12:20 pm.

An Air Force car and driver met them at the executive jet facility at the Washington airport and drove them straight to the Whitehouse where they were shown to the situation room. They were the last two to arrive.

After showing their ID to two Marines guarding the door they were allowed to enter. It was a meeting of the highest order. Present, besides the President, were the other Chiefs of Staff, Secretary of Defense and Chairman of the Joint Chiefs. Except for the President and the Secretary of Defense all were military. Now, add one more civilian, Scott Wilson.

"Gentlemen," the President began. "I asked Mr. Wilson to attend this meeting because he has direct communication to Piot. During his trip from Florida this afternoon he gave permission to reveal that to you. I don't need to tell you that information does not leave this room but, I will anyway. That information gets the highest classification, Cosmic. It does not leave this room."

When Skip and Scott were seated the Secretary of defense took over the meeting.

"We have a lot of traffic and excited voices that terrorists have a weapon of mass destruction and are preparing to use it. We don't know where or when or who. We need all assets on this at once. The FBI, CIA and NSA have been briefed as well as other law enforcement agencies and Interpol. We have also notified other countries who could be targets. As I said, we need hard intel and we need it now."

The meeting lasted fifteen minutes with everyone working together to coordinate their intelligence services. This was no time for territory squabbles and they all knew it. When the meeting was over Scott was wondering why he was asked to attend. He was about to find out.

He was the last to leave the room and as he did was handed a note by a security agent. All it said was, please follow this man. He did so and was soon at a familiar looking door. The agent knocked twice then opened the door and stood aside for Scott to enter. Yes, it was a familiar door, the same one he used when he entered the Oval Office the night of the cocktail party.

"Yes Mr. President?" said Scott.

"As you can see Scott, we have a major problem here. I asked you to join the meeting so you could see the gravity of the situation. Is there anything in Piot's arsenal that can help us?"

"We'll attempt to contact Piot as soon as we get back to Florida Mr. President. I will notify you as soon as we do."

"Thank you Scott."

When he left the oval office he found Skip waiting for him in the foyer

"Are you heading back to Florida now"

"Yes, the plane is ready to go and so am I."

"I have a driver waiting outside for you. I had the feeling you'd waste no time getting back to the island. Good luck Scott, I'll let Beth know we are tied up for awhile."

"Thanks Skip, and good luck to you."

It was a fast trip to the airport. When he boarded the crew had filed their flight plan and were calling for taxi clearance which came in the form of "Citation two four Romeo Charlie is cleared to taxi runway 16." The ATIS had given them the active runway, altimeter setting and winds. They had also received their flight plan clearance.

"Roger ground, two four Romeo Charlie taxiing."

When they reached the end of the runway they called tower and reported ready for takeoff.

"Citation two four Romeo Charlie you are cleared for takeoff, maintain runway heading to ten thousand, report reaching then cleared on course."

"Roger, Romeo Charlie."

A very short time later, "Departure control, Citation two four Romeo Charlie, ten thousand turning on course request frequency change."

"Frequency change approved Romeo Charlie."

Scott settled back in his seat and picked up the satellite phone to call Beth on her cell phone.

"Hello," she answered.

"Hi. Are you free for dinner this evening?"

"Where are you?"

"I'll be landing about seven thirty. Can you meet me at the hanger?"

"Oh, that's good news and I'd love to have dinner. I'll be waiting at the hangar when you arrive."

He then called Steve. After a few pleasantries Scott got to the reason for the call. "We have a situation and I could sure use your help, yours and Tim's. I can't tell you anymore now for security reasons except that we'll be wearing our suits."

Steve knew he was talking about pressure suits, not business suits. "We'll take the chopper out first thing in the morning. Beth is meeting me at the hanger at seven thirty. If you and Tim can meet me I'll give you both a briefing then. Beth and I are going to dinner but I'm sure you and Tim will have a lot to do."

"See you at the hangar," said Steve and hung up.

Scott then called Tim and had a similar conversation. He too will be at the hangar.

Both Steve and Tim had a very high respect for Scott. They felt he was extremely capable and competent in anything he chose to do. He was a man's man, a person who you considered it an honor to call a friend. Even though Scott had joined the Company long after them there was no jealousy or bad feelings whatsoever. Quite the contrary. They had great admiration for him. From his conversation, or lack of it, they both knew another combat mission was about to happen. Because of their confidence in his abilities and their feelings for him they would not refuse to go.

When the plane arrived at the hanger Scott saw the three of them waiting for him. As he deplaned, Beth left the group and returned to her car to wait for him. She was very astute he thought. She knew he would want to talk to Steve and Tim alone.

"Thanks for meeting me guys. I'll get right to the point. The terrorists claim they have a weapon of mass destruction and are about to use it. We don't know what the weapon is or where they plan to use it. All the free world governments are on full alert as well as the military, law enforcement agencies, coast guard and homeland security forces. All we know has been picked up from communications among terrorist groups and there has been a very high volume of traffic. There is an excitement in the communications. Time is critical in finding the weapon. If you agree to go with me our mission is intelligence eaves-dropping to find answers. If you have any improvements to equipment that will help us, we'll have tomorrow to install it. I don't anticipate any combat, just intelligence gathering. And, we'll be gone several days so supplies will be needed. This is strictly a volunteer mission but I need your answer now."

Almost in unison they replied. "Of course we'll go, don't even think of going without us."

"I'd like to take the chopper over later tonight with some equipment we'll need. I can start installing it tonight," said Tim.

"Me too," said Steve. "How about I meet you at the chopper pad at ten o'clock? Will that give you the time you need Tim?"

Scott just looked at them as he saw their excitement. "You guys are the greatest," he said as he turned and walked to the car where Beth was waiting.

He slid behind the wheel and turned to just look at her. "It's so good to see you," he said as he kissed her lightly on the lips. Someday, if the world settles down, he was going to have to get serious about this woman he thought. There hasn't been time for romance. Good things take time he thought.

They went to a small restaurant known for their excellent steaks and had a quiet dinner talking about her house hunting. Nothing was said concerning why her father had stayed in Washington or what was going on with Tim and Steve, she knew better than to ask. As they drove toward the Company, Scott went by the helicopter pad and saw Tim and Steve loading equipment. He stopped, got out of the car and visited with them a few minutes. When he returned to the car she knew what he was going to say but, before he could say it she was out of the car and retrieved his bag from the trunk and took it to him.

"Mental telepathy?" he said.

" It is scary how I can read your mind sometimes," she responded.

He took her in his arms and gave her a long but tender kiss. He then turned and walked to the chopper noting that Steve and Tim had everything loaded and were inside. He climbed in and the chopper lifted off and turned toward the island into a black night.

Beth stood where he had released her watching them disappear thinking, oh why did I have to fall so hard for this wonderful man as a tear rolled down her cheek. She knew the answer though, it was because he was such a wonderful man.

CHAPTER TWENTY-NINE

S teve and Tim worked on the ship until three in the morning while Scott made numerous phone calls to anyone who he thought could provide helpful information. All three hit the sack very tired men.

During breakfast the next morning they discussed the mission profile and objectives. They stocked the ship with provisions for seven days. This included food, water and other necessities. When they finished all the mission preparation they relaxed by the pool and later tried to sleep before their 10:00 p.m. takeoff time. None slept well in anticipation of the importance of the mission.

At exactly 10:00, p.m. they lifted off with weapons pod attached, closed the hanger doors and climbed toward an overcast sky on a very dark night. Soon the overcast became an under cast and the sky was ablaze with stars as they climbed to 150 miles high.

Tim was the first to speak. "We are approaching that piece of space junk soon Scott. As we planned, the time is near to try out your new toy. Turn your weapons selector to laser, go magnification on cross hairs, target at 027 degrees from our nose.

Soon there it was. Scott centered the cross hairs and pulled the trigger on the flight control stick. A pencil of light left the aircraft as they watched the magnified target on the holographic projection. The target was a fuel booster tank which quickly became a fire ball as the remaining fuel exploded from the heat of the laser. The new toy was an instant success.

"All right," yelled Tim. "If there are missiles in the air, we have a chance to get them without getting too close and blowing ourselves up too."

"Good job Tim," said Steve and Scott. "That's a relief to know we can knock them out from a safe distance," continued Scott.

When they arrived over the border between Afghanistan and Pakistan they remained stationary over a rugged mountain area and when it got dark gradually descended until they could pick up audio on their listening device. Steve and Tim had worked on extending the range. The improvement had increased the range to 10 miles. They turned the ship edge on to the ground which made them impossible to see with the naked eye. They descended lower and used their daylight radar and infrared capabilities. They had been picking up voices all day but nothing associated with any terrorist activities. They slowly moved up the border scanning several miles on each side and in the valleys.

"I'm picking up some of our guys Scott," said Tim. "Head up a little further, we should pick them up visually."

"There they are," said Steve. "Looks like about thirty five of them walking up that ridge. OH JESUS! They're walking into an ambush. Look at the side of that hill, its crawling with bad guys."

"Scan your com Tim and find their frequency, fast. We have to warn them," said Scott urgently.

"Got em Scott. Talk to them," responded Tim.

"U.S. troops moving up a ridge on the border, this is Friendly, over." No answer.

"U.S. troops northeast of Asadabad moving up a ridge, come in. You're walking into an ambush. This is Friendly, over."

"Who are you Friendly?" was the reply.

"This is Friendly. You are walking into an ambush up the ridge ahead of you. Turn your computer on and we'll relay our picture down to you. Our comm man will talk to you now."

Steve and Tim worked the com and forwarded the infrared picture to their computer.

"Ground this is Friendly. Do you see them now?"

"Yah., we see them. Man, we'd have been dead meat. Who the hell are you and where are you?"

"Move back to that pile of boulders you came through. They may have night scopes and are watching you now so move slowly and back. If you high tail it they may open fire. When you get there hunker down because we're going to drop CBU's. There will be a lot of steel flying through the air so protect yourselves, over"

"Roger Friendly. I don't know who you are but, thanks."

"Let me know when you're protected."

"Will do."

"Okay guys, the bombing is all yours," said Scott. "Figure the pattern and go for simultaneous detonation from a release of 5,000 feet. We have plenty of bombs so use what you need."

It took them about fifteen seconds to calculate the pattern and program the computer. These guys knew computers. "We're ready Scott."

Three minutes later ground called. "Friendly this is ground. We're covered."

"Drop them when ready guys."

"You drop Steve," said Tim. "You missed the last trip."

"BOMBS AWAY," yelled Steve.

"Ground, we have bombs away," transmitted Scott. "Keep your heads down."

The result was complete destruction of everything on the ridge. Nothing living could have survived.

"Ground this is Friendly, you guys okay?" radioed Scott.

"This is ground Friendly. Wow, that was really something."

"We have no movement ahead of your ground. You're clear to move into the area. We need you to look for papers, papers of any kind. If you find them get them to your command center as soon as possible. Call in a chopper to get them back."

"Will do Friendly and thanks for the help."

They moved further north into mountainous terrain where the many caves concealed the enemy. With no moon and an overcast sky it was a very black night. It reminded Scott of another very black night when an enemy guard lost his life instead of Scott when the guard lighted a cigarette revealing his position.

"I installed another weapon that might come in handy if we find some caves to explore," said Tim. "I haven't had time to fully test it so we might as well put it to a combat test."

"Okay", replied Scott. "We have everything on that might reveal a hot cave and we're only 100 yards from the side of the mountain."

Thirty minutes and two mountains later Steve called out. "I have a hot one at ten o'clock. There is a heat source showing on the scope. I can't identify it but it's definitely a heat source. Let's hold and watch it."

"Roger," said Scott. How nice it was he thought, to be able to remain stationery in the air with no noise. It was a great advantage over a helicopter whose engine could be heard from a considerable distance.

With their daylight scope they could make out a small opening in the side of the mountain. They waited for ten minutes with no change.

"I'd like to try out the other new weapon Scott," said Tim. "This might be the perfect test for it. Steve and I have been working on miniaturization of the propulsion system as well as audio and video capability. We call this first part of it a Scout. It's the size of a 38 caliber slug and we control the flight from a small control stick in here. It makes no sound and can relay both audio and video to us on a screen which we can transfer to the holographic projection. It also has a small sheathed needle containing enough poison for ten injections causing death within five seconds. In addition it has a self destruct capability in case we lose control."

"The other weapon we designed," chimed in Steve, "is called the Bang. It's the size of a medium sized pancake but two inches thick and packs the explosive force of ten hand grenades. We have flight control and screen viewing the same as the Scout. We see the scout showing us where the bad guys are then the Bang detonates in the middle of them after the Scout has made it to safety."

"This I have to see," said Scott. "Go ahead and see what's inside the cave."

Scott had no doubt that anything Tim and Steve came up with would work perfectly.

A small door the size of a quarter opened on the bottom of the ship under the flight crew station. From it appeared a small object shaped like a bullet. It hovered momentarily then moved toward the cave following the commands of Tim. It stopped just outside the cave while Tim adjusted the audio and video then proceeded forward entering the mouth of the cave.

The faint light shown from deep inside as the Scout moved slowly toward the source. After a ninety degree right turn the light was brighter and a faint sound could be heard. Steve hooked the voice translator to the audio so the voices would be heard in English. Suddenly the picture turned to a group of people sitting around a cook stove. There was a vent pipe going straight up venting the cook smoke to somewhere.

Scattered about the room were AK-47 assault rifles, rocket propelled grenades, boxes of ammunition, communication equipment and more boxes of something that could have been food or explosives. They were talking about how many Americans they were going to kill before they themselves would die. They did not mind dying as long as they could kill at least one American first.

"Let's see if there is another room off this one," said Tim. He kept the Scout in the shadows and moved it slowly around the room. Bingo! There was another. He entered a narrow hallway and carefully moved along one wall where it turned ninety degrees to the left and there was the room. There were fewer men in this room and they were discussing a map on the floor in front of them. They appeared to be the leaders and the language translator revealed they were planning an attack for tomorrow.

Around the room went the Scout looking for yet another room. Nothing. This cave had two rooms housing twenty-seven enemy, a sizeable cache of weapons and a group planning an attack. The Scout returned to ship, entered and parked itself in it's storage bin.

"One Bang for each room should be enough," said Steve as two Bangs exited the ship from a port the size of a plate. Steve controlled them both moving very carefully to avoid detection. He moved to the second room where he placed the first Bang on the low ceiling directly over the men. The second was moved into the first room and positioned against the wall over the heads of the largest group of men.

"We're in position and ready to detonate Scott," whispered Steve.

Scott moved out to a more than safe distance in case the explosion revealed there was more material than they saw.

"Okay, we're a safe distance away, touch them off when you're ready."

There was a tremendous explosion. Fire shot out the mouth of the cave and another spot 25 yards further up the mountain. That must be where the stove vented. There was no reason to send a Scout into the cave to verify the results, nothing in the cave could have survived. There were secondary explosions that continued for several minutes. They moved on looking for other caves.

They found seven more caves with the same result. Some had a greater number of enemy and some less. They were careful to confirm there were no women or children, only male enemy. The fifth cave they found was the most gratifying.

They sent in two Scouts and found five rooms. Four of the rooms held five to fifteen men each. The fifth room contained a huge supply of food, weapons, explosives and ammunition. The room was thirty feet long and twenty feet wide. The ceiling was fifteen feet high and stacked to the top with supplies. The entire room was packed. To be sure everything was destroyed, they place three Bangs in this room and one in each of the other four. They gave this one plenty of room before detonating the Bangs, it was good they did. The entire side of the mountain blew away. There was nothing left of the cave or it's rooms. Could that have been where the weapon was that all were looking for?

"You both amaze me", said Scott. "When have you found time to miniaturize magnetic propulsion? And in addition mating them with miniature audio and visual plus making them weapons. Just look at the damage we have done without risking our own necks. All of this, the ship, the weapons, none of this would be possible without you. The world owes you a debt of gratitude."

"We make a pretty good threesome", said Steve.

Before first light they climbed to 150 miles, ate dinner then reclined their seats and slept. All anti-collision and system detectors were activated. They would sleep and return to the mountain area that night for more cave hunting.

That night they found nine more caves occupied by the enemy and the following night only five. The cave hunting had proved to be most successful. They had hurt the Taliban and sent a message that their caves were no longer safe. It was all on video which had been sent to Mr. R who in turn saw the appropriate intelligence agencies received a copy. "Without these scouts and bangs we could never have done it," said Tim.

They set course for home and arrived just as the night covered their island allowing them to land in secrecy. After the usual post flight they stretched out in the living room with a cold Bahamas beer.

"This time we're going to wait until tomorrow to make our reports. I think we need time to reflect on what we accomplished over the last few days. We are a one of a kind vehicle with one of a kind weapons system that made it possible. This is a huge burden of responsibility we carry. We must be careful that we don't go beyond a line, a line that goes further than good, just, moral with the good of the people always in the forefront. Sometimes I feel like we're playing God and that worries me."

The three sat thinking about Scott's words while sipping their beer. One by one they left the living room and went to bed. A complete mission report was sent to the President and Mr. R the next morning. He would soon receive a complete report on any intel they had. There was nothing to do now but wait. As it turned out the excitement over the terrorist communication network had stopped. Someone had neutralized whatever it was that had excited them and no one was talking.

The next morning Tim And Steve went back to the mainland on the supply helicopter. Scott took the boat out to his favorite reef, dropped anchor and spent the rest of the morning swimming and laying under the Bimini canvass in deep thought. He thought about his life before the island and his life since. He thought about the people that now depended on him and the tremendous responsibility that went with that. Life was no longer simple with just a few concerns such as his children, his responsibility to his clients and the community. Now a huge Company and all it's people were depending on him to make the right decisions. The entire planet was trying to track him down to know who was responsible for the many missions he had flown. Who was it making the decision to destroy selected targets in the name of eliminating evil and at the same time killing or maiming many. He suddenly felt a tremendous weight on his shoulders. Was he capable of that weight? He needed to find the answer to that question.

CHAPTER THIRTY

When he returned to the house he called Beth and arranged a flight to the island for her that afternoon. She was greatly relieved to hear his voice.

After her arrival they sat on the edge of the pool with their legs in the water. They didn't need words as they held hands but Scott needed to talk. He wanted to tell her about his thoughts. He not only respected her comments but sought them. Their future was together.

So he began. He told her what he had been thinking and the thoughts that kept him awake at night. It took awhile as he chose his words carefully to let her know exactly how he felt. She said nothing but listened..

When he was finished he looked at her and saw tears running down her cheeks. "I'm sorry", he said, "I didn't mean to upset you."

"These are tears of relief. I was so worried that you might be coming addicted to combat which is not unusual. Some get an adrenalin high that they need and can't stop until they too are killed. I am so relieved to hear the way you feel and know you are not that way. I love you for the feelings you have. In time there will be others who will take your place and it will be hard for you to watch from the sidelines but, you will know that is the way it has to be. Until then, the world needs you to protect it from the evil doers."

A warm lingering kiss with deep feelings followed. There was truly love in those feelings.

CHAPTER THIRTY-ONE

The next morning Scott was awakened by the ringing of the phone. It was Skip calling asking if he was watching the news. He turned it on and was shocked by what he saw. Russia had attacked and invaded Georgia, a former border satellite country favoring the West and eager to join NATO. Scott and Skip talked about the why. One very obvious reason was oil. The other was the head of Russia's political force, Sutin, a former KGB big shot and eager to return Russia to the cold war days. They want their former satellite countries back under Russia control.

"Have to go Scott, emergency meeting in the situation room." The phone went dead.

Scott made an iced tea and sat by the pool to think about the situation. What could Piot do to diffuse the crisis? If he threatened Russia he would also have to threaten the United States and other Western countries or the world would think Piot was the US. He could warn the U.S. and the West to stay out of it or face consequences themselves. He could then take action against Russia if they do not withdraw. What those actions would be needed much thought. A plan was starting to form. Two hours and two more glasses of iced tea later he had a plan in rough form. He faxed it to Mr. R on a secure line. Mr. R replied a short time later with the words, DO IT!

Scott contacted Steve and Tim and asked them to meet him at his office tomorrow morning at 8:00a.m.. He would fly back tonight giving him time to refine the plan.:

At 8:00a.m. the next morning the three were at the conference table with Scott speaking.

"I asked you to meet me because of the Russian situation. I have a plan that I want to go over with you because if implemented I need your help. We will discuss the plan first then I will hear your comments and your decision whether or not you will go with me."

Three hours later the meeting was over with Tim and Steve having agreed whole- heartedly to go. They liked the plan and want at least two days to go over the bird and its systems, including weapons. It was important that everything work perfectly because the flight could get very hairy.

Before they left for the island they made a tape with Scott dressed as usual when taping. They warned Russia to withdraw immediately or pay severe consequences. They also warned other countries to stay away except for humanitarian help. This would include food, water, blankets, cots, tents even port-a-potties.

The next two days were 12 hour days and ended with all systems a go. The weapons pod was configured to give them every weapon they thought they could possibly need. The third day was spent catching up on sleep as takeoff was scheduled for dark time that evening.

It seemed that suddenly it was time. They were wearing space suits, strapped securely in their seats, the preflight done, weapons systems warmed up and checked again and the weapons pod attached. It was now dark hour and with a "everyone all set" they lifted off.

Russia was feeling the outrage from the rest of the world for its invading Georgia. They entered into a cease fire and withdrawal agreement but instead were sending in more troops and advancing further into the country. It was now time to show them that this action is unacceptable. Other former Russian satellite countries were very nervous wondering who would be next.

When they planned this attack they discussed taking out all of Russia's front line fighters and bombers. This would have to be done over several nights and the response was unpredictable. But taking out three should be a less violent response,

Their first target was the air base at Zhukovsky near Moscow where the Russians were meeting the next day with representatives from two countries to show them the best aircraft Russia had to offer. On the parking ramp were three turboprop Tu-95 MS Bear long range nuclear delivery bombers, three supersonic Tupolev Tu-160 White Swan nuclear delivery bombers code named Blackjack by NATO and three SU Flanker SU-30 fighters representing their best. Each set of three was lined up abreast with a space between each set. The plan was to take out the middle aircraft of each of the sets. This would show that they could have taken out all the aircraft but choose to show their precision strike capability and to serve as a warning to them to back off Georgia.

"OK guys, target in 5 minutes. No change in the plans. Tim on laser, Steve on back-up missile and video tape. Are you both a go?"

"Roger", they answered in unison.

Five minutes later they were over the aircraft parking ramp at 35,000 feet and looking at nine beautiful aircraft parked in three rows of three. They were ready to exit fast if detected but all was quiet and the ramp well lighted for security purposes.

"OK Tim, you're the man. You're cleared to fire when ready and remember guys, on the third shot we go into a fast climb. We don't want to risk a reflection of us off the fires".

Tim put the cross hairs on the fuselage of the turboprop Bear bomber. The laser was fully charged and ready for a deadly blast. He took a deep breath and let it out slowly then squeezed the trigger. He moved quickly to the supersonic Blackjack bomber and repeated the same prefire and squeeze, then to the SU 30 Flanker. No sooner had he fired the third shot than they were in a rapid climb pulling 6 plus G's. Steve was whooping and hollering during the climb.

"I know you guys were too busy to watch but he nailed all three right where planned. Beautiful shooting Tim. I'm replaying the video on the holographic screen now. Here it is, WOW, you squashed them, absolutely perfect. You broke the back of that Bear, and look at the Blackjack, it must have had a fuselage tank right where you hit it. I'm afraid there's collateral damage to the two on each side of him. Whoops, there goes the Flanker. Must have been full of fuel the way it blew. I'm thinking more collateral damage. Oh well, what the heck. We tried, they just parked them too close together. "

"I'd score it a ten on all three shots Tim", said Scott. "Now on to Georgia. Let's hope those tanks are still where the satellite pictures showed them to be. We'll know soon enough. The autopilot has the program running so cross your fingers. It will save us a lot of time if there is no change."

Thirty minutes later they were deep inside Georgia sitting over a tank that was the furthest inside the border. The plan was to heat the tank gun barrel with the laser with the intent of heating it so it would droop and be useless.

"Okay Tim, lock on the barrel and see what happens. Roll the video and timer Steve."

In five seconds it looked like the barrel had ED. The tank crew was scrambling out of their tent as the barrel must have made a load BANG when it landed on the tank body.

"What do you think those guys are saying about the barrel. They have to be scratching their heads trying to figure it out. Good shot Tim, now on to the next."

The autopilot was programmed with the GPS to fly to each tank in the shortest order. It took them two hours but they droop-barreled every tank shown on the satellite photos. They hoped the locals would get a chuckle seeing the Big Bad Russian Bear with useless tanks. Of course they still had their other weapons but they must be a bit embarrassed over their mighty tank.

"Time to head home guys with one small stop first. We need to pay our friend Chavez in Venezuela a visit. The Russians flew two of their Blackjack supersonic bombers there to impress anyone they could. I hate to destroy such a beautiful airplane but, Chavez has no peaceful purpose for buying them. I hope Russia financed them so they might get into a squabble over who owned them at the time of their destruction. I think Chavez will lose as he doesn't want to annoy the bad Bear but, I also feel he'll think twice about spending that kind of money for something that's going to be rubble shortly after landing. We need to convince him of that. This time Steve you're the man. Send two missiles into each of the birds. We have an hour and a half to target so let's do our after action reports and forward them and the video to Mr. R. I know he's waiting for them."

"My pleasure," replied Steve with a big grin

Before they knew it the reports were done and sent to Mr. R along with the video. A short message came back from him, "Well Done".

"Welcome to the skies over El Libertador, the main Air Force base of the Venezuelan military. Relay your scope to the holographic up front Steve so Tim and I can watch your shooting accuracy. They have a few F-16s, OV-10, King Air, Mirages, helicopters and look over at the south ramp. That's quite a conglomeration of old birds in a graveyard. Kind of sad isn't it? Well, the sooner we finish the sooner we can get home. If you have everything you need Steve the show is yours."

"Roger, selecting and arming missiles now, coordinates have been entered and picture memory entered into the missile noses. Here we go! Two missiles away on the north Blackjack and....two away on the south one. It won't take long. Contact NOW....and again Now! Scratch two Blackjacks."

"Right on Steve, remind me never to get into a shooting match with either one of you. You both are deadly. Anybody ready for a Kalik and bed?"

The next day they made a video for the news media and sent it out. As in the past Scott warned of retaliation against any aggressor and any country arming itself when there was no reason for it. He would love to have a bug planted in the Kremlin and hear the yelling. Then he thought…why not?

The press had a field day with pictures of the tanks with their main gun drooping as a man with erectile dysfunction. The local population was laughing and pointing causing the soldiers to hide inside their tanks. The mighty Russian bear was embarrassed.

CHAPTER THIRTY-TWO

R ussia is getting rich with their government-owned oil sales. European countries who depend on them for their oil don't want to do anything to antagonize them. They are afraid of the consequences if they disagree with anything Russia is doing. They need Russian oil.

Scott made three phone calls that were very similar in content and results. These were to the Board Chairmen's of Chrysler, Ford and General Motors. All three of these auto companies were on the brink of extinction if some miracle didn't happen soon. Scott convinced them that a meeting might produce the miracle they were hoping for. A meeting date and place in Michigan was agreed upon and Scott put his plan in motion.

The R Company had been testing a Chrysler 300, a Lincoln Continental Town Car and a Cadillac sedan with the electro magnetic motor. They each had over 150,000 miles on them with only tire and brake changes. These would be used as demos for the three

Chairmen. All three agreed to be picked up by a chauffer driven car produced by their Company. What they didn't know was that the engines had been removed and replaced with the electro magnetic engine. The meeting would take place at the R Company's new manufacturing plant. Scott asked Mr. R to run the meeting. He refused saying that this was Scott, Steve and Tim's show and the auto people should meet the new era regime. The meeting was planned for next Wednesday.

As the meeting drew near the final touches were put on the dog and pony show. Three of the R Company engineers familiar with the motor would drive the three cars and plan to arrive at the plant at the same time. They would have two way communications between the cars. A screen was installed in the back seat so a DVD could be played explaining in general terms the working of the motor while they were driving to the meeting. That would get the basics out of the way first.

The first pickup was Cliff Barrow of General Motors as he was the furthest away. Patrick Lane, the engineer driver parked in front and after entering asked the receptionist to let Mr. Barrow know his car was waiting. Patrick opened the rear door for Cliff to enter then walked around front and got in the driver's seat.

The first thing Cliff said as they pulled away was, "Why didn't you drive a new model? Can't the R Company afford it"?

Patrick couldn't help but laugh aloud as he replied. "Yes Mr. Barrow but, we have 150,000 miles on this one and it's hard to get that many miles on a new model just out. I will start a DVD which will explain the basics of why the meeting and a brief explanation of the motor. I am an engineer who has worked with the motor and can answer questions after the DVD unless you have a question before I turn it on."

"I'll watch the DVD first and we'll go on from there."

"Yes Sir, then here it comes."

It was about a ten minute recording which had Cliff's rapt attention. "My Heavens, is this thing really for real? You have it installed in this car and have put 150,000 miles on it with no problems?"

"Only brakes and tires Mr. Barrow. It certainly is quiet isn't it? Just for a demonstration I'll accelerate as if passing to show there is plenty of power."

Cliff was pressed into the back of the seat. "I see what you mean. It has plenty of get up go. How does it work other than the explanation that it is electro magnetic?"

"Basically a magnet drives the generator which produces all the electricity this car could ever need. It's more complicated than that but the engineering explanation is proprietary. The entire motor is a sealed unit with certain parts being destroyed if opened by other than a factory with a code. We want time for you three US auto makers to recover and help the economy by not laying off employees. We feel that a car that comes with a 100,000 mile guarantee of never having to fuel it will be very desirable. We want you to satisfy the US consumers before you ship any overseas. The first thing they will do is try to tear the motor apart to see how it works and with the safeguard it won't do them any good. The car is entirely electric Mr. Barrow."

"Are you saying we can make our cars as big a size as we want with as many accessories and options and the cost to operate would be no more that a small sports car?"

"That's correct Sir. Another interesting fact is that the 10 quickest cars in 2007 from zero to 60 miles per hour took 5.1 seconds to 5.9 seconds. This is pretty much the same for 2008. This big fella will do it in 5.2 seconds. Can't you see the face on some sports car driver when he can't beat this in a race to the next stop light? I don't recommend doing that but I do have first hand knowledge that their mouths hang open."

Each car gave their estimated time of arrival over their two way radio and increased or decreased their speed accordingly. They had big grins on their faces as they entered the plant parking lot at the same time. They pulled up parallel to each other, opened the rear doors and raised the hood so their people could see the motor. All three were shaking their heads as the motor was much smaller than the customary engine.

"We don't need to make them with a gas tank." One of them yelled. "We'll save money there."

Then they all started talking at once and laughing. Their mood had changed. Maybe there was indeed hope at the end of the tunnel. They were escorted into the conference room and at the front was a motor on a wheeled cart. Scott stepped up beside the motor and introduced himself then they shook hands.

"Thank you for coming gentlemen," he started, "I trust you all had an enjoyable and quiet ride over. I would like to introduce you to Steve and Tim who are responsible for the development of the electro magnetic motor. They have their names on a number of patents and are an amazing pair." They shook hands all around.

"We think this motor can be a big help in the recovery of the U.S. automobile market," continued Scott. You no longer have to be concerned with emissions control, gas mileage or even gas tanks in the cars. We'll look at our manufacturing plant here shortly but we are already producing these motors on a limited basis. It is our plan to meet with the manufacturers of your present engines and discuss licensing them to manufacture the motor. We can also use some of their subcontractors to manufacture parts for them. We'll do whatever we can to maintain job employment. The R Company already has several plants here in Michigan producing various items. When the time comes they will also be able to manufacture conversion models. Once the motor manufactures are able to satisfy your needs and after market needs they can then start producing for the export market to countries that we have not licensed. In other words, the U.S. comes first then, our friends and never our enemies. You will have a monopoly for several years."

"We hired two well respected economists to complete studies of the effect of this engine on the economy of the U.S. and the world. The opinion for the U.S. is that the effect of the engine will be gradual over the years. Business will adapt as they did with the coming of the auto and the air carrier industries. The horseless carriages converted to building auto bodies and as we know the railroads are expanding with container hauling and high speed passenger service. We also have few homes heated with coal thanks to natural gas and oil. It is interesting to note that before the auto came, New York City had 750,000 horses and what to do with all the manure was a huge problem. The automobile solved that problem. The world will solve the global warming concern as there will be fewer pollutants injected into the air."

"The oil producing countries of the middle east will still have a demand for oil but not to the degree they have now. Dubai is going after the tourist business even as we speak.

Others won't have the extra money to support terrorism and they will be competing with each other for the sale of oil. This will be a refreshing shoe on the other foot. Their royalty may not be able to have a mansion in every resort and the customized aircraft to get there. The US will be able to produce the oil it needs so no need to import. More and more oil is used in the production of other products which count into the many thousands."

They toured the plant, answered a multitude of questions, gave cost estimates, production quantity and time to ship. The three executives were ready to leave just before noon. They wanted to know if they could keep their cars for demo to the board of directors and other officers. They received permission to take the cars and the three left excited as little kids with a new toy. They planned lunch and for the first time they were working together.

There was much work to do yet such as meeting with and licensing the engine manufacturers. These are things others could do that would not involve Scott. He was looking forward to reporting to Mr. R of the positive reaction from the three executives. There was also much to be done in preparation for the upcoming meeting at the Bahamas Atlantis Hotel and Resort. Ahhh the Bahamas, it was time to get back to them and Beth. However, a problem was about to raise its ugly head. It came by a phone call from George Hutcher.

"Hello Scott. Call it my CIA training or just my lack of trust of certain people but, I bugged the three cars you loaned the CEO's of the auto manufacturers. One car made an interesting call to the White House Secretary of State, Secretary Painter. They and certain politicos in congress have very large investments in the oil industry and will talk of ways to put a stop to your plans for the engine. Physical convincing is not ruled out."

"Thanks George, see if you can discover the names of the players. If you need additional manpower hire it. I would like to give the Secretary the option of selling all his stock and retiring immediately. He was a good man in the past but growing older and greed has changed him. He got carried away with his own power. I'll see you in Florida."

That problem would have to wait as he was meeting Beth for dinner and didn't want anything on his mind but her. She had found a house for her and her father and was very excited. Dad would be down tomorrow to put his stamp of approval on it then they would all fly to the island for the weekend. Life was good, for now.

CHAPTER THIRTY-THREE

S cott, Beth and Skip were joined by Senator Chris Thomas and his lovely wife Pam on the island. They were having a wonderful time swimming, snorkeling and scuba diving. They brought back plenty of lobster, grouper and conch. In the evening they barbequed around the pool with cocktails while bringing the Senator up on the happenings of the Company. After all, he was one of the advisors.

On the second evening BBQ the Senator brought up a bombshell. The current administration was approaching the last year of its second term and the party had approached him to run for the Presidency. He had not given them his answer and wanted to see the reaction of those present. Even though he was fairly young for presidential consideration, he had all of the other qualifications. There was certainly no question of him passing the smell test. The Senator was squeaky clean. He was looking for a running mate with the same qualifications. He wanted their opinions on who that could be. The names they came up with were very interesting and Chris appreciated their input.

Pam had to return home for a child function which left the four of them for steaks on the grill with Kalik beer and rum drinks that evening. The subject of politics came up again. Skip was grilling the steaks, Beth was preparing the conch salad and Scott was bartender when Chris dropped the bomb.

"If I run, and I haven't decided yet, I appreciate your input on a running mate but I have a name in mind of someone I feel would be infinitely qualified and very well prepared to be President if required." They all stopped what they were doing and looked questioningly at him.

"My first choice would be Scott." The steaks were forgotten, the salad making stopped and the rum drink Scott was making was running over the rim with rum. They all looked from Chris to Scott who was speechless.

"Oh, Wow Chris. I appreciate the compliment very much but it is not possible for me to join you. There are things you don't know that makes it impossible." He looked at Skip and Beth and said "I think it is time to tell Chris the why. Do you agree?" They nodded.

"Chris," he began, "since you arrived on the island you have been in a foreign country. The name of that country is Piot." He paused to see the reaction Chris would have but there was no startled look on his face.

He just continued looking at Scott and said, "Why does that not surprise me. When you asked me to pass a note to the President I had the feeling that there was more to this man than meets the eye. When you two walked out of his office with his arm around your shoulder I was further convinced. I didn't know what but, I felt there was now a deep secret between you two."

"Folks, let's finish preparing dinner so we don't burn the steaks and we'll continue this discussion then. Skip and Beth know everything and it is time you should know too, especially if you become President. But, you will know why I can't be your running mate. And, I want you to know that I am deeply honored by your thinking of me."

Scott started at the beginning and told the whole story. Chris held his questions until Scott finished an hour later. Finally Chris spoke. "What you have accomplished for the benefit of all mankind has been nothing short of astounding. I don't look at you as a war monger or think you should be tried as a murderer, quite the contrary. You should be regarded as a hero to the world. Relieve yourself of these concerns. Where would we be today if you had not taken action against these rogue nations? Even though there are still hot spots today the main problem countries are no longer a threat to the world thanks to you. And now, thanks to Steve and Tim and your Company, the world has a revolutionary new engine that does not use fossil fuel and causes no pollution and will substantially cut down on green house gases and global warming. I am proud to be an advisor to your Company as well as your friend."

"Thanks for your comments Chris, they mean a lot me. Now that's settled, I won't drink this drink I made earlier so I can take us all flying tonight after dark. I'm anxious for Chris to experience the wonders of our ship. Would you like to do that Chris?"

"I certainly would.. I am really curious to see what it looks like."

It was very dark when they entered the hangar. They walked all around the ship explaining items of interest before boarding. The explanations continued in the interior until they took their seats. Scott and Skip sat in the two pilot seats while Beth and Chris sat in the passenger seats. So far Chris had said nothing, he just kept shaking his head back and forth in wonder. They opened the clamshell roof and departed climbing into the night. The stars were exceptionally bright tonight as they climbed through scattered alto cumulus clouds.

Since you are our guest Chris, you get to choose our destination. It can be anywhere in the world. It won't take long to get there wherever it is.

"Mentally I'm still back on the ground," replied Chris. "This is amazing. It's science fiction only it's not fiction, it's reality. Where to go? How about a trip down the islands of the Caribbean? I love the islands and the life style of the people."

"Great idea, let's start with Bermuda then the Bahamas then the Turks and Caicos and on down the chain. We'll turn on our daylight feature and present it in holographic 3D in front of us. We can go lower and magnify anything of interest. All anti-collision equipment is turned on so we will have ample warning to avoid any other aircraft headed our way."

The evening was a great success. Everyone enjoyed the tour and was sorry when they headed home and parked the ship in the hangar. Chris was still shaking his head as they entered the house. He was speechless for awhile but gradually recovered as the others started talking about the tour.

The following day they all returned to the mainland by helicopter and went their separate ways agreeing to do it again. Scott, Skip and Beth were all busy with Company business and Chris met Pam in Washington DC and returned to his senate duties. Time passed quickly as they were all very busy.

Unfortunately, during this period of time, the Vice President was taken very ill and his recovery was doubtful. They decided not to replace him as long as there was any hope for recovery. There was a lot of discussion on this decision but the wait and seers won out. The president was reported to be in excellent health so there was not a lot of concern.

This placated feeling was shattered a month later when it was announced that the President had suffered a major stroke and not expected to recover. And, with the Vice President out, that turned the reins of government over to the Speaker of the House of Representatives. Unfortunately Naomi Pulaski was not a favorite personality with the public. She was an egomaniac in the eyes of many and a real dove concerning American security. Congress and the people were concerned that some kind of attack against the Country was imminent with her as President. Someone would test her. The only salvation was that the elections were just seven months away when a new President and Vice President would be elected. It would be a matter of damage control until the new President would take over.

CHAPTER THIRTY-FOUR

"Hello Chris, nice to hear from you. How are things in Washington?" Scott said as he answered the phone on his desk.

"A bit tense Scott. Rumors are flying. We are hearing bits about Chavez's replacement President Maduro and Russia. Keep your feelers in motion. My campaign is progressing well and the numbers are good if you can believe them. November will be here before we know it. I'll be glad when election day is over. This campaigning is tough on the body."

"I'm sure it is. You've got the votes from here. All the employees know you are an advisor to the Company and of course that will have to terminate when you become President."

"Thanks Scott, I appreciate the vote of confidence. Please continue to keep your ear to the ground as we discussed before."

"Will do Chris."

Scott had made sure that all sources of information were on full alert.

The fears of many were soon realized. Intelligence picked up communication traffic between Russia and Venezuela. After a month of following this traffic it was confirmed that a shipment of military hardware was to be shipped to Venezuela. This would require a large transport as the amount of hardware was huge. They would sail under a Liberian flag to make Russia look innocent. There was also talk of a Russian war ship trailing the transport in case of any difficulties. What was meant by difficulties?

Scott called an emergency meeting of Skip, Beth, Tim and Steve at the home of Piot. He did not invite Senator Chris Thomas as it was time to separate him from Piot and the Company. The election was too near to take any chances of tainting his reputation.

Scott started the meeting by bringing them up to date on the latest intelligence. He had a plan but wanted input on their part. He respected their ability to analyze his plan and make suggestions.

"My plan is this," he began. "I will make a video that will go out internationally to all news media. I'll now read the message".

"This is the Country of Piot speaking to you .With the change of Presidents in the United States the security of the world is being tested by Russia and Venezuela. Russia is shipping a large amount of military equipment to Venezuela in a sea going transport under a Liberian flag. The Liberian flag is supposed to disguise their involvement. Russia is also trailing this transport with a fully armed destroyer in case of any difficulties.

I want to make something very clear to the United States, Russia and Venezuela. This shipment will not reach the Country of Venezuela. We will not tolerate any interference on the part of these countries. If it means sinking both the transport and the Russian war ship we will do so. Remember what we did to North Korea and Iran. We will not tolerate a threat to world peace. My Country's survival depends on peace."

"Turn these ships around Russia and send them back to their ports or we can not guarantee the survival of them or their crews. You are gambling with these sailors lives and you have no right to do so. Equipping Venezuela with war materials and putting them in the hands of a mentally deficient person is very dangerous and we will stop it."

"This is the only communication we will issue until this crisis is resolved."

"Okay folks, your comments please whenever you are ready."

"Are you really willing to sink both ships?" asked Tim.

"If they continue to come on I would first damage the steering of the warship. The purpose is to put the ship dead in the water. We could do that with the laser. This will require a sea going tug to take it back to port for repairs. Russia's war ship is now out of the picture."

"If the transport does not turn around we will first stop it in the water and give the crew time to abandon ship in life boats. After the crew is safe in the boats we will sink the transport. This will happen in the sea lanes so passing ships can pick them up. I am not worried about their survival, they will be safe. We can direct nearby ships to them. Whoever owns this hardware is going to see a lot of money go to the bottom of the ocean."

"If they fly transport planes to Venezuela we will destroy them on the ground so the crews will be safe. If any hardware gets through we will destroy it in their storage facilities.

We will not allow Maduro to have the capability of waging war in South America."

"Anyone else have any comments?"

In the end they all agreed the plan was sound but be prepared for the unexpected. They discussed what could go wrong. They covered every scenario they could think of and were finally satisfied.

They then went to the hangar to prepare the ship. Every system was checked and rechecked and the correct bombs and missiles were loaded. As usual Tim and Steve insisted on going. They did not want Skip going because of his military history and there was no question that Beth would not go. They would fly tomorrow night and locate the two ships to see if their warning had turned them around. If not, they would attack.

No one slept well that night. They were up early and started the discussion over breakfast. What if this, what if that.

"Okay guys, we've beat this to death. It's time to change the subject. I vote for a relaxing time on the beautiful water snorkeling or shallow water diving. Shallow water because we will be flying tonight and in the event we have to go high it won't mix physiologically with diving. It will relax us and we can nap in the sun to catch up on the sleep we didn't get last night."

They all agreed it was a good plan however, because they were flying that night they would have to leave the cooler full of Kalik beer on shore.

The plan worked. They returned late that afternoon in good spirits after snorkeling, diving and napping. They felt rested and pumped for the mission tonight.

That night when they met at the ship they high fived each other and boarded in good spirits. As they cleared the hangar with the weapons pod attached all were serious now with their duties.

"Scott, the GPS coordinates of the Russian ship are in the computer. Your heading bug will take you to it."

"Roger, we're on our way. When we get close be sure you are strapped in tight as we may take fire from the Russian ship. If they do fire on us we return the fire."

Time passed quickly and they were lifting into the night with the weapons pod attached. As expected the two ships were still steaming towards their destination. The three looked at each other and shook their heads. Why do the leaders of some countries have to keep pushing their aggressiveness on others in spite of world opinion to the contrary? They are like a school bully, they will keep it up until someone stands up to them. Most of the time they then turn into cowards.

Suddenly Scott spoke and brought them out of their what if thoughts.

"Okay guys, we're 5,000 feet directly over the destroyer. She is making 15 knots on the same course as the transport and thirty miles behind. We'll have to play this by ear. It is pretty dark out and no moon for us to be seen. I'll drop down to wave top height with our daylight vision on. Tim, the laser should turn the rudder and propeller to powder. Everyone be ready for a high G escape if needed"

Tim watched the stern of the ship as the swells caused the rudder and propeller to partially show. She must have been a little low on fuel as she was riding high in the water.

"I believe I can get a good shot at the running gear as the swells bring it out of water just high enough. Tell me when I'm clear to fire."

"Fire when ready Tim. Make sure the recorder is running Steve."

"They are running Scott."

Tim took his time and settled into the rhythm of the swells. He waited until maximum height and fired. They all watched the daylight screen to see the results. It was spectacular. The rudder disappeared and two blades of the three blade propeller were melted off.

"Nice shooting Tim," they both said.

"I'll climb back to 5000 feet and we'll watch for a bit. Monitor radio frequencies to see if they call headquarters and what they have to say", said Scott.

"They are putting a man overboard at the stern," said Steve

"After they bring him back aboard we'll see what they have to say to their headquarters. If we know they are going to be delayed for at least an hour we'll have time for the transport," said Scott

It didn't take long and the radio transmissions started. Moscow told them they would fly a diver and equipment to see if a patch job could be done and last until they returned to home port. At the same time they would send a ship to tow them back if the patch could not be done. The diver and equipment would be flown to Venezuela. The transport would have to be on it's own. Fortunately everything was paid for before the ship left port.

Scott laughed and said, "That will really hurt them when the transport goes to the bottom. I suggest we now take care of the problem."

"Thanks to the fine shooting of Tim the destroyer was no problem," said Steve.

"Fine laser work indeed" said Scott. "Strap in and we'll be on our way."

They flew at 1000 feet for the short trip to the transport. There she was, cruising along at 18 knots unaware the destroyer was no longer protecting her. Moscow decided that nothing would be gained by informing them so they were in the dark.

"I will go close to her stern so we can read her name with the daylight infrared. Sing out when someone sees it," said Scott.

"Well look at that" said Tim." She is the MSC Venezuela. A very fitting target don't you think.?"

"Absolutely ," said Steve. "I'll see if I can raise them on the maritime radio. I'll have to try several frequencies but we'll find them. When I do Scott, we'll get the Captain on so you can talk to him."

"Go for it." replied Scott.

"MSC Venezuela this is the Shark, Over. MSC Venezuela this is the Shark. Over. MSC Venezuela this is the Shark. Over."

"Shark, this is the MSC Venezuela. I read you loud and clear. Over"

"MSC Venezuela, this is the Captain of the Shark" transmitted Scott. " I must speak to your Captain at once. This is an emergency."

"Stand by Shark. I will get him."

A short time passed and a huffing and puffing voice said, "This is the Captain of the Venezuela, who are you? What is the emergency? Where are you?"

"Calm down Captain. This is the Captain of the Shark. We mean you no bodily harm but we are going to sink your ship. The war material you carry will not reach your port. We are from the country of Piot and I am sure you have heard of us after the carnage we brought on North Korea, Iran and anyone who supports terrorist activity. This includes your country of Venezuela. You must begin immediately to abandon your ship of all souls. I can understand if you doubt what we are saying but, we are going to blow a hole in your bow to show that we mean what we say. I also suggest you reduce speed to zero to give your men time to lower the life boats. You will be interested to know that we disabled the Russian destroyer so she cannot help you. Moscow decided not to tell but leave you to your own fate. That fate is now in our hands and we are going to sink you."

"Okay Tim. One good sized hole in the bow with the laser."

"Venezuela, get those life boats in the water now. You are sinking already. The next shots will be your end."

"Okay guys" said Scott. "Count the life boats and crew members. We want to give them every chance to get off the ship."

'Steve, try the radio and see if you get an answer from them. If you do tell them they must get off now as more shots to finish them are on the way. Then call for any ships in the area to come and rescue life boat crews in the water. Give them the exact location."

"Will do Scott. Venezuela, Venezuela this is the Shark. Venezuela, Venezuela this is the Shark. Do you read? Over. No answer from her Scott. They must have left the radio room."

"I see life boats in the water", said Steve.

"Okay Tim. Give them 10 minutes to get far enough away from the ship in case our shots trigger an explosion. Then let her have it. We want her to sink fast."

When 10 minutes was up and the life boats were well clear Tim fired several laser shots. It didn't take long and the ship was very low in the water and sinking fast.

They received several answers to their call for help for the crews in the life boats. It was certain that they would be picked up and the transport was now out of sight and on it's way to the bottom in very deep water.

"Well," said Scott "That takes care of that problem. You two are really something. All this could not be without you both. Not just the creation of this bird but the way you handle crew duties in combat. None of this would happen without you. You deserve medals you'll never get."

"Oh, oh," said Steve. "What do you suppose he wants?"

"I don't know," replied Tim. "But whatever it is my answer is No."

"Sorry Scott. Flattery will get you nowhere."

"Alright, alright you two. Let's get out of here. Are you two up for a trip to Venezuela to see if we can pick up any chatter on our language gizmo?"

"Let's do it." They replied in unison.

They stationed themselves above the President's offices and noticed the big glass doors to the veranda were wide open with music and laughter pouring out.

" I have a toast. I have a toast," came a voice through the translator. "I wish to toast to our glorious ship the MSC Venezuela and her bringing us a huge load of military supplies".

"Hear Hear", others could be heard shouting.

"And I have a toast," said another. "A toast to our fooling that outfit Piot who threatened us. It is now night and she is running silent with lights out and due to arrive in a few hours."

They could hear the hoorays coming from the party. But not for long.

Suddenly a voice yelled out. "QUIET, QUIET everyone. I have some bad news. A Mayday call came from the Venezuela captain that they were forced to abandon ship as they were under attack by Piot and were sinking. That is all we know now. As more information is known we will tell you."

The music and laughter stopped.

"Well gentlemen, the party is over. It is time to head home. I believe we are due for a rest. Well done."

On the way back Scott broke the silence. "I have been thinking about something that should pose a real challenge for the two of you. This will take time but, if it can be done the results would be tremendous. Is there a way to bug the Kremlin offices? Something that does not resemble a bug in any way. It could be in paint on the walls or something of that sort. It can not be electronic if it could be found by an electric debugger. It would be good to know what that little chrome dome head Sutin is up to."

"That would be a real coup," said Tim. "A very interesting challenge. We'll work on it."

They lowered the ship with the pod attached and completed their post flight inspection.

"Let's get our after action report and video to Mr. R then we'll have a Kalik and beat around the thought of a Kremlin bug," said Scott.

They did just that then headed to bed for a much needed rest.

CHAPTER THIRTY-FIVE

W hen Scott entered his office at the Company headquarters he was informed that George Hutcher wanted a meeting. They made a meeting time for 10 o'clock.

"Hello Scott. Good to see you"

"Same to you George. You sounded pretty anxious for this meeting. What's up?"

"My friends tell that there is talk about you and the price of oil stock. Some people are worried about losing big bucks in the market if your new engine takes off and the need for gasoline takes a nose dive. They think if they get rid of you the problem will go away."

"It would not. The CEO's of the major auto companies are each having a custom made luxury car for their personal use and as a demo for their wealthy clients. The Hollywood group is making inquires even now about a delivery date. Industry leaders are doing the same. The demand is going to keep increasing."

"I know, that's the problem for the oil investors. I have the names of the people Secretary Painter contacted after he found out about the engine. That will be a place to start. My CIA friends are digging also. In the meantime I will be close at all times. We have made other arrangements for the island. Don't worry, you won't know we are there. I'll keep you informed of our progress."

"What about General Hathcock and Beth. Where will they be the safest?"

"They decide whether a one bedroom apartment for each or a two bedroom for the both here on the Company property. The General can stay on base in the BOQ when needed at the Pentagon. The CIA will be keeping a close watch on him."

"One other thing Scott, the CIA brought in Secretary Painter and the three people I taped him calling. I would not want to be in their shoes right now."

The four suspects were at CIA headquarters in the interrogation room. It was bugged and everything said recorded. Bird Drop started the interrogation.

"We know that one or all of you is involved in hiring a hit man on Scott Wilson. We want the name or names of those contracted. We will give you no more than 30 minutes to comply. If you don't, this is what will happen. You will each be handcuffed and led out of the building where reporters and camera people will be waiting for you. Your jobs will be lost, you no longer have friends for they don't want guilt by association. Your wives will be shut out of all social events. You will have to liquidate assets including your homes in order to pay legal expenses. Your lives will not be the same. The clock starts right now. You are playing with the big boys now."

He walked out, closed the door, and sat in a chair by the speaker. In addition to the audio bug there was also a video bug. The men in that room were going crazy. "Who put out a contract? Did you do it Painter? How do they know you called us? The car was bugged. How else would they know? Maybe your phone is bugged Painter. The CIA is involved and they have all the equipment to bug anything and anyone."

"Alright, Alright," Said another. "Here is paper and pencil for each. We don't have much time. Each of us write down every name we talked to about this including other oil investors. We have our lives as we know them at risk. I can lose the oil investment but I can't lose everything else. Don't leave off a name because it could haunt us later. Put your name at the bottom."

Exactly 30 minutes later Bird Drop entered the room and collected the lists.

"You may leave now. We will contact you soon."

When they left the building they were relieved no one was waiting for them. The CIA agents went over the lists methodically. The investigation had started.

CHAPTER THIRTY-SIX

B eth and her father took separate apartments. Skip would be spending most of his days finishing his projects at the Pentagon so he would spend nights at the BOQ on base. They knew the CIA had their backs so went about their activities.

A man phoned Scott's office saying he was a union rep and wanted a meeting with Scott. Mary told him she would have to check with Scott, He refused to leave his phone number and would call back late afternoon.

Scott called George Hutcher and told him of the call. It may be nothing but, they had no union contacts. George told him to set an appointment and he would join them.

The man did call back and could make a 10:30 am meeting. Scott passed the word to George who would be there. In the meantime George was reviewing photos of known and suspected hit men.

The man arrived on time and called himself Ron Austin. George led him into Scott's office with a hand on Ron's elbow to confirm he was carrying. As the man was starting to sit George kicked his legs out from under him. As he went down George pulled the weapon from Ron's shoulder holster and pointed the gun at his head.

"Hand me your wallet Mr. Austin and we'll see what name is on your drivers license. One suspicious move and I'll smack you with your gun. The police picture of you leaves no doubt who you really are."

George handed the wallet to Scott. The name on the drivers license was not Ronald Austin.

"Give the local CIA a call Scott. Our contact is an agent by the name of Fred Ekstrom. I'll keep an eye on our guest.. Empty your pockets Mr. Austin, everything."

As he reached for his back pocket he made a sudden move to hit George in the adams apple. George was prepared and deflected the blow and simultaneously hit Ron on the side of the head with the flat of Ron's pistol. He was knocked unconscious. They emptied his pockets for him. A notepad with a couple phone numbers would be of interest to the CIA.. Fred Ekstrom of the CIA arrived shortly and took Mr. Austin into custody. As it turned out, Secretary Painter had contacted Austin and completed the contract.

Secretary Painter had not put this mans name on his list. The others had made no attempts to contact anyone. Strangely, Mr. Painter resigned from government employ and moved to a small town near his daughter. He became a recluse. The other three were completely innocent and were thankful nothing was made public.

The R Company had a plane due back from Washington DC early the next morning, Saturday. Skip would be on it. Scott, Skip and Beth would celebrate at dinner that night at the private club that Scott was now a member.

CHAPTER THIRTY-SEVEN

"Thanks for coming to the meeting. It has been awhile since we discussed a bug in the Kremlin and other places. Are you making any progress?"

"A little. We have both talked to a Mensa person who has been working with radio isotopes. He says he is close to having a nonelectric bug. He is saying another 3 or 4 weeks."

"I have been thinking about several things." said Scott. "How do we get into the room we want to bug? Where is that room? Where do we plant the bug so it won't be seen? What shape should the bug be? How does the bug stay charged? Where can we get plans showing the interior of the building? What do you think of using your scouts to explore the Kremlin? We might find Sutins office and their situation room. It could look around at the various fixtures to find one where a bug might be planted. What are your thoughts on this?"

They thought the scout was a good idea but the needle should be loaded with knockout serum instead of the lethal kind.

"Let's try the scout on the Cuban presidential offices first."

They agreed and set a tentative mission date for two days from now. That will give them time to check out the scouts and be certain the serum is not the lethal kind.

"We also have another project which is the transceiver that the isotope will transmit to. Can we use it in place of a bomb so we have a way to release it? Since the transceiver will be in a geosynchronous orbit we will need more than one. The first will transmit to the second which will in turn transmit to us at Piot."

Scott went to his computer to look up what he could find on the Cuban Presidential offices. He wanted an exact latitude and longitude to prevent any identification error.

He also called George Hutcher to ask if he had access to the Cuban or Kremlin government offices. The information received was very useful. The Cuban info contained the room info.

They were now ready to scout the Cuba offices.

They closed the hangar roof and climbed on course to Cuba through a very black night. They were as prepared as they could be.

"Scouts are ready and armed with non-lethal serum." said Steve.

"Monitors are on and ready" said Tim.

"Very good" said Scott. "We are now directly over the target so it's up to you two now."

"Two scouts are released and I have control of mine," Said Steve.

"I have control of mine", said Tim.

As the scouts descended they approached the front of the building. Someone was coming out the front door. Before the door could close behind the person the two scouts slipped inside.

"I'll go left and you right," said Tim.

"Gotcha"

Steve found the presidential office first. There was a sign on the door saying so. He told Tim, who came flying down an empty hall to join him. Now what? There was no room to get under the door so they would wait on the upper door trim until someone came or went.

They went. They dropped to the floor behind the person and hid under the desk in front of them. A woman was there typing on a computer. Now they would have to wait until someone went in or out of the inner office.

The woman's interphone buzzed and she said "uno momento."

The scouts followed the woman's skirt into the inner office. She leaned against the desk which allowed the scouts to fly out from the skirt and under the desk. There were two secretaries in this much larger room and another door to a second inner office. Another wait until the second inner office door opened. It was not long till the first secretary pressed her intercom and said she wished to enter. When she stood the two scouts went under and up her skirt a ways so the second secretary would not see them. She too went up against the new desk allowing the scouts to leave her skirt and duck under the desk. Now they were in the inner, inner office and assumed it was the president who was sitting in the chair above. The phone conversation the president was having was translated and appeared in English on the computer screens of Tim and Steve. There was nothing relevant in the conversation so they agreed to leave the building and return to the ship. This was done without mishap and the scouts put back in their cribs.

"Well done guys. What do you think about using that system in the Kremlin?" said Scott. They discussed it but cautioned about a scout falling into the wrong hands. If that happened they would have to detonate the scout which would almost certainly kill anyone close by.

They returned to the island, put the ship to bed and sat in recliners in their living room.

" I have an idea to discuss." Said Scott. "You know how vain Sutin is with the picture of himself with bare chest sitting on a horse. If we had an oil done of that picture, with a handsome wood frame with two sides of that frame drilled to a length that would hold the isotope bug. One on each side of the frame would give us more power. Then put a plug after the bug is inserted so a drill hole can not be seen. It would be a gift from the women of Russia who would be honored if it hung in his private office and shown to foreign dignitaries. This would save us from having to use the scouts and possible detection."

It was quiet for awhile before Tim said," An idea that just might work. What size hole were you thinking of drilling?"

"What is the smallest that could house the isotope?"

"I'll give our Mensa person a call in the morning for the answer. Then let's do one for a local person so we can see what problems there could be."

They all agreed. But, who should it be?

They agreed it should be someone whose bugging would be advantageous to someone. A person suspected of committing crimes would be good especially if the bug gave evidence of criminal activity. Or, a person who had a favorite pet or race horse or even a boat or plane. Let's do some research and come up with a really good name they decided.

CHAPTER THIRTY-EIGHT

C had Boomer was on the phone for Scott. Because of the economy the space program was being cut-back. The next space
flight was cancelled. That was Chad's flight. He was calling to tell
Scott.

"I am ready to retire from the Air Force Scott. Because of the
cut-back I have lost my place for a space flight. I can be there whenever you say. It will take me a couple days is all to file the paperwork
and clean up personal matters".

"I'm sorry to hear you are bumped from your space flight but
you will get plenty here. And, you won't have to check petri dishes.
If you have items that need shipping send them to the R Company
and we'll take care of them. When you are physically ready to come
yourself let me know and I will arrange your transportation. I look
forward to your arrival Chad."

"I am really looking forward to joining you Scott. Well, I had better get busy and get the things done that need doing. I will call you very soon. Goodbye Scott."

"Goodbye."

Scott called Max to inform him that Chad would be joining them soon and to allow time in his schedule to fly with Chad. He received an update on the second ship. It was nearing completion and would be a twin of the first one.

Since Steve and Tim were spending so much time on the mainland he would give one of the rooms to Chad. Max can use the other while checking Chad out in the ship. Won't that be something to have two ships in an attack?

While he was making calls he decided to call Skip to see how his schedule was coming along. The news was good there also. H should wind everything up in a week. The new Chief of Staff wanted to do things his way. Skip understood and there were no hard feelings.

Next he called Beth who was busy with the new house she and her father had decided on. They wanted to decorate the house their way before they entertained.

Tim called. The radio isotope was ready and worked well. The measurement of the bug is 5/16 of an inch in diameter and 2 inches long. They also built the transceiver to receive and transmit the data in voice. Now they could go ahead with the local tryout of a wood framed painting of whatever or whoever they bugged.

Scott decided to call Mr. R for any input he could give as to the who. He knew just the man. A fellow club member at his country club who threw money around and no one knew where it came from. "He has a beautiful home on the channel that went direct to the ocean," said Mr. R. "He is very proud of that home and enjoys entertaining in it. I think an oil of the front of the home would feed his ego. I know an artist if you don't have one in mind."

"Excellent . We appreciate the help. After it is done we'll have the frame made."

Knowing Mr. R, that painting will be done in a week.

Something was wrong. Things were coming together too well. Enjoy it while you can, he thought.

It was a very dark night. No moon, a perfect night for a relaxing joy ride in the aircraft. He did just that.

CHAPTER THIRTY-NINE

M ax and Chad were living on the Island while checking Chad out in the aircraft. Max said he was an excellent pilot and a very good choice for the R Company. Two more nights and Chad would be ready. Scott would then fly with him on missions before he would turn him loose.

The painting was done and so was the frame with the isotope inserted, It was wrapped for shipping and a note attached. A private company made the delivery to Jeff Carlson. The note said---

To Jeff Carlson,
You probably don't realize it but you did a huge favor for me a couple years ago. It made a big change in my life for the better. I have tried to think of a way to say thank you. I have been a guest in your house and know how proud you are of it. I thought a beautiful oil by an up and

coming artist hanging in your office for all your guests to see would be a fine addition.

Thank you Jeff,

From one who prefers to remain anonymous.

Word through the country club says he is thrilled with it and shows it to guests. The transceiver was placed in geosynchronous orbit yesterday. This was done with Chad flying and Scott working the hand held computer with a control stick. The ship had not been rearmed with bombs as the transceiver was placed in one of the bomb bays and released when over the target and at the correct altitude. Scott used the hand held computer with the joy stick to make small corrections to the exact position desired for best reception. It was decided to tape the conversations and deliver them to the proper law enforcement agency. They were sent in a plain envelope by US mail. They listened to a couple tapes and found them interesting. Jeff talked about coming ashore at places called Buick, Chevy, Honda and several others. Obviously code names. Other than that the R Company was out of it. Now it was time to put a plan in effect to bug the Kremlin.

The private delivery with the note worked well so they decided to do it again for the Kremlin. They wrote the following note---

To our Dear President Vladimir Sutin,

You have our sincere admiration, respect and unquestioning loyalty. We, an organization of Russian women, want to show you how strongly we feel.

Please accept this painting of you bare chested on your horse. We would be honored if you would hang this in your office where foreign dignitaries could view it. It will show them how much the people of Russia love you.

They would ship it by diplomatic courier and delivered to the Kremlin by a Russian service. A second geosynchronous transceiver would be put in orbit to receive the transmissions. The second one has already been built and on the island waiting for insertion.

Max and Chad were done with the checkout for Chad so a flight with Steve, Scott and Chad was planned for that night.

"You take the front pilot seat and I'll take the rear one," said Scott. "We are going to insert a transceiver in a geosynchronous orbit over Russia with the hopes we can record some of Sutins private conversations. The transmitter has been delivered and is in the bomb bay."

"Do you want to take the weapons pod ?"

"Yes Chad. We'll look for targets after the insertion."

They arrived over the Kremlin with Chad flying and Steve operating the hand held computer. They released the transceiver and Steve made minor corrections with the control stick and the insertion was done. They then flew to Baffin Bay and inserted another transceiver that would act as a line of sight booster. It would then transmit to the transceiver they had installed to record Jeff Carlson's conversations. The transceiver could handle several different bugs at once. All conversations were recorded in both

Russian and English. They were anxious to return to see if all was working.

"Since we are up here, let's take Chad to Afghanistan and Pakistan and show him cave hunting. He hasn't seen the scout or the bang in operation. Tim is monitoring the Russian transceiver and will brief us when we return."

"Good plan ", said Steve. "We haven't done that for awhile."

"Set a course for their mountains Chad. We can also start dropping to a lower altitude."

"Roger", said Chad. "The great thing about flying this bird is it doesn't take long to get from one side of the world to the other. And, you don't have to worry about fuel."

"You are right Chad. Fuel starvation is the cause of many accidents."

The mountains started showing up on their daylight vision which took the pucker factor out when flying at night in the mountains. They flew through the valleys looking up at the sides of the mountains for telltale signs like smoke, dim lights coming from tunnel openings or warn paths to an opening.

It didn't take long. About a third of the way up the side of a smaller mountain there was a faint light coming from the mouth of a cave. "Let's park about 40 yards from the cave and send a scout in. I've got the ship Chad. I want you to watch how Steve does this so you can do it in the future."

"You've got the ship."

"Roger, I have the bird."

Steve went through the steps in launching the scout and controlling it with the hand held computer which also provided the video. Steve flew the scout through the cave opening and an immediate right where several people could be seen and heard sitting around a fire.

It was a family. Steve turned the scout around and left the cave and returned it to the ship.

"We don't harm women and children. We'll find another one." They moved farther up the valley.

"Tallyho on the right." Said Scott.

"Ok Chad," said Steve." You fly the scout this time."

They stopped well back from the cave opening and Chad launched the scout. He maneuvered it into the cave and came to a opening to the left and one to the right. He chose the right. A few feet down it turned 90 degrees to the left . They saw a fire with eight heavily armed men sitting around. The talk concerned an ambush on an American patrol tomorrow. Chad was satisfied there were no women or children inside. He backed up and went down the left tunnel at the T. The cave opened to a room loaded with arms, ammunition and explosives. He returned the scout to the ship and launched a bang. He parked it on a crate labeled C-5 explosives US Army.

Scott moved the ship a safe distance away before they detonated the bang.

"Okay Chad. Your show, detonate the bang when ready."

There was a tremendous explosion that took the whole side of the mountain to the valley below. Nothing could have survived that. Chad was awe struck. He was also thinking that he was the one that caused the death of those men. Then he thought that he also saved the lives of many American soldiers who would probably been killed in the ambush by those same men.

They continued on for another hour and destroyed three more caves then set course for home.

When they left the hangar there was Tim with a big grin and three Kaliks in his hand.

"Welcome back great men of the sky. You have had a very successful night and a beer celebration is called for. I heard the after action tape you sent. Very impressive. But, what you don't know is the success of the bug in the Kremlin."

"Is it working?" said Scott

"Not only is it working but, it is working very well."

"Great news. Let's go listen to it."

They sat in the living room easy chairs as Tim piped the bug through that speaker. They heard a door open and close as someone entered the room.

"Yes Svetlana, what is it? " a male voice said.

"The American President is speaking on TV. I thought you might want to listen."

"I am too busy right now. Tape it and I'll listen later. All they talk about is more sanctions against us if we don't cooperate and leave the Ukraine. We know they don't have the will to do anymore than that. And that gives us a tremendous advantage which we will use."

"What are you thinking Scott?" said Steve.

"Is it possible to tap into Russia's pipeline where it enters Europe? Could oil and gas be pumped into the line and thus maintain oil and gas flow to Europe? What sea port would be best? If we cut their flow of gas and oil it will seriously affect their cash flow and tone them down."

"Another thought. What type of device could we use that would fit in our bomb bay and be launched as we did the transceivers? We could then attach this device to a satellite. The device would have a propulsion system or small rockets that when fired would propel the satellite toward the sun. Not only would this end their surveillance of the world but the cost to send up new satellites would hurt them. The reason they are so bullish now is that they are very flush with income. Whatever we can do to hurt their income will reduce their bullying. We could destroy their oil and gas flow completely by bombing it but, that would hurt other countries. If these other things don't work we could use bombing as a threat."

"And let's not forget we have the magnetic automobile engine. In the long run, this will do more than anything to cut oil consumption and hurt the Russian economy."

"Steve and I will get on the satellite idea," said Tim. I can hardly wait to hear Sutin when he finds his satellites are going missing.

That's a great idea Scott. We'll get working on the pipeline idea also. Our Mensa friends are most willing to help."

Later that day Scott called Mr. R to set a meeting for the next morning. Mr. R declined the meeting. He said that whatever they decided was fine with him. He had complete confidence in them.

They spent the rest of the day pre-flighting the aircraft and the weapons systems and confirming a max load of weapons was loaded.

CHAPTER FORTY

S cott awoke early and turned on the news.. By the time Chad and Tim got up there was a definite chill in the air. Their good humor was not equally received by Scott. For awhile Scott did not reply to the questions regarding his bad attitude this beautiful morning.

Suddenly he slammed his palm on the table. "I am really pissed", he said. "What is it about Russia and China. They feel that they can walk all over another country, at their whim, and the world is both glad and sorry.. Sorry for the country they are walking on but glad it is not them. We have punished North Korea, Iran and others but have done nothing to stop the two biggest bullies in the world. It's time we got our head out of the sand and helped these countries. So by God that's what we are going to do. They say to never go into a fight mad. I'm not mad, just pissed off. So, heads together at 11:00 am for a plan of action. I'll call Mr. R and see if I can get Steve back here for a couple flights. I want Chad and I to have one of you with each of us."

It was early enough that Steve made the morning helicopter and was there in time for the 11:00 meeting. They used the big conference table in the computer room and started exactly at 11:00. Scott opened the meeting.

"All of us have watched the news about Russia in the Ukraine now and who knows where in the future. We have read and heard about China's territorial claims in the Central and

South China Seas as well as the Yellow Sea. The only country with any power is Japan and they are no match against China. We need to discuss ideas which will make them think twice about their aggression. When we have written ideas I will meet with Mr. R and General Hathcock to discuss a plan."

"I'll start, then I want input from each of you."

1. "I suggest we neutralize their tanks by hitting all of them in the engine compartment with the laser. This will ruin their engines. Then we hit their guns with the laser to melt the barrels and give them ED."

2. " I think we should fly in the territories China is claiming," said Chad. "We go in with pads down so they can see us on radar. We can lock onto the radar sites, fire our missiles at them, retract the pads , climb, then see what happens. If they launch fighters we take them out. If they have a ship in those waters that fires on us, we sink it. I agree with Scott. It's time we got tough with those two countries."

3. 'I think", said Steve, "We should threaten to sink any Russian ships in the harbor of Crimea. We could give them 12 hours to leave or they will be sunk. This will give the Ukraine a

convenient port to bring in Arab oil and gas and pipeline it to eastern Europe"

4. "I agree with everything," said Tim. "But let's not forget our good friends the Israelis. Hamas is a big problem for them and they have been fighting alone for a long time. Let's find out discreetly a target or targets they would like destroyed without taking the blame."

5. "Don't forget the plan to send their satellites to the sun." said Steve."

"Good suggestions all," said Scott. "Let's let the dust settle and see if we come up with anything else. I am going to the mainland later today and will see the General and Mr. R. I'll be having dinner with Skip and Beth tonight if you need me."

"Today is Friday. I would like to plan our strikes for Monday night. Chad, you and Steve plan the China strike. This will give you time to get the appropriate maps and up to date on the situation. Estimate total time from takeoff to the strikes then eta back here."

"Tim and I will hit the tanks and check the seaport in the Crimea. We will warn Sutin today that the clock is running. I will find the location of the Russian and Chinese satellites for Monday night in case you come up with an attachment that will send those things way out of contact. This is going to be a very busy and intense time so get plenty of crew rest."

"Scott called Skip and Beth and invited himself to dinner to-night as he had important business to discuss. He offered to take them out for dinner but they insisted he dine at their home.

He caught a cargo flight to the mainland and found Skip waiting for him. On the way to Skip's and Beth's home he covered the part of the strike he didn't want Beth to hear. He thought she might worry too much.

Scott and Beth gave each other a big hug and was given a grand tour of the house. It was obvious a lot of thought went into the décor. It was a warm home that made you feel relaxed. Scott knew that Skip wanted to go on this strike in the worst way but he had to say no. He had promised no more combat flights for Skip. Skip said he would look into the Israel and Hamas thing and get the info to him. He was 100% in favor of the selection of the strikes.

Scott thanked them for a wonderful evening and after another warm and feeling hug left for his room at the Company. He would catch the morning flight to the island.

When he stepped off the helicopter the next morning he again got the wonderful, oh it's so good to be home feeling. Steve, Tim and Chad met him and were full of enthusiasm. This morning it was catching.

Time passed quickly and it was now Monday late afternoon. Preflights were done, weapons inspected, all personal gear on board including water bottles and light snacks.

Excitement was high. Then it was takeoff time. Chad would leave ½ hour before Scott.

Because of the time change they would both have to park at high altitude and wait for darkness.

Chad parked over the north part of the Yellow Sea and waited until dark. He had a good view looking south into the East China

Sea. It ran further south and became the South China Sea. This whole coastline is where China extended her territorial border.

Chad descended and lowered his landing pads. "Heads up Steve. We are now visible on their radar. When you pick up a site log it into a missile. We won't fire it until we get several more."

"Tick, tick, tick" said Tim. "I got three back there and more coming. These guys really believe in coast line radar."

"We'll keep going until we get to Ningbo." said Chad. "Then we'll go back to the start and fire the missiles at those you logged. That should stir up a hornets' nest."

There were 4 more radar sites and three at Ningbo. That's a total of 10 sites with the coordinates logged into the head of 10 missiles.

"Okay Steve. Here we go. Landing pads retracted. The firing is all yours. I'll fly the same course we went down on."

"Roger."

By the time they got to Ningbo the radio chatter was intense. They launched aircraft from Qingdao. It was obvious they didn't know where to go as the enemy was not showing a radar return. From Ningbo to Wenzhou there were 5 more sites. Then 25 more sites from there to Hong Kong. The Formosa Straight was especially active. Steve had entered all the coordinates in the missiles. Now they would go back, turn around and fly the same route firing their missiles.

"Okay Steve. Here we go again. Let them have it."

"Roger."

The destruction of the sites was total. Again the radio traffic was busy. Since they didn't show up on radar the confusion was also total. Aircraft were flying but they did not know where to go so they returned to their bases.

"We are going to fly across the Gulf of Tonkin now then fly the length of Vietnam. I'll lower the landing pads and see if we can get some fighters once we cross the Gulf."

It didn't take long to get a reaction. Fighters were climbing from the China border to engage the radar return. Chad watched his radar then retracted the landing pads just before they came in range. He then activated the night day and put it on the holograph display. Chad couldn't believe the one sided advantage he had. He quickly maneuvered to place himself on their tail. They were in two ship formation. He spoke on the language translator in Chinese.

"Are you Chinese pilots looking for me? Check six."

He startled them so much they both broke at the same time. They broke opposite ways, one to the right and one to the left, which was into each other. Both planes went down in a ball of fire. A flight of two others came rushing in thinking their buddies had shot down the intruder. Chad moved to their six.

He spoke in Chinese. "You just lost two of your planes. I hope you are better pilots than they were. Show me what you can do. I am on your six."

What happened next reminded Chad of the dog fight Scott had with the F-22. Check six. No matter how they twisted and turned he kept saying "check six". The result was he shot them both down.

Chad called on the translator, "Chinese ground control this is the aircraft you sent your fighters up to shoot down. They attacked me in international airspace not Chinese airspace. They left me no choice but to shoot them down. As long as I am in international airspace any aircraft you send against me will be shot down. I will not respect your sudden attempt to gain more territory. Send your inferior pilots up and I will end their existence."

"Hey Chad," said Steve. "We have company on the water trying to paint us."

"Is he in the old Chinese territorial waters or the new one?"

"The new but he hasn't attacked us yet."

"We'll see if we can change that. Landing pads coming down."

"Three missiles on their way to us."

Chad retracted the pads and took evasive action. The missiles missed.

"Well, Chinese person. Once again you have done the unthinkable. Your ship attacked us while we are in international airspace. We have every right to defend ourselves and we will. Why don't you inform your friends on that navy boat to abandon ship as we will sink them in 30 seconds."

"Okay Steve. One bomb in the bow, one midship and one in the stern. Use bunker buster so they will penetrate the deck and explode near the hull. That will blow the bottom out and sink fast."

"Bombs are away"

"Our bombs are on the way to your boat. I hope you told them to abandon ship."

They watched the action on the display. The bombs hit exactly where Steve had aimed. The ship did not stand a chance of staying afloat. They watched as the ship sank lower and lower until it went beneath the surface. The whole thing took less than 5 minutes.

"This is a warning to you China. The world will not tolerate your bullying and expanding your territory whenever you wish. If you don't reverse your course of action we will return with a larger force and have our way with you. You have lost 4 aircraft, one ship and many radar sites. If we have to come back the damage will be many times what you have suffered tonight."

"Okay Steve, time to leave. Did you and Tim have any luck with the hardware to attach to Russian and Chinese satellites."

"We did. It's a very simple affair and we have ten loaded on each aircraft. We also have the location of 20 of their lower altitude satellites. You can start climbing at your discretion. They are at varying altitudes from 150 miles to over 22,000 miles."

CHAPTER FORTY-ONE

Scott and Tim closed the hangar roof and climbed toward the low overcast. It quickly became an undercast as they climbed into the night sky with a million stars greeting them. The route they planned would take them over the east coast of the US, across the Atlantic, over England then on to the Ukraine. They planned to scout the Crimea harbor then locate all the Russian tanks on the border. They would also scout close airfields and determine the type of aircraft they might encounter.

They took turns napping as the ship was on auto pilot. When the action started they would be very busy so the naps should have them well rested. They entered the location of their targets in the gps which would let them fly direct to each one.

It was now very dark as they moved into bombing position over the two Russian ships in the Crimea harbor.

"Let's put three bombs on each target" said Scott. "Place one each on the bow and stern decks and one mid ship. Use bunker buster so it will blow the hull to the bottom. This should wake Ivan from his smug personality. All yours Tim."

"Roger, six bombs away."

They put it on the holographic projection and watched as the bombs detonated. Those ships would not be afloat long.

"Good bombing Tim. We need to keep a sharp lookout for fighters while we go to the tanks."

"Right. Course to the tanks is on the GPS. Sky is clear for now".

They lined up on the first row of tanks with the laser aimed at the rear of the tank where the engine is located. Down the row they went. Twenty tanks no longer had an operational engine. They reversed course and came back down the row but this time the target was the gun. As they fired the laser the gun barrels melted and dropped with a bang on the front of the tank. Any crews sleeping in the tank would be quickly awake thinking they had been shot. They went down each row until all rows had their engines and gun barrels destroyed. The count was sixty tanks put out of commission.

"We have company coming from the Russian side. I show four climbing in finger tip formation."

"Good radar eyes Tim. We'll climb while watching them on the night day screen."

After climbing they rolled inverted and watched the four fighters. They split with two going to the harbor where the two ships were sunk and the other two went to the tanks.

They followed the two going to the harbor.

"Put me speaking Russian Tim."

Scott flew low on their six then moved to about 50 yards behind and a little below their 2 ship formation. They were in echelon right. He keyed the mike transmitting in Russian.

"Who dat?"

"Two, is that you talking to me?" said the Russian lead.

"Negative lead, it wasn't me"

"Who said who dat?" said lead.

Scott keyed his mike. "Who dat who say who dat when I say who Dat?"

"I think we have a clown on our frequency two. We'll ignore him and look for the bandits."

"The bandit is on your six lead. Very close to you and in a far superior ship than that outdated 29 you are flying."

"Two break right and high."

"Two."

Scott could clearly see them both with his night/day vision. The lead broke high and left.

"Russian two." Scott transmitted." I will give you the honor of being shot down first. Prepare to eject."

Scott fired a burst of machine guns that tore into the engine of the 29. Fire started immediately. Number two ejected.

"Now it's your turn Lead. I am tight on your six. Would you prefer missile or guns?"

Lead was turning his 29 inside out to shake Scott. Whenever he stopped for a few seconds Scott would transmit, "check six.' and flash his landing light.

Time to put him out of his misery. Scott fired a short burst into the leads tailpipe from his machine gun which caused the engine to explode. Lead ejected.

"Let's go find the other two." Said Scott.

"They should show up on radar soon"

A short time later Tim said, "There they are Scott. They appear to be holding over the tanks."

"We haven't used our missiles on an aircraft yet. Let's take them out from maximum range and see how accurate they are. Program a missile for each aircraft and fire when ready."

Tim fired and they watched their scopes. Two explosions were seen and both aircraft disappeared from radar. Scratch four Mig 29's. The last two were 60 miles distance.

"Time to go satellite hunting Tim. Point the way."

Both crews were now in space hunting satellites. Chad and Steve had perfected their technique and were now hooking up to the fifth one. They would open the bomb bay door that housed the capture invention. It contained two minutes of a gas that was used to move the capture tool to the satellite. It had arms with hooks that secured it to the satellite. Steve used his laptop to guide the tool which contained two minutes of a rocket type propellant . When all looked good Steve hit the fire button and the satellite shot off in the direction of the sun. With 2 minutes of propellant it was well on it's way when burnout occurred.

"Let's save the other five for another time," said Chad. "I'm ready to call it a night. We'll park over the island and do our after action report. It will be dark by then so we can land.

"I vote for that," said Steve.

Scott and Tim in the other ship arrived 45 minutes later. After darkness came they landed in the hangars and met in the house for an after action meeting. Of course a cold Kalik was enjoyed by all.

Scott and Tim also launched 5 satellites to the sun. It shouldn't be long before Russia and China start pointing fingers at those they think may be responsible for their unresponsive satellites. They decided to make a video for the news media.

Our Air force flew again last night for the purpose of showing Russia and China that they can not walk all over other countries. Their bullying tactics will result in reprisals against them. We shot down several Chinese and Russian aircraft. We also sank two Russian and one Chinese ship. The Russian ships were at the dock in Crimea. The Chinese ship attacked us when we were outside their territorial waters. We don't recognize their claim of expanded territorial waters.

We also sent ten of their satellites off to the sun and have plans to send many more. We are going to turn the city of Moscow into a blackout city. This will be done by destroying the gas and oil pipe lines and destroying their electrical power source. It is suggested that you provide generators to your hospitals.

This can all be avoided by the immediate withdrawal of Russian troops, insurgents and other like persons from all parts of Ukraine. China must immediately rescind their statement of expanded territorial waters.

When we attack you will be helpless to stop us. You know that from the combat reports of your downed airmen and Navy personnel.

We will attack in two days.

"Please get that off to Mr. R as well as the after action reports. The General is flying over in the morning so we'll brief him then. Beth is coming with him so tomorrow fresh linen and off to the dormitory for us. I believe we are going to have need for another house soon. Good night guys, see you in the morning."

CHAPTER FORTY-TWO

When Skip and Beth arrived the house had been cleaned and fresh linen and towels provided. Colleen also came so the two women and Skip would occupy the three bedrooms in the house. The other four men would be in the dormitory.

They all gathered at the pool with large glasses of iced tea. The conversation was light and jovial when they heard Tim yelling from the house living room.

"Hey all of you. I'm going to send this to the pool speakers. This is a real time conversation from Sutin's office between him and his top military man, General Yuri Antonov. It is getting a little heated."

"Vladimir, you must get out of the Ukraine. We don't know who these people are so we can not counter attack. They have far superior hardware than anything we have. Look what they did to us the other night and we never saw them even on radar. You can't hit what you can't see either with the naked eye or radar. Blacking out

Moscow and cutting our pipeline is just the beginning. You don't plan to stop with the Ukraine do you? You want to get all the other countries back and put us in the terrible economic position we were in. I cannot let you do this. You are doing it for your own ego."

"I don't care what you think," said Vladimir. "I am head of the state and I'll do what I want to do. Anymore insolence out of you and you will be fired at best."

The next sound was a shot, BANG. Next, the voice of the general was heard.

"I could not let you do this to our country Vladimir. Our history is full of huge expenses after taking over other countries. Not anymore."

They all stood as is frozen.

"My God," someone said. "He shot Sutin. We just heard it in real time"

"Skip," said Scott. "The secure phone is yours. I imagine you have some important calls to make."

"Yes I do, and then I'm going to celebrate with something stronger than iced tea.," he laughed.

Scott said, "The bar is open."

He gave Beth a big hug, looked into her eyes and said, "Will you marry me?"

"Oh yes, yes, yes," she said.

ABOUT THE AUTHOR

Tom was raised in Michigan and attended Miami University**in**Oxford, Ohio. He received his degree in Business then entered the Air Force. He graduated from pilot training and received his wings as a fighter pilot. Strategic Air Command needed jet qualified pilots so he ended up flying the B-47 jet bomber. After 5 years he received an honorable discharge and promoted to the rank of Captain in the reserve. He then joined the Wisconsin Air National Guard and became a qualified F-89 pilot. He also received his license as a financial services rep.

After moving to Colorado, he obtained his flight instructors rating in single engine, multi-engine and instrument and was appointed as the States chief check pilot for the Civil Air Patrol. During this time he received his scuba diving certificate followed by an advanced scuba rating.

He and his wife Betty spend a couple weeks every year in the Bahamas scuba diving and free diving for lobster and grouper.

They also gather enough conch to make conch chowder, cracked conch and conch salad. They feed themselves from the sea.

He and his wife moved to NW Montana, truly Big Sky country, where they have lived for over 25 years.**